"Tautly suspenseful and sociologically fascinating, *The Forgotten Girls* demonstrates yet again that the finest contemporary suspense fiction emanates from Europe's snowbound North."

—*BookPage*

"Sara Blaedel's *The Forgotten Girls* is an emotionally complex police-procedural thriller set in Denmark. With a gripping premise, fast-paced narrative and well-developed characters, *The Forgotten Girls* is an incredible read."

—FreshFiction.com

"Tightly knit."

—*Kirkus Reviews*

"*The Forgotten Girls* is without a doubt the best the author has delivered so far...strikingly well done...The chances are good that *The Forgotten Girls* will become your favorite crime novel for a long time to come."

—*Børsen* (Denmark)

"[*The Forgotten Girls*] is gripping when it depicts some horrific crimes...[An] uncompromising realism...distinguishes this novel at its best."

—*Washington Post*

EXTRAORDINARY PRAISE FOR SARA BLAEDEL AND THE LOUISE RICK SERIES

"Blaedel is one of the best I've come across."

—Michael Connelly

"Crime-writer superstar Sara Blaedel's great skill is in weaving a heartbreaking social history into an edge-of-your-chair thriller while at the same time creating a detective who's as emotionally rich and real as a close friend."

—Oprah.com

"She's a remarkable crime writer who time and again delivers a solid, engaging story that any reader in the world can enjoy."

—Karin Slaughter

"One can count on emotional engagement, spine-tingling suspense, and taut storytelling from Sara Blaedel. Her smart and sensitive character, investigator Louise Rick, will leave readers enthralled and entertained."

—Sandra Brown

"I loved spending time with the tough, smart, and all-too-human heroine Louise Rick—and I can't wait to see her again."

—Lisa Unger

"If you like crime fiction that is genuinely scary, then Sara Blaedel should be the next writer you read."

—Mark Billingham

"Sara Blaedel is at the top of her game. Louise Rick is a character who will have readers coming back for more."

—Camilla Läckberg

THE LOST WOMAN

"Leads to...that gray territory where compassion can become a crime and kindness can lead to coldblooded murder."

—*New York Times Book Review*

"Blaedel solidifies once more why her novels are as much finely drawn character studies as tightly plotted procedurals, always landing with a punch to the gut and the heart."

—*Library Journal* (starred review)

"Long-held secrets and surprising connections rock Inspector Louise Rick's world in Blaedel's latest crime thriller. Confused and hurt, Louise persists in investigating a complex murder despite the mounting personal ramifications. The limits of loyalty and trust, and the complexities of grief, are central to this taut thriller's resolution. A rich cast of supporting characters balances the bleakness of the crimes."

—*RT Book Reviews* (4 stars)

"Sara Blaedel is a literary force of nature...Blaedel strikes a fine and delicate balance between the personal and the professional in *The Lost Woman*, as she has done with the other books in this wonderful series...Those who can't get enough of finely tuned mysteries...will find this book and this author particularly riveting."

—BookReporter.com

"Blaedel, Denmark's most popular author, is known for her dark mysteries, and she examines the controversial social issue at the heart of this novel, but ends on a surprisingly light note. Another winner from Blaedel."

—*Booklist*

"Engrossing."

—*Toronto Star*

THE KILLING FOREST

"Another suspenseful, skillfully wrought entry from Denmark's Queen of Crime."

—*Booklist*

"Engrossing... Blaedel nicely balances the twisted relationships of the cult members with the true friendships of Louise, Camilla, and their circle."

—*Publishers Weekly*

"Blaedel delivers another thrilling novel... Twists and turns will have readers on the edge of their seats waiting to see what happens next."

—*RT Book Reviews*

"Will push you to the edge of your seat [then] knock you right off... A smashing success."

—BookReporter.com

"Blaedel excels at portraying the darkest side of Denmark."

—*Library Journal*

THE FORGOTTEN GIRLS

WINNER OF THE 2015 RT REVIEWER'S CHOICE AWARD

"Crackling with suspense, atmosphere, and drama, *The Forgotten Girls* is simply stellar crime fiction."

—Lisa Unger

"Chilling…[a] swiftly moving plot and engaging core characters."

—*Publishers Weekly*

"This is a standout book that will only solidify the author's well-respected standing in crime fiction. Blaedel drops clues that will leave readers guessing right up to the reveal. Each new lead opens an array of possibilities, and putting the book down became a feat this reviewer was unable to achieve. Based on the history of treating the disabled, the story is both horrifying and all-too-real. Even the villains have nuanced and sympathetic motives."

—*RT Times* Top Pick, Reviewer's Choice Award Winner

"Already an international bestseller, this outing by Denmark's Queen of Crime offers trademark Scandinavian crime fiction with a tough detective and a very grim mystery. Blaedel is incredibly talented at keeping one reading…Recommend to fans of Camilla Läckberg and Liza Marklund."

—*Library Journal*

"*The Forgotten Girls* has it all. At its heart, it is a puzzling, intricate mystery whose solution packs a horrific double-punch…Once you start, you will have no choice but to finish it."

—BookReporter.com

THE
SILENT
WOMEN

THE SILENT WOMEN

SARA BLAEDEL

Translated by Erik J. Macki and Tara F. Chace

Previously published as *Call Me Princess*

GRAND CENTRAL
PUBLISHING

New York   Boston

Copyright © 2011 by Sara Blaedel
Translated by Erik J. Macki and Tara F. Chace; translation © 2011 by Sara Blaedel
Excerpt from *The Daughter* © 2017 by Sara Blaedel
Cover design by Elizabeth Connor
Cover image of suburban street © Paul Taylor / Getty Images;
cover image of women © Steve Smith / Getty Images
Cover copyright © 2018 by Hachette Book Group
Hachette Book Group supports the right to free expression and the value of copyright. The purpose of copyright is to encourage writers and artists to produce the creative works that enrich our culture.

The scanning, uploading, and distribution of this book without permission is a theft of the author's intellectual property. If you would like permission to use material from the book (other than for review purposes), please contact permissions@hbgusa.com. Thank you for your support of the author's rights.

Grand Central Publishing
Hachette Book Group
1290 Avenue of the Americas
New York, NY 10104
Hachettebookgroup.com

First published in the United States as *Call Me Princess* by Pegasus Books in 2011
First Grand Central Publishing Edition: September 2018

Grand Central Publishing is a division of Hachette Book Group, Inc.
The Grand Central Publishing name and logo is a trademark of Hachette Book Group, Inc.

The Hachette Speakers Bureau provides a wide range of authors for speaking events. To find out more, go to www.hachettespeakersbureau.com or call (866) 376-6591.

The publisher is not responsible for websites (or their content) that are not owned by the publisher.

Library of Congress Cataloging-in-Publication Data

Names: Blaedel, Sara, author. | Macki, Erik J.—translator. | Chace,
Tara, translator.
Title: The silent women / Sara Blaedel ; translated by Erik J. Macki and Tara
F. Chace.
Other titles: Kald mig prinsesse. English
Description: First Grand Central Publishing edition. | New York : Grand
Central Publishing, November 2018. | Series: Louise Rick series |
"Previously published as Call Me Princess."
Identifiers: LCCN 2018021724| ISBN 9781538759837 (trade pbk.) | ISBN
9781549141966 (audio download) | ISBN 9781538759820 (ebook)
Subjects: LCSH: Women detectives—Denmark—Fiction. |
Murder—Investigation—Denmark—Fiction. | Copenhagen (Denmark)—Fiction.
| Mystery fiction.
Classification: LCC PT8177.12.L33 K3513 2018 | DDC 839.81/38—dc23
LC record available at https://lccn.loc.gov/2018021724

ISBNs: 978-1-5387-5983-7 (trade paperback edition); 978-1-5387-5982-0 (ebook edition)

Printed in the United States of America

LSC-C

10 9 8 7 6 5 4 3 2 1

For my brother, Jeppe

THE
SILENT
WOMEN

1

The pain cut into her wrists, and she couldn't do anything because her hands were tied tightly behind her back. Terrified, she turned her face toward him. The blow struck so hard that her head hammered down into the bedding and rebounded back up for the next one. She tried to open her mouth to scream, but her lips were taped shut, which made her feel like she was wearing a mask.

The candles were still lit in the living room. The bottle of wine and the glasses were sitting on the coffee table. Blood trickled down her nose as she stared at the glow from the candlelight, her head turned to the side, and thought about the restaurant and their three-course meal from just a few hours before.

He had ordered calvados to go with their coffee, without asking her if she liked it, so she hadn't needed to admit that she didn't know what it was. They'd held hands over the table.

Pain shot through her as he cinched her feet together tightly. Something hard chewed into the flesh right above her ankle bone.

Later they had danced in the living room. Very close. He had held her face in both his hands and kissed her.

Dear God in heaven, help me!

The blood kept flowing, and she struggled to get the air in through her nose. She concentrated on her aim as she lifted her bound legs and tried to kick him off the edge of the bed. He was sitting with his back to her but managed to turn around and parry her feet. Another blow from his fist bruised her cheek and temple.

"Lie still now and nothing will happen."

He held on to her firmly, and angrily shoved her bound legs to the side.

His clothes were on the chair next to the wardrobe. Her own lay in a messy heap on the floor by the end of the bed. Piece by piece, he had slowly asked her to undress.

The left side of her face throbbed. The quiet music played on in the living room. Her fear felt like an iron grip around her gut.

She cried from pain and shame. Buried her face and body down into the soft comforter and wished it would swallow her up. Her tears mixed with the blood as he pulled her out over the edge of the bed so that only her upper body was resting on the mattress. The world and reality exploded as he shoved himself into her with a violent thrust.

The tape held her scream back. She fought to keep her nose free of the bed and struggled to inhale calmly, but she kept getting thrown out of rhythm by the pain. It threatened to destroy her. Her body began to relax as a fog slowly shrouded her and she lost consciousness.

2

There was a slight click as she pressed the switch, and a second later, the glass door to the emergency ward swung open. She walked quickly, her eyes trained on the floor. Out of the corner of one eye she noticed family members sitting and talking softly together. A lab technician wheeled a phlebotomy cart out of one of the exam rooms, and she only barely avoided crashing into him.

"Sorry," she said in passing and hurried past the glass windows surrounding the nurses' station, over to the reception desk.

"Assistant Detective Louise Rick, Copenhagen Police, Homicide Division, Department A," she said, introducing herself. "Whom should I be talking to?"

A young nurse stood up and smiled at her. "Just a second—I'll page the doctor. Why don't you take a seat for a minute?" She

3

pointed toward the white oval table covered in coffee-cup stains and crumbs from people's afternoon snacks.

Louise removed her sunglasses from where they'd been perched atop her dark hair, set them on the table, and watched the nurse page the doctor. Louise clasped her hands behind her head and exhaled heavily. She had grouchily struggled her way through rush-hour traffic along Kalvebod Wharf and Folehaven, swatting the steering wheel repeatedly in frustration when traffic ground to a standstill. It had taken an unusually long time to drive just six miles from the Copenhagen Police Headquarters out to Hvidovre Hospital.

It had been nearly five o'clock when the head of the Homicide Division, Lieutenant Hans Suhr, came into her office. She was writing out the list of things she needed to buy at the store on the way home, but when she saw the look in Suhr's eyes, she pushed her notepad aside and prepared to call Peter to ask him to pick up the groceries instead. Peter had suggested as much himself that morning as he drove her to work, but she had optimistically dismissed the idea, saying it would be no problem, she could run the errands for once.

"There's been a rape, and a brutal one at that. I want you to go check it out," Suhr said, sitting down on the hard wooden chair next to her desk.

Before he could continue, Louise pulled her notepad over again and tore off her shopping list. Lieutenant Suhr often called her in on rape cases: As it usually went over better to have a woman to take the victim's statement, and as there weren't that many of them in the division, the cases generally landed on her desk.

4

"The victim's been taken to Hvidovre," he'd said after she had her ballpoint pen ready. "She's a thirty-two-year-old woman from Valby. Her mother, who lives in the apartment upstairs, came down to her daughter's place at dinnertime and found her in the bedroom, gagged, with her hands tied behind her back. There was blood on the bed, and the daughter was nearly unconscious from the ordeal."

The lieutenant seemed to be considering whether or not there was anything else he ought to add. Then he said, "The mother took the duct tape off her mouth before calling the ambulance."

Louise studied him as he spoke, trying to prepare herself for how ugly it would be, whatever she was going to see. The fact that the victim had been hog-tied and gagged was enough for the downtown precinct to have contacted Department A, and the victim's condition automatically classified the rape as aggravated battery.

"Susanne Hansson lives alone. When the police arrived at the scene, the mother said that her daughter did not have a boyfriend or any friends she would have been sleeping with voluntarily."

Louise furrowed her brow. "What does the rape victim herself say?" she asked.

Suhr shrugged his shoulders. "Nothing. The precinct detectives tried when they got to Hvidovre, but they didn't get anything out of her. One of the female doctors has spoken with her a little since then, but I don't know how much she found out. Other than that the victim wants to report the rape. You'll have to talk to her, and then she'll have to go to National Hospital and be examined."

Louise nodded, satisfied that she would have a chance to build some rapport with the woman before they arrived at the Center for Victims of Sexual Assault downtown. Her experiences with previous aggravated rape cases told her that if Susanne had been roughed up as much as Suhr suggested, it would probably just traumatize her more to have to undergo the medical exam that same night. It would be good if they had a chance to make the woman feel at least a tiny bit secure again.

"What's her current condition?"

"Go find out," Suhr said. "I'm sending Jørgensen out to the woman's apartment on Lyshøj Allé. The crime-scene investigators are already there. Call once you have a rundown on what happened." He slapped his hand on her desk in closure, then got up and left her office.

Louise flung her jean jacket over her arm and glanced quickly at the stacks of paperwork on her desk. On her way to her chief inspector's office, where the squad car sign-out book was kept, she managed to get herself all worked up, worrying about what she would do if all the cars were already checked out and how then she'd have to go over to the garage and suck up to Svendsen. But no, thankfully there were two cars available. She grabbed a key and signed one out in the book. Silly to have worried about such a small thing, she thought as she headed down the stairs two at a time.

❧

"She's on her way now," the nurse said as she hung up the phone.

Louise thanked her and stood up. She stuffed her sunglasses in her pocket and pulled out her lip balm.

"Hi, I'm Anne-Birgitte," said a young doctor with gold-colored wire-rim glasses. Her hand was cool and her handshake firm, her long hair worn in a bun on the back of her head.

Louise felt sweaty and disheveled compared to the doctor, and she compensated by making her voice sharper and more detached than necessary. "How much has she told you?" Louise asked, instead of introducing herself, noting with chagrin the doctor's reaction. The woman's cooperative expression changed, but by then it was too late for Louise to change her more aggressive tack.

"Enough to know that it may be too soon to allow her to be questioned by the police."

They stared into each other's eyes, and Louise sensed a little bubble of respect forming and making its way up through her body. She let it radiate from her eyes just long enough for the woman facing her to be able to tell she was backing down.

"It's great that you got her to report it to the police," Louise said, flashing her a smile as the tension eased.

"If you have time, why don't I just fill you in on what I've jotted down in her case notes?"

They sat down next to each other, and Anne-Birgitte skimmed the loose pages she had brought with her.

"Her hands and feet were tied behind her back with strong plastic straps," she said. "The kind you would use to tie cables together or that the police use as disposable handcuffs.

"The ambulance guys cut them off before they brought her in, and the mother had already removed the duct tape that was covering her mouth. Her blood pressure was low, and we were able to ascertain that she was also suffering from dehydration, so we started a glucose drip, which is already helping. She's starting to come to."

The doctor finished, pushed the chart aside, and sat expectantly, ready to answer the detective's questions.

Louise nodded and tried to remember what else Lieutenant Suhr had said, and which other questions she still needed answers to.

"There was blood," she began. "How badly hurt is she?"

"Ms. Hansson sustained some violent blows to the face, which have bled a fair amount, and it appears there was some abdominal bleeding, but that's stopped. I haven't done a pelvic exam; that won't be done until she gets to National Hospital."

"How much has she told you?"

Anne-Birgitte spoke hesitantly. "Not so much. She's quite distressed, and either she doesn't want to say anything, or she can't remember what happened. To begin with, she wouldn't even confirm that there had been a crime. But obviously there's no doubt about that."

Louise noticed the doctor purse her lips to show that, in her opinion, there was no doubt that a crime had been committed. *Crime?* Louise wrote, moving her hand over the paper to hide what she'd written. "Do you know if she knew her assailant?" she asked.

"She was too incoherent for me to get that far. But she nodded when I asked if she wanted to report the assault to the police, so I passed that message on to the two officers who had brought her in."

Louise put her notepad back in her bag. The doctor didn't seem to have anything else to tell her. She might as well go in and speak to Susanne herself.

She stood up and waited for Anne-Birgitte to do the same, but the doctor remained seated, staring at the cookie crumbs on the table. "The patient is very distraught," Anne-Birgitte said, looking up. "She does not at all seem like a woman who would voluntarily consent to sex play that involved being gagged and having her hands and feet bound—and being beaten up."

Louise was about to interrupt her, but the doctor kept going. "She has been physically and mentally abused, and I would urge you to keep that in mind."

"Of course," Louise said, irritated. This wasn't the first time she'd been told off because the police were forced, for professional reasons, to consider both sides whenever a rape was reported. "I'm assuming it's all right for us to move her to National Hospital?"

"That should be fine," the doctor replied. "It shouldn't make her condition any worse. Shall we go in?"

Louise followed as the doctor led the way, but waited out in the hall while Anne-Birgitte went into the room to say that she was here. Shortly thereafter, the door was flung open and a woman in her midfifties rushed out and grabbed hold of Louise's arm. Louise quickly figured that this must be the victim's mother.

"You have to understand—something dreadful has happened," the woman said.

Louise pulled back slightly, but that just made the woman tighten the grip on her arm.

"I presume your daughter is the one I should be speaking to," Louise said, removing the mother's hand before gesturing to the row of chairs along the wall. "Why don't you wait out here while I go in and see her?"

She guided the mother over to a seat before the woman could inhale enough to protest. Louise gave her a friendly push down onto a chair.

"Once I've spoken with Susanne, she and I will drive over to National Hospital. At that time, it will be best if you go back home and wait for her there. If you give me your phone number, I'll give you a call when we're done with the exams at National Hospital and I've taken her statement at Police Headquarters."

She pulled her notepad out again and handed a blank page to the mother.

"I'm coming with you," the mother said, ignoring the piece of paper.

Louise squatted down beside the chair. "I can't keep you from doing that, but I want to prepare you. You'll be sitting around waiting for many hours, and there really won't be anyone who will have time to talk to you. Right now, this is first and foremost about your daughter, and of course you want to be there for her. But if we're going to have any chance at figuring out who did this to her, we need to have an opportunity to talk to her, and there are a number of exams that have to be done."

The woman looked as though she was starting to understand.

"Well, then I'll go home and tidy up her apartment a little," she said, mostly to herself.

Louise put her hand on the mother's shoulder and explained: "The police are still in her apartment, so it will be a little while before you'll be allowed in. I recommend that you go home. It must have been a big shock for you to come downstairs and find her like that."

The mother nodded, but Louise could tell that she was about to protest again, so she hurriedly wrapped up the conversation. "I'll call you later tonight," Louise said and scurried into the hospital room.

She'd been through this type of conversation many times before, so it hadn't taken her long to determine whether it was going to be a help or a hindrance to have this particular mother present during Susanne's medical exams and when her statement was taken: Everything about the situation told her that it was hard to see what the benefit could be.

＊

The hospital bed was near the window, the curtains fluttering a little in the light breeze coming into the room. Susanne was lying there staring outside, and she didn't turn her head until Louise was standing right next to the bed.

"My name is Louise Rick. I'm an assistant detective with the Copenhagen Police Department," she said to introduce herself, trying to keep her voice calm and soothing. "Could we have a little chat?"

Susanne turned and stared right through her. She had withdrawn into her own world.

Sad, Louise thought. *Things are much worse for you in there than they are out here.*

"You've just been through a terrifying experience," she said, looking down at the woman's battered face. "I know that you've already been examined a little, and I can certainly understand if you would prefer to be left alone right now, but I would really like to take you to National Hospital, where the Center for Victims of Sexual Assault is located. They're the ones who will do the official exam necessary to report the rape."

There was no response from the bed, so Louise continued. "If you're able to walk on your own, I suggest that we take my car. But I could also get an ambulance to take you, if you'd prefer?"

Finally, Susanne responded by letting her eye wander a tad closer to Louise's face. Louise quickly assessed whether she would do better to take a seat and pretend they had all the time in the world to wait until Susanne felt like she was ready to talk to her, or whether she should pressure the woman and provoke a response.

She decided on a compromise between the two.

"There's a coroner waiting at the center. He is going to examine you, and then the police will take your statement. And I was actually hoping that we could talk a little bit now, before the exam." Susanne interrupted her. Her voice was hoarse, and when the words came out Louise could barely see Susanne's mouth move. She had sores at the corners of her mouth that were obviously still painful.

"A coroner examines dead people. Why is he going to examine *me*?"

Louise leaned in to hear what Susanne was saying. She pulled her chair over to sit by the bedside.

"Coroners do perform autopsies on dead people, but they also examine the living," she said, trying to play it down, regretting her choice of terminology, forgetting that most people don't know the nuances of police lingo. "They are always called in whenever a rape victim is examined at the center."

The tears were starting to flow down Susanne's cheeks. Louise reached over to hold her hand, careful to avoid the woman's IV line. She reassuringly stroked her arm as she spoke.

"We want to make sure that we secure the evidence that the perpetrator doubtlessly left on you..."

Susanne began to sob. Her body was like a cavernous well, supplying bucket after bucket of tears.

Louise changed tactics. She would give Susanne the time she

needed now. Something was loosening inside the victim, and that was worth waiting for, she thought.

Finally, the crying subsided.

"I could ride with you," Susanne said, drying her eyes, "but I don't have any clothes."

She sounded apologetic, as if she was ashamed that she had been naked when she was brought to the hospital.

Louise smiled at her. "We'll have the nurse find you a bathrobe and a pair of slippers."

Susanne nodded, and Louise noticed that Susanne's eyes followed her as she stood up and went to find someone who could help them out with some clothes.

3

I n the car, Louise called Flemming Larsen's extension. He was
the coroner on duty, and she had already given him a heads-up
from the car during her drive out to Hvidovre.

"We're on our way in now," she said when he picked up.

"Good. What has she said?"

Louise avoided glancing over at Susanne Hansson, who was sitting in the passenger seat next to her. "Nothing."

Flemming was silent for a second and then asked, "Do you want
to take your statement before or after I examine her?" he asked.

"I'll wait until you're done. We'll head straight up to the division, so we'll see you there."

They agreed that Flemming would wait for her to call before
coming over to National Hospital from the building in back,
where the forensics unit was located.

Susanne sat staring out the window. Before they had left Hvi-dovre Hospital, the nurse had removed the glucose drip and given her a white bathrobe to wear over her hospital gown. She still looked dazed and battered. An aura of vulnerability and humilia-tion shrouded her, and it broke Louise's heart a bit.

Physically, Susanne would recover in a few weeks, but it would be a long time before that aura faded.

Louise contemplated whether it would help to start their con-versation while they were in the car. There wasn't any reason to pressure her or force her to remember the events of the night un-til she had made it through her examination. *She needs peace and quiet*, Louise decided, thinking about the standard uncomfortable questions that were part of taking a statement from a rape victim. *Are you sure that this was rape?* That was the last thing she needed to hear right now.

She stopped at a red light and looked again at the slumped-over shape in the passenger seat. She was having a hard time judg-ing how Susanne would respond psychologically to what awaited her during the next few hours. Right now, it looked as though everything had been taken from her. The quiet in the car was con-spicuous and awkward, but there was very little she could do.

Louise pulled in and parked in front of Stairwell 5, and she called the forensics unit once she had locked the car. They took the elevator up to Gynecology and continued down the corridor until they came to the small section that housed the sexual assault center.

Louise went up to the desk to say they had arrived.

The nurse at reception came out and gave Susanne her hand. "Do you have any family members with you?" she inquired.

"No," Louise said, avoiding looking at Susanne.

The nurse clearly understood that Louise had seen to this, and that she and Susanne had come alone because Louise needed to get Susanne's statement. She did not try to hide her disapproval of Louise's seemingly callous action.

Louise was irritated at being yet again cast in the "bad cop" role, but she bit her tongue. She still found it inconceivable that people who dealt professionally with these kinds of serious assaults didn't fully appreciate how important the medical examination and the victim's statement were. If they were to have any hope of catching the perpetrator, having a mother sitting on the sidelines possibly dissuading her daughter from giving the police a full statement was not going to help.

"The doctor will be by in a bit to take a look at you," the nurse told Susanne.

She avoided using the term *coroner*. Louise had not been as tactful, but she just didn't think there was any reason to hide from Susanne exactly who would be performing the examination.

"If you want it, we've got a bed where you can lie down until he comes," the nurse continued, glancing at her watch. "I'm sure he's probably on his way up now. You could also wait out here, or go on into the examining room."

That last part was directed at Louise.

At that very moment, Flemming Larsen walked in, wearing a white lab coat that fluttered around his legs. He introduced himself to Susanne and asked her to follow him.

"You wait here," he told Louise as the two of them went over into the little office that served as the examining room.

Louise had made up her mind to be present, although she knew that Flemming would not be happy about having so many people there as he performed his portion of the exam. A gynecologist and a nurse would also be present, so the room would be crowded, to say the least.

Still, she nodded and watched Flemming, who was almost six foot six, gently guide Susanne Hansson in, letting the door slide shut behind them.

If it had been any of the other doctors, she would have put up a fight. Eavesdropping on the examination could be a gold mine. Sometimes the victim included information that would be much more valuable at the time than later on when it eventually showed up in some report. But she had a good working relationship with Flemming and knew that she could count on him to give her a proper account of whatever information Susanne provided.

She went into the little conference room and sat down to wait. When the coroner was done, the staff from the sexual assault center would take over and offer Susanne a chance to take a shower and meet with their psychologist before proceeding to Police Headquarters to give her statement. In the meantime, Flemming would fill Louise in.

Louise pulled out her phone. Of course, she wasn't quite sure which sections of the large hospital were exempt from the cell phone ban, but she decided that phones must certainly be allowed in the conference room.

"Well, so much for grocery shopping," she said when Peter answered. She had already sent him a text message while waiting for the doctor out at Hvidovre, so he was prepared.

"You were really holding out hope, huh?" he said with a laugh,

SARA BLAEDEL

adding that he could swing by Føtex and pick up what they needed on his way home.

"Thanks," she said with an exaggerated sigh and then added that she might be quite late after all. She promised to call when she had an estimate of how long it would take.

"I'll make some dinner and put it in the fridge for you," he said, and she sent him a kiss over the phone, hoping that it wouldn't be drowned out by the weak signal, which was making the connection between them crackle.

Drunk on champagne on New Year's Eve, Peter had made a solemn resolution to be more understanding and accommodating whenever Louise called to say she couldn't make it home as planned.

The image of him holding the glass in his hand flashed before her eyes. It had irritated her a little when he'd made the promise, too, because he had already promised the same thing when she'd agreed to let him move in with her after he returned from nine months working in Scotland. He had originally accepted a job that had required him to move to Aberdeen for six months to launch a new product for the international pharmaceutical company he worked for, but then somehow it had become another three months, until finally he hadn't returned to Denmark until just before Christmas.

"Right back at you," he said, and she smiled at the phone as she hung up and put it back in her bag. She browsed a little through an old magazine and read an article about a young woman with leukemia who needed a bone-marrow transplant to survive. The problem was that the worldwide donor registry didn't have a single donor with the exact same tissue type as this girl. Hardly the mood-lifting reading material she was hoping for.

18

After an hour, Louise guessed that they were probably finishing up with the examination, and went out to the corridor to see if she could find a pot of coffee and a couple of cups somewhere nearby.

"Good thinking," Flemming said ten minutes later as he sat down across from her.

She poured coffee into a cup and pushed it toward him. "How is she?" she asked.

"She went through something pretty violent," he said.

Louise had already set a notepad and pen out on the table. She pulled them toward her and looked at him expectantly as he blew on his coffee.

"There was both vaginal and anal penetration," he said, setting his cup down in front of him.

She started taking notes.

"There are fresh bleeding tears in the posterior wall of the entry to the vagina, and three tears in the skin radiating outward from the anus."

"Did you find any semen?"

Their tone made it sound as if this were the kind of stuff ordinary people talked about, day in and day out, but without this seemingly cavalier handling of the grim medical aspects of assault, it would have been impossible for them both to keep *doing* this, day in and day out.

"Nothing immediately visible, but she had some fluorescent stains on her back that may have come from semen, so I secured samples of those."

Louise looked up from her notepad and asked, "Was there any in her pubic hair?"

Flemming shook his head and said, "He could hardly have penetrated her from the front the way her legs were lashed together. I think he penetrated her only from behind." Then he added, "But in this case, if he *had* approached her from the front, we would probably have found some evidence."

Apparently, to Flemming's great annoyance, it no longer seemed to be fashionable for women to have any pubic hair at all. That information made Louise chuckle in spite of herself, and made her feel extremely old-fashioned.

"What about the rest of her body?" Louise sketched a human body, ready to mark the locations where Susanne had been assaulted.

"There are bleeding erosions from the gag that he stuffed into her mouth," he said.

Louise marked this on her sketch before he continued.

"Its ends were jammed against both corners of her mouth and cut their way into her skin. I'm assuming that the gag was left in the apartment and that it's already been brought in to Forensics," he added.

Louise had seen the forensic unit's impressive collection of gags, and the mere sight of all the horrible things perpetrators had come up with to stuff into their victims' mouths to keep them from screaming made Louise's cheeks burn as if she had been gagged as well. There was everything from wooden blocks in socks to various heavy wires wrapped in duct tape or bandages. "And then there are two small blisters in the rectangular area where the duct tape had been—a hypersensitivity response, I'm assuming," Flemming said. He continued: "In addition, she took some powerful blows to the face."

"Was it someone she knew?" Louise asked, setting her pen down in front of her.

"His name is Jesper Bjergholdt," the coroner said, glancing down at his notes, which he had stashed in the pocket of his lab coat, "and he lives on H. C. Ørstedsvej."

Frustrated, Louise pulled out her phone and dialed Lars Jørgensen. She should have asked Susanne herself while they were in the car. While she waited for her partner to answer, she urged Flemming to keep talking.

"They went out to dinner last night, Monday night, but I wasn't able to really find out whether they had known each other for a long time or whether they had just met," he said, a little apologetically. "She made a big point of explaining that they had had a nice evening and that she doesn't understand what suddenly happened."

Louise nodded to indicate that she was still listening.

"As we were finishing up, she started hinting that it may not actually have been him at all," the coroner continued, gesturing with one hand to signal his doubt, "but she can't explain what became of him and how another person could have gotten into the apartment."

He paused to weigh his words.

"She's pretty upset, though; there's no doubt about that. She's talking with the psychologist right now."

"Could this Bjergholdt have slipped something into her drink?" Louise asked.

"That is definitely a possibility, but at the moment I don't think so. We took a blood sample to send to the lab."

"This will just take a sec," she said into the phone when her partner finally answered from Susanne's apartment. "The suspect's name is Jesper Bjergholdt, he lives on H. C. Ørstedsvej, and they had been out to eat."

She looked at Flemming and asked, "Where?" He shrugged and shook his head.

"I don't know where," she said to Jørgensen, "but I'll call you once I've talked to her. See you later."

She was about to hang up when it occurred to her that Susanne would probably appreciate leaving the sexual assault center in something other than a bathrobe. She added, "Do you think you could find some clothes in her closet and make sure they get over here? Then I'll bring her back to headquarters."

She put the phone in her bag and looked at her notepad to remind herself of how far they had gotten. Then she asked Flemming to continue.

"There are skin abrasions around her wrists and ankles, all the way around, about one centimeter wide, consistent with her hands having been bound behind her back with cable ties."

Louise took notes in the same clinical language.

"There are also ligature marks from the cable ties because he had pulled them so tight. My guess is that her hands were dark purple and swollen when the paramedics cut her out of the bands, but by the time I examined her, the swelling had gone down and the color was normal."

Once everything had been written down, they sat and talked a little about the summer vacation Flemming was planning to take with his kids. It was the first time they would be going on vacation alone without his former wife since the separation, and the kids were excited about the idea of spending it in a covered wagon that would drive them through the forests of central Jutland.

"They really want to sleep in tents and cook their meals over a campfire," he said, shaking his head before standing up and following her back out into the corridor.

They had just said goodbye when one of the psychologists affiliated with the center called down the corridor after Louise.

"Right now, she's suppressing what happened," the psychologist said when she caught up with Louise. "She's clear on most of the evening; but once they reach the bedroom, the chain of events gets foggy. I've referred her to a private-practice psychologist and recommended that she contact him in the next couple of days." Louise nodded and prepared herself for what could be a long victim's statement if they were first going to have to make their way through a layer of repressed memories. *Maybe we're not going to get anywhere.*

She knocked on the door as she entered the small examining room where Susanne was lying.

"Some of your clothes are on their way over here," she said, coming closer to her. "Once you're dressed, we'll drive over to Police Headquarters."

Susanne closed both eyes. The whole left side of her face had swollen up so severely that Louise doubted Susanne could open that eye at all. The skin on her cheekbone was a mess.

"I know you're tired and aren't feeling particularly well, but it's important for us to talk about what happened," she said, feeling sorry for Susanne and sorry for herself, too, that she had to keep pushing her. "It's important because we'd really like to find the guy that did this. But it's also important for you to get everything you've got pent up and eating away at your insides out in the open. It helps to talk about it."

She hoped that her words were making their way in past Susanne's closed eyes. Right then someone knocked on the door, and Louise stepped over to open it. Outside stood a uniformed officer with a bag in his hand.

"Thank you so much," Louise said, smiling and taking the bag, deciding not to let him into the room. She stepped back over to Susanne.

"Holler if you need help getting dressed," she said, setting the bag on the foot of the bed.

Susanne had accepted the offer of a shower once Flemming had finished his examination. Now her short dark hair was plastered against her face. "I can do it," she said, carefully opening her one good eye as she slowly pushed herself up onto her elbow.

"I'll be right outside," Louise said as she stepped out and closed the door behind her.

4

"A re you hungry?" Louise asked. They were in the car on their way to Police Headquarters, and it had occurred to her that it might have been more than twenty-four hours since Susanne had eaten. She knew that the most they would find in the break room was a box of crackers, so she didn't mind stopping to pick something up, but Susanne shook her head.

When they got to the office that Louise and her partner Lars shared, Louise asked Susanne to take a seat and went out to check whether anyone else was still there at this late hour, but the place was totally deserted. Lieutenant Suhr's door was locked, and the lights were off in Henny Heilmann's office, although the chief inspector had left Louise a message that she could be reached at home after eight. Louise looked at her watch. It was almost eleven. She would wait and update Heilmann in the morning.

She got two bottles of mineral water from the little kitchenette behind the break room and returned to her office. In the hallway she heard footsteps in the stairwell and waited to see who was coming up before she went back to Susanne. She smiled when Lars walked through the revolving doors.

"Did you find him?" she asked before he'd even made it all the way over to her, since the force had had an hour to locate Jesper Bjergholdt.

"There's no listing for a Bjergholdt on H. C. Ørstedsvej—or anywhere else in Copenhagen, for that matter."

"Fuck," Louise grumbled. "Are you guys done at Susanne's apartment?" she asked, hoping in vain that maybe something promising had turned up there.

"The investigators are still out there."

Louise nodded toward the door to their office.

"She's in there," she whispered. "I think it's best if I speak with her alone."

"Of course. I have her computer and cell phone. I'll get a warrant tomorrow so we can copy her hard drive and get a printout of the calls on her cell phone and landline."

Louise nodded and turned to go back into the office with the two bottles of water.

"Could you just ask her if she has a phone number for him?" he called softly after her. "I'll be sitting at Toft's desk, running some more searches on the name."

"Sure," she said and then walked into the room.

If anyone had asked her a year ago, she would have had a hard time imagining that she would appreciate Lars as much as she now did. She had been full of reservations when he had been assigned as a temporary replacement for her previous partner,

26

Søren Velin, who was taking some time off from the team. But she had forgotten about her aversion to the change with remarkable speed, and since then it had been business as usual when Lars officially replaced Søren after he was transferred "on loan" to an elite national police task force, Unit One, and away from the Copenhagen team.

❧

"Now I'd like to ask you to tell me about Jesper Bjergholdt," Louise said after she set the water and a glass on the table in front of Susanne. "Did you talk to each other on the phone?"

If we could get a phone number that Lars could use to track him down tonight, that would be undeniable progress, Louise thought.

"No, I never had his number."

Well, that was that. Louise turned on her computer, and her screen flickered a little before it slowly made up its mind to work. "I'm just going to tell my partner that," she said, picking up the phone.

A shadow slid over Susanne's face, and she seemed to deflate a little. It struck Louise that it hadn't even occurred to Susanne that at that very moment there was a whole team of people working on her case, probing into her entire life, shattering what little remained of her privacy.

When Louise hung up, she tried to strike up a conversation before starting the actual questioning. A lot would be riding on whether or not she would be able to establish a trust-based relationship with Susanne.

"First I need to ask if you would like to have a victim services counselor present when you give your statement."

It took a little while before Susanne reacted. "No, I don't want anyone else here," she finally concluded.

"You might be grateful for it someday when the case goes to trial," Louise said, just to make sure that Susanne knew the implications of her decision.

Susanne shook her head again, staring stiffly at one of the piles on Louise's desk. "No, thank you," she repeated.

"Okay," Louise said. She was having a hard time reading Susanne's apathetic expression. They were past the tears and the sobbing, but there was still pain several layers down, and in brief flashes Louise got the sense that Susanne wasn't withdrawing from the present, from reality, just because of the physical assault and her battered face. The walls sheltering Susanne from the outside world were not only there to protect her from her own bruised psyche and hide the violation of the brutal attack; the expression Louise glimpsed every so often in those matte-blue eyes was more of a person who had trusted someone and been brutally betrayed, and she could not understand why.

"So, who is Jesper Bjergholdt?" Louise asked, once she'd given up on getting a regular conversation going.

Susanne kept her eyes trained on the desk, sitting absolutely motionless. She squinted her one open eye dramatically. It made for a grotesque grimace with her swollen face, as her other eye was now completely swollen shut and purplish red.

Louise tried again. "You knew him. You went out to eat. How well did you know him?"

Finally, a response. "We had known each other for over a month." Susanne stared at the wall as she did the calculation. "A month and a half," she corrected herself. She looked at Louise with her one good eye.

But he didn't seem like the type of guy who would..., Louise thought, continuing the next sentence in her head when the words came out of Susanne's mouth a second later.

"No, of course not," Louise responded. "Otherwise you would never have invited him home." Louise's voice did not contain even a hint of sarcasm. She leaned over her desk and tried to catch Susanne's eye. "But we agree that he raped you?"

No reaction.

"There aren't many women who, of their own free will, go in for being subjected to what you have just been through. *Obviously*, he wasn't like that when you went out with him." She let her statement hang for a moment before continuing. "And the worst thing is that there was no way anyone could have predicted he could be like that." Louise very intentionally used *anyone* to make clear that it wasn't just Susanne who hadn't seen it coming.

"No," Susanne admitted softly. "I certainly didn't see that coming. I don't know what I did wrong."

"Did he rape you?" Louise asked again without commenting on Susanne's last comment.

Again, a long pause before Susanne finally nodded.

Louise's patience was starting to fray around the edges, but she kept her voice under control, like a horse being led around a dressage arena. Slow, steady, deliberate. "Could you please try to describe what Jesper Bjergholdt looks like, and then describe for me how you two got to know each other?" She smiled, extremely aware that her tone of voice could also come across as too controlled if she kept this up. "First, tell me how you met," she suggested a little more pointedly.

"He has dark hair, and his eyes are deep..."

They were talking at each other and not really getting any-where, but it was better than nothing.

Susanne looked at her, her eyes filled with sadness and shame. "I can't remember what he looks like," she continued unhappily. She started to cry. Tears streamed from her good eye. She hid her face in her hands. "It's like it didn't happen, as if it was just my body that was there. I can't picture him."

Louise stood up, went over to her, and sat down next to the chair, putting an arm around Susanne's shoulders. "It will help when you stop blaming yourself. It's completely understandable that your mind is repressing what happened. It was a very trau-matic experience. But you need to try to help by telling us what you can." She took a deep breath. "When we file a rape report, it is important that we close in on the perpetrator as quickly as possible. And the best way to do that is with your help." She stood up and went to get a box of Kleenex, which she set in front of Susanne, and then continued. "We can't find a Jesper Bjergholdt on H. C. Ørstedsvej. Have you been to his place there?"

Susanne blew her nose and looked around for a trash can. Louise pushed it over to her with her foot.

"I've never been to his place, but he said that he had an apart-ment there."

"Ah," Louise said. She was starting to get a sense of where this story was going. "Did you meet him on the internet?"

It took a little while for Susanne to answer, and the words came out reluctantly and hesitantly. "No...we met each other...downtown...at a café."

"At which café? When? And how did you end up talking to each other?"

Susanne stared at her. "I can't remember that, but he came over to my table."

Louise eyed her for a long time, then excused herself, stood up, and walked out. As the door closed behind her, she walked over to the only other office with a light on and asked Lars if he wanted a cup of coffee.

He gave her a questioning look.

"I need a break," she said. "I'm just going to go put on a fresh pot of coffee."

She slowly walked out to the kitchenette. She opened a bag and measured, pressing the little button on the side of the coffee maker, then stood by the wall and leaned her head back with her eyes closed while the coffee maker started gurgling.

Peace and quiet, she thought, trying to figure out what feelings were creating the roadblock in Susanne's mind. She thought about ways to break through the walls the woman had set up to protect herself from what had happened.

Over the years, Louise had struggled to avoid empathizing too much with other people's sorrows and emotions. Being involved in the aftermath of other people's tragedies had formerly affected her terribly, but she'd learned to deal with it. *Perhaps a little too well*, she thought. It could also be a strength, the ability to recognize the feelings people were struggling with. But there was something about Susanne that she couldn't put her finger on.

"What's going on in there?" Lars was standing in the doorway looking at her.

She opened her eyes, still leaning against the wall. "She may need to talk to a psychologist before I proceed. She's really completely blocked."

31

"So, we have to wait until she can get in to see Jakobsen?" Lars asked.

Jakobsen was Department A's standard crisis psychologist at National Hospital.

Louise shrugged her shoulders. "That might be best."

She pulled three dirty mugs out of the dishwasher and washed them by hand before pouring Lars a cup. Then she poured the rest of the coffee into a thermal carafe and went back to her office.

Susanne was still sitting there, staring at the desk.

Louise put down the carafe and the cups. "I think you need to talk a little more with a psychologist before we can proceed," she said. She knew full well that a visit to Jakobsen would cost them time, but it seemed to be the only solution if they were to get some concrete answers. She poured a cup for herself, held the carafe over the second cup, and gave Susanne a questioning look.

"Thanks," Susanne said with a nod.

"I suppose we could put the rest off until tomorrow, if you'd prefer," Louise suggested after tasting her coffee.

"I don't want to go home," Susanne burst out. "I'd rather talk now."

Finally, the words were coming out coherently, without the guarded hesitation. Louise took that as a good sign.

"On the internet, yes. There's no reason to hide it," Susanne said. "He's the first person I've met that way and gone out with." She was practically radiating shame. The whole story of the café and their first meeting had been a lie, one more layer of protection.

What a terrific introduction to the world of online dating, Louise thought. She looked Susanne over, from her short, dark hair that always fell to the one side, to her slightly rough facial features that were battered and swollen. It struck her that Susanne didn't look like the kind of woman who hung out in bars. She was pretty—Louise could see that, even through the bruises. Still, she wondered why Susanne was having such a hard time admitting she had met a man online, because it seemed obvious that that had something to do with it having ended so badly. Instead, it seemed as though Susanne considered it a defeat to meet a potential boyfriend that way, even though Louise thought that online dating had lost much of its previous stigma.

In fact, only a couple weeks ago Louise's friend Camilla Lind had been talking about her profound respect for people who put their profiles up on the internet.

"I mean, you have to be really creative just to come up with a username that isn't already taken," Camilla had said over the phone, sounding impressed, after the lifestyle editor at the Danish daily *Morgenavisen* had asked her to write a series of articles about online dating. "The people who are putting themselves out there in that world really aren't the 'fresh off the turnip truck' type."

Camilla had compiled a series of happily-ever-after dating stories that she'd shared with her readers, perhaps inspiring some people to give online dating a try. Maybe Susanne was one of them.

Louise had smiled as she read Camilla's pieces. "It's a very popular way to meet a potential partner these days," she had written with conviction. "You can express your attitudes and opinions up front, laying the foundation for a good relationship. Not like couples who meet each other out on the town after a few too many drinks," Camilla wrote in one article. Later on, she admitted to Louise that she would never personally look for a boyfriend online. She could see the advantages, but she couldn't even dream of writing a little sales blurb about herself. *That must be how Susanne had felt, too*, Louise thought. Susanne hadn't struck her as someone who'd fallen off a turnip truck. More as a timid, inexperienced woman who had ventured out into the big, wide world.

"I think there's something degrading about meeting a man that way," Susanne said, breaking Louise's train of thought. Then she asked for a little more coffee. "I don't care if people find that out about me now. But Jesper seemed like a decent guy, even though I did think he was too young for me at first."

Louise pulled her notepad over and started taking notes.

"We wrote to each other almost every day," Susanne continued.

"Was this the first time you'd met in person?"

Susanne's good eye seethed at this insult. "No! I wouldn't have invited him back to my apartment if it were. We'd been out twice before—well, just for coffee," she added.

"How old is he?"

"Thirty, but he looks younger."

"So, he's two years younger than you. That's not that unusual," Louise said.

"He was looking for someone older than him."

"I see. Had he been out with a lot of people before he met you?"

"No, it was his first try, too. Okay, we both agreed that there must have really been something there that made us both fall for each other." She tried to smile a little, but Louise could see that it hurt her.

"Do you know where he works? Or what he does?"

"Something with computers, but I can't remember if he said where."

"That's okay," Louise said. "It may come to you."

"We mostly talked about books, art, and…" She drew it out a

little. "…life. He was nice to talk to—or, well, write to, since that's all we did. He knew lots of stuff and had traveled a lot. It was exciting to hear about all that."

I wonder if he isn't the type who passes himself off as a pilot even though his only flight experience is as a passenger on some discount airline, Louise thought. *Some people have an uncanny and occasionally creepy ability to paint a picture of the life they want to live.*

"Can you try to describe what he looks like?" Louise asked.

"He has dark hair, slightly dark skin."

"Is he a foreigner?"

"No."

Dark hair and slightly dark skin, Louise noted. "Dark in what way?" she fished.

"Just, you know, a little darker. Sort of a bit of an olive tone to his skin."

"Does he have any distinctive features? Like a tattoo, or an obvious, visible scar, or any birthmarks?"

Susanne closed her eyes as she contemplated this. Then she shook her head and said, "I don't think so, but I'm not sure. Maybe a tattoo."

"Which of you made the first contact, in the beginning when you first started writing to each other?"

"Him." Her answer was prompt, without hesitation. "He wrote. He said I sounded like the woman of his dreams."

Louise could tell that Susanne's memory had finally been jogged and the words were finally flowing. Louise smiled and said, "Just describe him as best you can. What color are his eyes?"

"Dark blue, gray…" Susanne hesitated before adding, "They might have been brown. They were big and deep. That was one of the things I fell for."

"But you can't remember what color they were?" Susanne shook her head again.

"And his height? Just, you know, ballpark."

"He's a good bit taller than me, and I'm five foot four. Maybe eight inches taller. I came up to his shoulders."

"So, he could also be a foot taller?" Louise gestured with her hands how much a foot was and measured from her own shoulders to illustrate.

Susanne nodded. "I guess that seems more like it."

So you have no idea, Louise thought, sighing to herself and leaning back in her chair. It was almost one in the morning, and they weren't really getting anywhere. The description was too vague to be of any use, so they might as well stop.

"I suggest that we make an appointment for tomorrow after you've had a chance to rest. Then we can look at some pictures together. Maybe it will be easier for you to describe his features if we have something to compare to," she said.

Susanne yawned and nodded.

"Can you go home to your mother's place at this time of night?"

"She lives upstairs from me in the same building, and I'm sure she's sitting up waiting, so I definitely can. But I'd rather go back to my place," she said after a second, "if that's all right."

"I think your apartment is still sealed off, and it would be best if you weren't alone."

It didn't look like Susanne agreed, but after a bit she nodded anyway.

"Let's agree that you'll come back here at two o'clock tomorrow afternoon. And now I'll just arrange for someone to give you a ride home."

Louise called up the operations desk and asked if there was

someone who could drive Susanne Hansson back to her mother's place. Then she drummed her fingers as she waited for a response.

"Great," she said into the phone, once it was all arranged. Then she stood up. "I'll walk you down to the main entrance, and a car will pull around to pick you up."

They walked down the corridor together. Louise was surprised to see that Lars was still sitting in the office next door. After she saw Susanne off, she went back to find out if he had come up with anything.

"I just checked the Criminal Register," he said, "but we don't have anyone by that name. That would almost have been too easy."

He stood up and offered her a lift home.

"Yeah, thanks," she said. "I'm sure it would do me good to ride my bike, but it'll be fine parked here until tomorrow."

❧

She tiptoed in so she wouldn't wake Peter. He'd left a note on the kitchen table with a big arrow pointing to the refrigerator and the words *midnight snack* written in red felt-tip pen. She smiled and opened the fridge. She found Danish sausage, sliced ham, and different types of cheese neatly arranged on a plate. She cut herself a slice of bread, took a beer out onto the back steps, and sat down with the day's newspaper, which by this point was almost twenty-four hours old. She hadn't felt hungry earlier and didn't really now, either, but she needed to sit and unwind for a bit. As she finished eating, she suddenly felt tired. She yawned, folded up the paper, and went to brush her teeth.

5

"Is there no limit to women's naïveté?"

Michael Stig had sat down on the corner of Louise's desk. She considered for a moment asking him to get his butt off the table, but instead she forced a smile and asked what he meant.

They had accessed Susanne's email that morning, looked through her Outlook inbox, and seen that Jesper Bjergholdt had written to her from an account he had set up on Yahoo. They also determined that the two had not exchanged photos. That would help explain some of Susanne's vagueness when it came to how he looked.

Louise stifled a snort, but it irritated her that they had gotten their hopes up in the first place, because obviously Susanne would have mentioned it if she'd had a picture of him.

Now she leaned back in her chair a little, preparing for one of her colleague's sexist tirades by tuning him out to keep herself from becoming even more irritated.

"It's pretty fucking hard to imagine the man who would send an email from his personal account in a situation like this," he began, waiting to see if she was with him before continuing.

"They set up a Yahoo or Hotmail account so they don't have to divulge their identity. But it's so typical—women just hand out their email addresses without a thought—let alone their phone numbers and physical addresses," he added, rolling his eyes. "It fucking amazes me it doesn't end in disaster more often."

He hopped down off the desk and stepped behind Louise's chair to study her bulletin board, where she had pinned up some personal photos of her and Peter in Scotland and one of Camilla leading her seven-year-old son Markus on an Icelandic horse.

"If you don't have anything else, I'm actually kind of busy…," Louise hinted.

Before Stig could comment on the various photos, she got up and moved so close to him that he stepped back instinctively.

At that moment, her phone rang. She nodded toward the door to get him to leave.

"Department A, Louise Rick speaking."

"This is the front desk. You've got a visitor."

"I'm not expecting anyone, and I'm just on my way out the door."

She had an appointment with Lars to drive out to Susanne's apartment so they could walk through it together.

"It's a Susanne Hansson. She says she was here last night and"—the guard lowered his voice—"she doesn't look like she's doing that well."

Louise sat down and scooted her chair into her desk. It was

eleven thirty, so her appointment with Susanne wasn't for another two and a half hours. She felt a sense of alarm mixed with some reluctance. She hoped there wouldn't be too many problems with this case, glancing down at all the files piling up on her desk. Susanne's report was straightforward: aggravated sexual assault in the first degree, and no real way so far to identify the assailant.

"Send her up," she said into her phone.

Louise popped over to the break room to find Lars and tell him he could take his time finishing his lunch.

Susanne was wearing a baseball cap which in no way matched the outfit she had picked, but it did conceal a little of her battered face. She sat down in Lars's chair across from Louise.

"It's not right," Susanne said. She didn't waste any time on pleasantries, didn't even say hi.

Louise's head sank; an ominous thought started throbbing in the back of her mind. She was sure Susanne had changed her mind and decided not to report the rape after all, and how the hell could Louise stop her?

She took a deep breath and nodded at Susanne. "What is not right?" she asked in her most even-keeled, gentle voice.

"I can't put the blame on him," Susanne said defiantly.

Louise contemplated her for a moment and asked, "Have you spoken with the psychologist you were referred to at National Hospital yesterday?"

Susanne shook her head. "Don't need to. I may well need some help at some point, but not right now."

Louise rolled her chair over, next to Susanne's. "What do you mean?"

"I went along with it," Susanne admitted. "I can't back out now, because I let it go too far." Her voice was quiet but determined.

Louise took a firm hold of Susanne's arm and pulled her toward her. Susanne's response to the physical contact was for tears to well up in her eyes.

"Are you into S and M?" Louise demanded. "Did you tell him it turns you on to be bound, beaten, and raped?"

Susanne yanked her arm back. Her response was so forceful that she pulled Louise, and her chair, as well.

"Why are you saying that? Why are you accusing me of being into that kind of thing?" Susanne exclaimed, starting to cry.

When the door opened and Lars walked in, Susanne turned her back to them and rolled her chair all the way into the corner.

Lars stood in the doorway, trying to figure out what was going on.

"Should I go?" He gestured to Louise, who shrugged.

He closed the door and sat down on the low bookshelf next to the door.

Louise turned her attention back to Susanne and proceeded. "I'm not saying this to upset you. But since you just came in here and told me that you yourself are responsible for what happened, there are a few things we're going to have to get out in the open."

Not a sound from the corner.

Louise rolled her chair all the way over to Susanne. Whatever she said next would either get Susanne to relax or make her feel so cornered that she would decide to flee from the office. She cautiously laid her hand on Susanne's shoulder and calmly said, "You didn't ask for anything. You didn't invite him to mutilate and humiliate you, and you *definitely* shouldn't blame yourself." She gently stroked Susanne's back and sat there quietly, just waiting for her to stop crying.

"I should have realized that something was wrong," Susanne

eventually said. "And in a way, you *are* asking for it when you bring a man home with you without getting to know him properly first."

"Who the hell has been telling you crap like that?" Louise interrupted, so angrily that it made Susanne jump and sit up in her chair, frightened.

"It's obvious," Susanne responded meekly.

Louise spun Susanne's chair around so they were facing each other, and Susanne did not protest.

"Susanne, is this something that your mother put in your head when you went home last night or something? Where is this outrageous blaming-yourself stuff coming from?"

No response.

Louise turned to Lars, who was sitting perfectly still, trying to attract as little attention to himself as possible.

"Would you mind calling Jakobsen and telling him he needs to find time to talk with Susanne within the next hour?"

Lars frowned pessimistically. It was fairly short notice to give the crisis psychologist, but Lars headed out the door anyway, and when he came back a moment later, he nodded.

Technically, Louise was supposed to ask Susanne if she felt like talking to Jakobsen, but it would be beyond all reason to give her any choice in the matter right now.

"We're going to drive you over to National Hospital. They have a good psychologist you should talk to. There is absolutely no reason for you to be so hard on yourself, let alone *blame* yourself for what happened. While you're with him, we"—she pointed at Lars and back at herself—"will drive over and take a look at your apartment. It'll be easier for us to get a sense of what happened once we've seen where it took place. Is that okay with you?"

Susanne nodded and found her keys in the pocket of her jacket.

In the car, Louise asked where she and Jesper Bjergholdt had had dinner on Monday night.

"We were supposed to meet at seven o'clock in Tivoli Gardens, but I don't know what the restaurant was called. It was right next to Plaenen, the open-air stage there."

Louise was going to suggest that they take a drive over there after they had looked at some pictures to try to come up with a better description of the perpetrator, but stopped herself. The suggestion could wait; the priority now was for Susanne to talk to Jakobsen.

Lars, who had come with them in the same car, waited while Louise escorted Susanne up to the psychologist's office, and when she came back down they drove out to the Valby neighborhood in southwest Copenhagen, to Lyshøj Allé. Unfortunately, there hadn't been fingerprints either on the bottle of red wine or on the two glasses that were still on the coffee table when the police had arrived at the apartment.

"He was exceedingly aware of what he was doing," Louise said as they walked up the stairs to the second floor.

"I'm curious to see how long it will take for them to get the results back on the hairs they found on the bed." Lars ran his hands through his own short hair as Louise unlocked the door to the apartment.

"It might take a couple of weeks. Anyway, it'll take that long for the semen samples Flemming thought he found on her back to get in," she said, looking around the front hall with curiosity as she shut the door behind them.

The crime-scene investigators weren't there right now, but were still keeping the apartment sealed. It would be another day or two before they were done. There was some technical equipment lying around, but otherwise the crime had left behind only an aura of emptiness.

"He knew what he was going to do to her all along," Lars said. "From the moment he packed his 'rape case.'"

That was the name Flemming had immediately given to the small black briefcase Susanne said she had seen Jesper Bjergholdt pulling gags and duct tape out of.

"He had it under his arm when they met at Tivoli," Louise added. "Hard to imagine anything more cynical or calculating than that."

They were standing in the living room of the one-bedroom apartment. Louise went over and opened the door to the small balcony. She stepped out, looking over the bustling transit hub on Toftegårds Square.

"He had Susanne undress herself," Lars continued from the living room. He started getting into his reenactment, moving around the apartment as he described what had taken place. "He opened the wine, brought it in here, and set it on the table, but he got rid of his fingerprints. And Susanne was the one who poured it into the glasses. He was sickeningly aware of where he put his hands," Lars said as Louise came back into the living room.

Louise took a seat on the couch. There was a bookshelf that took up one whole wall. In the middle of it was an empty desktop where Susanne evidently usually kept her computer.

"Do you need to see anything else?" Lars asked from out in the hallway. Since the crime-scene investigators were still working on securing the evidence, Louise and Lars had to make do with just a quick glance into the bedroom.

Louise stood up. The apartment was quite girly, exactly as she had expected, without even the slightest masculine touch anywhere. The kitchen had a bunch of white porcelain canisters with floral designs on the labels and the words *flour*, *sugar*, and the like printed in a swooping typeface.

She stood, looking around. There was something modest about the way Susanne had furnished the place. Nothing in the apartment came across as ostentatious in any way.

She turned and walked back out into the front hall. "Nah. Let's just go," she said.

"Should I swing by Tivoli after we pick up Susanne?" Lars asked once they were seated in the car. "While the two of you go look at some photos?"

She thought about it.

"I think we should bring her to Tivoli with us, if Jakobsen doesn't have any objections. There's a chance that some part of what she's repressing will make its way to the surface when she finds herself back in the place where they had a good time together."

But when Louise checked in with Jakobsen's secretary to pick up Susanne, Jakobsen came out to let her know that it was probably going to take another hour or two before he was ready to let her go. He looked serious.

"Detective Rick," he began, "the guy who raped her was kind enough to make it clear that he was just giving her what she had asked for," he said.

Louise sighed. *Oh God, poor Susanne, it's so unfair.* Previous experience told her that repressed memories could have two outcomes, and in some cases one of these was quite striking: The victim would simply push the traumatic event out of her mind. But it could also have the opposite effect, as in this case, where she had obviously repressed the details of what was going on when she said he was "just" giving her what she had asked for. As far as Louise understood the psychologist's explanation, Susanne had somehow gotten it into her head that she had actually asked to be raped.

"This is obviously very harmful to her mental state," Jakobsen continued, "and I have to smash that notion before I'll allow her to leave."

Louise could only nod and accept that there was nothing she could do about it. Jakobsen always got his way. It was more important for Susanne to be able to continue living with herself than for them to get a good description of the suspect right this very moment. *More important from a human perspective!* she thought, repressing her inner cop.

"Tell her to call me when she gets home, and we'll make a new appointment."

46

6

They parked on Otto Mønsteds Gade, entered Police Head-quarters through the side door next to the municipal courtroom where they held preliminary hearings, and continued on up to the second floor to Department A.

"So, we're essentially in a holding pattern," Lars said, flopping down into his chair. "It's irritating that there isn't a crowd of witnesses to help us identify this perp. On the other hand it's just fucking weird not to have to go through a ton of witness statements."

"So why don't you go down to Tivoli and ask if anyone saw anything?" Louise suggested absentmindedly as she checked to see if they'd gotten any messages while they were out. "Although I don't know what picture you would take to show people." She glanced over at him. "We only have pictures of Susanne in her battered state. There's not a soul alive who could recognize her face that way. And in terms of the perp, it's not like we have much of a description to go by. I would assume there were quite a few dark-haired men among the couples dining there Monday night if you were to ask at the various restaurants. If going down there would make you feel more productive, give it a try. But first, drive back to her apartment and find a picture that actually looks like her."

Just then there was a knock on the door, and Heilmann walked in.

"We traced his emails," she announced.

Sergeant Henny Heilmann was fifty-seven and had been the head of Group 2 for the four years Louise had been working in the Homicide Division. When Heilmann's husband had fallen seriously ill last year, she had taken some time off to stay home and take care of him toward the end. He passed away in less than a week, but it took three months for her to come back to work. She'd told Louise that she'd spent the first month slowly trying to adjust to the idea that she was alone. And that twenty-six years of marriage were over. After that, she'd spent some time visiting her sister in France, and for the last several weeks before she returned to work she'd done a few different things—including a fourteen-day yoga-and-meditation retreat in Vrå. When she returned to work, she got in the habit of starting her day with a jog past the Little Mermaid statue along the Langelinie promenade, losing about fifteen pounds. Her body, which had been in good shape before, was now fit and muscular in her short-sleeved T-shirt and short skirt, which stopped just above her knee.

Louise had always had a great deal of respect for her chief investigator, and when Louise heard about the yoga retreat, her already admirable opinion of Henny increased. She mostly thought of Heilmann as fairly reserved and a hard worker. Louise found that the image of Heilmann sitting in the lotus position meditating, with her middle finger and thumb together, gave her boss a whole new dimension.

"Where did Bjergholdt write from?" Louise asked.

"From an internet café on H. C. Ørstedsvej," Heilmann responded.

Lars had gotten up and was standing in the middle of the office. "Bullshit!" He angrily slammed his right fist into the palm of his left hand.

"But if he wrote to her from that location every day for the last month, then there's a reasonably good chance some of the other regulars or whatever you call them could recognize him or positively ID him," Louise suggested.

"He actually wrote from multiple locations," Heilmann said. "We traced most of the emails Susanne received from Bjergholdt's email account back to IP addresses that belong to that café, which has about twenty computers. But we also found an IP address that matches a computer at Frederiksberg Library and another one from the Copenhagen Main Library."

"He really went out of his way to make himself hard to track down," Louise exclaimed, watching her I'm-sure-someone-will-recognize-him theory crash and burn.

"You can say that again." Heilmann nodded. "We've got to get a solid description, and then you have to go find out if anyone at any of those locations noticed him."

Louise said that Susanne was having a session with Jakobsen, so they would have to wait a bit before they took her to look at pictures.

Heilmann, who was leaning against the door, stumbled forward when Police Commissioner Willumsen suddenly pushed the door open.

"We need ten people out in Nykøbing Sjaelland. You guys are coming. We're leaving in half an hour."

"That's going to be difficult," Heilmann said coolly.

"We located the suspect in the murder of that immigrant woman that people thought would remain cold," he continued, ignoring her.

"That's nice," Heilmann said calmly. "We're busy getting a description of the perp in a rape case, so you'll have to take people from one of the other groups."

There were five investigative groups in the Homicide Division, so in principle, there were plenty of people to choose from. It just wasn't in Willumsen's nature to inconvenience himself by bothering to find out who had time to help out on a case. He took whoever was closest.

"Your case will just have to wait," he said, looking at his watch. "Make sure you're ready. Our guy left town and is at a summerhouse out by Rørvig right now. There's no telling how long he'll be there."

"I don't have anyone to put on that." Heilmann was composed, but Louise could see her temper starting to flare below the serene surface. Willumsen gladly took advantage of Heilmann's lack of authority: His rank was higher than hers.

"You don't even know who you're looking for; it's not like the case is going anywhere," Willumsen said. The senior sergeant turned on his heel and started to leave.

"On the other hand, since you know exactly where your guy is, you could just get the police in Nykøbing to go pick him up," Heilmann called after him, "and then search the house at your leisure afterward."

Willumsen stopped and slowly turned around.

"It's our case. The murder happened in Copenhagen, so we'll apprehend him ourselves."

Heilmann sighed and gave up. She suggested tersely that if he were going to take anyone from her group, he ought to take Toft and Stig.

"I don't fucking have time to run around looking for your men," he said. "Besides, they're probably out bowling. Isn't that what those two spend most of their time doing?"

Louise was just about to let loose on him for his snide insinuation, but managed to bite her tongue. Everyone in the division knew that Thomas Toft and Michael Stig spent quite a bit of their free time roaming Denmark's various bowling alleys to procure gold medals, to the delight of the Policemen's Bowling League, but it was never at the expense of their duties.

Willumsen continued in the same tone, addressing Heilmann. "I expect you to come, too. We're heading out there together in three squad cars."

Louise wondered if Willumsen grasped how abrasive he was when he was in this mood. He could be so unreasonable when he commandeered personnel from the other investigative groups, but then he always made a big stink whenever Lieutenant Suhr ordered him to hand over a couple of *his* officers if one of the other groups needed extra staff.

Heilmann kept a straight face when he left.

"Toft and Stig are on their way up," she said as his footsteps faded away. "They were there when CCU analyzed Susanne's computer. We might as well accept that we have to go to Nykøbing, so we'll pick up again with the photos tomorrow."

The Computer Crime Unit was the official designation for the experts who could trace any activity that had occurred on a computer. Sometimes the detectives could do it themselves in-house, but since Susanne's computer was pretty much the only lead they had to follow, it had been sent over to the CCU experts in the Fraud Unit.

"Jeez, I cannot stand that guy," Lars said after Heilmann left. He was sitting with his phone in his hand, and Louise guessed he was about to call his wife at home and let her know she was going to have to pick the kids up.

Lars had twin four-year-old boys whom they had adopted from Bolivia, and the first time they had visited the office with him, they had pretty much managed to tear the place apart. During a second of inattention, they dumped the contents of several green case folders onto the floor, and when Louise returned from the bathroom they were sitting side by side, tossing the loose pages around—cute as anything, but clearly not conducive to professional productivity. She got the sense from her partner that he didn't always mind being asked to stay late, although he loyally maintained that he did.

Louise tried to call Peter, but his cell went straight to voicemail, so she just left a quick message and added that she would call him again when she knew when he could count on seeing her. Then she stood up with a big sigh and went to join Willumsen's group.

⁂

The location of the summerhouse had been marked on a map. When they were about a quarter of a mile away, Willumsen turned on his blinker and pulled over to the side of the road. He waved the two cars following him to pull over, too. Everyone gathered around the hood of his car.

"We got a tip from the local police this morning," he said. "We've been searching for this man, and an officer who lives in this area recognized the picture we sent out, and he called it in."

Louise moved in a little closer, listening as Willumsen handed out assignments. Like Heilmann, Louise was having a little trouble understanding why he didn't just have the local Nykøbing police bring the perp in and wait to take over himself once they were sure that they had the right guy.

"The summerhouse is on a dead-end street," Willumsen continued, poking the map authoritatively with his finger.

Louise gave up on trying to make out all the details on the map and decided listening would be enough. Willumsen nodded at the officers who would take up positions around the house, then at the two officers who would go in after the man.

"Once we've got him, we'll search everything. We've got good reason to believe he brought the things he wanted to dispose of with him. We'll have to go over everything with a fine-tooth comb."

Louise had already heard that there wasn't anything at the woman's address or in the suspect's home that could connect him to the murder. Her body had been placed on a post near the suspect's car, an older model white Peugeot 309. Louise stood so she had a good view of the front door of the summer home.

Willumsen looked around once before walking up to the front door and knocking. Everyone had their weapons drawn, and when the senior sergeant raised his hand and knocked again, Louise suddenly felt the weight of her pistol and holster. Arrests usually went off without a hitch, but she'd also seen them get out of hand, and it only took a second for that to happen.

❧

The man was wearing sweats and denied having any knowledge of the woman Willumsen was talking about. Gesturing wildly with his arms, he uttered a bunch of loud complaints before two officers grabbed him from either side and led him back into the living room.

Louise stood behind the white Peugeot, waiting. A second later, her colleagues came to the door again with the man between them. Now he looked obstinate and furious as they led him over to one of the police cars and put him in the back seat.

Willumsen walked over to Louise.

"You and Jørgensen drive him back to headquarters. I'll stay here and lead the search."

"Aren't you going to question him?"

They'd been looking for this guy since Saturday, and now suddenly there was no hurry to get him to talk?

"Of course, but he'll have to wait until we've searched the house."

That made sense, but Louise didn't understand the division of labor. The most obvious thing would be for Willumsen to take him back to Police Headquarters and get started with the questioning while the others conducted the search.

"Just get a move on!" he ordered.

What the fuck is he thinking? Louise wondered, not believing her ears. She looked around quickly for Heilmann, furious at having been roped into serving as a fucking chauffeur for some arrogant senior sergeant when she could have been using this time to go through photos with Susanne instead. Seething, she walked right past Willumsen to tell Heilmann that they were leaving.

Louise found Heilmann hunched over a dark brown leather suitcase. Wearing white latex gloves, she was fishing out articles of clothing one by one. She just nodded absentmindedly at Louise's apologies and kept going through the clothes, completely wrapped up in her task. The small wooden summerhouse was tense as officers methodically searched every room for hidden items. Louise gave up. Through the window, she saw Lars standing next to the car, looking for someone—likely, herself. She walked out to him.

The whole way to Copenhagen, the suspect sitting next to her in the back seat didn't say anything, but as they approached Police Headquarters, he started talking loudly and quickly. "What do you want from me? Why are you doing this?"

"It makes sense that the police want to talk to you," Louise interrupted. "Your wife was just murdered, and we haven't been able to locate you until now."

"I loved my wife. I'm grieving," he yelled.

Louise tuned him out even though he kept on talking. Lars was sitting stiffly in the driver's seat, like a robot, maneuvering through traffic. At some point, the suspect started crying. Louise turned and shot him a dirty look.

"Should we put him down in the basement?" Lars asked over his shoulder.

"Yeah, listening to this is unbearable. Willumsen will have to come get him when he gets back."

They agreed that Louise would take the man down to the holding cells in the basement under the headquarters building while Lars drove the car over to the parking garage.

When they met up again in their office afterward, Louise cast a tired glance around at the bare walls and noted that their office needed painting. It had only been a couple of months since their 1970s-era desks had been replaced by a newer style, with desktops whose height could be adjusted, but that just made everything else look even more out-of-date. The only personal touches were the two bulletin boards that she and Lars had covered with personal photos and souvenirs from some of their more spectacular cases. For example, they had put up the formula for how to make a light-green narcotic, called "green dust," which had been a scourge throughout Copenhagen. Uncovering green dust was a case Louise's friend Camilla had been very involved in and that had nearly killed her.

Off on the right side of the bulletin board was an access card for an EU summit meeting. Louise thought that had been one of the most horrifically boring things she had ever had to do, but it was one of the compulsory duties that were occasionally part of being in the division.

She sat for a bit, collecting her thoughts as she let her eyes rest on her desktop, where there was a written phone message from Susanne, confirming that their appointment had been moved to the next day.

She called Peter at home and let him know she was on her way.

"I'll put on a pot of tea," he offered right away. "Have you eaten?"

Sometimes his motherly concern got on her nerves. She didn't remember anyone ever making such a fuss over whether or not she'd eaten before she and Peter moved in together. For some reason it made her uncomfortable. She convinced him that a cheese sandwich would be just fine.

7

Louise poured some coffee and passed the thermal carafe to her right. Most of the people attending the morning briefing in the break room already knew about the arrest at the summerhouse outside Nykøbing Sjælland for the murder of the immigrant woman, something they had been working on for several weeks. The ones who hadn't been there or who had only heard about the man's interrogation, which had lasted until late into the night, were sitting and listening with interest to Lieutenant Suhr's account.

"The couple had been separated for a good seven months. They've got two kids who were living with the mother in the apartment she was renting temporarily. There really wasn't any problem at all, until the day she made it clear she didn't want to get back together with him."

"We think," Willumsen interrupted, taking over, "that he must have picked the kids up on Saturday morning and dropped them off somewhere before going back for his wife. That fits with the racket that an upstairs neighbor heard from the apartment around one o'clock in the afternoon. It's hard to say if he planned to stab her to death or if it was an argument that got out of control, but she was murdered, stabbed nine times. He says he was with their kids until late Saturday afternoon, when he came back to drop them off, and he found her lying in a pool of blood in the living room."

"How does he explain running off to a summerhouse that no one in his circle of friends knew about?" someone asked.

"He doesn't. He says he didn't run off. To the contrary, he says he withdrew a little to 'work through his grief.'" Willumsen made air quotes with his fingers. "The CSI folks found his fingerprints all over his wife's home."

"You need to find the knife or some clothes with her blood on them," Suhr said, standing up from where he'd been leaning on the edge of the table. "It's not that hard to imagine him denying his guilt the whole way through and claiming that his fingerprints were obviously in her home since he regularly spent time there."

Willumsen nodded. That was exactly what he himself had said before they arrested the man last night. Without any direct evidence, they would be in a weak position when they presented their side in court later that morning.

"I'm sure we'll find something," Willumsen said, "but there wasn't anything at the summerhouse."

"How is it going with the rape case?" someone asked.

Suhr came and stood by the end of the table where Heilmann, Louise, and Lars were sitting.

"*Morgenavisen* called me this morning. They'd like to know what we're doing to track down the suspect."

"How do *they* know about that case?" Louise demanded, lurching forward in her chair as she fought to slow her racing heartbeat and keep herself from blushing. She made a concerted effort to maintain a professional distance from *Morgenavisen*, where her friend Camilla Lind was a reporter, so that no one could accuse Louise of leaking stories to her: Camilla had the Copenhagen crime beat at the paper.

"That lady journalist of theirs got a call from Susanne Hansson's mother last night," Suhr said.

Louise sighed and closed her eyes for a moment.

Suhr had walked back over to the giant dry-erase board hanging at the far end of the break room.

She opened her eyes again but avoided looking at him. She didn't feel like listening to whatever he was about to say.

"The mother of the victim was extremely upset that the police, quote, 'weren't doing anything to find her daughter's assailant.'"

Louise could hear in his intonation that the mother hadn't spared any details. "That bitch," she muttered, gulping down the remainder of her mostly cold coffee.

"How far have you guys gotten on a description of the suspect? And what do we have that can identify him?"

He stood ready in front of the blank dry-erase board with an uncapped blue marker in his hand.

"We still don't have a usable description," Heilmann said. "The plan was for Rick to have Ms. Hansson go through photos yesterday, but then the Nykøbing Sjaelland operation came up, so we had to postpone that until today."

Heilmann calmly explained that they still didn't know if there was enough biological material to run a DNA analysis, but the DNA lab was hoping to have the results later this week or early next week. She said this a little hesitantly, because in reality it might also take until the week after next, and no one really wanted to think about that.

"Could you then just explain why you guys went to Nykøbing when you've got more than enough on your plate here at home?" Suhr asked with an undertone that Louise couldn't interpret. Either Heilmann had told him how ridiculous it was that she, Louise, and Lars had been ordered to go to Nykøbing when all they ended up doing was chauffeuring the suspect back to headquarters, or Suhr had had no idea that Heilmann's team was out there during yesterday's arrest.

"We were assisting because we were ordered to," Heilmann replied, gesturing by faintly nodding her head that the request had come from Willumsen. She stared directly at Lieutenant Suhr as she spoke.

Willumsen followed the whole thing, unconcerned.

"I want to have something actionable after lunch," Suhr continued, bellowing. "There is a lot of attention on rape cases these days, especially when the parties met each other online, and a case like this one might drag out over several weeks if the media latches onto it. We can assume they'll publish that the victim was gagged and bound. The mother obviously isn't planning on keeping her mouth shut about the way she found her daughter, but apparently she doesn't know that her daughter met the perp online. Her version makes it sound like a complete stranger forced his way into her daughter's apartment. The story will undoubtedly blow up if it comes out that the victim invited the suspect in."

Louise knew Suhr was already picturing the headlines.

"You need to close this case, and I will not tolerate you spending time on other cases before this one is out of the way. If you've got anything pressing on your plate, you'll have to hand it off to someone else." Suhr cast a quick glance at Willumsen. "And it has to come through me."

Louise glanced at Heilmann as they stood up, but she couldn't tell whether she was satisfied with the lieutenant's direct rebuke of Willumsen.

"Let's just meet in my office and touch base on this," Heilmann said on her way out the door.

"Was your pal Camilla the one who called the lieutenant?" Michael Stig asked as they sat around the desk in Heilmann's office.

"I don't know. I haven't spoken with her," Louise answered defensively.

"Maybe it'd be a good idea for you to call Camilla Lind and find out what the mother is saying and why she went to a newspaper with the story," Heilmann said.

Louise was about to suggest that someone else should make that call, but then it occurred to her that she didn't want to draw any more attention than necessary to her relationship with Camilla.

"Okay, I'll give her a call, but I've got an appointment with Susanne at ten. She's coming up here so we can try to nail down a description."

"The perp's online profile isn't up anymore," Toft informed them. "I went into Susanne's profile to check her inbox, and the messages she had gotten from Bjergholdt, and as far as I could tell his profile has been deleted."

"That was probably one of the first things he did after he wiped off her blood," Stig interjected.

"Shouldn't we also see if we can find any other women Bjergholdt was in contact with via the dating site?" Lars suggested.

"We should track any accounts that exchanged messages with 'Mr. Noble,'" Toft said.

Louise raised her eyebrows, wondering if Bjergholdt's username were somehow an allusion to his being from a blue-blooded family. Or whether it meant he was an attractive guy or something else.

"Come to think of it, what was Susanne's username?" Louise inquired, curious.

"'Snow Wite,' without the *h*."

"Ah, the spelling with the *h* was probably already taken," she remarked.

"The website's administrator can trace any messages exchanged with 'Mr. Noble.' If they balk at that, we'll sic CCU on them."

This made Louise think of the guys from *Ghostbusters* showing up with those vacuum-like gadgets on their backs, exorcising ghosts. *It's actually kind of the same thing*, she thought; *we're looking for something that can't be seen.*

"Have you told the photo lab you're coming?" Heilmann asked, looking at Louise.

Louise nodded and asked Heilmann if having Susanne look at the photo archive would jeopardize her ability to pick the perp out of a lineup later on. In cases where the victim has a lot of doubt about the perpetrator's description, they frequently run into big problems with defense attorneys claiming that the reliability of the recognition is weakened when they present the victim with a series of pictures in advance. And it happens too often that when the police show pictures to a victim, it affects the victim's memory.

"Do we have any choice?" Heilmann said, looking at her. "No, we really don't," Louise answered, annoyed that witnesses were so bad at recognition. People are terrible at remembering details accurately. Dark-haired men become medium-blond. A face that one witness remembers as having pronounced features is remembered by another as having weak features.

"Or do we go to the press?" she suggested, interrupting the silence that had settled over the conference table. "We could describe the crime and look for other women who had something similar happen to them, and then hope they've got a clearer image of the suspect in their minds."

"Are we *looking* for other women?" Lars asked, as if he had been suddenly awakened from his thoughts.

"Not yet."

Heilmann had apparently already given this thorough consideration. "There is no doubt that when the story hits the papers, there will be a massive chorus of folks saying Susanne herself is to blame for what happened to her. We can agree, can't we, that there is no reason to subject her to that as long as it can be avoided?" Everyone nodded. Not just for Susanne's sake, but also because the uproar would make it hard for them to do their work.

"We need to get her to give us a description, and we'll look after the rest ourselves," Heilmann said, and then told Louise, "but find out what the mother is saying."

When they stood up, Heilmann asked Stig to drive out and have a word with Susanne's mother. The way she said it left no doubt that she meant he should drive out there and get her to shut up.

Louise asked Susanne to sit in the chair in front of the yellowed screen that the photographs would be projected onto.

In the room next door, the technician was pulling out the photos that matched the information they had given him: male, dark complexion, high forehead, dark eyes, smooth face. Those were the characteristics that had been noted in advance; height was plus or minus four inches, and age was plus or minus five years.

Before they got going with the slides, Louise wanted to show Susanne photos from the sex-offenders file.

"They're using it in the room next door, but you can have it after we've been through the slides," the technician said when Louise asked for the file.

He snapped the slide carousel into place with a loud click and handed Susanne the control with the button that advanced the carousel.

"Let's just forget going after a specific person," Louise told the technician before they got started. "Susanne is too fuzzy on what he looks like. We're looking for a type."

The technician nodded.

"Okay, we're ready now," Louise said. She took a pad of paper out and sat next to Susanne, explaining that she should just advance through the photos at whatever pace she wanted and take her time.

Susanne nodded and pressed the button to pull up the first photo that the technician had found in the comprehensive offenders' index that the police maintained.

"He didn't look at all like that," she exclaimed emphatically, sounding irritated.

Louise considered whether she should tell Susanne that in fact he was an exact match for the description Susanne had given them, but Louise knew it was hard to understand how precise a description had to be before you could pick out a person who even vaguely resembled the person you were looking for. It wasn't that easy to explain the wide range that "dark" and "dark hair" actually covered when someone described it that way, based on an image in their head.

Susanne clicked to the next image.

"His forehead wasn't that high, his temples are even higher," she said, studying the photograph of a sleepy man with tousled hair. It wasn't any easier to recognize people when many of them were groggy and disheveled because they were usually photographed the morning after their arrest.

Louise took down Susanne's comments on her pad of paper. "His eyes are prettier!" Susanne exclaimed.

"How so?"

"More honest."

"How so?" Louise repeated.

"They're more attentive."

"Explain."

"They aren't set as close as his." Susanne pointed at the screen.

Eyes not close-set, Louise wrote on her pad.

An hour later, she handed a piece of paper to the technician. Three times Susanne had exclaimed, "That's him!" The first time she had started sobbing, after which she'd sat for several minutes staring out into space.

Each time, Louise had suggested they take a break. The monotonous clicking when a new picture was called up was grating on their nerves, and sitting in the dark was making them sleepy. Each time, Susanne had quickly composed herself and said they should continue, but when Louise asked why she thought it was him, it turned out she wasn't sure.

"He looks like him. The mouth and nose are the same."

The technician came in and handed them a piece of paper with the names and details on the three people she had picked out. The first man, Karsten Flintholm, had done time for rape, and that made Louise's adrenaline surge. His picture would undoubtedly also be in the sex-offenders file. The two other men hadn't been previously connected to rape.

Flintholm was the only one Susanne had immediately responded to as she sat flipping through the blue binder of sexual offenders, but she looked hard at the pictures that came up each time she turned a page. *As though she's memorizing the faces*, Louise thought, wondering if Susanne thought maybe she could learn to see the evil in them if she paid enough attention. Louise felt sorry for her and hoped it was some consolation that many of them looked quite average. There were only a couple where you could tell by looking that you probably wouldn't want to meet them on a dark night.

Louise called Lars and asked him to check the three names in the Criminal Register so they could see whether they were currently in or out of jail.

In addition to the three specific men, Louise described the general type of face Susanne had pointed out for the suspect. From Susanne's comments about a high forehead, eyes not closely set, and the other details that Louise had written down on her pad, the technician pieced together a description in the room next door and handed her a printout.

She took Susanne downstairs. Her face was hidden in the shadow of her baseball cap again, concealing her dark bruises. Initially, Susanne said she would be taking sick leave from work for the rest of the week, but the crime-scene investigators had said that they had finished at her apartment that day, so she could move in again if she felt she was ready, and she was now contemplating going back into the office.

"Maybe you should stay with your mother until you've gotten a little distance from the attack?" Louise suggested before they parted ways. She considered mentioning that Susanne's mother had contacted the newspaper, to see if Susanne was aware of that.

"I'd rather go home."

"How is your mother taking all this?" Louise asked, curious. "It must have given her quite a fright."

"She called a locksmith so I could get the keys changed, and had a peephole and chain installed on my door. She doesn't know I was out on a date with him."

Susanne shifted her weight from one foot to the other. "Are you trying to keep that a secret?" Louise asked.

Susanne carefully touched the wound on her left cheekbone. "It's no secret. We just don't talk about stuff like that," she said after a long pause.

"You're not close?" Louise asked.

"Yeah, I guess you could say that. She has created her own image of what my life is, and it's not that easy for her to see beyond those preconceived notions."

Louise pulled her over to a bench on the landing. They spoke softly so their voices wouldn't carry through the stairwell.

"What does she want your life to be like?" Louise prodded.

"The way things usually are. I've lived alone for twelve years. I moved to the apartment downstairs when I was twenty, when I got my job at the bank. We've got our rhythm, my mother and I, and she really likes things this way. Everything's become routine."

"A routine you don't dare—or don't want—to break out of?"

"There's no need to change anything until there's a reason to," Susanne replied evasively.

"Did you know that your mother got in touch with the press and told them your story?"

Louise still wasn't sure if it was a good idea to bring this up, but this was the closest thing to a heart-to-heart they'd had so far, where Louise was able to get some insight into the life that Susanne had been living until Monday night when she went out to dinner with the man who called himself Jesper Bjergholdt.

At first Susanne didn't respond to what Louise said, but then she kicked the toes of her shoes together.

"I didn't know that," Susanne admitted with a sigh. "But she can't understand why he hasn't been arrested." She glanced at Louise out the corner of her good eye. "She's afraid he'll come back."

"Are *you* afraid he'll come back?" Louise asked. Susanne shrugged.

"I don't think I'm afraid…and yet…I don't feel anything. I might also run into him on the way to work, or he could be standing there when I get home."

She took off her cap, set it in her lap, and shook her short hair.

"It didn't occur to me in the least that that night could have ended in such a disaster, and it may sound strange after all that's happened, but I can't really imagine it happening again, either." Louise watched her as she spoke. There was naïveté and a protective shell around her that evidently had been there for many years, but at the same time she sensed that now there was also an awareness that you can't always control what life has in store for you.

"Maybe it's time you took responsibility for your own life," Louise suggested, noticing how absurd it was that Susanne had been so deeply hurt the very first time she had made an attempt to do something slightly out of the ordinary.

"Maybe."

"At any rate, you ought to talk to your mother. I don't think either of you should be talking to any more reporters," Louise said, looking for a way to make her next point so it wouldn't sound as harsh. "But now that the story is out, you're going to have to resign yourself to the possibility that the fact that you knew the suspect in advance and that you had been out together will come out."

Susanne put her cap back on and nodded. "And there's nothing wrong with that, either," she said, sounding like she was trying to convince herself.

Susanne walked off and Louise headed to her office.

Louise threw the printout onto Lars's desk.

"Something along these lines," she said, sitting down.

He read the descriptions while he updated her on what he had found out while she was gone.

"Karsten Flintholm was released seven months ago," Lars began. "We've got both fingerprints and DNA for him, so it might be easy to match if it turns out anything is still usable from Susanne's place. The second face she picked out is Nils Walther. He's been out for over a year, but, as I said before, he's never been involved in a crime of this caliber before. He's mostly interested in things that can be converted into cash."

Louise pushed her chair back and propped her legs up on the edge of her desk.

"The last guy, Søren Matthisen, is still in prison. He has another year to go for rape, so he's out of the picture."

"He wasn't on weekend release by any chance and failed to return on Monday?" Louise brainstormed.

Lars smiled, shook his head, and said, "I checked."

"I'll try to get hold of Camilla."

She was a little afraid to hear what Susanne's mother had told Camilla, and recalled what Susanne had said. Louise recognized the feeling of irritation from her own past when her mother had been a little too controlling, but she knew it couldn't compare. Here they were clearly dealing with a mother who had seized control of her daughter's life. She lived right upstairs, which in and of itself was enough to make Louise cringe. A mother who was involved in controlling what her daughter did, what relationships she had, and what opinions she held. She probably also knew all the people Susanne hung out with—and there most likely wouldn't be many of them. It must feel like living in a gigantic straitjacket.

"Poor Susanne," Louise mumbled, noticing that Lars was looking at her with a questioning expression on his face. To a certain extent, she felt sympathy for Susanne and how she had secretly tried to forge a path out of her mother's domination by carefully trying to create her own happiness and look for a husband and family. In her peculiar living situation, the only refuge that was free from her mother's ever-watchful eye was the internet. Her seemingly uncharacteristic turn to online dating now made more sense than ever.

8

Camilla answered her phone so fast, Louise suspected she'd been sitting there with her hand hovering over the receiver.

"What did Susanne Hansson's mother say when she called you?" Louise began, without even saying hello.

"Susanne Hansson?" Camilla feigned ignorance.

"Knock off the subterfuge," Louise insisted. "I really want to know what her mother told you. I just don't get why she even contacted you. What did she want?"

The length of time it took Camilla to respond told Louise that her friend was considering whether or not she could get something in exchange for her information.

"She didn't understand why the paper hadn't reported the assault," Camilla finally said. "She feels like all you ever read about is rapes, but then no one was interested in such a crime against her own daughter."

"She really ought to be grateful for that," Louise huffed.

"Well, she wasn't!" Camilla said, sounding serious. "It sounds like an awful story. I haven't been able to get Lieutenant Suhr to confirm the chain of events, which I'm assuming means I'm pretty close…or maybe the actual details are even worse, and that's why he's being so tight-lipped about it."

"It may also have something to do with the fact that we'd like to keep things quiet, so we can work the case," Louise interrupted.

"I'd be happy to fill you in on what the mother said, if you'll tell me what happened."

"Enough already, Camilla. I'm not telling you anything. Whatever you get on this one has to come from Suhr. But I have the feeling that there'll be some information later today. Your phone call put enough pressure on Suhr that he's insisting we come up with something to tell you."

"Good," Camilla said, clearly satisfied that her call had triggered a reaction. She filled Louise in on the details of the mother's phone call.

"She told me she found her daughter in a pool of blood, with her hands and feet tied behind her back, beaten, and gagged. The guy who did it had tried to suffocate her by stuffing a block of wood in her mouth—"

"Stop!" Louise cried into the phone. "No pool of blood, no attempted suffocation! Outside of the police report, I mean. You don't need to tell me any more. Save yourself some trouble and don't put your name on that garbage; you'll just end up having to retract the whole story later."

Camilla was so audibly disappointed that Louise guessed she must have finished writing most of the article already.

"It's nowhere near as sensational as all that," Louise said, trying to sound convincing as she pictured Susanne's puffy face. "The most dramatic aspect of the case is that the girl has a mother who is an unbelievable blabbermouth—"

"Maybe," Camilla cut her off, "but obviously the mother didn't fucking arrange for her daughter to be raped so she could enjoy her fifteen minutes of fame."

"No, of course not; but now that the opportunity *has* presented itself, she certainly doesn't seem to be shy," Louise countered.

"That may be," Camilla said pensively. "I think I'm going to have another chat with her."

"You won't get anything out of her. Michael Stig is with her now, and he is usually quite effective at persuading people to put a lid on things."

"Ha," Camilla said drily. "Okay, I'll agree to sit on the story until after I've talked to Suhr. But not if I can read it anywhere else."

Louise understood that agreeing to sit on a story involved a calculated risk.

"And I would appreciate your keeping me in mind, once you guys are finally able to talk about whatever actually happened to that poor woman. Oh, and hey, is there any chance you could watch Markus this weekend?"

The change in topics was so abrupt that Louise shook her head, trying to switch gears. On the spot, she couldn't think of any fixed plans they had for the weekend, so she nodded to herself and said, "Sure thing."

Camilla sometimes had to work weekends at the newspaper,

and then she had a childcare situation because she lived alone with Markus. The boy's father, Tobias, had him every other weekend, and he was usually able to help out whenever Camilla had to work. When he couldn't, Camilla was forced to make other arrangements because her mother lived four hours away in Skanderborg, Jutland, and her father was not interested in shuttling grandchildren around.

"Drop him off on your way to work," Louise said.

"I'm not actually going to work. I'm going to be home, but I'm having some company."

"You don't say," Louise laughed, surprised. "What's his name?"

"Now let me just think for a moment if there's any reason at all for me to share that information with you," Camilla replied sarcastically.

Louise pictured Susanne's battered face for a second and said, "As long as this isn't someone you met online." She had just finished her sentence when Camilla suddenly went ballistic.

"What the fuck is that supposed to mean? You're the one who's always harping on me to find someone I want to go out with."

Louise couldn't remember ever pressuring Camilla to date.

Camilla continued her rant. "Now I tell you I actually have a date, and suddenly it can't be with someone I met the same way over half a million other people meet? What's so wrong with that? If that even *is* how I met this guy."

"Nothing," Louise said, trying to sound conciliatory. "I just wasn't aware that you'd caved and started doing the whole online dating thing," she said, immediately regretting the use of the word *caved*.

"Well, I'm not saying I have or anything, but it is the most obvious way to meet someone new."

Louise tried without success to get a word in edgewise, but Camilla continued with her tirade: "I just heard about a couple where the husband is the CEO of a big grocery-store chain and his wife is some important sales mogul for the fashion industry. Nice people, both with cushy incomes, and they actually met each other online because they didn't have time to go hang out in bars."

Louise refrained from commenting on the torrent of words filling her ears. Instead she focused on trying to find a way to say that, obviously, there was nothing wrong with it all the times it worked out well, but it could also end really badly if you were unlucky. She knew full well that she couldn't say that, because Camilla would immediately detect that the warning had something to do with Louise's job—and her good friend was sharp enough to guess the rest. All the details Susanne's mother didn't—and probably shouldn't—know.

"There's nothing wrong with meeting people online. I just mean that you should exercise a little caution when you decide to meet the actual person who's been hiding behind the profile."

"Oh, for Pete's sake, you sound like some ridiculous pamphlet from the Council for Greater Water Safety." And that was the end of that.

❧

"I think this might be one of those cases where the person we're looking for just vanishes into thin air. This Jesper Bjergholdt doesn't exist," Louise said to no one in particular after she hung up with Camilla and reflected on the entire situation.

Lars was busy reading a stack of papers and looked over at her, confused. "Doesn't exist?" he asked, a little taken aback. "Well, Susanne certainly didn't hog-tie herself."

Louise smiled at him and explained: "Of course it *happened*, but this Jesper Bjergholdt could be anyone. He's made-up. We don't have a goddamn thing to identify him with. He could live in Ålborg and be named Bjarne for all we know. If there's no DNA match in the system, and his fingerprints aren't in IFIS, then he's out of our reach." IFIS was the Danish police database containing hundreds of thousands of fingerprints.

"We'll just see," Lars said, setting down his stack of papers. "It's pretty rare for people to completely disappear."

"We've seen it before," Louise said again. "And even in a case that was similar to this one."

"You mean that guy Kim from Hørsholm?"

Louise had told him about this cold case before, which had involved a woman from Rødovre in suburban Copenhagen who had met a man online. He had called himself Kim Jensen and claimed that he came from Hørsholm. They had started a relationship that had ended with her horrifically brutalized. When the police later went after him, it was like he had vanished from the face of the earth. His profile had been deleted, his cell number wasn't in use, and there was no evidence other than fingerprints and a DNA sample, which they couldn't identify.

"His sample is stored in the archives, just waiting," Louise said, nodding toward their unsolved-case files. It frequently happened that they would catch a rapist because he was brought in for some other type of case that necessitated checking his fingerprints. And then, voilà, the computer would find a match, and in a split second they would have a name and Danish national ID number for the perpetrator.

"I can't remember her description of that perpetrator," Lars admitted, "but if he had dark hair, then we'd better get in touch with her. Perhaps it's a serial-type thing."

Louise was already out of her chair, trying to remember which one of the thick three-ring binders the Rødovre case was filed in. She found it in the third folder she pulled down from the steel shelves, which took up a whole wall in their office. She'd been on that case two years ago and remembered at the time fearing that there would be many more like it. You never knew who, or where, the people you were talking to were anymore. You thought they were sitting at home when they called, but really, they were calling from a summer home way up on the north coast of North Zealand in Rågeleje or something.

Louise had experienced that once herself, one time when she'd been riding her bike home from work and had just pulled out onto Gammel Kongevej when her cell phone started ringing. It was Peter, and she knew he was at a sales seminar in North Zealand. She stopped and was leaning on her bike on the sidewalk as they talked. After a couple of minutes, he suddenly exclaimed that it was wonderful to see that she smiled when they talked to each other. At first, she hadn't responded, but then it occurred to her that he must be able to see her. And, sure enough, he'd come home early and had just walked out of the corner grocery store when he spotted her on her bike.

At first she grinned, but then she was struck by an uneasy feeling. In her mind, he had been in North Zealand, and it had not occurred to her in the slightest that he could be anywhere closer. It was very unsettling to find that he was right there, watching her; when she thought about that, she realized how often people assume they know where people are. When those assumptions are shaken up, the whole picture in your mind crumbles.

❧

Louise went in to see Heilmann and took along a photocopy of the suspect's description. She gave Heilmann a quick report on what Susanne Hansson's mother had told Camilla.

"I don't think any of what Jesper Bjergholdt told Susanne about himself was true," Louise said, reminding the chief investigator about the similarities between Susanne's assault and the Rødovre case.

"Looking into that case again is a good idea," Heilmann said. "They may be related. If we profile the kind of perpetrator who would commit this type of crime, he would probably be flagged as a potential repeat offender. If he gets away with the crime once, he'll try again—sooner or later. It's part of the psychological power play that goes on between the rapist and the victim. He possesses and exercises his power, and when he succeeds, it whets his appetite to possess again, and the cycle begins anew."

"Couldn't he just be a sexual deviant? Maybe he craves that power element?" Louise suggested. She'd never done much with profiling, herself, but she respected Heilmann's contributions whenever a case called for it.

"He had handcuffs and a gag with him in his bag, which definitely constitutes forcible means," Heilmann explained and started reading the description of Jesper Bjergholdt.

"The description isn't all that great," Louise hurriedly admitted.

"It may be dangerous to try and push this guy out of hiding," Heilmann continued. "If he starts feeling threatened, his need to control will increase, and then there's no telling what he may do."

"We've got to find him," they heard from the doorway, where

Lieutenant Suhr was somehow now standing, although neither of them had noticed his arrival. "We lure him out on a date using Louise as bait, and have her nab him, right before he has a chance to off her."

There was something shrill about his voice, and they both looked up at him but didn't respond. *Okay, that would be crazy*, Louise thought, and suspected that Suhr also sensed that they were facing a case in which the perpetrator had appeared out of nowhere, like a genie from a lamp, and then vanished again into thin air. Suhr could tell what this case was going to require and didn't want to accept that it was turning into one of those complex cases that drained all his resources.

"I just talked to the forensics lab about the DNA," he said in a more normal tone of voice. "They're working on the hairs that were found, and we shouldn't count on there being enough material in the semen stains for them to extract any DNA, but they promised to expedite it. We'll have something at the end of next week."

Louise sighed. She had been hoping the lab would have their DNA profile ready sooner.

"Until then, we should be approaching this from all angles," he continued, an edge of frustration already in his voice. "He can't be fucking impossible to find. Toft and Stig will contact the regulars at the places he emailed from. We have a list of IP addresses. He must have fucking talked to somebody or at least been noticed, God damn it."

Heilmann nodded. They obviously agreed on how to approach the case.

"You have to get Susanne to say more," Suhr told Louise. "Familiarize yourself with how people meet online, if you're not already up to speed on that."

He didn't look at her as he spoke, so there was no point in her shaking her head to convey that she'd never even looked at any of the numerous online dating sites people were using these days.

"If we're going to do a thorough search, that will take time," she said, thinking about the massive amount of work it would require to go through all the relevant profiles that matched Susanne's vague description.

"So take the time!" Suhr blurted out, throwing his hands up in the air. "Print out pictures and profiles of everyone who sounds interesting. Show them to Susanne. Maybe she'll recognize someone."

Louise sighed and was about to leave when he changed the topic.

"What are we going to tell the press?" He started pacing around Heilmann's office. "I think we're going to have to tell them that they knew each other," he said, without waiting for a response.

"We could also just not tell them anything," Heilmann suggested. "You could say that she was raped in her home by an unknown assailant, and that we have more or less no leads."

"That's not...," Suhr broke in, irritated. He hated looking like he didn't have any leads.

"Yes, it is," Heilmann said decisively. "We need some peace and quiet so we can work. We don't need anyone fanning the flames until we've managed to contact the other girls who have been exchanging emails with our guy. Toft is already working with the people who run the website, and thinks they'll have a list for him later today. After that, we can go to the press, but right now it's too early."

Suhr just stood there, mulling over Heilmann's argument. "Fine," he said, turning on his heel.

Before he reached the door, Louise asked if she'd understood him right, that he wanted someone to run pictures over for Susanne to look at, of all the dark-haired men in the right age range who had posted pictures online at the various dating sites.

Suhr turned back and looked at her in irritation. "Obviously I don't want that. Just the relevant…the ones that match Susanne's description."

Louise put her hands to her temples, picturing thousands of dark-haired men flashing in front of her eyes. In a huff, she kept her distance as she left Heilmann's office. She sensed him standing there, watching her go, not sure what he'd said wrong.

9

I think we ought to stop by Tivoli and see if we can find out which restaurant they ate at," Louise suggested.

The stack of papers in front of Lars had grown. He put his finger down to keep track of where he was on the list he was studying. "Do you mind going over there alone? I'm trying to figure out what times the perp was online, logged in to his profile. I was hoping that there might be a pattern, but at first glance the times seem to be completely random, all different times of the day and night. But I haven't included any of these yet"—he placed his hand on the pile of papers—"so it's too soon to give up."

Louise stood there for a moment, contemplating. She should drive out to Valby to pick up a decent photo of Susanne, but maybe that wasn't necessary. She pulled out the pictures taken when Susanne was examined at the hospital. One of them showed her from her less-swollen right side. Louise stuck it in her purse and said that she would be back as soon as she'd asked around at the restaurants in Tivoli.

It only took a second to walk from Police Headquarters to the back entrance of Tivoli Gardens, across the street from the red-brick Glyptotek art museum. She flashed her police badge to the cashier, who gave her a friendly nod and let her in. The screams from the roller coaster near the entrance drowned out all other sounds in massive waves, so she could only feel the crunching of the gravel under her feet as she weaved along the path among the strollers and amusement-park visitors munching cotton candy. She'd been counting on the restaurants not being busy, since it was late afternoon, but as she approached the concert lawn at Plaenen and the restaurants came into view, she realized she'd been completely off. Obviously, the majority of the lunch rush must be over by now. After all, it was after four thirty. But there were still tons of people eating. Some people were having a traditional afternoon coffee and cake; others were eating a late lunch or an early dinner. At any rate, the square was packed.

Louise stood in the doorway of the first restaurant, somewhat at a loss as she tried to figure out who was in charge. But all the employees looked the same, so she decided it didn't matter too much whom she approached.

❧

The headwaiter gathered all his staff together and asked the whole group who had worked the evening shift on Monday. Four people said they had, and they willingly came over to study the picture Louise was holding out. None of them recognized Susanne, but they assured Louise that that did not mean the woman in the picture hadn't been there.

"We had three turns per table that night," one of the waiters said, his brow thoughtfully furrowed.

Louise waited for a translation. She wasn't sure what he meant by "turns."

"Every time you seat a party at a table, serve them, and then clear the table, that's a turn. On a night with weather like we had on Monday, each table gets turned about three times, on average. So, if there's nothing that really stands out about the customers, it's almost impossible to keep them all straight."

She nodded in understanding and thanked him before proceeding to the next restaurant, no longer feeling optimistic. Susanne was not the kind of person you would notice in a crowd, and she figured this Jesper Bjergholdt would have done as little as possible to attract attention to himself.

Louise stopped to look at the oversize flowerbed with its enormous blossoms, standing with majestic pride. She cast a quick glance at her watch and strolled over to a bench to sit for a second and enjoy the view. She closed her eyes and turned her face toward the sun, feeling the warmth permeate her. Without a thought in her head, she let herself be carried away by the light.

She opened her eyes and watched the patrons dining at Perlen with its big windowed façade. She was lost in thought and actually wasn't all that surprised when she suddenly caught sight of Peter.

He was sitting at a table right by the window, and a blond girl was just sitting down across from him. Louise leaned forward a little on the bench. Based on the length of her hair, it could be Camilla. She decided to go in and say hi, but as she got closer, she realized that the girl sitting across from Peter was his sales rep, Lina. They must be sitting there waiting for a client. Louise quickly sat back down and hoped they hadn't noticed her, because she had no desire or time to be introduced and then be forced to explain that she was working, looking for witnesses at the surrounding restaurants.

She then walked over toward Balkonen, which had a large outdoor patio on the ground floor, with just a stone balustrade separating it from Plaenen's lawn and footpaths. Before she went in, she pulled the picture of Susanne out of her purse again and took a deep breath.

"Well, let me just find out who was here on Monday," the waiter said willingly, once she'd explained why she was there.

She stood there, looking around. A young woman was balancing a tray full of beers, the tray the size of the bottom of an oil barrel. She held on tight as she wove her way through the restaurant over to a table where a group of young guys was seated, teasing each other about how many beers they could drink without throwing up when they rode the Demon afterward.

Louise thought back to one time she'd come to Tivoli with Camilla and a group of guys about the same age as these. Back then, one of the group had thrown up on the roller coaster, although thankfully it had not been her. She didn't have a chance to draw her memories fully out of the fog, because suddenly the waiter was beckoning her toward the very back of the restaurant.

"Olsen," he said, pointing to a man with an enormous mustache, who was talking to somebody standing in the kitchen.

The waiter disappeared again, and Louise stood there waiting for Olsen to finish his conversation.

"I totally didn't think she'd be back for it herself," he said after studying the picture for a second. Before Louise had a chance to react to his cryptic comment, he turned around and disappeared again toward the kitchen.

Irritated, she started to follow him, but stopped when he returned a moment later with a lavender cardigan in his hand.

"Here it is," he said, holding the sweater out to her.

Louise started to explain she wasn't here about a sweater. She was looking for the man who had been dining with the woman in the picture.

Olsen was still standing there with the sweater dangling, and it didn't seem like he was interested in hearing any more about why she was there. She guessed that they must be serving the meals for the staff in the back, so he was eager to get rid of her as quickly as possible.

"So, this woman in the picture was here?" Louise hurriedly said to keep his attention.

He nodded and hung the sweater over her arm. "We stuck it in the lost and found for her in the back, once we realized she'd left it."

So far, Louise was following him. She found it a little odd that Susanne hadn't mentioned that she'd forgotten her cardigan. "Can you remember who she was here with?"

"Nope." Olsen glanced over at the staircase that led up to the balcony on the upper floor. "But I can show you where they sat."

Louise followed him, hoping it might jog his memory if he showed her where they'd eaten.

"They sat over there in the corner." He made a gesture with his head. "She was with her boyfriend, I assume," he said, sounding like he was striving to say what he thought she wanted to hear. He wasn't particularly convincing, and Louise got the sense that he was guessing instead of telling her something he actually remembered.

"What makes you think they were boyfriend and girlfriend?" Louise asked, studying him closely. "What did he look like? Were they holding hands, or was it something one of them said?"

Her questions were curt and terse, meant to emphasize that he should keep his guesswork to himself and share only concrete information he was sure of.

"Obviously I'm not sure…," he said after thinking about it for a moment.

"So, on Monday night you served the woman in the picture and the man she was with?" Louise fished slowly.

Olsen was starting to get irritated now, too. "You couldn't really say that. It wasn't my table. I had that group of tables over there." He pointed over toward the opposite side of the room. "But I noticed them, because she forgot her sweater. I closed that night, so I took over the tables that were left so the other waiters could go home."

"Great," Louise said and pulled a chair back from a table, which had already been set, to lean on the backrest. "Can you remember what the man looked like?"

Olsen glanced over toward the table he said Susanne had been sitting at. "They were a calm, quiet couple. I think they had kind of a pricey meal."

"How did he pay?" Louise asked, maintaining eye contact with Olsen. "Try to remember if he paid with a credit card," she asked.

"He didn't. I'm sure of that. He paid in cash, and I'm not all that sure that he was Danish." Something suddenly occurred to him. "When I put the sweater into our lost and found, I told the other waiters that no one was ever going to come claim it…and I said that because I felt like they were tourists."

Louise was losing hope that this would lead to anything at all. If nothing else, Susanne would have at least noticed if Jesper Bjergholdt had spoken with an accent.

Olsen shrugged. "You'll have to excuse me, but I couldn't really tell you that for sure. We see too many customers in here for me to be able to keep them all straight, and especially when it comes to customers I didn't even serve. But I'm sure it was her." He pointed to Susanne's photo. "And I'm sure she was sitting with a dark-haired man, who I assumed was a foreigner. I can't tell you any more than that with any degree of certainty."

Louise thanked him and stuffed the photo back in her purse. Then she started toward the exit with Susanne's sweater over her arm, thinking it would probably be a good idea to send it down to the crime-scene investigators. Not that it was very likely they would find anything on it, but it was worth a try.

❧

"Restaurant Balkonen," she said in response to the hopeful look Lars gave her. Then she shook her head and added, "Nada."

She stuffed Susanne's sweater into one of the CSI's paper sacks, wrote the case number on the outside, and put it on the bookshelf by the door so she would remember to drop it off.

"They ate there, and she left this. Bjergholdt paid in cash. Strangely, the waiter was able to remember that, but otherwise his recollections were pretty limited."

She went in and dropped off her report for Heilmann.

"I've got the names of twelve women who exchanged messages with 'Mr. Noble,'" Lars said when she walked back in.

"Have you contacted any of them?" she asked.

"Not yet. But when you set up a profile, you have to provide an email address." He showed her a piece of paper with a list of email addresses on it.

"Do you have to give your own email address?" Louise looked at him in surprise, assuming up until this point that people could just set up dummy accounts.

"It's only visible to the company that runs the site, so they can send information to their customers."

She noticed a quiet germ of anticipation starting to sprout. They hadn't hit a total brick wall. Once they pinned down the description a little more, she would talk to Susanne again, and then they could go to the press and search for him. She felt a primal joy at the thought of interrogating him after they caught him. *Just you wait, you sadistic pig*, she thought and went over to find the folder for the case on Kim Jensen from Hørsholm, the man who'd disappeared into thin air. Karin Hvenegaard was the name of the woman he had raped. She lived in Rødovre. Louise wrote her phone number down on a notepad and picked up the phone.

She sat drumming her fingers on her desk while she waited for someone to pick up. A quiet click told her it had gone to voicemail, but instead of the subscriber's own voice, there was a recorded operator's voice saying that the number was no longer in service. Louise sighed and hung up. She called information and asked if there was a new number for that name.

"It's unlisted," the woman replied.

Louise went through the slightly complicated procedure the police used to circumvent the standard security measures and access unlisted numbers.

"She doesn't have a landline, and there's no cell-phone number listed for that address," the woman said after a pause.

"Thanks," Louise said and hung up, thinking it might not hurt to drive out to the address the next day. She dialed Heilmann's extension and explained that Karin Hvenegaard no longer had a phone. She could tell from Heilmann's voice that she wasn't going to sanction Louise putting this off until tomorrow, so she hurried to add that she'd find her in the Danish national population registry and then go pay her a visit in person.

She knew she wouldn't make it home in time for dinner now, but Peter was prepared for that, and it occurred to her that she didn't even know if he was home. His New Year's resolution seemed to be working, because it had been a long time since he'd complained about her unpredictable work hours.

She packed up her bag and nodded absentmindedly to Lars, who was talking on the phone. Thoughts of Peter were running through her head. She didn't have the least desire to live apart from him, but she also didn't feel any pressure to spend time with him, either, now that he lived with her. Although they'd been going together for six years, she'd been afraid, when Peter moved into her apartment, that living together would start making her feel chronically suffocated; but to her own surprise, she was actually enjoying his presence. She had quietly admitted to herself that her dread of his being a ball and chain had proven to be unfounded, and she had slowly forced it out of her mind. She was starting to have a much more relaxed view of their future together.

10

Blommevej. Louise was driving out along Roskildevej, the highway from Copenhagen to Roskilde, keeping her eyes peeled for Tårnvej, where she was supposed to take a right. From there, she was supposed to find the road that went down to the neighborhood with all the row houses. She was concentrating on driving and looking for the right address; although she was close, she was having a hard time seeing any system to the numbering. So she decided to park and search for 211F on foot.

The first conversation she'd had with Karin Hvenegaard two years earlier had been at the Center for Victims of Sexual Assault, the same place she'd taken Susanne. Karin had come in to Police Headquarters a couple of times since then, but Louise had never been out to her house before.

She pulled over in front of a small cluster of two-story houses.

Number 211F was on the second floor, but there wasn't any name on the mailbox. Louise was starting to suspect that Karin didn't live here anymore, or maybe she'd just listed the Blommevej address as her permanent address and lived someplace else that they didn't have on record. Louise rang the doorbell and leaned against the railing while she waited.

When the door opened, Louise recognized Karin right away, even though she had a totally different air about her now than the way Louise remembered her. She hadn't shrunk in a physical sense. And yet there wasn't much left of the woman who, even in the battered and miserable state she had been in two years earlier, had projected so much more vitality than the woman standing in the doorway before her now. She was hunched over and had fear in her eyes, which were looking more downward than straight ahead. It was obvious that she remembered Louise, but she did not seem surprised or curious. She just stood there, with a neutral expression, waiting for whatever was going to come.

"Could I come in?" Louise asked after a second. Karin stepped aside.

It had been a long time since they'd talked to each other. The last time they'd spoken, Louise had told her that she didn't think they were going to be able to find Kim Jensen, her attacker, and Karin had seemed to accept that. She said something about that being the way things went when you swam out where you couldn't touch the bottom and the current carried you away. She had nodded and thanked them for trying, and then she'd been given a lift home and had disappeared from Louise's life and thoughts.

Until today, Louise hadn't even wondered how she was doing, or even whether she was still alive, and that realization stung a little as she stepped into Karin's apartment.

Karin still hadn't asked why Louise had suddenly turned up, and Louise couldn't discern any glimmer of curiosity in Karin's eyes to suggest that she might ask. Instead, once they'd reached the living room, Karin asked, "Would you like a cup of coffee?" Lunch was sitting in a pan on the table along with two plates and a pitcher of juice. Karin lived alone with her young daughter.

Louise did the math and calculated that she must be almost four.

"Yes, please," Louise replied.

The place had an open floor plan, so the living room and kitchen were one space. Louise said hello to Karin's daughter, who was playing on the floor of her room, and then joined Karin in the kitchen, taking the two mugs Karin handed her from the cupboard.

"I came to talk to you about Kim Jensen. We're dealing with a rape case that is sort of similar to what you went through. Obviously we don't know if it's him," Louise hastened to add. "But I've read through your police report again, and there are some similarities that indicate it *might* be the same perpetrator. So I've come to see if I could get you to provide a few more details, even though we went through all of this back then."

Karin finally turned around and looked right at her.

"Do you think you're up to talking about it?" Louise hurriedly asked when she saw the blank look in Karin's eyes. Not that that would make it any better if Karin's answer were no, but Louise didn't want to push her too hard.

Karin nodded and shrugged her shoulders. "Of course. If I can help."

She walked over to the table, gathered the plates and glasses onto a tray, brought them back to the kitchen, and started washing the dishes. All without uttering a word.

Louise took a deep breath. "How's work going?"

Karin had been working at a day care when they last spoke, the lead teacher in her classroom. She was a slender woman, thirty-one years old. A woman who had seemed fully committed to whatever she was involved in. While taking her statement, the police learned she had been raising her daughter alone since the little girl was almost two and that between work and her child, it was nearly impossible to find time to date. She had decided to look for a boyfriend online in the hopes of making a family again.

"I'm not working anymore," Karin said in a monotone as she pulled out a kitchen towel and started drying the dishes.

Louise was starting to get an uncomfortable sense of what had happened during the two intervening years, or perhaps more accurately what hadn't happened. It had struck her the instant she'd stepped into the living room: There was something stagnant about the place. A stack of magazines lay under the coffee table, but there was no energy in the room, no spark, no spirit. Just emptiness, like a vacation home that had been closed up—and yet there were two people spending their days here.

They sat opposite each other around the coffee table. Louise had her notepad ready, and she scrutinized Karin, trying to determine what was going on inside her shut-down exterior. How was she responding to being contacted by the police again? Was she hoping that Kim Jensen would finally be caught, or was she indifferent after all this time?

"I want to ask you to think back and try to describe Kim Jensen's physical appearance for me in as much detail as you can. In the police report you said that he didn't have any particularly distinguishing features, but try your best to describe what he looked like."

Karin sat there, staring at the coffee table. "Since it happened, I've been trying to erase him from my memory. I've closed my eyes many times and imagined his face being swallowed by flames, but it has never worked. His eyes keep burning into me. They follow me everywhere, watching everything I do."

She spoke softly, slowly, as if it took a great deal of effort to choose her words. "He had dark brown hair, short, slightly wavy, sort of a little combed back." She closed her eyes and sat there in silence for a moment. "He had really pretty eyes, greenish brown, and heavy, dark eyebrows. He had soft, full lips. Not really big lips, but they were unusual. If he'd been a woman, I think you would say he had a sensual mouth. Do people say that about men, too?"

A shiver ran down Louise's spine. Karin's voice had suddenly changed. There was a passionate warmth to her words, one that shouldn't be there because she was describing the man who had practically murdered her.

Sick, Louise thought, *she must be sick.* Something was very wrong. The woman across from her was drowning, and it didn't seem like anyone was doing anything about it. To the contrary, it seemed like a process that Karin was calmly, quietly succumbing to.

"Six foot one and what people online call an average build." Karin made a little face at the impersonal description.

"Was he dark-skinned?" Louise asked, interrupting Karin's steady stream of words.

Karin looked surprised and shook her head. "No. He was Danish, if that's what you mean."

Louise hastened to explain that that wasn't what she'd meant— just if he had a dark or fair complexion. "Fair."

"When did you meet?"

"In early December, but he didn't come over here until January."

Louise turned to a fresh page in her notepad, and asked Karin to repeat the story.

"We exchanged emails and met at a café downtown, and then I invited him to dinner. He brought flowers and champagne. By that point, I had already fallen in love with him. We agreed that he would spend the night, and everything was as it was supposed to be."

Again, that warmth popped up in her voice, and the small hairs on Louise's arms stood up. She had read through the chain of events in the report before she drove out here, but sitting across from Karin, who was almost ardently describing the events of the night that had ended so badly, was another matter.

"It wasn't until quite late that he suddenly changed," Karin said, as if she could tell what Louise was thinking. "At first, he was kind, and everything was good. We smoked in bed afterward and cuddled."

She hid her face in her hands and sat perfectly still.

After the cigarette in bed, the assailant had tied her hands to the bedposts with his tie and raped her for hours, with and without paraphernalia.

Once Karin calmed down again, Louise thanked her for the coffee and said that they were in the middle of an investigation. She prepared Karin for the fact that they might need to talk to her again if the case turned out to involve the same man.

"Have you talked to anyone about what you've been through? Have you been in therapy?" she asked on her way to the front door.

Karin gave her a look that said she had overstepped her bounds, and grumbled, "That won't change what happened."

"You may be right about that," Louise said, "but it may change what happens in the future. It can make it easier to move on."

"I've gotten used to it. That's not what was supposed to happen, and now it's best for things to just be calm here." She'd opened the front door and was waiting for Louise to exit.

It hurt to say goodbye. It wasn't hatred that hung like a fog around Karin: It was despondency. She clearly no longer believed in the good in people, and it would take more than some everyday conversation to restore her faith in their goodness.

Louise felt glum on her way back to Police Headquarters. It was simply unfair that a guy who had caused so much damage was free, she thought, strongly suspecting without any concrete proof that Kim Jensen was the man who had attacked Susanne. She tried to throttle her instincts. There were similarities, but surely there were a shitload of dark-haired rapists out there with appealing features. As she drove down Hambrosgade and drove the car into the precinct garage, she thought about the even larger number of dark-haired men who had put their photos up on the various on-line dating sites. *This sucks*, she mumbled to herself as she parked. She waved at Svendsen, who'd been in charge of the fleet of squad cars here for many years. She wasn't surprised to see him so late in the day. He watched over those vehicles as if they were his own private property.

❧

Heilmann was in her office when Louise came up.

"Jørgensen got hold of the women who we know were in contact with the suspect," Heilmann said. "He made a list of them. Those women are coming in tomorrow. But then Jørgensen's wife called. One of the twins is in the emergency room, so he had to go home to watch the other one," she said. "I doubt we'll see him back here before Monday; you'll have to talk to some of the women when they show up."

Louise nodded. "I haven't had a chance to start searching for dark-haired men yet," she reminded Heilmann. "If we need that right away, someone else will have to take over."

"That's fine. That can wait. The girls' statements are more important. And." Heilmann paused for effect. "I really want to have you talk to Karsten Flintholm. We have an appointment with him tomorrow afternoon. He says he wasn't even in town last Monday, but he has dark hair and dark eyes, and was one of the three men Susanne picked out of the books. If he doesn't have a watertight alibi, we'll do a lineup on Monday."

That suited Louise just fine. She relished the thought of talking to him. *Even just hauling his ass in here will be fun.*

"How many of the women are coming in tomorrow?"

"Nine. I'll divvy them up between you and Stig."

"It doesn't seem likely that a woman who's been subjected to the kind of assault we're searching for would keep her profile up online," Louise said. "Wouldn't she go in and delete it right away?"

She had a hard time imagining what kind of information could be gained from interviewing the women, and how much of a description they could get. But, of course, you never knew.

Heilmann rubbed her forehead and said, "We don't have anything else to go on. The crime-scene investigators didn't get anything else from Susanne's apartment. Suhr is pacing around the division unable to decide if we should ask the public for help or wait for the lab results to come back on the DNA and just hope we find a match in the database. Right now, we have nothing, so we just have to work with what we've got and hope more leads turn up over the next few weeks."

With that outlook, Louise realized there would be time to enjoy a quiet Friday night with Peter and a pleasant weekend with Markus; before she even left Heilmann's office, she started planning a little trip out of town to visit her parents. Markus and Peter would both enjoy that.

She went in and studied the list Lars had compiled. Four women to interview, the first at ten o'clock. She turned off her computer and locked the door behind her.

Her bike was still parked outside the building and the air was still warm. She rode down across the cobblestones on Halmtorvet Square and felt like stopping for a cup of coffee at one of the cafés. She pulled off to the side and called Peter at home to see if she could entice him to join her.

"Doesn't that sound nice?" she asked convincingly. She could sense him trying to find a way out of it, and when he finally did say yes, she was sure it was more to humor her than because he really wanted to. They'd hardly spent any time together all week because she'd come home so late each night. They agreed she would go in and order, and he would leave right away and be there shortly.

She waved as he came striding up the sidewalk. He looked tired, but like he was trying to snap out of it.

"Hi, honey," he said, kissing her and taking a seat.

The coffee was already on the table, and she filled him in on her plan to go visit her folks out in the country the next day.

"What did Camilla say about Markus coming with us?" he asked, taking a cautious sip of his coffee.

"I haven't asked her yet, but I can't imagine her having any objections. He loves going out there. Camilla's meeting a guy, so I bet she'll just be glad to know that Markus is in good hands and being entertained. That way, she can relax and enjoy her weekend."

Peter looked at her in surprise. "She's seeing someone? When did all that happen?"

"I don't actually know," Louise said. "I was just thinking she's been a little distracted lately. You know her. She usually calls several times a day, and now I hardly ever hear from her. I talked to her briefly earlier today, but it was mostly about my current case. And then she said she was having someone over on Saturday and asked if we would watch Markus."

"Well, we'll see how it goes," Peter said, smiling. He sat for a bit, lost in thought, until he eventually stroked her cheek and then asked the waiter for a refill.

11

"Can I take the car?" she yelled from the bathroom. "I won't be late getting home, and *I'll* stop and pick up the groceries on my way."

Normally they kept their weekends free for each other, and Peter was the one who usually did the grocery shopping and cooking. They would eat breakfast together on Saturday, and afterward they would sit on the sofa talking about everything they hadn't had time to do during the week.

Peter came back out of the kitchen holding a cup of coffee and dug the car keys out of his pocket. When he turned back toward her, she noticed dark circles under his eyes. She'd heard him get up at some point during the night and assumed he had been up working while she was sound asleep.

"I'll suggest to Camilla that I pick Markus up today," Louise said. "That way, we can get an early start tomorrow morning. You look like someone who needs to unwind and relax a little."

Having practically inhaled the first one, Peter turned around and went back to the kitchen to pour himself a second cup of coffee. "Okay," he said from the kitchen, and then a moment later added that he wasn't sure when he'd be able to get away from the office.

"I'm doing interviews all day, so I'll be at Camilla's place around five," Louise guessed.

Peter stuck his head into the bathroom when he was ready to leave. "I'll call when I know when I'll be home," he promised before turning to go. Louise heard the door click shut behind him.

"Let me fucking tell you something, you fucking bitch. I wasn't anywhere near Tivoli or Valby on Monday or any other day." Louise was losing her patience. For the last hour, Karsten Flintholm had been screaming and yelling and swearing at her. He'd been aggressive from the moment she sat down across from him and had pretty much repeated the same few sentences for the whole session.

"I told you. I was an hour away from Copenhagen in Ringsted with my wife and new baby."

It turned out that he had gotten married during his last stint in jail. He had gotten a barely legal woman pregnant just before he went in, and now they were living in a glorified shack of a cottage out in her allotment garden on the outskirts of Ringsted.

Louise let him talk. Toft and Stig were on their way out to the address to see if the girl could give him an alibi, and until they had talked to her, Louise was going to keep Flintholm under close observation. He hadn't known in advance what the police had wanted to talk to him about, so he hadn't had a chance to coach his young wife on the answers. However, Louise was prepared for the possibility that he might have instructed her to back up his story: that they'd been together the whole time since he'd gotten out of jail.

"Here I am starting a family and settling down, and you're all over my fucking ass here because of my past." He sounded like a petulant child, but certainly didn't look like one with his unkempt hair and tattoos covering most of his exposed skin.

"We're not all over your ass," Louise said calmly. "We just want to know where you were Monday night. You were identified, and you ought to be familiar enough with how things work to know that we have to check out your story."

He leaped out of his chair and lunged at Louise, but she was on her feet before he got to her. She grabbed his arm and twisted it behind his back. She gave it an extra jerk upward, which really wasn't necessary, but he could take that as thanks for all the shit she'd had to sit here listening to him spew for the past half hour.

He glared at her but backed down. She sat down again, ready to proceed. He was thirty-two, but looked much younger. His short, dark hair was gelled back. When he looked at Louise, there was a measure of detached evil in his eyes, but she had no doubt that some women would find him charming. He had an attractive nose and soft lines around his mouth, although it was a little hard to see anything charming about him right now. There was something unsympathetic and cold in his face. He had a lack of respect and an obvious desire to show it.

"And you still don't want to tell me what you were doing Monday night? You, your wife, and your child?"

He didn't respond, didn't bat an eye. She didn't want to get all worked up. She was very conscious of her own short fuse.

Louise calculated that the others would soon be at the location down in Ringsted. It couldn't take more than an hour to drive down there and find the house. Before she'd started questioning him, she had arranged with Toft and Stig to call when they arrived and let her know if the young woman was home; when the phone call came, the phone hardly had time to ring once before she had the receiver to her ear.

"They're there and getting started now," Heilmann said. Louise hung up and sat silently for a moment, watching Flintholm. He had been staring daggers at her, trying to figure out what was going on from the moment she answered her phone.

"They're in Ringsted," Louise said. "Now we'll just wait and see what your wife has to say."

"She won't say shit!" he snorted, and his tensed jaws relaxed a little.

"Well, that'd be dumb," Louise said, "because then they'll haul her in here, and your child will be placed with social services."

She held her breath, a little nervous that this would provoke a new outburst, but he seemed to have regained his composure. So, she continued: "If she feels any shred of responsibility, she'll talk. And if you're sure she's going to confirm your story, then everything will be fine."

"You obnoxious bitch!" he hissed, but he stayed in his seat.

"You'd best shut up. Otherwise I might start getting the impression that you're hiding something."

She made a show of picking up the stack of interview summaries from the women she'd spoken with earlier in the day. As she'd predicted, none of them had met "Mr. Noble," only exchanged emails with him. But two of them had kept up their correspondence long enough that they'd swapped email addresses with him instead of writing via their dating profiles.

She knew that CCU was already working on the two women's computers to see where Mr. Noble had written from. It didn't take them long to figure out that he had used a different publicly accessible computer each time. She kept reading, intentionally ignoring Flintholm, who grunted or swore periodically.

One thing both women had in common was that they were similar to Susanne Hansson, personality-wise. They were introverts and weren't all that self-confident. Since her first chat with Susanne, Louise had been struck by the fact that Jesper Bjergholdt had never planned to exchange photos. He'd written to her that he preferred what was inside a person to what was on the outside.

Two of the women Louise had spoken to that morning had also fallen for that wording, whereas the other two had written him off for that same reason. They'd apparently assumed it meant he didn't consider himself attractive, and they'd consequently lost interest in him.

She thought it was striking that Mr. Noble had insisted that they write to each other for a long time before they considered meeting in person. Experts usually advised people involved in online dating to meet relatively quickly, or at least to talk to each other by phone after writing for a week. This can help them figure out if they have any chemistry sooner rather than later. But Mr. Noble and Susanne and these other women took the completely opposite route.

Louise could appreciate how the former would be very hard to gauge through a computer screen. Online, it was all too easy to fall for a person who was good at expressing himself in writing. When you finally met in person, it might turn out that you'd fallen in love with the words and not the person—hence the encouragement to make contact outside of cyberspace as soon as the spark struck. However, for Mr. Noble, women falling in love with his words was exactly what he wanted.

Mr. Noble hadn't given his phone number to any of the women Louise or Stig had talked to that day. Only one of the five women Stig had interviewed was still in touch with Mr. Noble. The rest had all quickly brushed him off as uninteresting or weird. The one that was still interested was yet another woman who was hungry for his words of reassurance: that perfectly ordinary people could find happiness, too. And she seemed to feel like things were finally going her way.

The phone rang again. "Let him go," Heilmann's voice said. "His wife says he was home. Her parents came to visit, which has been confirmed. But make sure he knows we'll call him in for a lineup if necessary."

Louise hung up. She sat and looked at him for a minute before nodding to the door.

Finally, something happened in his eyes. He leaned forward a little and glared at her before saying anything. His voice was malevolent: "If I ever get involved in a situation that makes you guys lock me up again…" He let his eyes roam provocatively up and down her body. "I think I'd pick someone like you."

Louise quickly counted to ten in her head, extended that to fifteen, and then stood up. "Goodbye."

She stood there watching him as he shuffled out the door. *Fucking asshole*, she thought. An obnoxious idiot, he didn't have the balls to really attack her. It was pathetic. She'd just read up on his previous sentences, and according to the police reports, the women he'd raped had all been weak targets. He'd assaulted one of them right as she left a bar, so drunk that her stomach would have been pumped if a medical evaluation had been requested. He'd pulled her into the bushes and raped her. Afterward, he'd run off and left her lying there. The woman hadn't come to until the next morning, and even though she was pretty incoherent about what had happened, he was quickly apprehended. His DNA in her vagina made it impossible for him to deny the assault, although he'd claimed she was depraved and had gone to great lengths to lure him, a total stranger, into having sex with her. From the very first interrogation session, he'd claimed the sex was consensual, but witnesses from the bar had confirmed that the victim, eerily also named Louise, had not been in any condition to say what she wanted when she'd left the bar. His defense attorney had finally conceded that point, leading to a plea bargain.

There was no reason for Louise to stay and wait for Toft and Stig to return from Ringsted. She agreed with Heilmann that they would meet on Monday after Lieutenant Suhr's morning briefing to see where their group stood with the investigation.

A couple of guys from the Computer Crime Unit had stopped by Heilmann's office late in the day with the results of their search of the three women's computers. Determining that the women had exchanged email addresses with Mr. Noble had given them all hope, but even from the very end of the hallway Heilmann could read, from the faces on the CCU team as they walked into the division, that the search hadn't come up with anything useful. Mr. Noble had used the internet café on H. C. Ørstedsvej and the Østerbro Library on Dag Hammarskölds Allé, so they were back to square one. A couple of detectives from the downtown precinct had been assigned to check in at those locations regularly. They were supposed to meet with the regulars Toft hadn't yet spoken with, to look for anyone who might have noticed the dark-haired man, but that was a shot in the dark, as Suhr would say.

"People who go to places like that do it precisely to avoid contact with other human beings. They're only fucking paying attention to what's on the screen in front of them," Suhr had said when they originally decided to ask around for people who might have noticed Jesper Bjergholdt. "But, of course, it's one of the things we ought to try," he conceded in the same breath.

Camilla had said *"Great!"* right away when Louise asked if it would be okay if she picked up Markus that night, instead of early Saturday morning, so Louise had driven to the grocery store to get something to fix for dinner for the three of them.

"We'll be home about four thirty, so I'll have his bag packed when you get here," Camilla had said, sounding excited that her son was getting to go out of town for the weekend.

Maybe her excitement also had something to do with the fact that she had suddenly been given a whole Friday night to herself, Louise thought, smiling as she parked in the garage underneath the Kvickly mart on Falkoner Allé. She was still thinking about her friend as she navigated her shopping cart along the refrigerated cases, trying to decide what to make. She sensed that Camilla was very eager to meet this new acquaintance. It wasn't like her to be so secretive, and that made Louise curious. Camilla normally didn't hold back on details when she met a man, but it rarely lasted longer than a couple of dates, and she often had long dry spells in between her relationships.

Louise had occasionally suspected that Camilla went on these dates just to please her friends—and especially her mother in Skanderborg, who never hid her opinion that her daughter spent too much time on her career and way too little time on herself and her own needs. On the other hand, the few times Camilla had kept her dates to herself, it was usually because they meant a little more to her. Over the years, Louise had learned that, in those cases, there was no point in asking.

She gave up on the idea of anything that required more culinary skill than turning on the oven. She'd spoken with Peter before she left Police Headquarters, and he still couldn't tell her when he would be home. He'd been curt, and she'd hurried to say that she would fix something for herself and Markus, so he shouldn't feel any pressure to rush. She grabbed a bag of chicken wings from the frozen-foods aisle, deciding that that would be a good thing to eat in front of the TV.

Louise parked in front of the main entrance to Camilla's building and rang the buzzer.

"Is it you? Come on up!" Markus's voice yelled through the speaker on the entrance phone.

She noted her own happiness as she hurried up the stairs. A loaner kid was really the perfect arrangement for the way her life was set up, she thought, before preparing herself for the maelstrom of a reception she usually got.

"Mom's in the shower," Markus said when they finished hugging.

Louise smiled at him and said that they'd best not bother her then.

"You're not bothering me at all," Camilla said, sticking her head out of the bathroom with her hair wrapped in a green towel. A second later, she came out into the hallway wearing a short terry cloth bathrobe, smelling of perfume, and gave Louise a kiss on the cheek.

"Markus is looking forward to this," she said, going out to the kitchen to turn on the oven.

Louise followed her and stood in the doorway. "Is your date coming over here?" Louise mimed so Markus wouldn't hear her question.

Camilla nodded.

Markus was off packing the toys he wanted to bring.

"He asked if I'd rather meet at a café, but it's a little less formal if he comes here," she said, putting a bottle of tonic water into the fridge to chill.

"Since you're meeting for the first time, don't you think it would be wise to meet somewhere public with other people around?" Louise suggested, almost knowing what would come next.

Camilla sprinkled flour on the kitchen counter and was rolling out some puff pastry with a rolling pin when she turned around. "You know I have written several pieces about the safety tips SafeChat.dk recommends you follow when you meet someone you've only had contact with online," she said with a joking scowl. "So nice to know you read my articles."

She kept rolling until the puff pastry couldn't be stretched any further.

"Well, since you've written about them, I would think you'd follow them!" Louise tried, having a hard time seeing how the one thing precluded the other.

"Those safety rules are meant for children and teenagers: 'Don't meet someone you met online without telling a grown-up.' I *am* a grown-up, so I've been told, and I can just shoo him out the door if he's up to no good," she continued.

Louise was in no doubt about Camilla's ability to shoo men out, but it still sounded risky to her.

Camilla opened the fridge and took out a jar of Glyngøre lump-fish caviar. With a teaspoon, she placed dollops onto the puff pastry at regular intervals and then rolled it up like a jelly roll before cutting it into thin slices, which she laid out flat, like Danish, on a baking sheet.

"Should I bring my video games?" Markus shouted from his room.

"Take your Game Boy so you'll have it for the drive," Camilla answered. "Besides," she said to Louise, "he's just coming over for a drink. We're going out to dinner tomorrow night, but if it turns out there's no spark there, then we can skip the dinner." She opened the oven and put the baking sheet in, then quickly glanced at her watch and asked if Louise and Markus shouldn't be going.

Louise smiled and called out to Markus.

Camilla was getting out her hair dryer when Markus ran into the bathroom to say goodbye to her while Louise stood at the door holding his bag over her shoulder, waiting until they were done with their goodbyes.

"Can I sit in front?" Markus asked when they got down to the car.

Louise gave him a smile and tousled his hair. "We'll have none of that, young man. You know I'm a police officer," she said, making her voice sound very authoritative.

He bowed his head in a theatrical sulk and opened the back door. His whole goal had been getting her to say that she was a police officer. It surprised her a little that he still thought that was a big deal, and she thought she really ought to enjoy her rock-star status for as long as it lasted.

❧

Markus was lying on Louise's sofa watching cartoons on TV while she got out their plates and her travel bag. She hadn't been planning on taking much at first, but her mother had called and said that she wanted to take Louise's visit as an opportunity to get the whole family together, so she'd invited Louise's brother and sister-in-law and their two children.

She thought fleetingly about Karsten Flintholm and could still hear him gloating—really, taunting her about the fact that she was going to have to let him go. It was bugging her because she was usually pretty good at leaving her "work hat" at work and not bringing it home with her. She'd picked up the technique from a training seminar for homicide detectives and investigators. The "imaginary work hat" helped people who tended to dwell on their cases even when they were off work. In the beginning she'd had a hard time getting used to this new technique, but now it had become a ritual for her, one she quite unconsciously relied on at times when brutal crimes might otherwise linger in her thoughts overnight. Thoughts of Susanne Hansson and Mr. Noble were soon placed far into the recesses of her mind as she went to the kitchen to get a bag of candy and returned to the living room to watch TV with Markus.

Later, she only just barely heard Peter come home. Markus had been asleep for ages, as had she. She noticed the mattress yield to his body as he cautiously lay down, taking care not to wake her. She reached over and found his hand, but couldn't climb out of the tight embrace sleep held her in.

12

She saw it coming but couldn't pull her arm back in; he was too fast. He positioned his weight over her back and then pressed down until she couldn't breathe. She gasped as she heard something snap in her shoulder. The pain was so intense that her muscles quivered.

He gripped her left arm tightly and tugged her back so that she rolled onto her stomach. Pinned underneath his body, she went limp and her muscles relaxed.

"Lie still."

She could feel his breath at her ear.

She noticed that his weight eased up slightly off her back as he leaned over to get a better grasp of the arm under her. She quickly flipped over onto her back, making him lose his balance. Then she pulled both legs up and kicked him as hard as she could. The impact sent a jolt through her body. He reflexively grabbed hold of her ankles and cinched the cables tight. It felt like a knife cutting in deep.

She instinctively scratched at him, hitting out whenever he was close enough. His cheek was bleeding. She could see the aggression radiating out of his dark eyes and prepared herself for another blow.

She had vaguely sensed that something was wrong, but had ignored the warning signs. He had been attentive and courteous. She had found it strange all along that he didn't want to exchange pictures, but she had taken that as a compliment, since he had written in one of his first emails that he could tell from her tone she was different from the others.

A reproachful voice popped up in the back of her mind and mixed with the fear: You're playing with fire. Fight!

She had enjoyed it; she'd flirted. It had been titillating and exciting to write back and forth, looking forward to their first meeting.

She screamed as he tied her wrists together, and kept on screaming as he pushed her down onto the floor. The fitted sheet had come off on one side.

She had seen the transformation happen when she had taken control in the bedroom. It had turned her on that he was so nervous, so hesitant and slow in taking off his clothes. A diamond in the rough, *she teased him in her mind as he stood next to the bed fumbling with his shirt buttons.*

"Here, let me," she had said affectionately once she had taken off her own clothes. She had started undoing his buttons, and that's when she had noticed him change. Something had settled in between them like a chill in the air she was breathing. He stood motionless as she slowly undressed him.

She had smiled at him as he pushed her onto the bed, not seeing what he was hiding in his hand. She thought it was a condom that he was too embarrassed to let her see. Now she realized it had been the sharp bands that he used around her ankles and wrists.

She struggled further onto the floor until he yanked her back up, intending to push her down onto the mattress. She managed to keep her balance despite her tightly bound legs, and with tremendous force she swung her arms at him. The blow knocked him down, and she was afraid the rage she had ignited in him would kill her.

The silence following their struggle hung thick in the bedroom as he sat, just in his boxers, straddling her chest and arms as he forced something hard into her mouth. He reached over for the roll of duct tape he had set on the bed and bit off a piece of tape as she writhed beneath him. She felt his arousal distinctly, and noted to her own astonishment that the fight had also left her own groin quivering and tingling. This helped her relax a little, thinking it would be over soon. It was a game that was exciting to both of them. She had just underestimated him; she hadn't thought he'd be into this kind of thing, and they hadn't gone through the rules of the game because she had started undressing him too quickly. So, she let him put the tape over her mouth.

She interpreted it as conciliatory, as an expression of their mutual enjoyment, when he stared intensely into her eyes, leaning forward toward her face. But then he pulled back a little, forced her knees apart, and jammed some hard object up into her. Everything went black. Her already-contracted muscles tensed further, so the only reaction was a small jerk that made her arms and legs twitch. She had been so stunned by the pain that was tearing her apart that she hadn't given a thought to the fact that she would suffocate if she couldn't breathe through her nose. She frantically turned her head to the side; the pain stopped, and she heard him drop something onto the floor. The dildo she kept in the drawer of her nightstand fleetingly entered her mind; that might be what he had found, but before she could finish the thought, he placed *his hands around her neck. Tears blurred her vision as she looked at him to see when it would stop. He wasn't squeezing, just letting his hands rest there as he settled on top of her with his full weight and plunged deep between her thighs.*

She relaxed a little again. Now it was done: He had had his orgasm. She tried to signal to him with her eyes that it was okay, she had gotten through it, but even before he yanked her over so she was hanging off the edge of the bed, she could tell he had no intention of stopping. Rage shot through her with the same intensity as the blow she had laid into the side of his head. She gathered her strength, and when he tried to flip her onto her stomach she kicked out at him again. Furious, he turned his back to her and left the room.

With difficulty she got up onto her legs and looked around for a weapon, but before she made it around the bed she sensed him behind her. It happened so fast that she didn't have a chance to parry the blow. Nausea set in as the next blow thundered into her face, and she hit the floor. She could hear him getting dressed as she lay there behind the bed with her eyes closed, feeling nausea overwhelm her.

She tried to hold it back by taking steady, deep breaths. Her relief at hearing the main door slam shut behind her made her relax a bit, but it was too late to stop the powerful wave of vomit surging through her. Her immobilized body flinched reflexively, and she fought for air. The next minute felt like an hour.

Another wave of vomit came, but she was no longer aware of it. Unconscious, she lay heavily on the floor and didn't notice her throat fill up and her cheeks distend.

13

We're going fishing," Markus bragged as he bounded out of the car and into the yard.

Louise's mother came out to welcome them. Peter walked over and gave her a kiss on the forehead.

"Hey, you!" Louise's father called from the farmhouse. She waved at him and gave her mother a hug.

Her parents had traded in their apartment in Copenhagen for an old rundown country house before Louise and her brother started at the local elementary school. Now it was hard to imagine that her parents had ever been city dwellers, and it was perfectly all right with Louise that they had continued to live in the country. Occasionally, she would get an intense urge to sit out in the yard under the enormous apple tree and walk through the fields, which were surrounded by woods. On the other hand, she had a hard time imagining that she would ever move to such a rural area, even though the landscape had become a part of her and filled her with an inner peace so pronounced that she noticed the change the second she stepped out into the yard. She took a deep breath of the fresh air and started carrying their bags in from the car.

"How're you guys doing?" her father asked as they sat down around the garden furniture on the patio. Louise smiled. Everything was as usual. She sighed contentedly and dragged her chair over into the sun. From out in the yard, she could hear Markus mowing some grass with the ancient manual lawnmower. It always amazed her that children were so willing to push it back and forth. She herself would do anything to get out of it.

"The kids won't be here until around five thirty," her mother announced, "so you guys can enjoy a little peace and quiet before the tornados arrive."

Thank God, Louise thought. Her two godchildren really could wreak havoc on a place. She had teased Mikkel and Trine many times, saying that just because there was a lot of space available, that didn't mean they should raise their kids to use every last inch of it. She meant that in all seriousness, but either they thought she was joking, or they refused to see the problem. Instead, they always got back at her by asking if she and Peter were going to have any children, and the conversation always ground to a halt right there.

Peter had an easier time finding things to talk to Louise's brother and sister-in-law about. After dinner, he asked with interest how things were going with their house, but by that point Louise had already disappeared into the kitchen to start cleaning up and making coffee. She was so rarely in the mood to listen to her brother and his wife talk about their staid life and big circle of friends, with one social event after another. This never bothered Peter. He took the whole thing in stride, and even remembered whatever they had told him the last time they were together. She smiled at him as he sat there nodding at whatever her sister-in-law was saying. It wasn't until they stood up to say goodbye two hours later that she realized it had actually ended up being quite a pleasant evening.

Markus was sleeping, so she persuaded Peter to join her for a moonlit stroll through the woods. It was extremely dark out, except for the bright moonlight that filtered down through the trees and lit up the paths so they could find their way. It was still too early in the year for warm summer evenings, and before they made it back to the house the cold had crept through her clothes, making her speed up a little when she saw the light from the windows.

"Don't you think we should buy a vacation house?" Peter suggested as they turned into the yard.

She stopped, surprised. They had talked about a lot of things for their future, but this one was new. She tried picturing herself as the owner of a vacation house, but she wasn't wild about the image that came up.

"I don't really think I'm cut out for that," she said, but she couldn't tell whether he was seriously considering the idea or whether it was just a whim, so she hastened to add that they might consider getting onto the national forest agency waiting list and hope to be picked for one of the old gamekeepers' cottages. That would be a little more her style: more land and not so stereotypical.

The gravel on the path through the yard crunched under their feet as they walked hand in hand. Peter was looking up at the stars, seemingly not listening to what she said. *So much for that idea*, she thought, squeezing his hand.

Up in their room, Louise dutifully checked her cell phone.

The screen said eight missed calls. The phone had been in her bag with the ringer off since Friday night when she had done her packing, and she had forgotten to switch it back on. She sat on the edge of her bed and pulled up the missed-calls list. One call from Camilla, the rest were from Police Headquarters. *Fuck*, she thought, dialing to retrieve her voice messages, a sense of anxiety spreading through every cell in her body.

Heilmann had left the first message about quarter to five on Saturday afternoon. After that there were two more messages from Heilmann's cell, and the rest were from Lars. In Heilmann's last message at eight thirty, she asked Louise to call the next morning. No hint about what was going on, just that short message.

Heilmann's irritation was clear in her voice. There was noise in the background, but not enough to tell where she was calling from. Louise looked at the clock; it was almost one in the morning. They had sat in the living room with her parents and had a couple of gin and tonics after their nighttime stroll. *Fuck*, she thought again, feeling Peter's eyes burning into her back. She was still sitting there with her cell phone in her lap.

"That was Heilmann," she said without turning around. "She's been trying to get hold of me since this afternoon."

"You're off. They can't expect that you sit around waiting for them to call all the time. You know that," Peter said, defending her. "If you're off duty, you're off duty!"

"Yeah, but they ought to be able to reach me if something happens."

They did not call her this way very often, but it did happen.

And anytime she wasn't one of the first ones to come running back into work, she felt instantly guilty—even though it was perfectly legitimate for her not to have been home.

"They'll manage," Peter said, yawning. "I'm sure she would've called twice as many times if she hadn't managed to get someone else."

Louise tossed the phone back in her bag and climbed into bed. The feeling of relaxation was gone. They both knew that she would get up early and be ready to leave as soon as she had spoken with Heilmann. She took a deep breath before she snuggled up to Peter and started to gently nibble his ear. He lay as stiff as a board as she tried to get the warmth from her body to spread to him. Her tongue had slid down and started tickling his neck before he gave in and pulled her close to him so their bodies melted together. It had been a long time since they'd made love. She hadn't thought about it before, but quickly calculated that it must have been almost a month since the last time. *That's too long*, she told herself as she let the pleasure carry her away.

14

There was a tense silence in the car. Markus was sitting in the back seat with a comic book, munching on a snack. Peter was driving. Louise was staring out the passenger-side window. Given the situation, there wasn't enough tenderness left over from the previous night to defuse the strained atmosphere between them.

Louise had gotten hold of Heilmann at eight that morning. She'd briefly told Louise to be at the pathology lab in time for an autopsy that would start at ten.

"A rape," Heilmann said. "The victim was found gagged and bound with cable ties."

Louise had quickly packed their bags. She'd waited until the bags were stuffed into the car and they were ready to leave before waking Markus. They had agreed that they would drop her off at the lab first, and then Peter would take Markus back to their place. It was too early to drop him off at Camilla's.

On the way out to the car, Louise's father told her that Roskilde would have a new police chief. "When Nymand is out of there, maybe you should think about whether that might be a nice place to work."

Louise gave her father a stiff smile, replying that it would take more than Nymand's departure for her to consider transferring from the Homicide Division in Copenhagen to the Criminal Investigations Division in Roskilde.

He tried to smooth things over by saying that he just thought she wouldn't be under so much pressure if she worked somewhere other than Police Headquarters.

She explained that the opposite might well also be true, and then she took a deep breath before continuing. "Now, quit feeling sorry for me. I love my job." She couldn't stop the defensive tone that made her voice rise.

As they drove away, she turned to Peter and said, "And this is just part of what living with me means." And then she thought there was really no way in hell it should be coming as a surprise to him.

The mood was definitely wrecked, and it irritated her because she was also angry that their Sunday had been ruined. It wasn't like she had planned for it, but then it also wasn't like this was anything new.

❧

"The body will be up soon. They're just weighing her, down in the basement," Flemming Larsen said as he let Louise in the main entrance to the lab. Louise took a seat in the lobby. The lab was closed on Sunday, and she guessed that he had tried to postpone the autopsy until Monday but Lieutenant Suhr had insisted on having it done ASAP. That was a recurring theme. Whenever they got a body after hours, it took a lot of doing to get the pathologists to perform the autopsy right away. Their argument was that they could see better in the daylight. Suhr would maintain that he had an investigation to get started on. Then they would grumble back and forth until Suhr would finally pound his fist on the table and snarl, "If you have trouble making out the fucking details, why don't you turn on some more goddamn lights."

And then he would get his way.

"She wasn't brought in until about nine o'clock last night," Flemming said. "They had a huge contingent of CSIs over at the crime scene, so for once everyone agreed that we wouldn't do the autopsy until today. They just needed a couple of people available to come in here and assist."

Louise nodded. The pathologists couldn't start until Forensics sent a couple of people to watch the autopsy. And, of course, she knew that all available resources would initially be allocated to securing the crime scene. Other than that, she still didn't know anything beyond the fact that a woman had been found dead in an apartment.

"Was it her own apartment? Where was it?" she asked. Heilmann had been very snappish when they spoke that morning. "You'll have to wait until the briefing," she had said when Louise started asking her questions.

Now, Louise turned her barrage of questions toward Flemming instead. He shrugged and said, "I think it was her own place, out in Frederiksberg."

When he said Frederiksberg, it suddenly occurred to Louise that she hadn't called Camilla back yet.

"What was her name?" she asked.

"I haven't gotten that far. She's still being called 'Emergency, Frederiksberg.'"

Louise thought that even if it did turn out that Camilla's date had been with a guy she'd met online, she wasn't the type of woman their perp would dare attack. There was nothing timid or insecure about her friend Camilla. The opposite. And they were talking about a person who put a great deal of effort into selecting and grooming his victims. He would have long ago determined that Camilla didn't meet his criteria. Louise looked at her watch.

"Are you guys going to be sticking to the schedule?" she asked. It was a quarter to ten and she hadn't heard the elevator doors, so she assumed the victim's body was still down in the basement.

"We may have to push it back a little. Suhr told us to wait for him, and he hadn't left the victim's apartment yet when I spoke to him a little while ago," Flemming replied. "He may be coming with the pathologists."

Louise and Flemming sat down across from each other in silence, waiting by the front entrance to let everyone in when they arrived.

"So, aside from this, did you have a good weekend?" Flemming asked.

Louise shrugged her shoulders. The nice part of the weekend had vanished the instant she listened to Heilmann's phone message.

"We were down at my folks' place in the country. Why?"

"I was on duty yesterday, too, so I was doomed to spend my weekend in here no matter what."

Louise had often wondered what Flemming Larsen was like when he was at home on his own time. She knew he lived alone after a divorce two years earlier, but she didn't know if there was anyone new in his life. He had two sons who were about five and seven.

Flemming and Louise had a great professional relationship, but they never saw each other outside of work. The only time she had seen him away from the office was at an event the year before when a group from work had gone bowling and had some beers.

"Who found her?" she asked, changing the conversation back to the professional.

Flemming shrugged and said, "I don't know. There weren't any witnesses on-site when I arrived. I think Suhr mentioned a female friend. There were a few indications that this time there will be quite a few clues to go by. The victim fought like crazy. Things were knocked over, and he left prints in several places."

That was the most encouraging news Louise had heard all day.

"It looked like the situation sort of got out of hand for him, so he was less careful this time," Flemming said.

Just then, they heard the buzzer from the other side of the glass sliding doors. Flemming stood up to let the people in.

Louise sat for a moment before following him. She heard Suhr's voice and was glad he was there. For the more spectacular cases, Suhr tended to come observe the autopsies in person, along with one of the people from his office. In addition to this, two people from the Forensics Unit would attend, one photographing the body during the procedure and the other asking questions and taking notes.

"We need every single shred of information," Suhr's voice thundered as he entered. "Now we'll catch him."

The others were eagerly debating whether the tissue someone had already noticed under the fingernails on the victim's right hand would provide enough DNA.

Louise joined everyone, saying hello to the lead forensic investigator, who set down her large bag and held out her hand to Louise. She had transferred to Copenhagen the year before from the Forensics Unit at Ålborg in northern Jutland. She was petite and slender; the first time Louise had met her, she'd mistakenly thought the woman was a trainee. She had to quickly reassess the woman's delicate appearance, however, because it turned out Åse had a lot of experience and was only slightly younger than Louise.

Just then, the elevator started making noise. The body was on its way up from the basement for the autopsy.

Louise nodded to Suhr and Klein, the no-nonsense forensic investigator on duty. She didn't recall ever having seen Klein without his lightweight blue windbreaker on. In the summer he would push up his sleeves, and there they would sit, wrapping his arms like sausages, right above his elbows. In the winter he would wear several layers of sweaters underneath, but even when it was bitterly cold he just wouldn't wear anything over that windbreaker.

Louise and Flemming chatted on their way up the stairs to the second floor, where the autopsy rooms were located, just beyond the changing room with its lockers containing sterile scrubs and gowns. It was quiet as everyone walked through the open door into the changing room.

Louise adjusted her pant legs inside the scrubs, gathering her long, thick hair and twisting the unruly curls before pulling a hair-net over it all. She had already stuffed her feet into a pair of blue plastic shoe covers, and finally, she tied the mask on so it sat securely over her face.

As they started the autopsy procedure, she sat down toward the back on a lab stool with her notepad on her knee. The body lay under a white sheet on the autopsy table in the middle of the room.

Flemming removed the white sheet. The first thing Louise spotted was the long blond hair that hung down like a curtain. The sight was like a fist to the gut. Camilla's apartment flashed before her eyes, sealed off with red and white crime-scene tape. She jumped off her stool and brusquely shoved Åse aside. Åse was just getting her camera ready so she could start photographing the body before they removed anything. The tape was still covering the victim's mouth, and her arms and legs were tied together with heavy-duty plastic strips. Åse said, "Hey, watch it!" after Louise's shove.

Both Flemming and Suhr knew Camilla Lind. Obviously they would have responded if the image that Louise suddenly pictured in her sick imagination had turned out to be true, but by the time she realized it wasn't Camilla, it was too late for her to stop herself from rushing over.

"Sorry," Louise mumbled.

She put a hand on Åse's shoulder before quickly withdrawing, scolding herself for letting her thoughts run rampant. She had managed to see the face with the closed eyes and the thick piece of tape over the mouth. The deceased didn't look like Camilla at all.

Her notepad had fallen to the floor when she leaped up.

"Her name is Christina Lerche," Suhr stated, looking at Louise. Louise felt like she had been found out. She tried to get a grip on herself as she bent down to pick up her notepad.

Back on her lab stool with the pad on her lap, she followed along as Flemming took the forceps and cut through the cable ties.

"Easy! There may be evidence in the closures," Klein said. He held out a bag the coroner could drop the ties into.

"Now I'll remove the tape," Flemming announced, leaning over the victim's face. Very cautiously he loosened one side. He could never have done it so quietly or slowly on a living person. With his white-gloved fingers, the coroner checked inside the victim's mouth. When he was done, the vomit ran out, forming a little puddle on the shiny surface of the stainless-steel table.

He turned toward them and observed, "The gag isn't sitting flat."

At the scene, he had determined that the victim had vomit in both nostrils and concluded, "Suffocation by vomit."

"The gag must have slipped far enough back into her mouth that it triggered her gag reflex." He bent over the body again. "The duct tape formed a complete seal, so she suffocated."

Louise concentrated on taking notes while simultaneously reaching a conclusion in her own head: The perpetrator hadn't suffocated his victim. He had certainly *caused* her death, but was it premeditated murder?

Before Flemming proceeded, it was Åse's turn again. She photographed the body's back and right and left sides, this time without the cable ties or gag.

Klein cut the victim's nails and took a sample of her hair while Flemming dabbed her nipples with a cotton swab to secure evidence. Louise studied the woman's neck and chest. Those were areas where rapists often kissed their victims. Flemming placed the long swabs back into the carton and closed it carefully. When he was finished, he asked the lab technicians to come open the body.

Louise followed the others out into the hallway to wait. Their steps echoed faintly as they walked past the open tiled autopsy rooms: high ceilings, stainless-steel tables, sinks, hand-held showerheads with extra-long hoses for rinsing bodies and body parts. The whole place was clinical and cold, and ultimately completely utilitarian when you were in the middle of it.

She leaned against the wall and eavesdropped on Suhr, who was chatting with the forensics people. In the background, a saw started. Normally other tools and running water would have drowned the noise out. But today the insistent drone echoed through all the empty autopsy rooms before reaching the "murder room," as they called the last one because it was twice the size of the others and thus had enough space for everyone who had to observe a forensic autopsy.

Louise was used to being there while the pathologists did their work, but something about that lonely sound from the saw, cutting through the silence, made her turn and face the other way. On weekdays when people were walking around working, the cold, clinical feeling was usually humanized some. But the Sunday morning quiet made the sound of the saw too persistent to block out of her mind the way she would have liked.

Flemming called everyone back in, "We're ready."

The two lab technicians came out of the room removing their armor-like iron gloves. They hung them up side by side in the changing room. Louise backed up a little to give them room to get by, accidentally bumping into the row of white rubber boots the

131

pathologists wore when they were working. She nodded to them as they left, and Suhr came over to her.

"I'm heading back to headquarters now; you'll have to give the report on Flemming's exam," he said.

Louise nodded and watched him disappear, his steps precise and determined, making his gait a little stiff. The others had already taken up their positions around the steel table when Louise entered, walking back over to the lab stool, ready to continue taking notes.

Oral cavity and nasopharynx filled with vomit. Same color as gastric contents, she wrote, listening as Flemming explained that this was a case of asphyxia secondary to an internal obstruction. The victim would have lost consciousness quickly, probably within one minute.

"She was dead after about five minutes," he said.

Louise's hand was getting tired from writing in this awkward position, perched on a stool with her pad balanced on her knee.

"He used a hard object in her vagina. I'm guessing it was the dildo we found on the floor next to the bed. There are incised wounds, the edges are reddish, and there is blood around the opening," Flemming announced.

Louise let the words flow onto the paper, but avoided looking over while the woman's gynecological examination was going on.

An hour later, they were done. Flemming didn't pause during the exam, but he did look over at Louise when he determined that the victim would still be alive now if the tape had been removed from her mouth.

She nodded, following his train of thought: *Did the perp sit there, watching her suffocate?*

Louise accompanied Flemming back to his office after they said goodbye to Åse and Klein on the stairs.

She sat down in the chair across from his desk, her notepad still in her hand. She followed him with her eyes as he checked his messages and looked around for any notes that might have been placed on his desk.

Flemming sat down. His tall body made the desk and the chair under him look small. His desk was stacked with paper and folders, a hilly landscape leaving almost no free space on the desktop. They sat there in silence for a moment before he finally confirmed what she had pieced together herself.

"The vomiting occurred right after the gag in her mouth shifted, triggering her gag reflex."

Louise didn't say anything, waiting for the rest.

"When you look at the blows she sustained, it is reasonable to assume that the gag shifted because he hit her…"

She completed his thought for him: "So he watched her die and didn't help?"

Flemming shrugged and said, "That's a reasonable supposition."

Louise shivered.

"I don't think he likes women very much," Flemming added. His comment interrupted Louise's train of thought and fed the rising wave of the hostility in her.

"No, you don't say," she exclaimed sarcastically. "He assaulted her, raped her, and then sat and watched her suffocate. Yeah, you don't need to convince me that he feels nothing but contempt for the opposite sex."

They agreed to talk again when the autopsy report was finished, if there was anything in it that required further clarification.

※

They parted ways outside the main entrance to the lab. Flemming walked her out and then went back inside. As the glass doors closed behind him, it occurred to her that Peter had dropped her off that morning, so she didn't have her car or her bike with her.

Irritated, she started walking south down busy Blegdamsvej. It was almost one in the afternoon. She flipped open her cell phone and called Heilmann to say she was on her way back in.

Heilmann asked, "Could you go out to Susanne Hansson's place and tell her what happened so she'll be prepared when it leaks to the press?" Louise stopped for a moment as Heilmann spoke, but then slowly turned and started heading toward a bus stop. "I just spoke to her at her mother's apartment, and I asked her to stay put until we arrive," Heilmann continued. "And I explained that a new situation had arisen that we wanted to brief her on."

Louise nodded, looking straight ahead. *A new situation!* You could certainly call it that. At any rate, it was now clear that the perp was far more antisocial than they had previously assumed.

"Maybe we should find out if there's somewhere else she could stay until we catch him," Heilmann suggested. "Given the developments, there's a good chance he may decide to go back and stop her from telling us anything else."

"The only thing I'm certain about is that there's no limit to what he may do. The stakes are definitely higher now," Louise responded as she fished out her bus pass, thinking how ridiculous it was that she was being forced to take the bus to see a witness.

"Are you going to stop by headquarters before you go back out to Valby, then?"

"Nope. I just got on a bus. I'm going straight there." Louise could hear Heilmann's smile.

"I'll ask Lars to drive out there and pick you up when you're done talking to her. Then you two can also stop and check out the most recent crime scene."

15

There are numerous indications that Jesper Bjergholdt"—
Louise and Lars had decided to continue calling him that
until they determined his real identity—"has just committed another very serious crime, which cost a young woman her life."

Louise spoke slowly, gift wrapping her words. She rolled,
folded, and tied little bows around each individual sentence. Still,
there was no mistaking her meaning. It could have been Susanne
who ended up on that stainless-steel autopsy table. That was really
what she was saying, and Susanne got the message—although she
tried to distance herself from it emotionally.

"But you're saying it was an accident that she died?" Susanne
said hesitantly.

Louise nodded, but her gesture was not convincing. Then she
continued: "He didn't plan for the gag to slide back into her mouth

and make her throw up. But he didn't help her, either, when it happened. He did nothing to save her. To the contrary, he let her die."

The indifferent expression that had clouded Susanne's face since the first time Louise met her at Hvidovre Hospital had returned. Susanne's eyes moved slowly. Just from looking at her, the amount of effort it took for her to pull herself together before she finally said something was evident.

"How can you know it's the same person who did this?" Susanne asked.

"We can't know for sure yet, but it's the same MO," Louise replied. Realizing Susanne didn't understand what she meant, she explained, "The details of what happened to you have not been made public. No one knows about the cable ties he used or the gag you had in your mouth. So, it's reasonable to assume that this is the same man, not a copycat."

Susanne's head made a couple of small, mechanical nods as Louise spoke, but it didn't seem as though any of it was registering. Her whole body had started trembling. She wasn't crying, just sitting there shaking as though a fist were rattling her body from head to toe. In silence she rocked back and forth with her arms wrapped tightly around herself. She shut Louise out and disappeared into her own hollow world.

Louise contemplated going to the living room and calling Susanne's mother, but instead she remained seated, laying her hand on Susanne's shoulder. *Maybe this wasn't the right time to talk about moving to another location*, she thought. It seemed almost abusive to force this fragile woman to deal with anything else by highlighting the risk that her assailant might come back looking for her in the near future. On the other hand, Susanne might be thinking these same thoughts right now, on her own. Maybe her fear of this was provoking all the shivering. She might even find the idea of moving somewhere else comforting.

While Louise sat there thinking this through, she pulled out her cell phone and texted Lars that he would have to be patient because she couldn't leave Susanne quite yet.

"Of course you feel scared because he's not in custody yet," Louise tried.

No reaction.

"Our sergeant suggested it might be a good idea for you to move somewhere else while we look for him," Louise continued. She spoke in a subdued voice and patted Susanne's shoulder until she started to calm down and the tension in her body abated a bit.

"Do you have someone you could stay with for a while?" Louise asked gently.

Susanne seemed to consider that, but then shook her head. They sat in silence for a moment.

"Is he going to come back?" Susanne asked, looking up. She no longer had the vacant stare, but Louise couldn't interpret what her eyes were hiding. Maybe fear, but Louise didn't think so. Perhaps doubt, or failure to comprehend. Or a fear of something else that Louise just couldn't relate to.

"I don't know," Louise answered honestly. "But there *is* a risk. You do know what he looks like, so you could identify him."

"Yeah, but I can't remember!" Susanne burst out.

"True, but he doesn't know that."

"Then say that. Get them to write that, that I can't remember anything." Her tears welled up and her voice was desperate.

Louise squeezed Susanne's shoulder and started patting her back again in a soothing motion. "Well, maybe that's what we should do. But then your whole story will come out, and that might not be that pleasant. Worse, perhaps."

Susanne's shoulders relaxed a little. "That doesn't matter," she said hoarsely, wiping her nose. "It's worse walking around like this, without anyone knowing why." Silence settled between them before Susanne started to explain what she'd meant.

"I went to work on Friday..." Susanne had to push the first few words out, but once she got started, it came out as a torrent. "But it was no good. I left again after two hours. People were staring at me, and I could tell they were all talking about me. But no one came over and asked me why my face looks this way. Everyone was avoiding me, even though their eyes were following me everywhere. I couldn't stand it, so I left."

"I think you should seriously consider staying somewhere else for a while," Louise repeated, overcome with compassion. She knew how weird people could get about other people's suffering and how this weirdness could create a distance that is often painful. Plus, the weirdness always happens right when the person can least cope with feeling rejected by friends and co-workers.

"I can also check to see if *we* could find someplace for you to stay for a while," Louise offered, collecting her things. Susanne was so calm that Louise thought it would be all right for her to leave now.

"Think it over," Louise urged. "We can talk about it tonight or tomorrow. Also, I picked up your sweater that you forgot at the restaurant in Tivoli, but the technicians are looking it over right now. As soon as they're done with it, you can have it back."

Louise wrote her cell number on a piece of paper and told Susanne to call if anything happened that made her feel unsafe. "Or, if you think of someplace you could stay," she added. "You're also welcome to call if you just want to talk to someone."

Louise rarely included that last comment in her standard spiel to witnesses, because there were people who took it as a standing invitation to call and go on and on about whatever. Louise decided to offer it to Susanne because it seemed to her that Susanne wasn't going to get anything out of talking to her own mother—in fact, it would probably be better for Susanne if she didn't bother.

Thank God that woman had to go do some shopping, Louise thought. Before she left, Susanne's mother had actually stuck her head into the room to nag Susanne to reassure Louise that she certainly appreciated the wisdom of keeping the press out of things for now. But Susanne's mother had also said that she would not tolerate the police putting the case on the back burner—as she had also explained to "that delightful gentleman the police had sent over."

"If you don't find that man who *molested* my daughter," Susanne's mother continued, "then I'll be forced to go to the press again and ask for their help." She sounded like a patient defending her right to see a dentist to have an abscess removed.

During her entire tirade, the mother had not once noticed Susanne rocking side to side, her eyes completely vacant.

Louise couldn't be bothered to respond, which offended Susanne's mother, who slammed the door behind her as she left in a huff.

Louise gave Susanne's arm one final squeeze and then stood up and said goodbye.

Down on the street below, Lars was illegally parked in the narrow drive that led to the building's inner courtyard. Louise slid into the passenger seat and sat there in silence as they headed out to Frederiksberg.

"How's your son?" she asked as they made their way over Valby Hill. She was watching the bicyclists struggling up it, their legs working in labored strokes.

"He needed seven stitches," Lars replied. Louise nodded, still looking straight ahead.

"And now the other one has a fever!" Lars continued.

"Oh, thank God I don't have kids!" Louise blurted out. Louise usually kept these types of thoughts to herself, but she didn't manage to catch this one in time.

Her partner glanced over and smiled indulgently—and a tad enviously, Louise suspected.

She was waiting for him to ask about the autopsy, but since he obviously figured she would just start talking about it, the silence ended up becoming awkward.

"He could have saved her," she began. "Flemming thinks the gag slipped back in her mouth when the perp knocked her over. If that's true, then she died within five minutes, and there's no fucking way he couldn't have noticed. She lost consciousness almost immediately."

Lars's jaw muscles tensed. "We have *got* to get this guy."

That indulgent smile he had given her as they discussed sick children was suddenly gone, replaced by an expression of determination.

"Toft and Stig are looking through Christina's computer," Lars said. "They'll hand it over to CCU tomorrow. This time, there *must* be some fucking leads to go on. Every move he makes can't be so carefully thought-out. He's bound to slip up on something."

Louise shrugged. Lars noticed this out of the corner of his eye and put more resolve in his voice.

"He must have written something we can use," he continued, turning to look at her.

"He could have written all kinds of things. It doesn't necessarily mean we'll find him," Louise retorted. "He could be sitting in an internet café God knows where, luring his next victim into his trap at this very moment, and we have no way of knowing he's at it again."

"Why are all the fucking streets out here one-way?!" Lars growled, testily backing up.

Louise was astonished and didn't respond. Her partner rarely lost his temper like that. But they were both worked up, professionally and personally, and aggression was a natural way to deal with that.

She inhaled all the way down to her stomach and slowly exhaled before continuing.

"We have to persuade Suhr to warn the public about this guy," she said. "And then he'll have to assign extra personnel to watch the phones if he doesn't think we'll have time to talk to each of the frightened women who will inevitably call in and start indiscriminately reporting men by the truckload…"

She took another deep breath. "I wonder how much he already has planned out as he sits at the computer writing emails to lure these women into his trap," she mulled.

Her voice had grown calm again, and that clearly rubbed off on her colleague.

"I wouldn't be surprised," Lars said, "if he has pictured, to the smallest detail, what it will sound like when he tightens the cable ties around the women's hands and feet. How the plastic teeth will slide through the locking mechanism with small, sharp clicks." Lars made smacking sounds with his tongue to illustrate. "The mere fact that he brings his 'rape case' with him on dates shows that he's planning to go all the way before he even leaves home," he concluded. Then, after a short pause, he added, "Anyway, none of my male friends bring plastic strips, duct tape, and condoms along with them in their briefcases."

He pulled into some angle parking under the trees on Adilsvej. The quiet street in the Frederiksberg neighborhood wasn't far from where Camilla lived, so Louise knew the area. They walked toward the entrance.

One of the crime-scene investigators' blue emergency response vans had pulled over between two No Parking signs. Christina Lerche had lived on the second floor.

Louise tried the handle of the locked main door before calling up on the security phone. She stood there peering up at the building while they waited to be buzzed in. Upstairs in the entryway of Christina's apartment, they stepped over a toilet and bathroom sink that the CSIs had removed to inspect the drainage pipes and sewer line underneath.

"Have you found anything?" Louise asked from the hallway, calling into the bathroom where two investigators were leaning over the open drain.

"We can always hope that he was dumb enough to flush the condom down the toilet. Or maybe he took the time to rinse his penis in the sink before he packed up his things," said Niels Frandsen, the lead forensic specialist. He smiled optimistically and waved at Lars before going back to concentrating on the drainpipe.

"What about fingerprints from the bedroom?" Louise asked.

for them in our database, so it's not a guy we've dealt with before."

Well, that definitively rules out Karsten Flintholm, Louise thought. His fingerprints were in the archive. She watched Frandsen as he got up to join them in the hallway. He fished his pipe out of his white overalls before walking off toward the bedroom with it. It wasn't customary to smoke at a crime scene, and Louise had never seen him actually light the pipe.

Louise stopped in the doorway to the bedroom, astonished. A large hole had been cut in the wall between the bedroom and the living room.

"It's not a load-bearing wall or anything," Frandsen said, smiling and taking the pipe out of his mouth. "There was evidence of the struggle on that section. I didn't want to risk not getting the whole thing, so we just took the wall down and ran it through the superglue-fuming chamber."

Louise nodded. In another case, she herself had helped examine a section of attic wall they had cut out and hauled into the forensics lab, where a technician put the section of wall into a large, airtight chamber along with fresh superglue in a heated reservoir. She had been amazed at the results: The glue vaporized, and the vapor adhered to any latent fingerprints on the surface of the wall. The prints were then clear and relatively easy to see and photograph.

Louise walked over to the foot of the bed. "Is this where you think they fought?" she asked, turning toward Frandsen.

He nodded, and she studied the narrow space between the bed and the wall.

"She must have kicked him with her legs together, and if she hit him, it would have been with the sides of her arms and palms, or

144

she could also have pushed straight into him with her fists clasped together," he said.

"Flemming found subcutaneous bleeding on her arms, so it seems conceivable that she swung her arms at him or used them to block his blows," Louise said.

A wicker laundry basket was tipped over. She guessed that it had been on the right by the foot of the bed opposite the door. There was a chair in the corner with Christina's clothes on it.

"It's strange that he didn't stand things back up again before he left, to make it less obvious that there had been a struggle," Frandsen said, puzzled.

Lars joined them.

"He was very meticulous the first time," Louise said. "Is there anything in the other rooms?"

She walked into the living room, where a door was ajar. It looked like it led to an office.

"No, they went right into the bedroom."

"She had a pretty high blood alcohol reading. They must have had drinks somewhere," Louise informed the others as she walked over to the desk. There was an empty spot where the computer had been. The investigators had been studying the thin layer of dust that covered the top of the desk like a membrane.

"We thought he might have tried to delete something from her hard drive before he left. But he obviously knew we could probably recover whatever he deleted, because he didn't go anywhere near her desk—we found only her fingerprints in this area."

"Eureka!" The shout came from the bathroom, and when they got there, one of the forensic guys was sitting on the floor holding a condom he had fished up out of the toilet's drainpipe using a pair of thin, curved tweezers.

Louise and Lars stayed back while Frandsen went in and squatted down to study the find.

"Well, would you look at that?" Frandsen's excitement was contagious, filling the room with anticipation.

Still, Louise couldn't help but ask, "Can the evidence survive sitting in the sewer pipe for almost two days?"

Frandsen got serious again.

"Even if it takes a month to clean it up, we'll get a DNA profile out of it," he said, still with a confident, victorious air to his voice. "But you're right, it's harder to get DNA from a sample that's been kept wet. The forensic pathologists have to cleanse the cells, and they often have to cleanse the impure cells many times before they're pure enough to get a profile from. But, shit, we will do whatever it takes."

He moved his pipe back to the corner of his mouth.

Louise's cell phone rang, and she stepped away from the group a little before answering.

The enthusiasm in Heilmann's voice was infectious. "One of Christina Lerche's girlfriends, who has keys to her apartment, found her yesterday afternoon. She's coming in here in an hour. Can you come talk to her?" Heilmann asked.

"We're leaving soon," Louise replied. "I'm in Christina's apartment now, and the CSI guys just found a used condom in the drain under the toilet. It's starting to look like we're getting somewhere."

Adrenaline coursed through Louise's bloodstream, and she pushed the faint pangs of hunger that had sneaked up on her in the apartment from her mind as she started mentally running through the interview she was about to conduct.

"I think the friend might have something interesting to tell us.

It appears that Christina Lerche was not particularly tight-lipped when it came to talking about her conquests, so we can hope that she described the suspect to her circle of friends, if she had met him previously," Heilmann continued without stopping. "It would be great if you and Lars both came back, because I would really like Lars to be there when they go through her computer."

"Where's Stig?"

"He's busy with the MTP and won't be back until Wednesday of next week," Heilmann said.

Louise felt her lips purse. It still irked her to no end that Michael Stig had been selected for the police department's Management Training Program, which meant not only that he was out of the division about two days a week, but also that he could one day be her boss. *God forbid*, she thought. Plus, she knew that Lars had also applied but had been passed over. That had caused some tension in the group, what with Stig gloating and Lars grumbling.

"I'll tell Lars," Louise said.

She went back into the living room, where her colleague was studying the victim's CD case.

"Heilmann wants us back at headquarters. I'm going to do an interview, and you need to be there while they go through the victim's computer."

He nodded and looked around to solidify the details of the scene in his mind. The apartment was nice, simple, without any knick-knacks, and tastefully furnished. The furniture might be from Ikea, but, combined with the lamps and the framed photographs on the wall, it looked fashionable. No piles of stuff, no mess, no throw blankets draped over the arm of the recliner.

"What did she do?" Louise asked as they started toward the front door.

"Realtor," Lars said. He had flipped through a couple of the folders on the bookshelf in the office. "She worked for one of the big agencies north of Frederiksberg on Falkoner Allé."

Louise went to retrieve her purse and jacket from the victim's kitchen. The Realtor thing didn't surprise her, because there was quite a bit of truth to the notion that you could learn a lot about a person by looking at their stuff. Every item in the room had clearly been picked with care—from someone who knew quite a bit about interior decorating. That would make sense for a Realtor.

Louise peeked in on the two CSI guys, who were both leaning over the drainpipe under the sink.

"Good luck, guys. See you later," she said and waved.

"Yup," Frandsen said, giving them a farewell salute with two fingers to his temple as she and Lars left.

16

I could tell this guy was different from the others. Christina didn't talk about anything else after her first date with him."

Marianne With was sitting on the very edge of her chair. Christina Lerche's friend had twisted up her dark hair and secured it to the top of her head with a clip. She had a nice complexion and wasn't wearing any makeup. She was thirty-three, just like Christina, and they had worked together for four years.

"She really enjoyed herself. She was a happy person. I envied her that."

Marianne seemed to slump, staring off into space and receding into her own thoughts before she continued. "But she was also the kind of person you could easily think was sort of overdoing it. She was totally obsessed with online dating. She had profiles on God knows how many different dating sites, and she never made any secret of it. She sometimes went out with several guys in the same week, although she rarely went on more than one or two dates with the same guy. It was as though that first meeting was the only part that interested her. After that she'd toss them aside, and the next day she'd be at it again with someone new."

Louise observed the dark-haired woman as she spoke. There was no doubt that Marianne did not approve of her friend's behavior, but Louise also detected a touch of envy in her voice. Christina's behavior, at least the way Marianne was describing it, was not unusual, though. A little while back, the division had held a Friday continuing-education meeting where a Swedish lifestyle researcher gave a talk about the increasing number of people who were becoming addicted to online dating.

"But it wasn't like that with *this* guy," Marianne continued. The vaguely disapproving tone was gone from her voice. Now she just sounded sincere, and sad.

"I think he charmed her with his chivalry. She made it sound like him walking her back to the subway was some heroic deed."

Marianne slumped again. She sat staring at the floor before straightening up and saying, "Sometimes I thought she deserved a good slap on the wrist."

Her voice started sounding choked up, and Louise braced herself for a bout of sobbing.

"She would get all irritated whenever a bouquet of flowers would show up at the office from one of her rejects," Marianne continued, her voice not breaking after all. "She lost interest so fast that the guys totally didn't get that the relationship was over." She paused briefly. "I really shouldn't be talking about her like this," she sniffled.

"What day did they see each other?" Louise asked, all her senses heightened, ignoring the witness's self-reproach. Her question was so abrupt that Marianne looked at Louise in confusion.

"What do you mean?"

"Tell me when Christina went out with him," Louise explained. "Where did they go, and when did he walk her back to the subway?"

"It must have been Monday or Tuesday."

"Do you mean only three or four days went by between when they met for the first time and when he murdered her?"

Louise was champing at the bit, but trying not to push Marianne too hard so she wouldn't freeze up.

"It felt like more time had passed," Marianne said, "but it must have all happened the same week. We were at a training seminar the week before that. And they hadn't met each other yet then. But she did say she'd been emailing a guy who sounded interesting. I'm quite sure now that it was Monday. They were supposed to get together after work in front of those quaint old pubs along the quay in Nyhavn."

"Did they go out to eat?" Louise urged. "Or did they see a movie?" Louise searched her memory, trying to think of other things people might do on a first date.

"Uh-uh," Marianne said. "That was one of the things Christina thought was so great about him. They just went somewhere and talked, and it seemed like she was impressed to meet a guy who was both well-read and gentlemanly at the same time. She told me about how they had chatted for a couple hours before he politely asked if he could take her out to dinner on Friday. After she said yes, that was when he walked her back to the subway."

"So that was late afternoon or early evening?" Louise prodded.

Marianne nodded.

SARA BLAEDEL

Louise wrapped up the interview, saying goodbye and thanking her for coming. Then she popped into Heilmann's office.

"We have to review the subway's security footage," Louise said before she was even seated in the chair opposite Heilmann's desk. Then she plopped down and gave Heilmann a quick summary of the interview with Christina's friend.

"We'll start by watching what the CCTV cameras recorded on the platforms at the Kongens Nytorv station, and then if they don't show up there, we can always try the cameras from the escalators leading down to the platforms."

"Hell, yeah!" Heilmann interjected. She didn't use words like that often, but she had been a little less formal ever since she'd returned from her leave of absence.

"First thing tomorrow morning, we'll have to ask them to save all the subway CCTV surveillance footage for us," Louise continued excitedly. "They keep the recordings for a week, and after that I think they record over them."

Heilmann nodded.

"I'll call the subway security office first thing in the morning."

Louise smiled and sank back in her chair.

"Now we'll get him," she said and starting humming to herself.

"Lieutenant Suhr just went home to spend Sunday evening with his family," Heilmann said. "But he prepped a press release for us to go public with tomorrow morning. We're asking for witnesses who had contact with a man matching the description of our suspect. And women who experienced the same type of assault but didn't report it. We're also warning people about him. It's just too dangerous not to."

"If we find him on the surveillance tapes, we can put out an APB for him with a picture as early as Tuesday," Louise said. "Actually, I could head over there right now. But do you think anyone would be there at this hour on a Sunday to pull the surveillance footage for me?"

They agreed that it made the most sense to review the tapes on-site, using whatever equipment the subway security folks used for that purpose. Otherwise, standard procedure was to copy the surveillance footage to DVDs that they could bring back to Police Headquarters and review there, but the transfer reduced the image quality.

Heilmann looked at her watch. It was almost seven.

"I doubt it. It'll have to be the very first thing we do in the morning. You and Jørgensen can make an appointment with Metro Security right after the morning briefing."

Louise went to find her partner. He was sitting with Toft, still working on Christina's computer.

"We're not going to get anywhere else with this until CCU looks at it," Toft said. "We can tell that they were emailing each other for about fourteen days, but we need to trace the emails he sent her. Our application turns up a number of different ISPs, but we're not getting anywhere beyond that. Besides, we'll have to get a warrant before the four service providers will turn over the details on the IP addresses to us. That'll take a couple of days."

Toft sounded discouraged.

Louise smiled and patted him on the shoulder.

"Then it's a good thing we've got another way to track this guy down."

Toft pushed his reading glasses on top of his head and pulled his eyes away from the computer screen. He could already tell from the tone of her voice that she had something new.

"What's up?" Toft asked. Lars didn't react. He kept on scanning through the printouts of the emails that Christina and Jesper Bjergholdt had exchanged, and Louise figured he assumed she was referring to the condom they had found at the apartment.

"Tomorrow we're going to go pick up a picture of him," she told Lars. "And you're coming with me."

"'Pick up'?" Lars and Toft exclaimed in unison.

"The same day our guy had dinner with Susanne Hansson in Tivoli, he also spent the afternoon with Christina Lerche drinking beer in Nyhavn. And then—wait for it—he walked her back to catch the subway at the Kongens Nytorv station and invited her to go out on Friday. We're going to look through the station's surveillance footage for Monday between five and seven p.m. Her friend can't remember what time this all happened, but we know when he was in Tivoli having dinner with Susanne, so it was probably sometime just before that."

Both men sat listening attentively to what she was saying.

"It will be interesting to see whether he knew how to evade the cameras. It's actually not that easy to do," said Toft, who was the person in the division with the most camera surveillance experience.

"Well, we'll cross that bridge when we come to it," Louise said, interrupting him in her sunniest voice. "He's not untouchable; he showed us that in his last attack when he lost control, leaving his fingerprints on the wall and later being stupid enough to flush his used condom down the toilet. He *thinks* he's in control, but he slips up now and then."

They nodded, and she continued: "Now at least we've got a lead."

Before heading back to her office to straighten up after her interview with Marianne With, Louise told Lars and Toft that she was on her way home, so if there was anything else that they needed from her, they should say so now.

"No, I think we're all set," Toft said. "We're going to drop off the computer now, and then we'll have to wait and see what the experts can get out of it." She waved goodbye and hoped they had a good rest of their Sunday evening.

❧

"Hello," Louise called, opening her front door. She heard voices, and a moment later Markus came running in and gave her a hug. Camilla and Peter were sitting in the kitchen sharing a bottle of red wine. Their empty plates had already been cleared and were sitting on the counter, along with a pan. A large unwashed skillet was soaking in the sink.

"Well, bon appétit!" Louise mumbled under her breath. She quickly glanced around at the mess and suddenly felt tired. She went to the bathroom to freshen up a little. The autopsy, crime scene inspection, and witness interview had all taken their toll.

"Have you eaten?" Peter called from the kitchen.

She had grabbed a piece of crispbread out of her desk drawer before Christina Lerche's friend arrived, but otherwise, she hadn't had any real food since leaving her parents' house that morning.

"Nope. Is there anything left?"

She walked over and peered down into the pan. In the bottom were a couple of uneaten boiled potatoes. She grabbed two slices of rye bread, buttered them heavily, sliced the potatoes, and seasoned everything with sea salt.

"Wine?" Peter offered. He was having a hard time hiding his

irritation at their weekend having been cut short, but he was making an honest effort.

Louise shook her head to say *no, thanks* and stepped out onto the landing of the back stairs to grab one of the lukewarm cans of beer they kept out there. Only after she opened it did she realize that Camilla had been watching her without saying anything. She hadn't even stood up to give her a hug hello. It gave her the creepy feeling that they had been sitting there talking about her and that maybe Peter had been venting. She just wanted to take her food into the living room and plop down in front of the TV, but that would not go over well, she thought.

With a forced smile, she took her beer and plate over to the round kitchen table and joined them. They had lit candles, and the bottle of wine was almost empty. *They've been sitting here for a while*, she thought. Markus was glued to Peter's PlayStation in the bedroom, so they only heard the occasional cheer of triumph from him.

"Is something wrong?" Louise asked Camilla, wondering why she was being so quiet. "Did you have a good weekend?"

Finally, her friend smiled.

"I had a really great weekend—thank you for watching Markus," Camilla said.

"Oh stop, I wasn't fishing for a thank-you," Louise said. "You know how we love having him. So…pray tell. Who is he?"

Camilla blushed a little, which Louise noticed immediately. Camilla didn't do that often.

"So, what kind of guy is he?" Louise said, trying to prod her along.

Peter stood up and started loading the dishes into the machine.

"His name is Henning—" Camilla started.

"Henning?" For the second time that day, Louise had spoken

before she could stop herself. It was just such a dweeby name, she thought, and hastened to ask whether he had a last name as well.

"Yes, Henning Zachariassen. He's got a daughter about Markus's age who spends weekends with him."

"Where did you meet him? Where does he live?" Louise asked.

"Okay, okay, easy now!" Camilla protested.

Peter turned toward them and explained. "Camilla's been politely waiting for you to come home before giving us the scoop, so give her a chance."

"All right, all right! Start from the beginning, then. I want to hear all the details...well, except for, you know, the *intimate* details," Louise added quickly.

"I only just met him," Camilla said.

The smile that Louise had put on to encourage her friend to start talking froze, turning into a scowl she had trouble concealing. She gave up on taking another bite of her food, and instead set her fork down onto her plate.

"Does he have dark hair?" she asked, suddenly serious.

Camilla nodded dreamily and purred "Mmm" in a deep, mellifluous voice. She had always described her dream man as dark and a good deal taller than her own five foot seven.

"Did you meet him online?" Louise's voice, stripped of any hint of encouragement or approval, cut through the pleasant mood in the kitchen. Peter, who was washing the frying pan, dropped it into the sink with a bang and turned around in indignation.

"Would you give it a rest?!" Peter exclaimed. "Has it escaped your notice that the internet is a completely normal way to meet someone?" he asked, looking at Louise accusingly.

Louise didn't even deign to look at him, continuing, in her stern tone, "Do you have a picture of him?"

Camilla shook her head. The purr in her voice was now replaced with grumpy exasperation. "No, I don't," Camilla said. "What the fuck is wrong with you, anyway? Can't you just be happy that I met a guy I want to be with?"

"Yes, of course," Louise said, a tad defensively.

Peter gave up on washing the dishes and came back over to sit down.

"Under normal circumstances, I'd be thrilled for you—" Louise began, trying to clarify.

"But, what, in your mind the internet isn't a 'normal circumstance'?" Camilla blurted out before Louise could finish. Louise held up both hands to try to calm the situation.

"That has nothing to do with it. I would be over the moon for you if I hadn't just been watching the autopsy of...standing over the corpse of a woman just a couple years younger than you who invited a dark-haired man she met online home with her...Friday night..." Louise raised her hand again to keep Camilla from interrupting her. "A dark-haired man who was in all likelihood the same guy who bound, gagged, and raped Susanne Hansson on Monday. Both of those women had one thing in common, and that was that they fell for him online. So, you'll have to just excuse me if I'm not gushing with enthusiasm."

Everyone was quiet. Louise no longer needed to fight to get a word in edgewise. "The victim even lived in Frederiksberg. When they wheeled the corpse into the autopsy room this morning," she continued, "for a minute I fucking thought it was you lying on that table, Camilla!"

"All right, that's enough! I don't want any more details," Camilla burst out in fear.

158

Peter put his hand on the back of Louise's neck and stroked her with his thumb.

Then Camilla's horrified expression changed, her eyes revealing the steely glint of a journalist on the trail of a new story. Seeing this, Louise hastened to add that that was all she was going to say about the two cases.

"Lieutenant Suhr will be putting out a press release tomorrow," Louise said. Camilla, in full crime-reporter mode, completely ignored this last comment.

"There are two victims? So, does that mean you're hunting for a serial rapist?" she fished.

Louise nodded, but obstinately insisted that she would say no more.

"What time does Suhr come in to work in the morning?" Camilla asked.

"Just before the morning briefing at eight," Louise replied.

"Fuck it—I'm going to call him tonight," Camilla said, sounding enthusiastic.

The wistful, dreamy look was long gone from Camilla's face. Now a professional spark had been lit. She had apparently moved her own love life to the back burner, faced with the prospect of a case that would undoubtedly fill the front pages of the newspapers in the coming days. She was about to stand up when Louise put a hand on her arm and asked her to sit back and tell them more about her date.

"What do you know about Henning?" Louise asked.

"I know plenty about him," Camilla said, a tad defensively. "He's good-looking and doesn't seem very criminal. Even if you seem to think that."

"I don't think anything," Louise said, tired. "All I know is that, at this very moment, a guy with a special knack for charming his way into the panties of women he meets online is ravaging the city. He's brutal and calculating and a sadistic fuck. And to top it off, he's sneaky. So far, he's made sure we can't even trace where he's emailing from."

"Well, then you can rule out Henning," Camilla said triumphantly, drinking the last of her wine. "He writes me from his living room out in Sorø."

"Sorø! Henning's from Sorø? Really, Sorø?" Louise teased, smiling.

"What's wrong with that? Have you ever even been there?" Camilla countered. Sorø was a sleepy lakeside bedroom community about an hour west of Copenhagen, not exactly the hip, urban neighborhood Louise would have expected Camilla to pick a man from.

"I'm sure there's nothing wrong with Sorø," Louise said. But now she was laughing. Peter shot her a look and she tried to stop, but small, shivering twitches in Peter's cheeks revealed that even he was only just barely able to suppress his own chuckling.

"Maybe Henning walks around wearing white gym socks with Tevas, too," Louise managed to say between guffaws. Her laughter released all the tension that had been building up in her gut since she walked into the kitchen, and now it washed over her, robbing her of any chance of regaining her composure.

Camilla slid her chair back over the kitchen floor in a huff. "I don't have to listen to this! He fucking does not—and, anyway, so what if he did? A guy can still be hot even if he walks around wearing lame-ass gym socks."

The last comment finally pushed Peter over the edge, and he dissolved into laughter as well.

It had always been Camilla's mantra that she would rather "end up an old maid than fall in love with some hick who goes around in gym socks and Tevas."

All the laughter and Camilla's angry outburst brought Markus storming in. "What is going on in here?" he demanded.

"Nothing," his mother said. "Louise and Peter are just goofing around."

He lingered in the doorway, but eventually gave up and went back to his video game without finding out what he'd missed.

Louise grew serious again. "Not to be paranoid, but you actually have no way of knowing whether Henning is sitting at home in Sorø writing to you just because that's what he claims he's doing."

"Why would he lie about that?" Camilla asked, more subdued. A small trace of uncertainty had crept into her voice, and she had apparently stopped taking Louise's comments personally and was now listening instead of being defensive.

"I'm sure he probably wouldn't. But our suspect had his victims—well, his first victim, at least," Louise said, correcting herself, "convinced that he was sitting at home in his apartment, even though he was actually emailing from a public computer. So, it's hard to be sure. Was he at your place all Friday evening?"

Camilla was about to defend herself again but relented and instead just said, "Yeah...until about eight o'clock. Then he said he had to meet someone."

"Who?" Louise asked.

Camilla shrugged and admitted that she hadn't asked. After all, it was just their first date.

"I know tons of great stories about people who met each other this way," Camilla said after a moment's silence. Peter got up and went back to doing the dishes.

161

"And I've only heard a couple of bad stories," she continued, "and I'm sure there are only a tiny number that sink to the level you're describing."

"Obviously. I know that," Louise said quickly and a tad defensively.

She also knew plenty of heartwarming stories with happy endings, and she actually did have a soft spot in her heart for single people who preferred writing to a potential boyfriend or girlfriend online as opposed to trawling the picked-over crowd that hung out in the city's bars weekend after weekend.

Mollified by Louise's comment, Camilla conceded that there were obviously some con artists out there who were really living it up, doing whatever they wanted under identities that existed only in their imaginations.

"This one time, I wrote a piece about a girl who met a man who really 'thought outside the box,'" Camilla said. "He convinced her that he was building a big hacienda in Spain. She lent him money several times because he claimed the banks in Spain couldn't figure out how to transfer money from his Danish accounts. She was happy to pay, believing that he was sending her money to the contractors in Spain, so the swimming pool would be finished by the time they went down there on vacation."

Camilla sighed, thinking about the woman.

"The relationship ended as soon as she realized that he didn't even own a planter of flowers in *front* of a hacienda. Her money was gone, and so was he, the minute she closed her wallet."

"Some people are just naïve," Peter said to her from over by the kitchen sink.

Louise shook her head slightly. "It's inevitable that misfits and psychopaths will be attracted to a venue like the internet. The problem is just that it's so fucking hard to spot them on a screen," she philosophized.

"Well, if you've got such bad judgment, you have to hire a private eye!" Camilla said.

"No, seriously, some people really do that," Camilla explained when Louise laughed. "There has been a big uptick lately in that kind of work at all the detective agencies."

"Well, maybe just to be safe you should hire a detective to take a little look at Henning," Louise suggested, knowing at the same time that that would spoil the pleasant, joking atmosphere they had managed to recapture.

"It's not him. He's a perfectly ordinary guy, definitely not a serial rapist," Camilla said and then got up and went into the living room to tell Markus they were going. After a brief debate, he came back out with her and started putting on his shoes.

Louise had gotten up and was standing in the entryway. Camilla stood in front of her and put her arms on Louise's shoulders, shaking her slightly as Markus went out into the kitchen to say goodbye to Peter.

"Can't you just give it a rest? Sometimes I get the feeling that you don't want me to be happy."

That stung. Camilla might not have meant it that way, but it felt like her friend had just kicked her in the stomach. She pulled herself together and then wrapped her arms around Camilla and pulled her close.

"There's nothing I want more. I'm just saying you should be careful."

"You think I've got crappy judgment," Camilla said, her voice now a whisper.

"That's not what I meant," Louise protested. "I'm sorry. I just don't feel like getting called out to your apartment and finding your arms and legs tied behind you. But I guess enough is enough. Even I can tell that I'm being too much of a busybody."

After they said goodbye, Louise lingered in the doorway, watching them go down the stairs. Her body felt heavy and her mind felt groggy after what Camilla had said. She shut the door and went into the kitchen to help with the last of the cleaning.

Do I really not want her to be happy? she wondered. Of course, that wasn't true, but sometimes Camilla plunged into things without thinking them through, and that's what worried her.

She started the dishwasher and headed to the bathroom to brush her teeth.

According to the statistics, Camilla wasn't an obvious rape victim and did not match this lunatic's perceived "type." But Christina Lerche hadn't been one, either, which just meant that their initial theory that the suspect targeted quiet, insecure women who dreamed of a man and a stable, secure relationship had already been shot down.

Peter sat down in front of the TV to watch a movie that sounded like it was well under way. Louise went into the bedroom to put on her pajamas. It struck her that she actually did not know what Camilla had written in her profile. Maybe she just said that she'd lived alone with her son for years, and that she longed for someone to share her life with. Maybe the take-charge, independent, urban side of Camilla—a woman who wouldn't dream of putting her precious feet into shoes that cost less than several hundred dollars—was hard to spot through whatever wishes and desires she expressed when looking for a life partner. Louise had no idea, and it really wasn't any of her business, either. Of course she wanted Camilla to be happy, even if it meant dating someone from Sorø.

She returned to the living room and flopped down onto the couch with Peter, pulling the afghan over her.

"What movie is this? What have I missed?"

Since he had been watching for only ten minutes himself, Peter's summary was somewhat vague, so she gave up on following the movie and closed her eyes instead.

17

"You can use this room here. We're just pulling the tapes. From what I understood, you want to see both ends of the platform at Kongens Nytorv, as well as the escalators?"

Lars confirmed this.

The security manager in charge of the surveillance archives had been waiting for them when they arrived. He led them down past the Copenhagen Metro's security office, where they monitored the surveillance footage from all stations continuously. A little farther down the hall was the archive itself, with its narrow steel shelves full of surveillance tapes from all the subway stations.

"There are monitors and two players in the next room." He pointed into a room the size of a cigar box. "The footage has also been burned onto DVDs, so you can take what you need to use back to Police Headquarters if that'd be more comfortable," he offered.

"No, this is fine. We'll watch them here," Louise said. She was impatient to get started and didn't think it would take them long. They had a time window of about two hours, and there was CCTV coverage from two angles, so they could each concentrate on one section of the station. For the moment, they were interested only in the north side of the platform where the trains heading toward Vanløse station stopped, since Christina Lerche had lived in Frederiksberg, four stops before Vanløse.

"Knock yourselves out," said a short, fair-haired man who came in and powered up the machines. "This is some scintillating stuff!"

They thanked him and remained standing until he left.

When they'd left headquarters after the morning briefing, they'd driven past Christina's apartment, and Lars had run upstairs to leaf through the photo album he had remembered seeing on the bookshelf in her bedroom. He was holding three pictures when he came back down to the car. Vacation photos of a happy, very much alive woman. Two close-ups of her face, and one showing her full body. They set the pictures on the table between them and started figuring out how the Metro Security machines worked.

"Do you guys want some coffee?" the archivist called in to them.

"Please," Louise said, turning around to smile at him. "Could you just show us how to put the machine on slow and pause?"

She had quickly inspected the basic functions, but knew that she would need to slow down the tape each time passengers flocked in and out of the subway cars. The pace was fast and the station was quite crowded with people on their way home from work.

"That button on the far right slows the replay down, and if you hold it in, the machine will freeze the frame."

He set two plastic mugs on the table, and Louise noticed him lingering over the pictures of Christina they'd brought.

Lars noticed it, too. He covered them with his elbow and forearm and said, "Thanks for the coffee!" with exaggerated politeness.

"No problem," the archivist said, slowly withdrawing. "Just holler if you need anything."

Louise and Lars got organized and hit play.

"How typical. The time of day we have to review is rush hour, when the trains are arriving every minute and a half. It's one train after another," Louise said, sounding a little grumpy. Her nose was right up against the screen as she followed the people coming down to the platform with concentration. Every once in a while, she stopped the machine when there were several people so close together that some of them were hidden from the camera lens.

After a good half hour, as she was starting to develop a headache, she jumped a little when Lars finally spotted something.

"There she is!" Lars said, shattering their focused silence.

His finger followed the stream of people on their way down the escalator from the round plaza at Kongens Nytorv.

Louise accidentally knocked over one of their coffees as she spun around to see his screen. She jumped up and grabbed the pictures of Christina.

"God damn it!"

The archivist came rushing back in to ask if anything was wrong.

"Do you have something I could wipe this up with?" Louise asked, trying to stem the little river that was heading for the edge of the table.

It only took him a second to whip out a roll of paper towels. In

168

the meantime, Lars had turned so his back was blocking any view of the screens. He stayed like that until the short man left again.

"Sorry," Louise apologized. "Can I see?"

Lars rewound a little. The camera didn't cover the top of the escalator, but halfway down, a blond woman with a large bag over her shoulder came into view. She was leaning against the handrail, her head turned back over her shoulder. They could see she was talking to the man on the step behind her, but they couldn't really see her face. It didn't make it any easier that as the two stood there, a steady stream of harried commuters hurriedly walked down the escalator steps past them, each one temporarily obstructing the camera's view of them. Louise immediately estimated the man's age as midthirties. His dark hair fell down, covering his face, as he leaned forward to hear what the woman was saying.

They did not get a good look at the couple until they reached the landing at the bottom and walked around to continue down on the last section of the escalator.

"That's them!" Lars announced emphatically, freezing the frame.

Louise moved in close to hold up the full-body photograph of Christina Lerche so they could compare. The man was standing with his back to the camera.

"That's her," her partner repeated, advancing the images at half speed.

People started moving again, their movements exaggeratedly slow. Christina stepped forward so the camera caught the right side of her face from an angle.

"Stop," Louise exclaimed. "Stop right there."

She held the photograph with the close-up shot next to the screen.

"That fucking isn't Christina Lerche!" Louise blurted out, shaking her head. "That woman's smile is completely different. I think Christina's hair was longer, too. That woman's is only shoulder length."

"Maybe she got a haircut," Lars suggested, sounding a little irritated.

"I just saw her yesterday," Louise exclaimed. "True, her hair was hanging off the edge of the autopsy table, but it must have at *least* reached her shoulders, probably farther."

Lars grumbled, clearly not convinced.

The dark-haired man was tilting his head down and concentrating on where he put his feet.

"Let's look at them on my tape when they get to the platform."

Louise rolled her chair back over to her own screen, ready to see them appear, but they didn't show up. She compared her time stamp with the one showing on Lars's machine. They were almost identical, so the couple should have been there.

"They're gone!"

"Rewind and try again."

"I would've seen them if they were here," she said in a tone that really left no doubt. "They must not have taken the train toward Vanløse station after all. Maybe they went the other direction, toward Amager Strand? We can look and see if he shows up again. He should, if he was just there to see her off," Louise speculated, trying to tamp down her irritation a bit.

"I wrote down the tape number and the time stamp, so I can find them again. Let's just keep looking," Lars said, as if he was giving in only grudgingly. "If we don't find anyone else who resembles her, we can have her friend Marianne look at this couple."

"Good idea," Louise conceded.

Their concentration was shot. Their eyes laboriously followed passengers as they climbed on and off trains. After another fifteen minutes, Louise punched the freeze-frame button on her machine with a hard jab of her thumb.

"There!" she cried out.

A couple was standing on the far end of the platform talking. "They must have taken the elevator down, not the escalator," Louise said, staring at the young blond woman. Now there was no doubt. It was Christina Lerche, smiling eagerly and nodding at what the man said. She gave him a quick hug before they parted ways, and then she started walking down the platform to get ready to board the train. At the same time, he forced his way into the elevator between a stroller and a bicycle to go back up again.

Louise stopped and rewound a little. She and Lars sat together watching in deep concentration, following the man. His dark, collar-length hair was slightly wavy.

"Six foot one," Lars guessed.

"Come on, turn around so we can see you!" Louise urged, drumming her fingers on the tabletop. The man didn't seem to realize he was being filmed, she thought, and yet he kept his face pointed away from the station camera the whole time.

Lars rewound the tape and they watched the scene again.

It'll be hard to make the description any more specific using this, Louise thought. She noted that he was thin. He was too far away to let them see his facial features clearly, but there was something aristocratic-looking about him. He had a bit of a Roman nose, and his lips were full.

Lars was sitting with his face in his hands. It just wasn't enough to go by; they both knew that. A rear view and a blurry silhouette weren't enough to print out and take to the press. Louise wound the tape all the way back, and neither of them said anything. There was no reason to leave the results of their search queued up for that little archivist, who would no doubt be in here trying to figure out what Louise and Lars had been looking for the second they left.

The archivist appeared in the doorway and nodded at the monitor, which was off. He asked, "Are you looking for that woman the papers wrote about today?"

Louise was about to deny it. Then she pictured him playing the tape back until he found Christina Lerche and comparing her with the old photo one of the newspapers had managed to obtain. Louise had no reason to believe he would do this, but she was annoyed that they hadn't gotten more from their search and she felt like blaming someone. So she nodded that he was right, even though she didn't know how much the newspapers had managed to find out.

"Awful story," he mumbled, following them to the stairs, where he disappeared back into the security office.

❧

"Why don't we go to that singles mixer event on Friday?" Camilla asked as she and Louise were sitting at Cafe Svejk that evening, waiting for Peter. Louise listened to her friend without taking her eyes off the river of people strolling down Andebakke Path into Frederiksberg Park.

"If he's such an enthusiastic online dater, then there's a chance he'll turn up when they hold the next singles mixer," Camilla explained. "It's a way to meet other people who have profiles on the website."

"I don't really think it's all that likely that he'll show up if every newspaper in Denmark is reporting that the police are looking for him."

They were drinking Czech draught beer and had been lucky that an outside table by the little pond was free when they arrived. Peter thought it was a great idea to go out for a beer, but then he had called when they were on their way out there and told them he would join them later. Markus was sleeping over at a friend's house, so Camilla wasn't in any hurry to get home.

The morning's disappointment was still weighing on Louise. When they got back to Police Headquarters, Suhr had trouble accepting they hadn't gotten anything useful from the surveillance footage. He'd stopped the press release that they were about to issue and insisted on watching the recordings from the subway station in person. Louise had sat in Heilmann's office, cursing Suhr for second-guessing their ability. She knew the whole thing would end up with the DVDs being brought in, and then he would see with his own eyes that the images weren't useful. He came to her office late in the afternoon and stood in the doorway, admitting it would be hard to use anything from the CCTV footage from the station to hunt for the perp, and deciding to stop the press release because it didn't include a useful picture of the suspect.

Before he left, he asked Heilmann to set aside time after Tuesday's morning briefing so they could discuss how to word the warning. He had decided that they would look for other women who had experienced similar assaults, which was the original plan, but Suhr apparently decided that warning women about meeting face-to-face any dark-haired men who were about thirty and whom they had only met online would be casting too broad a net. And, although Louise had been trying to keep her disappointment to herself all day, the setback had taken an even greater toll on

Suhr. After bragging to the chief of police in the hallway outside the Homicide Division's offices, claiming they were already getting close to solving the case, Suhr had later been forced to explain that they might not have gotten as far as they'd first thought.

"We have to get Suhr not to release this," Camilla exclaimed when she heard about the warning the police were about to send out.

Louise stared at her blankly.

"If he waits before he goes public with this warning, then the suspect can attend that mixer thing at no risk," Camilla added.

"The man just committed a rape and a murder. He's not going to show up at a mixer," Louise scoffed, shaking her head.

Camilla took a sip of her beer and then scooted her chair a little farther back toward the fence around the pond so the afternoon sun could hit her face.

"Dating is apparently a subject you have rather limited knowledge of," Camilla said in her best schoolmarm's voice, looking at Louise. "It's got its own culture. There's a solidarity among daters. You can take part and still be anonymous. People show up at these events with their username on their shirt, so you go over to TruckerBob and say, 'Hi, it's me, Anemone. We've exchanged emails.'"

Although Camilla was speaking as though she were giving a detailed lecture at the university, she could tell Louise still didn't really get it.

"You get kind of, I don't know, addicted to it," Camilla continued. "And then at these events you have a chance to see all the people whose usernames you know from the internet. If you don't want anyone to recognize you, you show up under a new identity and say you just thought you'd give dating a try."

"How many people come to one of these events?" Louise asked, having no real sense what the number would be.

"A thousand, maybe two," Camilla guessed and then ordered two more beers, but upped it to three as she noticed Peter walking up right then.

Louise greeted him with a kiss and pulled a chair over from the neighboring table. She could certainly see Camilla's point, but it was just too dicey compared to letting the public know there was a brutal rapist on the loose. After all, there was no guarantee he would show up at a social event like that. And even if it did turn out that he was there, it would be hard to spot him in the crowd.

Louise was about to ask Peter if he'd had a good day, when Camilla commandeered his attention, asking what he thought about her plan. Louise smiled at Camilla's enthusiastic arguments, finished her beer, and took her wallet out to pay for the next round, which the waiter was just setting on the table.

Peter nodded slightly absentmindedly.

Louise thought that Suhr's professional vanity might keep him from holding his announcement from the press until Friday.

"What the hell other alternative is there?" Camilla wanted to know, gesturing with her hands for emphasis. "You don't have anything. That's fucking worse. A murder, a rape, and a psychopath who hog-ties women and stuffs crap in their mouths! This is really going to be fun for Suhr once the slow news days of summer start. The press is going to go to town with this story. They're going to rake him over the coals. He's not going to fucking enjoy that very much."

Louise grinned. Camilla was right. He wasn't going to fucking enjoy that at all. Then she grew serious again.

"First of all, you don't know what we have—and you won't

know that, either, until you hear it from Suhr; and, second, if I pitch your idea to him, I will do so without any input from you. We don't team up with journalists when we do things like this. So, you can just stop looking forward to that Saturday cover piece you're dreaming about."

Camilla sat back a bit in her chair, offended, and fumed. "I wouldn't dream of getting mixed up in all this, but I just might invite Henning to the event on Friday, and Suhr better not fucking stop me."

Peter smiled as Louise sighed. She decided not to present Camilla's idea to Suhr, but also wouldn't tell Camilla she wasn't going to. She really wanted to ask some more questions about Henning, but she held back since Peter was there.

The first of May was as warm as if it had been August, and people were strolling home with picnic baskets and blankets over their arms. It had been a long time since she and Peter had had dinner in the park. Even though it was so close to where they lived, they rarely went. Actually, it had been quite a while since they had done anything so wholesomely ordinary and enjoyable together. A little devil on her shoulder whispered that the spontaneity had vanished...after they'd moved in together. She looked at him and thought maybe it had happened *before* they moved in together. Their everyday lives had taken over. Work kept them busy. Peter had been working a lot of overtime, and he tried hard to keep his weekly badminton date. Most of the week was taken up that way, without much time for them to just be there for each other.

She reached for his hand. Every once in a while she longed for a little more togetherness, but mostly she enjoyed the sense of freedom she felt. She didn't need them to do every last thing together. What she loved most about their relationship was just knowing they were on the same team, knowing that they loved each other and that he was always there for her. Doing everything together wouldn't necessarily strengthen those feelings.

"I presume you'll let me know what Suhr says about my idea," Camilla nagged. "Or, obviously, I could call him and ask him myself."

"We'll have to wait and see how far he and Heilmann get tomorrow," Louise said evasively. She thought about how Camilla's suggestions often seemed very simplistic. Camilla went after ideas or stories without thinking about their consequences. They had known each other for many years, and Louise knew it didn't matter what she said: Camilla always did whatever she wanted anyway. But Louise tried to be a little bit of a grounding influence by bringing up the consequences and realities that went along with the ideas in her friend's blond head.

Later, all three of them strolled along Smallegade up to Falkoner Allé. Peter followed a few paces behind them.

"There's one major flaw with your idea," Louise told Camilla as they parted ways. "He has enough time to attack one more victim before Friday if we don't do something before then. And Suhr won't be happy about that, either. I'm sure that would get a lot of fucking play during the slow summer news cycle."

18

I really want to talk to you before the morning briefing." Heilmann had come over and tapped Louise's shoulder as she stood
pouring herself some coffee in the little kitchenette off the break
room where her colleagues were showing up for Tuesday's morning briefing.

Heilmann looked tense and serious, and Louise noticed how
she was bracing herself for whatever was coming. *Fucking asshole*,
she thought, picturing the back of the suspect's head with its dark
wavy hair, and then followed Heilmann into her office. Louise
took a seat on the edge of the visitor's chair and noticed she was
clenching her jaw. She opened and closed her jaw a few times and
massaged just below her temples to get her jaw muscles to relax.

Heilmann was watching her.

Self-consciously, she slowly lowered her hands into her lap.

"Susanne Hansson tried to commit suicide last night," Heilmann said.

The silence was oppressive. Louise's arms felt heavy.

"She's been admitted to Hvidovre Hospital. Actually, the police aren't involved with this at all, but obviously there's no doubt why she felt driven to do such an unfortunate thing. Her mother was the one who called the ambulance."

Exactly a week after she found Susanne the last time, Louise thought, her heart sinking. She pictured the slightly awkward, battered expression on Susanne's face, and it struck more of a chord in her than she would have liked.

There was a knock on Heilmann's door, and Suhr stuck his head in. "You guys coming?"

"We'll join you in a minute," Heilmann replied, waving him away.

"Susanne's mother called Suhr at home at six this morning. She must have gotten the number out of the phone book," Heilmann continued, smiling wanly. "I think you should drive out there and talk to Susanne. I'm sensing maybe there's something she hasn't told us. Something that's really bothering her. This was a cry for help. We'll also need to offer her some counseling."

Louise nodded, completely in agreement.

"Not that you should push her too hard," Heilmann continued, "but maybe she's remembered something that could help us. Something she repressed originally because of the shock. We see that all the time."

"Of course, I'll talk to her. I can go right now," Louise said.

"You should attend the morning briefing first. You can drive out to Hvidovre after that," Heilmann replied, standing to retrieve the vehicle logbook off the bookshelf behind her. She wrote in

Louise's name and tossed her a set of keys. They walked together over to the break room, where the briefing was already under way. They had just sat down when Willumsen flung the door open and interrupted Suhr.

Louise followed along with interest as Willumsen, whom she was still angry with for forcing her to waste a whole day traipsing out to Nykøbing Sjaelland, unleashed a torrent of profanity. He ignored everyone else in the room, addressing only Suhr.

The murder of the immigrant woman had been officially categorized as "solved but not closed," since they had taken the woman's ex-husband into custody. Now it turned out that the witness who said she had heard all the noise coming from the victim's apartment around one o'clock had broken down and confessed that she'd only said that because a reporter was asking her a bunch of questions the same day the body was discovered. The reporter, along with a photographer, had settled into her kitchen, and since they were there, the witness felt under a lot of pressure to make some kind of comment on the appalling tragedy that had happened in the apartment below hers. So, she'd made up those comments about the noise. The paper ran with that the next day, and when the police came back to ask why she hadn't mentioned the noise the first time they talked to her, she was too afraid to admit she had gotten carried away and made it all up. Her lie had just snowballed out of control.

"Fucking idiots!" Willumsen snarled. "Now we don't have *shit* to hold this guy on."

Willumsen turned, surveying the officers of the Homicide Division's five investigative units, and stormed out of the break room again. Louise wasn't really sure who the phrase *fucking idiots* referred to—the witnesses or the reporters. She shook off his angry outburst and concentrated on Suhr, who was reviewing what the other units were working on. As he wrapped up the briefing, she got ready to head out to Hvidovre.

❧

"You're driving my daughter to her death!"

Accusations were being hurled across the hospital room. Susanne's mother was on her feet, coming at Louise before she even managed to close the door again.

"She can't live like this," Susanne's mother continued. "We read it in the paper—there's a vicious sociopath on the loose. And you're not doing anything—aside from sitting around drinking coffee in people's homes! First, he came after *us*, and now he's gone and murdered some poor young woman…"

Susanne's mother's voice was agitated and shrill, but devoid of even the slightest hint of sadness.

Louise looked over at the hospital bed. Susanne was just lying there, the same as the first time Louise had met her. Susanne turned her face toward the door to see who had come in, but avoided looking in her mother's direction. That sent a twinge through Louise's heart. The mother's accusations had the same effect as one of those awful little yappy dogs: It's all you could do not to kick it in the rump to get it to shut up.

"I'd like to ask you to step out of the room while I speak to Susanne." Louise kept her face calm and spoke with all the official police authority she could.

"No way," the mother fumed. "My daughter has suffered enough. I insist on being here to protect her. You've certainly demonstrated that you can't." She made a big show of walking

181

over and sitting down on the edge of the bed. Susanne did not acknowledge her mother's presence.

Again, Louise tried to get the mother to wait outside while she spoke with Susanne. But the mother started getting all worked up; when she began blaming the police for her daughter's suicide attempt, Louise gave up.

"I'm just going to step out and call my partner, so he can remove you while I do my job," Louise calmly announced.

That seemed to hit home; the mother finally dropped her voice. "Someone has to take care of her," she said in a half whimper.

That was the last straw for Louise. She walked over, grabbed hold of the woman's arm, and escorted her out of the hospital room. Susanne lay there watching her, and Louise thought she saw a little glimmer of amusement deep within those expressionless eyes.

Louise pulled a chair up to the bed and sat in silence for a moment as she searched for the right words, wondering whether she should be more professional or more personable.

"We've got to stop meeting like this," she said.

Her words did not elicit any response. Susanne had swallowed a whole jar of Tylenol and ten of her mother's sleeping pills, but because she'd started vomiting not long after, the pills hadn't had a chance to have any serious effect. Her mother showed up and shook Susanne until she admitted what she had done, and then called an ambulance. Under normal circumstances, a patient like this would probably have already been on her way home again with the number of a therapist in his or her pocket, but because of her experience with rape and because Susanne refused to say a thing to the doctors who tried to talk to her, she now had to wait for a psych consult.

"Would you rather drive over to National Hospital and talk to Jakobsen instead of the psychologist on duty here?" Louise offered. Louise had no idea if that was even possible. All she knew was that Susanne had clearly benefited from talking to Jakobsen before, and she might find it easier to talk some more to him.

"Yes, please," Susanne said, nodding weakly as she turned her head to look at Louise. Although it had faded from purple to a dark yellow, the bruising was still obvious. At least the swelling had gone down. There was something about her expression that made Louise feel like Susanne was starting to disintegrate—like Karin Hvenegaard from Rødovre, who had been similarly assaulted two years before. Louise held out her hand and gave Susanne's arm a little squeeze to reassure her that she wasn't alone.

"I'll just check if he's in, and then I'll arrange things with the nurses here," Louise said. "Do you want to tell me why you did it before I go out and make my phone call?"

Silence. Susanne's eyes were blank again.

Louise waited, then asked, "You're thinking about the girl he killed? Are you afraid he'll come back?"

"I didn't want to die!" Susanne said.

"Is that why you threw the pills back up again?" Louise asked.

Susanne finally turned her head. "No, that's why I took them in the first place!" Susanne practically screamed.

It was hard to make any sense out of her words.

Susanne lowered her eyes to stare at the blanket. She looked like she was disappearing back into her own world; Louise worried that the conversation was over.

But Susanne shook her head and quietly said, "I would rather be beaten to death by him than be suffocated by the life I have now." Tears flowed noiselessly down her cheeks.

Louise stroked her arm as the full weight of Susanne's grim admission settled in her chest like a tombstone. Susanne didn't need to say anything else. Her message had been understood, and it was utterly bleak.

"Susanne, you don't need to kill yourself to keep your mother from suffocating you. You can move out and break your ties to her—for a while," Louise hurried to add before continuing. "Tell her you're a grown-up and she has to stop butting into your business."

Louise hoped she hadn't been too forceful.

"She teases me for trying to find a man that way." Susanne's words filled the room. "I wish I'd died last Monday, because then at least it would have happened with someone other than her."

There was nothing else to say. Louise sat for a bit, stroking Susanne's arm. Louise was already plotting how quickly Susanne could move to a new address. Not just to prevent Jesper Bjergholdt from finding her again, but also to get her away from her mother. She'd have to fill Heilmann in on how this all fit together, and Susanne needed to talk to Jakobsen. If the crisis psychologist wasn't in his office at the hospital, she would drive Susanne over to his house. She contemplated whether someone ought to talk to the mother and make her aware of *her* part in all this.

But Louise knew there was no point. The mother was undoubtedly old-school enough that she wouldn't listen to anything unless it came from the chief of police himself. Louise predicted Susanne's mother would spew all her accusations against the police and their inability to protect poor innocent victims who were at a high risk of suicide. *Maybe Lieutenant Suhr could put her in her place*, Louise thought as she stood up to walk over to the door.

"Don't go!" Susanne pleaded.

Louise turned and smiled reassuringly. "I need to talk to a nurse to get permission to take you with me," she said.

"I don't want *her* back in here," Susanne said.

Louise walked over and pushed the call button on the table next to the bed, and a second later a nurse came through the door. Louise saw Susanne's mother stand up, about to follow the nurse in. Louise held up her hand, as if she were a traffic cop motioning for a vehicle to stop, and to her surprise Susanne's mother sat back down.

"I would like to bring the patient over to National Hospital to speak to the crisis psychologist she spoke to last week. Is there any way we can make that happen?"

The nurse looked at Louise in surprise and said there was no reason they couldn't do that.

Louise smiled and thanked her.

"You'll have to take her records with you," the nurse said. "Susanne was examined last night when she arrived, but we haven't had a chance to do anything else yet."

"The patient would like to rest until we're ready to go," Louise said. "That means she doesn't want any visitors."

The nurse smiled and said, "I'll just go let her family know that."

Louise wondered if she ought to take the time to call Heilmann and Jakobsen before she and Susanne left, but decided she could just do that from the car. If Jakobsen didn't have time, they would wait at Police Headquarters until he had a slot he could fit her into.

"Do you have any clothes here?" Louise asked, afraid she was going to have to whisk Susanne away a second time wearing just a hospital gown, but Susanne nodded, pointing over toward the closet, where her clothes hung neatly. Louise brought them over and laid them on the bed.

"I'll wait outside while you get dressed."

"I'd rather you stay." Susanne's pleading tone worried Louise. She guessed that under those words lurked a panicked anxiety about being left alone with her mother. So she stayed, walking over to look out the window and give Susanne the privacy she could. Susanne swung her legs over the side of the bed and was getting dressed when the nurse came in and set a copy of her case notes on the bedside table.

"We were planning on discharging Susanne after she spoke to the psychologist, but, as the doctor noted, we also planned to schedule a series of counseling sessions. Those could just as easily be conducted at National Hospital if she's already started a course of treatment there." The nurse paused for a bit before lowering her voice and proceeding. "It's my sense that quite a few sessions will be necessary," she said, tipping her head slightly toward the door.

Louise nodded, thanked her, and said goodbye before taking Susanne by the arm and preparing to escort her out.

"I asked your mother to go down to the waiting room," the nurse called after them. "You can just follow the hallway down to the right. Then I'll go let her know you've left."

On the way down to the car, Louise took out her phone, realizing she had better fill Heilmann in on developments sooner rather than later. She helped Susanne into the passenger seat and shut the door before dialing Heilmann's extension.

"It's such a heartbreaking story. It's almost unbearable," Louise said, briefly summarizing how the attempted suicide was motivated by Susanne's desperation to escape her mother's need to overprotect, dominate, and manipulate her life and activities.

"That's terrible. Death felt like the only way she could escape. I'll call Jakobsen and let him know you're on your way," Heilmann said as Louise opened the driver-side door and climbed in.

"Thanks," Louise said.

"And if it turns out he isn't free until later, then come here," Heilmann added after a moment's thought. "I'm just about to meet with Suhr to decide how much information we'll release about the suspect and discuss the wording of the warning we've prepared."

Louise rashly blurted out that it might be a good idea to wait. "If we hold off on the warning, I might run into the perp on Friday." She regretted it right away—mostly because it sent a shudder through Susanne, who was leaning forward, completely on edge. Louise sensed that her words had sent a tremor through the phone connection back to Police Headquarters as well.

"I think you'd better explain what you mean by that," Heilmann said.

"I'd rather not go into the details right now," Louise said.

She needed to figure out how she could present the idea so Suhr didn't think she was deranged and transfer her to Arson or something.

"There's a social mixer event for one of the big online dating sites this Friday," Louise explained, "and I think he might decide to attend. It's just an idea, but you have to get Suhr to wait until we've discussed it as an option."

187

"Yeah, yeah, yeah," Lieutenant Suhr grumbled impatiently, holding his hand up in the air to stop her. "Camilla Lind already explained the pros and cons. And I think she's right. We ought to give it a try."

Louise hid her hands behind her back, pinching her index finger hard to keep herself from fuming. *Oh, that Camilla! She promised she wouldn't say anything. That woman just can't help herself.*

"The question is really whether we dare keep this from the public any longer, now that we've got two serious cases on our hands," Heilmann said rationally.

Louise still had not quite regained her composure. She had just dropped Susanne off with Jakobsen, who had been waiting for them in the doorway to his office, ready. He had put his arm around Susanne in a fatherly way and shepherded her inside. Once he'd gotten her settled on the comfortable couch, he came back out and let Louise know that he was going to keep Susanne for a while, so Louise didn't need to wait. They agreed that he would call when Susanne was ready to go.

The whole way over to headquarters, Louise had contemplated how best to pitch Camilla's idea without revealing that the idea had come from a reporter. She could have spared herself the trouble.

"Of course, the trouble is that we might not recognize him," Suhr said. "We saw only a glimpse of him on the CCTV footage, and we didn't get much from that."

It caught Louise by surprise that Suhr was evidently taking Camilla's idea seriously, already envisioning apprehending the guy.

"True," Louise agreed, "but I saw enough of him that I'm sure I would recognize his distinctive silhouette and posture if I saw him again. You need—"

Again, he gestured with his hand to stop her. "We'll bring the girl," Suhr said.

His statement hung in the air until Heilmann and Louise grasped what he meant, and then they both yelled in unison, "Absolutely not!"

Louise shook her head and added indignantly, "She just tried to commit suicide, Lieutenant."

"Not because of him, if I understand correctly," Suhr retorted.

Louise stared at him for a moment. He was usually such a considerate person to work with. His tone was far from the gruff style Willumsen had made part of his image. And yet, every once in a while Suhr would make seemingly callous and unfeeling decisions. At the same time, Louise could appreciate why he had made this suggestion.

"We'll just need to see what Jakobsen says about that," Heilmann cautioned.

"Maybe we should just skip that and stick to the original plan for the investigation," Louise suggested.

"No, I think we damn well ought to give this a try," Suhr argued. "There'll be an ungodly uproar when we go public with the warning, especially since our description of the suspect is so vague. No, we'll do this social event on Friday. If we don't get anything out of it, then we'll go to the public.

"Sergeant, you update Jakobsen on this and see what he has to say," Suhr continued. "We'll have another meeting once you've planned out our approach. Take Toft and Stig with you. They could stand to get out a little."

"Wasn't the idea for Lars to go, too?" Louise asked. "I mean, at least he's seen the footage."

Suhr nodded absentmindedly. He had already moved on to the next thing on his to-do list.

Just as he turned to leave, Louise asked how things were going on the investigation of the immigrant woman's murder. Suhr turned around and glared at her, his lips pursed, but then took a breath and just shrugged.

"We haven't gotten anywhere. Unfortunately, the guy lucked out and got assigned John Bro as his public defender for his prelim."

She felt for Suhr and Willumsen. It made all their cases absurdly more difficult when they got stuck with aggressive defense attorneys. She had encountered Bro herself one time when he was representing one of the biggest drug dealers in Danish history, but Bro's efforts to find evidence to exonerate his client had indirectly saved Camilla's life. Louise didn't have anything bad to say about him—but it was a fact that you needed to be on top of things and have truly rock-solid evidence when facing him in court.

"What happened to the woman's children?"

"Her sister is taking care of them, which the husband is furious about. He'll tell anyone who can be bothered to listen that he's going to be sending the children out of the country soon. He claims it is to ensure their safety and help them regain the peace and balance their mother destroyed when she moved out."

Louise was on her feet. Heilmann had already returned to her office.

"Well, who did it, then, if it wasn't him? Do you have any other suspects?"

"It was him," Suhr said and looked like he was about to say more but stopped himself. Instead he simply said they'd gotten statements from everyone in the murdered woman's family and circle of friends.

"We also think that it may have been some kind of honor

killing," he said. "Not because she refused to marry someone her family had picked, but because she had brought shame to *his* family by *leaving* the marriage. Her own father might also have a motive if he didn't accept his daughter's divorce, because it went against the choice he made for her," Suhr said, shrugging and making a face. Then he concluded, "If we hadn't relied so much on the witness statements and thought the murder had happened around one o'clock, we would have had him. He probably did pick up the kids earlier that morning as he claimed, but we think he went back sometime between eleven and twelve. Or maybe in the afternoon, just before he said he found her. We don't have any witnesses who saw him come or go, and no one saw anyone else enter or leave the woman's apartment."

Suhr grumbled and added that the man ought to send a nice bottle of wine to his ex-wife's media-happy upstairs neighbor, whose story had gotten him out of jail. He thumped his hand against the doorframe in frustration and then walked back to his office.

Louise went back to hers. Her head was buzzing. Her irritation at Camilla for getting involved had abated, but she decided not to tell her that the police would be at the mixer on Friday. And especially not that they might be bringing Susanne.

19

Louise knew the second she let herself into the apartment that Peter was home from the soft music coming from the living room. It surprised her. It was only six o'clock, and he usually didn't come home until eight at the earliest.

"Hello," she called from the entryway, pleased that they could finally spend a whole evening together. They could either go out to eat, or get takeout and have a picnic in Frederiksberg Park, she thought. The weather had been surprisingly nice for May.

She smiled and went in to give him a kiss, but stopped in the doorway, shocked to see three empty beer bottles on the coffee table and a fourth that Peter was close to finishing. He looked like someone had punched him squarely in the chest, forcing him back into the soft cushions on the couch. His eyes were red and puffy and avoiding her.

"What happened?" she asked, frightened, walking over to sit down in the armchair next to the couch. There was something about the way he looked that kept her from sitting down on the couch next to him, a wall of despair that made him seem sealed off in his own private world.

He still hadn't looked at her. He just sat, staring down at the top of the coffee table, frozen and distant. Finally, he pulled himself together and looked at her.

"I came home to tell you I've fallen in love with someone else and I'm moving out today."

She held her breath as his words hung in the air. She could hear what he'd said but couldn't process it.

Peter looked down at his hands, which were clutching his beer bottle.

Louise stared at him, expecting him to continue, but he had disappeared back into his vacuum. She would have thought her head would be bursting with questions in a situation like this. But there was just silence. Emptiness.

"Who is she?" she finally asked.

Her insides were frozen solid. She both did and did not want to know who had forced her way into his heart and driven Louise out. An icy awareness of her own self spread through her, warning her that worse was coming. She pictured herself and Peter. They'd always had a special vibe, such great chemistry between them, and she had let them both down by pulling away and prioritizing herself and her own life. Louise could see now that she had pushed Peter into someone else's arms.

He sighed deeply before responding, not even trying to pull himself together. She would just have to deal. He didn't try to pretend that he was the master of the situation, didn't act like he was merely passing on some information. Sorrow and pain radiated from him.

"It's Lina." His evasive eyes finally fixed on her. "I'm really sorry, but I'm in love with her."

Louise pictured Peter's co-worker's face enlarged and projected onto the living-room wall as though by a slide projector. Sales meetings. Overtime. Business trips. Louise felt neither sadness nor anger, just nausea. Her emotions were locked away in the block of ice that had settled in her gut.

"I tried to end it," he continued.

The image of the blond sales rep faded from the wall. Louise's memory was blocked—suddenly she couldn't remember the girl anymore or picture her face. She kept calling her "girl," but knew she must be somewhere in her thirties. Maybe a couple of years younger than she was, but definitely no more than that. Louise wasn't being dumped for some hot young thing, but for Peter's co-worker, an equal. *Which, it turns out, is every fucking bit as pathetic and heartbreaking*, she thought.

"I can't tell you how sorry I am," Peter repeated.

The block of ice started to melt, but Louise didn't feel like she was about to dissolve into tears. She felt cold and hard. She matter-of-factly acknowledged in her mind that things hadn't been right between Peter and her ever since he had come home from Scotland. Well, actually, not while he was living in Scotland, either, or even really before he had gone. They had made it this far because they had both been working toward the same general things, and they wanted to succeed. He had grudgingly accepted her decision to stay in Denmark. And she had visited him in Scotland as often as she could, even though they had spent most of her visits sightseeing and eating out, not really doing anything that could count as spending quality time on their relationship.

Then, when he came home, she had given in and let him move in with her, even though she would have been just as happy if he hadn't. And they had both struggled to live up to each other's expectations, to prove that moving in together was the right decision. She had lost herself in her work, and he had apparently found a more lascivious outlet, she thought, finally feeling a wave of anger. Frost had lost its grip on her insides, and now the full intensity of her feelings came thundering to the surface.

"You've been sneaking around screwing her this whole time you had me thinking you were working so hard? What in the fuck is wrong with you?" she yelled.

She should have known, she thought at the same time. He knew she would believe he was pouring his heart and soul into his work, and she had no reason to doubt his need for so much overtime, given her own workaholic tendencies.

"I totally understand that you're pissed at me," Peter said. "You've got every right to chew me out. But I just want you to know that I didn't do it to hurt you."

Louise went ballistic. *Oh no, do not tell me he is fucking sitting there feeling sorry for me.* Infuriated, she rose, pointed at the bedroom, and said with as much strength as she could muster, "You will go in there now, pack your things, and get out. I don't want to hear another fucking word about you or what you 'understand.'"

She was shaking and gasping for air as sobs overwhelmed her body.

"Out!" she yelled.

He got up slowly, walked over, and put his arm around her. She tried to pull back, but her body wouldn't obey. She sobbed into his shoulder and let him lead her over to the couch and sit her down. She hid her face in her hands as she tried to regain some semblance of composure. She slowly caught her breath, breathing deeply several times until she thought she could speak without crying.

"I saw you guys in Tivoli last week," she said as the image of them at the window table popped into her head. He sat a moment before responding.

"That was the day I broke up with her. I never meant for it to keep going. I'm not cut out for affairs," he said, trying to laugh. "I get paranoid."

Louise thought bitterly that he would probably get by just fine in life if that was his biggest problem. *Glad you figured that one out*, she thought, recalling all those nights he had come home late.

"I didn't think I would end up missing her so much," Peter said. "But this past week made it clear to me that I made the wrong choice. I haven't been able to stop thinking about her since Tivoli."

Louise thought about the passionless sex they had had up at her parents' house, cursing at him in her mind and wishing every cell of his body were far away from her.

"And I suppose she's ready to welcome you back even though you dumped her?" Louise asked.

Peter nodded and reached for her hand, which she quickly yanked back. "She wants to have kids and a real home life," he added.

As though that explains everything, Louise thought, staring at him incredulously. *He does not seriously mean he's trading me in for another woman who is willing to tend his house and bear his children. I would have borne his children...or child,* she thought, correcting herself. *One would probably have been plenty.*

"We've got the same outlook on life," he continued.

Louise didn't want to hear any more, but started when he said that at least Camilla had understood him when they had talked about it in the kitchen the other night.

"You told Camilla that you were seeing someone else?" Louise exclaimed in surprise.

Peter looked at her, confused. "Of course I didn't. But what we were talking about was making room in our lives for love and our dreams for the future, and doing what feels right."

He paused, as though weighing whether he dared continue. "You never really accepted...or maybe you just never really understood, how much Camilla really wants to find a man and have another kid."

Now Louise was doubly hurt. Her best friend had never told her she wanted more kids, and had chosen to confide in Peter instead. Now she knew where that barbed comment about her not wanting Camilla to be happy came from. "You should go now," she said, standing. "I don't feel like talking anymore."

She went into the kitchen and stood there a moment, listening to his footsteps as he left the living room. She heard him pull the big suitcase down out of the closet and open a drawer. It felt like a dream. She had no sense of time, no sense of how she was feeling. She sat down at the kitchen table and stared into space. She wanted to go outside for some fresh air, but the muscles in her body didn't respond when she tried to stand.

Peter stopped in the kitchen doorway. He was holding his dark brown suitcase in his hand, and suddenly she was afraid he might decide to kiss her goodbye. There was a limit to how much crap she was willing to put up with.

He stood for a moment, swaying back and forth, and finally said, "I'll call you."

She nodded without a word, and her mind kept reeling even after the door shut behind him. She considered calling Camilla, but realized that she needed to sit for a while by herself. She still wasn't convinced that the whole thing hadn't just been a figment of her imagination. She reached for the bottle of calvados and poured herself a very full glass. She took a swig, swallowed, and drank until her throat started burning. *So long, asshole*, she thought. Here she was struggling, compromising, and adapting, and he just went and threw in the fucking towel and took the easy way out. He was off taking care of his own needs, while she was making sacrifices. She took another big swig, pushed her chair back, and marched out into the hallway for her purse. She ran down the stairs and over to the newsstand to buy a pack of Prince Lights.

The whole way back, she kept thinking how pathetic it was to start smoking again, but, really, if getting dumped didn't make it okay, she couldn't fucking imagine what would. When she got back to the apartment, she poured herself another half glass of calvados and lit her first cigarette. She waited impatiently for the dizziness to hit her. People had been telling her for years and years how dizzy you get when you haven't smoked in a while. She was looking forward to that sensation now, to letting herself get carried away in a soothing fog. But nothing happened. It tasted just the way she remembered, but her body wasn't responding in any discernably positive way. The whole thing with Peter had probably short-circuited her pleasure centers or something, she thought.

Her ringing cell phone was just audible in the kitchen from the pocket of her jacket in the hallway. She was about to get up, but guessed it was Peter wanting to make sure she was okay, and she didn't have the energy for his concern. Still, she lit another cigarette and got up, driven by an unhealthy curiosity to check the display on her phone to see what she had missed. The call was from a number starting with thirty-five, so it was a landline in Copenhagen. It might have been National Hospital. She contemplated whether it would be wise to call back, considering the frame of mind she was in. She thought about Susanne and sat back down heavily as she pulled up the call log and had the phone dial back the last number.

She was about to cancel the call when she heard Flemming Larsen's voice. She sat for a moment without saying anything, listening to the coroner say, "Hello?"

"This is Louise Rick," she said. "Sorry, I was away from the phone."

"I thought you were always at work," Flemming teased.

She was about to say defensively that she was not, but he had already started talking again, apparently not sensing that something was wrong.

"I just finished the autopsy report, which has been signed off on and will be on your desk in the morning. But there was one thing that struck me..."

She tried to listen, but his words simply washed over her; she couldn't manage to stifle the sob that forced its way out.

Flemming fell silent abruptly, listening patiently as without any preface she explained in staccato phrases that Peter had just left her. In between sobs, she assured him that she was okay, although she heard how ridiculous that sounded.

"I'm coming over now," Flemming said. "Give me your address, and I'll be right there."

She told him where she lived, even though she didn't feel like company. They had good chemistry, but even in her frazzled frame of mind she knew that there was no way their work relationship would benefit from his seeing her at a time like this, when her world was falling to pieces.

She quickly hid her cigarettes in a drawer and drank a glass of water before brushing her teeth, in the hopes of getting rid of her tobacco breath before he arrived.

Peter had forgotten his toothbrush and shaving things. She grabbed a big paper bag and started raking all of his things into it. Once she had stashed all that on the back steps, she lightly dabbed some powder on her face and ran her fingers through her thick, dark curls. She pulled her long hair back into a ponytail, annoyed that she hadn't told Flemming not to come. *Pull yourself together*, she told herself as the intercom beeped. She went over and buzzed him in.

From the depths of the stairwell, she could hear him bounding up the stairs as she stood in her doorway, waiting to receive him.

"Hi," she called with all the cheer she could muster. Flemming leaned forward and pulled her into a hug, and they stood for a moment swaying back and forth before he let her go. "I brought these," he said, tossing a pack of Prince Ultra Lights onto the table, even though he knew she didn't smoke.

Louise looked at him surprised, guessing he had categorized her as the kind of smoker who had only just managed to fight her nicotine addiction.

She was just about to decline, to avoid revealing her weaknesses to him, when he beat her to it and said, "It helps to have some kind of bad habit you can beat yourself up about. It takes the edge off the other stuff. Plus, then there's something else going on in your life besides just being that poor thing who got dumped," he said, smiling at her.

She smiled back and took one. She had always liked people who could smile openly while breaking rules. It was liberating. Plus, Flemming knew what he was talking about. His wife had left him about two years ago now.

She decided she didn't need to hide her misery from him. She relaxed and started telling him about how she had found Peter sitting in the living room when she came home. His empty beer bottles were still in there, she noticed. She sighed and stood up to clear them away. She didn't want to be reminded of him.

"When you're in the thick of it, you may not be able to imagine something better waiting on the other side," Flemming said when she returned to the kitchen.

She listened without admitting she didn't understand what he meant.

"People have to hit bottom before something new can take root," he continued, "and maybe that new thing is what will make you truly happy."

He fidgeted a little in his chair before conceding that he was sure this wouldn't be much help to her at the moment, but still maybe it would bring her a *little* comfort now, when things seemed bleakest. "Anyway, it helped me."

She sat for a moment staring into space and then asked him if he was happy again.

"That's the whole problem with you, you know," Flemming said. "You're always so sensible and matter-of-fact; you won't let anyone squeak by with anything less than a concrete answer or hard-and-fast data. I guess, no, I'm still working on it. Give me time. But I have no doubt it's coming—and I've got a better life now living on my own than I did there at the end with my wife. It's hard to admit that when you have kids, but that's how it is."

Louise knew that Flemming's wife had gotten married again

right away. *Probably to someone who worked more normal hours*, she thought. She had the impression that Flemming and his wife—well, ex-wife—still communicated with each other well. But Louise realized she knew practically nothing about his personal life. Still, she decided not to ask him about it; she wasn't used to this new level of intimacy in their relationship, which had always been strictly professional.

"Um, so, anyway, why did you call me again?" she asked after they finished their lengthy discussion of failed marriages and relationships.

For a moment Flemming looked as though he had no idea what she was talking about, but then he figured out what she meant.

"I had an addendum to the autopsy report I just submitted. It's hard for me to say whether she died from the assault itself or afterward. It depends on when the gag he put in her mouth triggered her gag reflex and caused her to vomit. Her gag reflex could also have been triggered if she was lying there with saliva collecting in her mouth and then suddenly swallowed." He shrugged uncertainly. "It's impossible to say."

Louise nodded, promising herself that she would remember that no matter how tired she was.

It was late when he left. Louise felt a little dazed when she finally lay down in bed. She still wasn't quite sure she understood what had happened. There was something unreal about the hours since she had come home from work. She was bitterly aware of the fact that, after six years, her Peter had chosen to move on without her. And she really had no fucking idea how she felt about that.

She turned off the lamp next to her bed and rolled onto her stomach. It had occurred to her as she sat there talking to Flemming that she was not that unhappy about the prospect of a future without Peter. All the relationship pressures and always having to feel guilty about everything would end. But she had been with Peter because she loved him. *And what would happen now?* she thought before, exhausted, she slipped into sleep.

❧

Her temples were pounding when she woke up the next morning. She had gone to the bathroom at some point in the night, and on the way back to bed her legs had steered her into the living room and to the couch where Peter had been sitting with his beer bottles. She'd sat down, the intensity of her sobs shocking her. In a daze, she had staggered back to bed once the tears had slowed a little. Her eyes were so swollen that there were only two narrow slits left, and she deliberately avoided looking at herself in the mirror when she finally decided to get up. Half-asleep, she called in sick to work, and then she went back to bed and slept hard until almost noon. In the kitchen she put the kettle on, took out a large mug, and filled the infuser with loose tea leaves. The persistent pounding in her temples had spread to her forehead, so she swallowed a couple of Tylenol before turning on the hot water and stepping into the shower.

What the fuck was that fucking asshole thinking? she thought, lying back down on her bed, wrapped in a bathrobe and holding a steaming glass of tea in her hand. Peter, who was usually such a rule follower, had been screwing around behind her back instead of doing the decent thing and breaking up with her first before plunging into something new. It was like he was trying to hedge his bets, take a test drive before making his final decision. Asshole.

Late in the afternoon, she got up again and started getting rid of Peter's things as they caught her eye as she moved around the apartment. She'd have to live with his furniture, but she tossed everything else into a giant heap in the guest room that she would ask him to come pick up in a few days while she was at work. She got a kick out of seeing the mess she had made of his things: books, CDs, folders, knickknacks…all randomly strewn on top of each other. *This will piss him off*, she thought before shutting the guest-room door and going to look up the number of the pizza place around the corner to order dinner.

When she went to bed that night, she felt better. She would survive. *He can go fuck himself.* She would focus on her work, and he could focus on his domestic bliss. She repeated this to herself a few times; she could tell it didn't sound totally convincing yet, but it was a start.

20

W e can't force you to go. Personally, I don't think you should do it." That last part slipped out before Louise had time to change her mind.

"I'm coming," Susanne said, with a conviction in her voice that indicated that the matter was settled.

She'd spent two days at National Hospital and had had many long conversations with Jakobsen during that time. Louise noticed the change right away. There was something calm and open about her movements. Her face also didn't bear such clear reminders of the assault anymore, although the area around her left eye and cheekbone was still discolored.

"I've wanted to go to that party all along," she continued after a little pause. "Ever since I heard about it. If he comes, I want to see him again."

Louise stared at her. She didn't have a chance to launch into a dismayed tirade, because Susanne put out her hands to calm Louise.

"Not like that," Susanne reassured her. "But he's in my mind all the time, and it's bugging me that I can't picture him. I can't remember what he looks like. Jakobsen calls it normal repression," she said in a tone that revealed that she did not agree that it was helping to protect her. "But I don't think I can move on until I can picture him and accept that what happened wasn't my fault."

Louise thought it was amazing what a crisis psychologist could accomplish, but she wasn't completely convinced by this new Susanne who was so enthusiastically on display before her. If Jakobsen hadn't stopped by Police Headquarters that morning to participate in the discussion about whether or not it made sense to take Susanne to the party, Louise would not have wanted to even consider the option.

Jakobsen had given his permission for them to ask Susanne if she wanted to help as he simultaneously filled them in, confidentially, about Susanne's hellish adult life of constant suffocation by a mother whose husband had left the second she uttered the *p* in pregnant.

The mother had raised Susanne to believe that the two of them belonged together, thus forcing Susanne to completely fixate on her mother in the most abominable way, a way that would have relegated many young girls to psych wards with their wrists slashed or that would have sent them spinning into terrible rebellions, probably with consequences for the rest of their lives.

But Susanne did not rebel. She put up with it, adjusted to her mother's compulsive possessiveness, and gave up her childhood— along with a sizable chunk of her adult life—before she finally ventured out, trying to escape her biological straitjacket. But then things went so horrendously wrong that there was almost no chance in hell she could cope with it, Jakobsen concluded, stroking his beard with a sad look on his face.

"She's getting out of that environment now," he continued. "I stopped by to talk to her mother and find out how aware she is of what she's doing to her daughter's life. It's almost as sad to report that she's using her daughter to fend off loneliness and to hold up as a trophy to taunt the man who left her. Even though he'll probably never even realize it. The mother ought to be in treatment, because when you get right down to it, she's a sick woman."

Louise could only nod in agreement to that. She'd thought the same thing whenever she had encountered her.

⚭

"Here's what will happen," Louise explained as she sat facing Susanne in the cafeteria at National Hospital over a cup of coffee. "I'll come pick you up tomorrow night, and we'll go out there together."

Susanne was going to be discharged the next morning. Jakobsen had found her a temporary place to stay at an undisclosed address, which would be ready for her on Monday, but until then she would stay in her own apartment on Lyshøj Allé in Valby.

"When we get to the mixer, we'll look around and hope, of course, that he's there. We won't do anything else. If you see him, let me know, but under no circumstances should you go over and talk to him. If he sees you, we'll leave. We won't apprehend him while he's inside, and maybe he'll follow you if he sees you leaving the event. We'll have people ready to apprehend him outside. But remember," Louise added when she noticed Susanne nodding in concentration, "that this whole thing is a shot in the dark. There's only a minuscule chance that he'll be there. He's just committed two very serious crimes and is probably in hiding."

⚹

Before Louise left National Hospital, she considered calling Flemming Larsen to ask if he wanted a cup of coffee. She hadn't talked to him since he left her apartment, and now, since she was here anyway…But maybe it was best if they brought their relationship back to a professional level.

The night before, she had called Camilla to update her on her personal life. At first, her friend had refused to believe Peter had found someone else.

"He's an idiot!" she'd finally exclaimed in irritation, and then suggested that she try to talk him out of it.

"Are you insane?" Louise cut her off. "You're not going to persuade him to come back. The only way he's fucking moving back home is if he wants to and decides it's the only right choice. But I'm not so sure he'll try," she concluded.

"No—I'm sorry. You're not some consumer product with a money-back guarantee," Camilla said affectionately. "Anyway, you don't come crawling back to someone unless you're prepared to have the door slammed so hard in your face it hurts."

Louise smiled. She wasn't sure she was that tough, but she also didn't picture herself as the kind of woman you leave and then come crawling back to.

She gave up on the idea of a cup of coffee with Flemming and went back to headquarters instead.

"I'm picking Susanne up at her apartment. Should we come back here first, or just go straight to the mixer?" she asked, standing in the doorway to Heilmann's office.

"We'll all meet here. Then we'll go through what we'll do if he's there, and I will make sure everyone understands that we're not going to do anything inside the event—aside from looking."

Louise nodded and was about to say goodbye when Heilmann asked her how she was doing. When she showed up for work that morning, Louise had noticed that her boss had picked up on the fact that something was wrong. It hadn't taken Lars long, either, to see that there'd been a change in his partner's behavior. He had discreetly raised an eyebrow when she tossed a pack of cigarettes on the desk, assuring him that she wouldn't smoke in the office they shared. He had just nodded and refrained from asking any questions, presumably expecting that Louise would provide the answers when she was ready. Which she did after lunch, when she stopped pretending that she was able to do her job effectively.

The first thing Lars said was, "It's okay with me if you smoke in here." Then he started trying to lift her spirits with a bunch of encouraging words, which she started tuning out.

All the same, she dutifully trudged outside when she felt like she needed a cigarette.

"I'm fine," she said evasively when Heilmann asked, not up to giving anyone else the lowdown on her personal life.

She could tell that Heilmann didn't buy it, but she was tactful enough not to ask anything else.

21

Louise picked up Susanne on Friday evening, a half hour before they were supposed to meet the rest of the group in Heilmann's office to finalize their plan. The dating mixer was being held in a big warehouse in Holmen, an old navy base that had been redeveloped into an artsy residential district. When they got there, they all parked in a small lot next to the building, where they would have a direct line of sight to the entrance.

Louise and Susanne strolled over and got in line. There were only two people ahead of them. Lars stayed in the unmarked car, waiting until after they were in to get in line himself. Louise said, "No, thanks," when a young woman offered her a marker and a blank name tag.

"Just for your username," the young woman clarified, already starting to help the next person.

Louise saw that Susanne had taken a name tag and was busy writing on it before Louise even had a chance to tell her it wasn't necessary. Louise pulled Susanne through the crowd of people that had gathered just inside the door.

"We're only here to look," she reminded Susanne, repeating what they had discussed in Heilmann's office before they left.

"We'll fit in better if we act like everyone else," Susanne pointed out once they had made it through the throng.

Louise didn't respond. Instead, she walked over to a tall table that was in front of the bar. She positioned herself so she had a good view of the people coming into the room. The large warehouse space was far from full, but the event organizer had assured them it would be when she and Lars had gone out to talk to him that afternoon to map out the exits, see how the space would be laid out, and find out how many people were expected to come.

The organizer was definitely not thrilled about the police being at the event. He was probably worried that it would harm the reputation of his dating site and his periodic mixer parties if people found out that rapists found their victims this way. He was only slightly mollified when they assured him that they would not make any potential arrests inside the venue.

"But what about the press?" he had spluttered at them. "I've invited quite a few reporters!"

"Well, that is the risk you run when you go looking for media attention," Louise had answered on her way out the door. She avoided turning around to look back at him. He was the last person she was going to feel sorry for.

"Would you mind?" Susanne asked, reaching for Louise's cigarettes.

Louise was so surprised, she just watched as Susanne awkwardly extracted a cigarette from the pack.

"Help yourself," she finally replied, sliding her lighter across the table toward Susanne.

"Well, you're certainly opening up to new experiences," she continued with a quick smile. She had no intention of quashing any curiosity that was beginning to emerge from Susanne's emancipation. "Have you ever tried smoking before?"

Susanne shook her head, holding the cigarette clumsily between her fingers.

"To begin with, then, don't inhale. Pull the smoke into your mouth and then blow it out again. Once you've gotten used to the taste, then you can start drawing it down into your lungs," Louise explained in her best teacher's voice, scarcely believing that she was instructing someone on how to best acquire what was a very bad habit.

It had been more than twenty years since she had taught anyone how to smoke. And even then, it wasn't because she had been especially experienced as a teenager. As far as she remembered, she had been one of the last ones in her class to give in and follow the pack. But after she started, she hadn't been shy about helping others pick up the habit.

There were more people in the warehouse now. The big crowd just inside the door had spread, and people were streaming in, visible only as vague silhouettes, lit up in brief glimpses by the flashing, flickering lights that followed the thumping beat of the music.

"Let's walk around," Louise suggested in a few minutes, after they put out their cigarettes.

Louise and Susanne meandered slowly through the space, trying not to appear like they were looking for something, but Louise quickly discovered that that was exactly what separated them from everybody else. Everyone was scanning the room, staring unabashedly at the name tags of each person who walked by. Groups had formed around some tables, while other people stood by themselves, waiting for someone to come talk to them.

The dance floor was already packed. People weren't pushing their way across it. Instead, they skirted around it and continued on into a little alcove off the back of the large hall. The alcove had been set up as a lounge with pillows on the floor and soft music, which was barely audible in contrast with the thunderous noise from the enormous club speakers in the large hall. Susanne and Louise sat down a little restlessly, peering around until they had scanned the whole alcove, and agreed that he wasn't there. Then they made their way back to the bar area and found a table to stand near.

"He's not coming," Susanne said and asked for another cigarette.

Louise shook one out of the pack and was inclined to agree. "How long are we going to stay?" Susanne asked.

"Until it's over. There's just as much chance he'll show up during the last thirty minutes as now."

Lars came over and stood by their table. He shook his head and turned the corners of his mouth down discreetly.

"It's going to be a long night, but I'd be a jerk if I didn't at least flirt back a little," he said, letting his eyes wander through the crowd. "And it's even more horrifically boring standing outside."

He jumped as a pair of female hands covered his eyes from behind, pulling his body back into an embrace. He quickly spun around and found himself face-to-face with Camilla, who was only a few inches shorter than him.

"Hi!" Camilla crooned.

Lars seemed bashful, but smiled. They had met several times at Police Headquarters, and after he'd become Louise's partner, Camilla had added him to her list of police sources—which he put up with, good-naturedly. He seemed to really like her, if his sudden attack of shyness was any indication.

"Do you have a lot of people here?" Camilla asked inquisitively, looking around.

Louise ignored the question, instead asking Camilla where Henning was.

"Oh, he just had to pick up his brother, but I think they'll be here in a bit," she said, making a face at Louise. "I'll introduce you!"

Louise smiled, and then remembered how Peter had accused her of not accepting the fact that Camilla wanted to find a man and start a family. So she hurried to add that she was excited and looking forward to meeting them. But something in the way she said it wasn't fully convincing, and she could tell that Camilla had picked up on that.

"I'm just going to go to the bathroom," Susanne said, interrupting the slightly tense atmosphere that followed Louise's statement.

"Aren't you supposed to be at work?" Louise asked Camilla, changing the topic yet again.

Camilla nodded and said, "I'm actually looking for the event organizer. I want to interview him briefly as part of the story I'm doing on this whole phenomenon."

They parted ways when Camilla spotted the photographer she had arrived with, and Louise started looking around for Susanne.

The place was packed. Louise tried to keep an eye on Lars's back as he disappeared into the crowd to search the room one more time. She caught sight of Susanne's short, dark hair by the door leading to the restrooms.

With her eyes trained on Susanne, Louise noticed the second Susanne's eyes locked onto something. She saw Susanne falter for a second and then stiffen.

Louise quickly looked over to see who had triggered Susanne's response, but it was hard to tell who she was looking at. Louise started pushing her way through the crowd, trying in vain to make eye contact with Susanne. Annoyed, she forced her way through the people blocking her way.

There he was.

Louise stopped short when she saw his wavy collar-length hair. He was talking to two women she estimated to be in their late twenties. Then he turned halfway around, and his profile was so clear that the adrenaline started pounding through her veins.

She wanted to run over to the exit and alert the team outside, but didn't dare leave Susanne. She quickly pulled her cell phone out of her jacket pocket and dialed Heilmann's number, but the call didn't go through. Irritated, she stared at the display and realized she had no service. There wasn't even one bar on the scale indicating signal strength. Of all the times...Louise searched feverishly for Lars but couldn't see him, so she turned back to Susanne to make sure she found her way outside quickly so she wouldn't have to confront her rapist.

Of course, they had talked about what she should do if she suddenly found herself face-to-face with him, and Heilmann's orders had been clear: "Do not speak to him. Turn around and walk toward the exit, so he doesn't have time to make any threats."

And yet Susanne wasn't heading toward the exit. She was standing there as if nailed to the spot, allowing herself to be jostled back and forth by the crowd of people heading toward the restrooms in a steady stream.

Louise could no longer see Jesper Bjergholdt when she finally reached Susanne, grabbed hold of her arm, and started pulling her along. She quickly realized that Susanne's feet were not obeying, so Louise put some muscle into it, practically dragging Susanne across the floor while irritatedly scanning the room for Lars. She thought she caught a glimpse of Jesper heading toward the lounge with the two young women.

Louise finally let go of Susanne's arm once they were outside, giving Susanne a moment to recover while she walked over to alert Michael Stig and Thomas Toft, so they'd be ready.

They came when she waved them over. She saw Heilmann coming from over by the cars, holding her phone to her ear. Louise guessed she was advising the extra people, who were on-site to assist, that the ball was in play and they should be on the alert if it turned out he was there.

"We'll go in and get him," Stig said the second Heilmann lowered her phone. Heilmann gave him a look and took charge.

"In a second we'll have two people stationed by the loading bay doors around the side of the building, and the three of us will stay here," she said to Stig and Toft. Then she spotted Susanne and walked over to take charge of her. Heilmann put her arm around Susanne's shoulder and led her quickly over to the car she was using as a base of operations, and opened the rear door on the passenger side.

"Rick, you go in and find Jørgensen. I'll keep an eye out for our guy," she said once she returned from the cruiser. "If Jørgensen doesn't have any reception in the warehouse, either, one of you will have to come out and let us know the second the suspect seems like he's about to leave."

Louise went back inside and started looking for her partner. She found him with Camilla by one of the tables near the bar. Slightly annoyed that he was standing there making small talk while the shit was hitting the fan, Louise approached and interrupted their conversation.

"Let's take another spin around the room," she said, worried that this would tip Camilla off that something was up, but her friend just waved at them and headed out into the crowd, as though she had been just waiting for a chance to slip away. Louise guessed that Henning had shown up or must be on his way, at any rate. Louise moved quickly, tugging Lars along, very aware that to other people she must look like a woman putting the moves on him.

"He's here," she said, letting go of her partner's jacket.

She quickly filled him in on what had happened and where she had last seen the suspect, and they headed purposefully toward the lounge, trying to look like a couple who had just met. Most of the places to sit were already taken. Small groups of people were clustered together sitting on the pillows on the floor, while other people were standing and leaning against the wall. Louise and Lars stopped just inside the heavy sliding doors and started scanning the crowd.

"He was wearing a white shirt," it occurred to Louise to mention.

That quickly ruled out most of the men, leaving only a few potential targets. It didn't take long to determine that none of them was their guy.

Louise still felt the adrenaline pumping blood faster through her body, and she recognized the tense expression on Lars's face. If he was there, they'd get him.

"He's not in here," her partner determined, and they left the lounge and went back out into the main room—an inferno of light, music, and people.

They stood for a long time watching people dance, concentrating on spotting the ones in white shirts who had dark hair. Louise craned her neck and thought she spotted one of the women the man had been talking to, but Bjergholdt himself was nowhere in sight. They started scanning for him, walking among the countless tables that formed small islands in the vast room, even though they knew at this rate they would be lucky to pick out a specific person in a crowd of two thousand. It was incredible enough that Louise had spotted him the first time—or, more accurately, that Susanne had.

Once they had been all the way around the room without results, they agreed to do the rounds one more time in case he had been in the bathroom, and after yet another round they decided to go outside. Louise stopped as they walked by one of the two women she had seen the suspect talking to, and she told Lars to go on ahead. She wanted to make one last try.

The woman knew who Louise was talking about right away. "Duke," she said, and repeated it when Louise didn't respond.

"That's his username."

"I thought it was 'Mr. Noble'!" Louise said, noting that either he really did have some blue blood in his veins or he was somehow preoccupied with the nobility.

The young woman shrugged and didn't seem to know or care what Louise was talking about. "He left a while ago," she said, seeming like she was wrapping up the conversation.

That really got Louise's heart rate up. "The other young woman you guys were with, is she a friend of yours?"

"Yeah," the woman said. At first, she stared blankly at Louise, but then a suspicious look crept into her eyes. "Why do you ask?"

It was obvious that she considered Louise a rival. She had already started walking away when Louise reached out and grabbed her arm.

"Did they leave together?" Louise asked pointedly and didn't have time to rephrase her question before the girl had twisted her arm free and started accusing her of a bunch of irrelevant stuff, which Louise didn't even bother paying attention to.

"Look, I'm a police officer, and I'm going to have to ask you to step outside with me," Louise said.

It was either the words *police officer* or Louise's tone that decided the matter, because the woman went with her without any further fuss as Louise took a firm hold of her arm and started to lead her out of the room.

"Do you know this Duke's real name?" Louise asked, after asking the girl her own name.

The girl shook her head, a little bewildered at the situation and also quite drunk, Louise now realized, although she was still with it enough to tell Louise her name was Annette.

"Did your friend leave the party with him?" Louise prodded. A shrug was the woman's only reaction, which caused Louise to lose her patience. Her tone grew sharp, and any friendliness she had so far made an effort to display disappeared.

"Annette! Tell me if your friend left the party with that man, the one who calls himself Duke."

At last the severity of the situation seemed to dawn on the woman. She seemed to grasp that *something* was going on and that it affected her friend.

She finally acknowledged, "Yes, they left together."

22

They climbed into the unmarked squad car so they could talk privately, and Louise could almost feel Susanne's eyes on them from the next car over.

"Did they know each other already?" Louise asked Annette, every single nerve in her body twitching to hear the answer.

"They've been emailing each other for a while…I've chatted with him, too, but he and I never exchanged emails."

"How long ago did they leave?" Louise demanded.

Annette thought for a long time before she estimated that it had probably been a good hour. That fit with when Louise had seen him.

"He was really drunk, you know?" Annette said.

That was not a particularly reassuring piece of information. "We have to contact your friend," Louise said urgently. "I presume she has a cell phone," Louise said, more as a statement than as a question, and Annette nodded.

"I'll be right back," Louise said. She got out of the car, knocked on Heilmann's window, and asked her to get out, too. Once Heilmann closed her door again and Susanne couldn't hear them, Louise explained that their suspect was very likely with a young woman right now, a woman he had been emailing for a while.

They stepped away from the cars and discussed how risky it would be to call her cell phone themselves. That might drive "Duke" or Jesper Bjergholdt, or whatever alias he was going by now, into wounded-prey mode. He might go into a rage or feel forced to attack—or maybe he would run away and try to hide.

"Her name is Stine Mogensen," Louise said. "She's twenty-five, and she left the party with our guy about an hour ago. He must have slipped out in the crowd before I managed to get outside."

Heilmann listened without showing any reaction.

"We have to assume that they went to her apartment," Louise continued, feeling the tension mounting in her gut. "If that was over an hour ago, something really bad may have already happened."

"Tell the girlfriend to call Stine on her cell phone and get her out of there," Heilmann said. "She could say she needs to see her right away. Or something like that."

"But then we'll lose him," Louise objected.

Heilmann hesitated for a brief instant before continuing, in an authoritative voice, "The most important thing is for us to make sure the girl is safe. I'll send the others out to her address."

Heilmann went to call her male colleagues over.

As Louise walked back toward the car, she caught sight of Camilla out of the corner of her eye, strolling out arm in arm with a man. Even from a distance, Louise could tell he was attractive, but instead of going over and saying hi, she hurriedly got back into the car so Camilla wouldn't see her.

"Where does your friend live?" Louise asked.

Annette was pale. "On Sverrigsgade in Amager," she mumbled.

Louise wrote down the address and apartment number and got out of the car again to find Heilmann.

Camilla and Henning had disappeared, and Michael Stig was already waiting in the car.

"You drive over there, siren and flashers off," Heilmann cautioned. "And make sure you have backup in place at the back door before you go in."

"Shouldn't I go, too?" Louise offered.

Heilmann shook her head. "You're going to stay here with me while the girl calls her friend on her cell phone, and then you're going to drive Susanne home."

Louise made another attempt to convince Heilmann, but the sergeant stood her ground even though she knew it would irk Louise to let other officers make the arrest in a case she had worked so hard on.

Heilmann sat down in the back seat of Louise's car and tried to strike up a conversation with Annette, who was gradually sobering up but was still deathly pale. She had apparently given up on understanding what was going on, apart from Duke being mixed up in something so serious that the police wanted to get hold of him. She didn't ask what he'd done but, understandably enough, was growing more and more concerned about what might happen to her friend.

"Call her now," Heilmann urged Annette.

Annette scrolled through her address book until she found

Stine Mogensen's number and then took a deep breath before dialing. She sat anxiously until she heard it ring, then her shoulders relaxed, and she waited.

Louise and Heilmann were so still, it looked as though they were both holding their breath.

"It's going to voicemail," Annette said after a second.

"Try again," Heilmann said from the back seat.

Annette called again and left an urgent request for Stine to call as soon as she heard the message.

Heilmann thanked Annette for her cooperation and climbed out of the car. As the car door closed, Louise heard Heilmann, already on her phone, ordering the team to enter the apartment.

"Check for sounds or light from outside. If she doesn't open the door, kick it in," Heilmann ordered before she was even back in her car. A moment later, Susanne came and climbed into the back seat of Louise's car, and they took off with Heilmann following so fast that the gravel flew.

The mood in the car was muted. Everyone was quiet, collecting their thoughts.

"What if Stine calls me back?" Annette asked, breaking the silence.

Louise was in the middle of contemplating whether she could just let Annette out there and then drive Susanne home or if she was obligated to drive Annette home as well. Annette's question resolved it for her, because it suddenly hit her that there was actually a small chance that Stine Mogensen and Duke were someplace other than Stine's apartment, and if that was the case, the police would still need Annette's help.

Louise turned on the ignition and started driving toward Annette's address in Nørrebro. Susanne hadn't said a word since she'd gotten into the car. Not *hi*, *hello*, or anything else. She just sat there staring out the window, as though her thoughts had transported her to another world.

"I'm driving you home now," Louise told Annette. "If Stine calls, tell her you need to talk to her."

Louise spoke as calmly as she could to avoid upsetting Annette any more than necessary. It was better if Annette didn't realize how important it was that they get this right. That would reduce the risk of her being so nervous she messed something up.

"My colleagues are at Stine's apartment now. If she's there, they'll explain why you asked her to call, and that'll be the end of it." Louise drove across Christianshavn Square before continuing: "If Stine calls you back, it'll be because she's not at her apartment when she gets your message. If that happens, then you should just ask her to come over to your place right away. And then call me immediately. *Immediately*," Louise emphasized.

After Louise dropped Annette off at her apartment and made sure she was inside and safe, she was itching to call Heilmann. Things were about to come to a head.

"You think he's doing it right now, don't you?" Susanne said.

Louise nodded as she started driving toward Valby. They were driving down Falkoner Allé when Heilmann called. Louise snapped the handset to her ear instantly before Susanne could hear Heilmann's voice come over the two-way radio's speaker.

"He wasn't there," Heilmann reported succinctly.

"Well, where are they then?" Louise asked, speaking quietly so she wouldn't be heard from the back seat. She glanced discreetly in the rearview mirror to see if Susanne had reacted, but she was leaning her head back against the headrest with her eyes closed.

"*She* was there," Heilmann said. "Half-asleep and very confused."

Louise had a hard time pinning down the feeling that came over her. It was a mixture of disappointment, relief, and frustration at being back to square one.

"They did leave the party together," Heilmann reported. "But they said goodbye when she got on her bike and he kept going on foot."

Louise's fingers tensed around the steering wheel. It was her fault Bjergholdt had gotten away. She should have stopped him from leaving the party before he had a chance to slip out. Self-recrimination filled her head. How stupid she'd been to rely on her cell phone in the warehouse when she knew there was a risk they wouldn't have any reception. She could have left Susanne standing there and hurried over to the exit instead of taking the time to bring her along.

Fuck, she thought, hitting the steering wheel, snapping Susanne out of her reverie. Louise tried to pull herself together, but her composure was crumbling. To her surprise, she longed to snuggle up against Peter, and that pissed her off even more because it forced her to admit she still needed him. Suddenly the emptiness started feeding on itself: She had nothing to go home to, no one to comfort her the next morning and tell her she'd done the right thing. Even though he, of all people, had no fucking idea what the right thing to do even was. It always used to help her feel better, not feel so exposed when she showed up at the morning briefing.

"We're almost there," she announced into the dark car.

Lyshøj Allé was just off Toftegårds Square. Louise parked in the middle of the narrow street and turned around to look at Susanne.

"Do you feel safe sleeping here alone?" Louise asked, with no clue what she would do if Susanne said no.

Luckily Susanne nodded and, in an even more convincing voice, said she was looking forward to being by herself.

"If you feel unsafe for any reason whatsoever, call the number we gave you. It's the direct line to Police Headquarters dispatch. They'll send a car over right away."

Lieutenant Suhr had arranged for dispatch to keep an eye on Susanne's apartment until she moved to her new address after the weekend.

Susanne didn't seem to be listening. She had gotten out of the car and was just standing there fidgeting, waiting for permission to go in. Louise couldn't blame her. It was four thirty in the morning, and she'd just been discharged from the hospital. There was no question that she needed to go to bed and get some rest.

Louise waved at her and put the car in gear, then decided to head home instead of returning the car to the garage. She could drop it off later that morning. She was sure the others were back at headquarters, rounding off the day with a debriefing, but they'd just have to make do without her.

23

So we'll go public and look for other young women he's victimized in the past."

Suhr's voice rumbled through the break room during Monday's morning briefing. Louise felt like she'd lost her grip. She'd woken up Saturday morning feeling extremely sick to her stomach and had thrown up numerous times over the next few hours. In the end, she'd swallowed her pride and called Camilla, even though she knew Henning was probably there and that she would be interrupting their Saturday plans. But Louise just couldn't bring herself to call her mother.

She hadn't told her parents much about the breakup. They knew there'd been a fight, but they didn't know what to make of Peter moving out of the apartment, and Louise still didn't feel ready to explain it.

Camilla came over Saturday afternoon and sat with Louise as she lay on the sofa, pouring out her grief and despair. Louise was astonished at how easily the tears came, but stubbornly insisted she wasn't crying about the breakup.

"Are you lonely?" Camilla asked cautiously, getting up to put in the Big Fat Snake CD she had brought over. Camilla firmly believed that their music helped *everything*.

Louise shook her head firmly and then closed her eyes, carried away by Anders Blichfeldt's amazing voice. When she finally opened them again, she reassured Camilla that she had been longing for a little solitude.

"I just feel like I've become so fragile inside. Like I might shatter if I get hit by a stone." That was the best way Louise could explain how little was left of the strength she'd always taken for granted.

Camilla was tactful enough not to bring work up while Louise was so upset, but questions about the previous night's singles event were looming behind her comforting words and nurturing tone. Camilla stayed until late afternoon, when she and Henning planned to drive out to his place in Sorø and spend Saturday night there. Markus was staying with his father.

The tears and the nausea had abated by the time Louise waved goodbye to Camilla from the stairs. Louise accepted that she had to live with her body's way of working through the breakup, but she set Sunday night as her deadline for getting over it. She thankfully still had one more day to wallow in self-pity, she thought to herself as she watched Camilla get into her car and drive away.

"Now we're closing in on him, and we won't back down until we've got him," Suhr bellowed on, yanking Louise's attention back to the morning briefing.

Her colleagues did not pile the blame on her when she showed up for the briefing as she had feared they would. When she woke up a few minutes before the alarm went off, she inhaled all the way down to her gut and decided that, from this moment on, her life would continue as it had before—just without Peter. Sadness, loneliness, and brokenheartedness were feelings she could have; they just couldn't be *all* of them. Then she got up and thought she was doing better. She managed to sound almost natural when Michael Stig passed her in the hallway and asked her—the only one who had done so—how the hell she could let Bjergholdt escape into thin air when it had been her job to keep that from happening.

"He left," Louise had said in a steady tone and walked off to the briefing.

"We'll show the CCTV footage from the subway station if we have to, but we'll start without it," Suhr said.

"Maybe I should check if Duke's profile is still up," Louise suggested, interrupting the lieutenant. "He doesn't know we're onto that name," she continued.

Suhr grumbled a little as he considered that, but finally nodded and then pointed at Heilmann. "We're going to meet after this," he said, nodding at Louise to indicate that she would attend as well.

❧

Louise was already sitting at her computer searching when Suhr knocked on the wall next to the open door to her office. Lars had gone to get coffee, so Suhr sat down in his chair.

"So, what are you going to do if you find his profile still up?" Suhr asked. He had suggested before that Louise go out with the perp. Now a deep wrinkle formed above his nose as he awaited her answer.

Louise mulled it over for a moment. What *did* she plan to do, actually? They couldn't trace him just from his profile information. If they really lucked out, he might have posted a picture, and then they'd at least have something to take to the public. If not…

"Email him," she responded. "Then maybe we can trace him." Lieutenant Suhr sat staring out the open door to the corridor. Louise assumed he was keeping his eye out for Heilmann, and knew he would feel better if Heilmann agreed that it was a good idea for Louise to contact their man.

"Although I haven't found him so far," Louise added, to Suhr's relief. "I need to get hold of Stine Mogensen and ask how she was writing to him, because he isn't listed on any of the online dating sites I've checked."

Just then they heard rapid footsteps. Heilmann turned the corner without stopping and was suddenly standing in the middle of the office with agitated red splotches on her cheeks.

"He was at Susanne's apartment!"

Heilmann had already sent a patrol car out to Susanne's address, and she asked Louise and Lars to follow it out there.

Susanne had been in her apartment since Louise dropped her off early Saturday morning. She hadn't stepped outside all weekend and hadn't had any contact with anyone—not even her mother. Monday morning, she stepped out to buy a few groceries, and when she came home a half hour later, she found an envelope that he'd slipped through her mail slot while she was out.

"He wrote very briefly that he had been thinking about her a lot," Heilmann said.

"A threat?" Suhr asked.

Heilmann shrugged. "That's sure how I'd take it," she said, "but we've seen how erratically he acts. It's hard to say whether he's dissociative or a sociopath. But we need to get her out of that apartment right away."

Then Heilmann looked at Louise and said, "I ran into Lars out in the corridor. He's waiting for you. Make it clear to Susanne that she's not under house arrest or anything. She's free to come and go, both down there and in the city, but she shouldn't go around broadcasting her new address."

Louise nodded, already on her feet. The apartment Jakobsen had lined up was on the outskirts of Roskilde, about a half hour west of Copenhagen. Heilmann leaned over Louise's desk and wrote the address on a notepad. Suhr asked them to call in when they'd gotten Susanne set up in her temporary residence.

Louise powered down her computer and decided she'd stay out in the field the rest of the day. She had tried breaking the case by scanning through men's profiles several times and was a little irritated that that approach wasn't panning out yet. She kept hitting dead ends and having to start over again with broader and broader search terms. At the same time, another thought had occurred to her: Maybe they could leverage the fact that Stine Mogensen had been in touch with Jesper Bjergholdt. But now that would have to wait, too, because once again something else had come up that took priority.

Susanne had a suitcase and a weekend bag packed and ready by her front door. She and Heilmann had agreed that Susanne would label the other things she wanted brought to her new place, and the police would have someone come and move them later in the day, but since the new place was fully furnished, she mostly just needed clothes.

Louise felt bad for her. This whole thing might be over by the end of the week, but it might also take months. After the morning briefing, Heilmann explained that the woman Jakobsen had borrowed the apartment from was out of the country, so Susanne could stay there for at least four months if need be. Jakobsen felt that, whether or not Bjergholdt was apprehended, Susanne could use some peace and quiet and the space to find herself. He advised her to give up her own apartment and find a different permanent place to live where she wouldn't be so close to her mother anymore. That was a significant step in her treatment, which was well under way.

Louise sensed that Jakobsen was concentrating more on the profound impacts and scars that Susanne's mother had inflicted on her daughter than on the comparatively superficial wounds and scrapes that had come from the rape itself, even though those were also serious on a different level.

"When can I get my computer back?" Susanne asked as they carried her bags down to the car, where Lars took them and put them in the trunk.

"You should probably plan on being without it for a little while. It's been submitted into evidence," Louise advised.

"Well, is there any way I could borrow another one in the meantime?"

"I don't know," Louise answered, holding the car door for her. She couldn't figure Susanne out. She didn't seem particularly bothered by the message Bjergholdt had slipped in her mail slot. Or by having seen him at the party. At least Louise couldn't really see any signs of anything resembling fear. Perhaps that could be ascribed to the freedom Susanne felt at escaping the overbearing clutches of her mother.

"What do you need a computer for right now?" Louise asked once they were seated in the car.

Susanne was on a long-term leave of absence from work while she underwent counseling with Jakobsen.

"Not for dating," Susanne said. "Just for fun."

Louise didn't respond, but decided that she would call Jakobsen to ask if there was any risk that Susanne might decide to get in touch with Bjergholdt if she had that option. She took some comfort from knowing that Susanne would have just as much trouble finding him as the police did.

"I want to try to find a new job and another apartment," Susanne said. "I don't want to go back to Valby."

Lars looked like he was about to say something, but stopped himself.

"First, you should get some distance from all of this," Louise said, wishing she didn't sound so much like a self-help book. But Susanne had a good point; Louise would have wanted the same thing.

After a long silence, Susanne casually mentioned that she had agreed to tell her story to a reporter from *Morgenavisen*.

Louise sighed deeply and hoped that Lars would say something this time, but he kept his eyes trained on the road as they exited the highway and drove through Røde Port, an industrial zone being redeveloped as a residential and commercial area.

"That's your decision, but don't invite any reporters down here. If an article mentions where you're living, it will undermine the whole purpose of moving you here. Agree to meet the reporter only back in Copenhagen," Louise suggested, feeling suddenly exhausted. She had such good advice for how other people should live their lives sometimes, but then when people didn't follow her advice, she would get irritated and shrug them off as stupid. "You do whatever you want in terms of this newspaper interview," Louise said, smiling at Susanne, "but make sure you get to read it before they print it."

Susanne obviously didn't grasp why that was important. *She apparently has no idea that that's the only way to guarantee they don't fuck up her story*, Louise thought.

Susanne's new apartment was on the ground floor of a two-story building surrounded by a landscape of paths that ran through a whole development of yellow buildings that all looked the same. It had two rooms, lots of natural light, and a little deck out back. Susanne entered cautiously, as though she was afraid of scratching the light birch flooring. She walked to the center of the room and inspected her temporary home.

"This is nice." Her smile reached all the way up into her eyes.

It wasn't until Susanne was in the kitchen that it hit Louise how utterly awful the woman's life must have been. Susanne Hansson was actually starting to flourish, Louise realized, lost in her own thoughts as she watched her. Susanne was about to bloom despite what she'd just been through—and had put herself through.

"I hope you'll settle in all right even though it's just temporary," Louise said before holding up her hand to wave goodbye.

❧

Louise spent the next two days on various online dating sites, scrolling through the profiles for all the dark-haired men who were about thirty. She even visited sites specifically intended to help farmers find girlfriends, and BeautifulPeople.dk, a site ostensibly for especially attractive Danes. She poked around through men who were searching for their soul mates.

Stine Mogensen and Duke had met each other on Dating.dk, and Toft had already been in touch with the people who ran the site, who had quickly reported back that the profile he was looking for had been deleted. It had been set up by a user with a Hotmail address, so there was no reason to assume the name, address, or phone number would be correct, but they were checking anyway. But they also determined that the username Duke was already in use again, this time by a twenty-year-old guy with shoulder-length blond hair, if you could believe his profile photo. Just to be sure, they checked him out and verified that he was the person he claimed to be.

Louise called Stine and explained that she had no idea how to go about chatting with someone on a dating site. She asked Stine to try to find Duke again, even though he might be using a different username.

"I don't think he's there anymore," Stine said. "I haven't talked to him for a couple weeks."

Stine had been very standoffish at first, not wanting to push Duke into the arms of the police. It wasn't until Louise explained she was investigating the murderer and rapist all the newspapers were talking about that she agreed to help, rather shaken.

"If you find him online, call me the second you're sure it's him," Louise said, adding that obviously this was something that should just stay between them.

"Don't tell Annette or any of your other friends that you're helping me with this," she said sternly.

Louise was astonished at how many different online dating sites there were. She hardly knew where to start. With Mr. Noble and Duke in mind, she paid particular attention to usernames that had anything to do with nobility or aristocracy, and she sat bolt upright in her chair when she stumbled across the Count, who according to his profile was a twenty-eight-year-old blond man.

Louise wrote and asked him to send a picture, explaining that she wanted to see who she was writing to, and very shortly a photo appeared in the inbox at her new Hotmail address, which Lars had set up precisely for this purpose.

The Count was soon ruled out, as were RedBaron and King, but each time she felt that rush and a wave of hope rising, and then fading again just as quickly when the incredible variety of photos appeared in her inbox.

Now she understood better why a number of girls had given up and stopped writing to Bjergholdt. Apparently it was quite common for people to just send their pictures. This caused some trouble for Louise as she tried to figure out how she could avoid sending her own picture. She ended up resorting to the most pathetic excuse of them all: *Sorry, I just don't think we're right for each other*, she would write whenever the guy she was emailing sent her his picture.

She felt bad and wondered if it would be fairer if she briefly explained that she was a police officer searching for a specific individual, but that didn't seem feasible either, she thought. You never knew. They might decide to go into a chat room and tell everyone there was a cop fishing around online. Weirdly, so far no one had asked her to send her photo first; she always brought it up.

Suhr had been buzzing around the corridors since Tuesday morning when his "wanted" announcement had appeared in all the big newspapers. He had decided to withhold the still from the subway CCTV footage. "That's the card we still have up our sleeve," he commented at Tuesday's morning briefing.

Many tips had come in that same morning from frightened women who said they had been in contact with him but had never met him in person.

Michael Stig loudly derided them as "all those annoying tips." Toft shushed him, taking him to task and saying he ought to welcome all tips. There was no telling which one might break the case.

Louise smiled as Toft talked his partner down in a calm voice. They had already started following up on the potentially interesting leads.

A phone call came in from a woman in her midthirties who for the last six months had been keeping a secret of the nightmare she'd experienced following what she had thought was a successful dinner date at her home.

As recently as March, another woman had had what she described as a "nasty" experience. But she wasn't sure it could be called rape since she'd "asked for it."

Even Lieutenant Suhr was shaken by how unsure the women were about where the boundary between rape and consensual sex was and what people were apparently willing to subject their bodies to. He sat in Heilmann's office, reading through the reports that were written up as the tips came in.

"If it hurts and you ask the man to stop and he keeps going anyway, then people have to realize that that shifts it from something consensual to assault," Suhr growled, infuriated, arranging the pages he'd read into a neat stack.

"It's just not that simple," Heilmann said without looking up. Obviously, Suhr was aware of that. It was just so clear, when you sat there looking at a whole stack of tips, that these women should have reported the incidents. The definition of rape had changed since online dating came onto the scene. The police saw more instances of cases where a couple had agreed to meet and to have sex. They just didn't agree on when to stop and how rough it would be. Proving that an assault had occurred could be difficult in cases like that.

They also received loads of messages about men who looked nothing like the suspect they had described. Blond, jet-black hair, short, fat, foreign, not foreign, older, younger. One of the junior detectives who had been tasked with answering the phone had to sort through all of them. He knew where to draw the lines for whom to include.

❧

"I want to see the messages Bjergholdt sent," Louise said, stepping into the doorway to Suhr's office on Wednesday afternoon. Suhr and Heilmann were sitting there quietly discussing which tips they should follow up on. "Maybe I can figure out what it is about them he responds to. There must be something or other that triggers him to target these particular women," she continued.

She had already made copies of the profiles of women Bjergholdt had contacted, and there *was* a pattern. They were reserved. Not a word about sex or decadence or expensive habits. They just wanted a couple of candles on the table, to spend time one-on-one with someone, and to feel safe. These women preferred movie theaters to bars, family togetherness and leisure activities to a career.

Suhr waved for her to come in.

"I need to figure out what turns him on," Louise explained. She needed more time and was glad she didn't need to fight for it. Suhr had already decided that she should continue her search while the detectives worked on the tips and talked to persons of interest.

"Toft has all the correspondence between him and the two victims. You can copy the whole stack," Suhr said, returning his attention to the papers in front of him.

The DNA results had come back from the pathology lab earlier that day. They showed that the semen in the condom and the pubic hair found on the floor of Christina Lerche's apartment both matched the samples collected from Susanne's back. Based on the suspect's signature, or MO, as Heilmann usually called it, they had already *assumed* they were dealing with the same man, but now they had concrete evidence. There was no doubt that this was an important step forward and a big relief for Suhr. In addition, another match showed that the man who called himself Kim Jensen, claiming to be from Hørsholm, who had raped and beaten Karin Hvenegaard two years earlier, was in fact the same person as Bjergholdt.

Three victims.

Louise was inclined to agree with Suhr that there were bound to be more. Maybe as soon as Stig got back from taking the statement of a woman whose description of an assault last year was strikingly similar to Karin's.

❦

Louise sat down heavily when she got back to her office. Fatigue washed over her. The sheer quantity of online profiles made the task seem insurmountable, and she still didn't understand what kinds of things made people respond to a certain profile. Maybe there were special rules that she just hadn't figured out yet as a newbie to the world of online dating. She picked up the phone and called Camilla.

"Hey, could I read your articles on online dating?" she asked. "That series you did, and anything else you've got in your archives."

Camilla seemed busy and touchy. It didn't sound like she was planning to set down what she was working on to comply with Louise's request.

"If it can wait until I get back in a couple of hours, I'll put together a packet for you," Camilla offered, intentionally packing up her things as audibly as possible as they talked.

Camilla had catapulted through the ranks on *Morgenavisen*'s crime beat in the last year. She had free rein to do what she wanted as long as Terkel Høyer, her editor, could count on as many front-page stories from her as possible. It had been a long time since Camilla had had to call around to the various police precincts to find out what was on their blotters for the day. It had also been a long time since she had been sent to a pretrial hearing; if she ever went to one now, it was to cover a story she had pitched herself. Otherwise, those sorts of mundane assignments now fell to the intern or to Ole Kvist, even though he had been with the paper a lot longer than Camilla.

"I'm on my way out to do an interview for a piece I'm writing tonight. So, I'll be here if you stop by later," Camilla said. "I probably won't have time to chat, but I can have the articles ready for you."

It wasn't hard for Louise to figure out that Camilla must be referring to the interview with Susanne. Printing her story while the investigation was still in full swing would obviously be a scoop. But Louise didn't comment on that.

The earliest she could pick up the material would be around six or seven, but she could head straight home from there and read it that evening. Maybe that would help her learn some of the unwritten rules of the online scene that she was ignorant of. Susanne hadn't been an experienced online dater, but maybe she had stumbled onto something because she had been so totally raw and honest about what she was looking for.

Louise had already read a couple of the emails Bjergholdt and Susanne had written to each other, but then she set them aside again, deciding to wait until she had read Camilla's articles. Now she was back to searching for dark-haired men, and she found herself lingering a number of times on profiles that captured her interest. Not because they struck her as anything Bjergholdt might be lurking behind, but because Louise found the guys' self-portrayals intriguing on a purely personal level.

Before leaving, she warned Heilmann that *Morgenavisen* was going to be publishing an interview with Susanne the next morning. Louise was just shutting down the laptop she had been issued for her searches when Suhr walked in.

"Hey, do you think you can get Camilla Lind to reprint the

information about the suspect we're looking for, along with the interview?" he asked. "It'd be good to keep that fresh in people's minds."

"I don't think I'm going to be talking to her," Louise said. *Why doesn't he fucking pick up the phone and call her himself?* she thought.

He muttered something she didn't catch before he turned around and disappeared.

❧

She enjoyed her bike ride up to Rosenborg Castle Gardens, just catching sight of the Renaissance verdigris spires over the wide-crowned trees, then turning north onto Kronprinsessegade, where *Morgenavisen*'s offices occupied a beautifully restored two-hundred-year-old neoclassical building. She parked her bike and headed up the stairs to the third floor, where the crime desk was located. Camilla was there, concentrating on writing, when Louise walked in.

Camilla looked up from her screen, but seemed in another world.

"Do you have time for a cup of coffee?" Louise asked.

Her friend shook her head and said, "My deadline is in an hour and I still need to get it okayed." Camilla nodded at what she'd written.

Louise was glad that Susanne had remembered to ask to read through the piece before it was published—if she indeed was the one Camilla had interviewed. Louise briefly contemplated mentioning that Suhr wanted her to reprint the description of the suspect, but decided to drop it.

"All right. Let's get together another time," Louise said, taking

243

the plastic binder containing the articles Camilla had printed out for her. Camilla had changed since Henning had entered the picture. She no longer had the same need to spend time chilling out with her friends, or maybe Louise just noticed it more since she was living alone now.

"Henning and his brother are stopping by tonight. You're welcome to come over. Markus will be there, too," Camilla said, explaining that Christina had picked him up from school.

That babysitter was God's gift to the single mother. She had known Markus since he was in kindergarten and jumped at the chance whenever Camilla couldn't pick him up from his after-school program.

"No, thanks, but that's sweet of you," Louise replied. She just wasn't up to it; she really did want to meet Henning—just not tonight. They gave each other a quick kiss on the cheek goodbye. Louise walked back down to her bicycle and rode south along the lakes separating downtown Copenhagen from Frederiksberg, turning onto Gammel Kongevej.

⁂

She wasn't much the wiser by the time she finished reading Camilla's articles about the dating culture later that evening, but it had occurred to her that the online dating scene could be divided into two groups: people who set up a profile exclusively to find a partner or companion, and people for whom this became a lifestyle. Susanne, Christina Lerche, and Karin Hvenegaard belonged to the former group, whereas Bjergholdt was in the latter. She still couldn't decide if it was meeting strange women that drove him, or the knowledge that he could hide his true identity—

or if he lacked those kinds of psychological motivations and was just using the internet as a supply source for his fetish. Maybe he had even started out with more genuine intentions and discovered how much freedom he had later. Either way, he was now icy and calculating and exploited the anonymity the internet provided. There was no way to know, she concluded as she tried to piece together a pattern in her mind.

On the other hand, she had no doubt that the internet and that type of online contact had now become a part of his life. He traveled in those circles. That's why he'd showed up at the mixer. Those two young women had known him. She still hadn't heard back from Stine Mogensen, so she must not have found him yet.

Louise tried to picture him. What the fuck kind of person was he? *Chivalrous, courteous, polite*, she wrote on a piece of paper. Orders multiple course dinners and calvados with his after-dinner coffee. Invites people to the quaint old wharf at Nyhavn, goes to hip dating mixers. He's urbane, she concluded. He's familiar with Copenhagen and knows his way around here. He walks his dates to the subway, and shows up at Susanne's apartment.

Something dawned on her as she was reading Camilla's articles. It didn't matter so much where you met online, but rather that you had a life in the virtual world at all. You met new people over the internet, formed new connections. People went online to play Yahtzee. Camilla had written about a woman who spent eight hours a day playing Yahtzee online with people she had never met in real life. Her best friends were people she knew from the site. As the virtual dice tumbled across the screen, they would write back and forth to each other and form close, intimate bonds.

When she had first read about that woman, Louise had had a hard time taking it seriously. She was about forty, was apparently quite normal-seeming and extroverted, and didn't have the least bit of trouble getting to know other people, either at work or in her free time. In the article, she discussed the world that had opened up to her when she started surfing the net. She talked mostly about her Yahtzee friends, calling those friendships both deeper and far more intimate than the ones she had with her friends who she hung out with in the real world. She made a big deal about saying that she had never felt a need to meet these online friends face-to-face. What they shared belonged in the Yahtzee universe, and it was better not to mix that with her everyday life. But that didn't mean that it was less important to her. She had made sure to emphasize that at the end of the article.

Louise understood exactly what Camilla meant when she compared the woman's two lives to people who had vacation homes somewhere remote but spent their everyday lives in the city. Those two lifestyles didn't necessarily have to merge, either. Maybe the appeal was just that, switching back and forth between rubber rain boots and stilettos, as Camilla had poetically put it. All the same, it struck Louise that living in a cyberworld to that degree could outcompete living in the real world. Scary, especially since Louise mostly used the internet only to Google things, check the weather, or email. With a sigh, she gathered the articles together into a pile and got ready for bed.

24

The Susanne Hansson article filled most of the front page the next morning, and Camilla's interview continued on a second page. Louise folded up the paper after a cursory skim. She also noted the box in the lower right corner with the photo of Suhr and a reprint of the description of the suspect, which had already appeared on Tuesday. *Contact the Police*, the heading read, and people did. Men and women both. In droves.

Louise shook her head in dismay at the men who called in claiming that they were the man the paper was warning people about. They started tracing those calls, but nothing had come of that so far.

And then there were countless messages from women who had been attacked by a man whose description or MO matched Bjergholdt's.

On the other hand, the flood of new, relevant tips had restored Suhr's optimism. "We have at least twice as many leads now," he said with satisfaction when the group gathered that morning to see where they stood.

They all agreed Bjergholdt was the person who had murdered Christina Lerche and raped Susanne Hansson and Karin Hvene-gaard. They were also pretty sure he was behind two of the tips they had received, but that would be hard to prove. They showed the victims the stills of him from the CCTV footage, and the victims confirmed that it looked like the same man, but that alone wasn't strong enough evidence to prevent a good defense attorney from picking apart the criminal charges even before the prosecution had a chance to present its case. Not that they were close to bringing anyone in at this stage anyway.

When Louise returned from the briefing, she sat down in front of her computer, her mind wandering. Her stomach felt empty, and it occurred to her that she had skipped breakfast. She just hadn't felt hungry, and by the time she finally was, she smoked a cigarette and drank a cup of coffee instead. Before, she would have gotten by on mineral water and apples, but that wasn't enough anymore. Peter called and asked if they could get together for a cup of coffee over the weekend so they could work out how to divvy up their joint savings account and the possessions they had purchased to-gether.

Suddenly the weekend seemed daunting. She caught herself wishing that something would happen so she could bury herself in her work and the time would fly by. After a lot of cajoling, she had agreed to go out with Flemming on Friday night. They had spoken only once since he had been over, and she didn't want to spend a whole evening talking about her failed relationship. On the other hand, she didn't have any other plans, and it would do her good to get out.

She felt another wave of nausea after she ate a slightly stale piece of bread with butter she found in the kitchenette. She only just made it to the bathroom in time to crouch over the toilet bowl. Once back in her office, she found the number and called her doctor. A nagging suspicion had been creeping into her consciousness the last couple of days. No matter how much she tried to ignore it, it pushed itself to the forefront of her mind.

"He doesn't have any openings tomorrow," the secretary at her doctor's office said emphatically, "and Monday the urgent cases from over the weekend will be coming in, so unless it's an emergency, the first available appointment is Tuesday."

Louise grudgingly conceded that it was not an emergency and made the appointment.

***

The next day, Louise forced herself to go along when Lars came in and said it was time for lunch and that he had to go to the cafeteria because he had forgotten his lunch on the kitchen counter at home. There was a throng of people and a heavy odor of food. Again, Louise's stomach lurched. She considered stopping by the pharmacy on the way home so she could buy a test and find out for sure, but the idea was so awful that she just couldn't face knowing. *God, what a sucky accident that would be*, she thought, following Lars to the end of the cafeteria line.

She stared dully at the fruit basket sitting next to the cash register and looked at the floor as the guys ahead of her filled their plates with steaming helpings of pork meatballs in curry sauce. She took a piece of rye bread and a banana and was ready to head back down to the office.

"Come on," her partner said, nodding toward the long cafeteria table.

Louise reluctantly followed. She really just wanted to go back to the office and eat there so she could keep working. She had just briefed the lieutenant on an idea she'd had the night before and wanted to get started.

"Fine by me," Suhr had said, hurrying on his way.

She suddenly realized that Suhr had been going easy on her. He's been babying her because she had told him Peter had moved in with someone else, and he thought searching dating sites would be easier on her while he had everyone else out searching for Bjergholdt and his victims. She was so furious at the special treatment that she couldn't stop herself: Before she knew it, she was standing in his office, taking him to task, and lecturing him about how the internet had become the preferred reality for lots of people. She was quite a way into her monologue before she noticed that Sergeant Heilmann was sitting in the chair across from Suhr, watching the whole scene with disapproval on her face.

"Uh, hi," Louise said, nodding at Heilmann.

Then she turned back to Suhr and continued, while slinking back toward the door, "I suppose I could just search more later if you'd rather put me on something else."

She stared him intently in the eyes with all the strength she could muster, hoping to convince him that she didn't require any special treatment.

Suhr looked like a man who was finally ready to admit that he didn't understand women. He had no idea what Louise was trying to tell him, so he decided to pretend she hadn't said the last part. Instead he just gave her a friendly, if slightly bewildered, nod and asked her to keep doing what she was doing.

Sitting at the table in the cafeteria with Lars, Louise discovered that she had forgotten how nice it was to listen to conversations at the lunch table. She put off her work, fetched a cup of coffee, and got an update on the case about the man they had charged with murdering his ex-wife. The charges had been dropped, and Willumsen was so frustrated that he had decided to take a long weekend with his wife. No one could remember him ever doing that before.

Everyone agreed that the most frustrating part was that there was practically a hundred percent chance that the guy was guilty, but because it was perfectly reasonable that his fingerprints were all over her apartment and because a witness had felt pressured into making a false statement, the whole thing had fallen apart. He'd walked out of Vestre Prison a free man and had already sent his children out of the country. Unless they found some new evidence, the police were going to be forced to accept that he would get away with stabbing his wife to death and they wouldn't be able to do anything about it.

"That's the way it is. We're going to have to close the case. You'll just end up beating yourself up if you can't let it go and admit that sometimes luck and circumstances favor the bad guys," said Detective Pihl with a resigned shrug. He'd worked closely on the case.

Louise agreed, though she didn't like hearing it. If they couldn't ID Bjergholdt soon, their case could land in the same cold-case pile, she thought. Their problem was just the opposite, though— they had the evidence, but not the guy.

❧

While she was in the cafeteria, Louise received a text message from Camilla: "Do you want to get out of town this weekend?" Camilla and Markus were going to Sorø, and Louise was tempted, but she was seeing Flemming that night and having coffee with Peter on Saturday, so she sent a brief text back saying she couldn't and then sat down at her computer.

Nightwatch.dk. She needed an account to get in, which meant she had to sign up. She wanted to get Lars to help her, but he had already left the cafeteria and wasn't there when she got back.

Well, I suppose I can probably figure it out on my own, she thought, trying to think of a username. She ended up using initials, just not her own. She stole her sister-in-law's. Trine had changed her last name to Rick after she married Mikkel, but she kept her maiden name as her middle name, and it grated on Louise's ears whenever she heard her say Trine Madsen Rick. It just didn't go together.

Louise typed in *TMR* and hoped the site would accept a username that was only three characters long. It didn't. There had to be at least four. She amused herself by deleting *Rick* from her sister-in-law's name, making her into Trine Madsen again. She then shortened that to *TRIM*, which the site accepted. A colorful welcome screen popped up, and the menu bar on the left explained how to navigate on the site and which bars, nightclubs,

252

and dance clubs you could visit on Nightwatch.dk. The goal was for late-night party animals to get photographed by Nightwatch's photographers, who roamed around the city, and have these photos posted on the site.

Obviously you could also use your own camera. The site had really taken off, now that so many people had cameras in their cell phones. So people texted their pictures to Nightwatch.dk and wrote who they were out with or who they had met at the bar and maybe a brief comment. You used your Nightwatch username, and the pictures were posted right away. So then if you were surfing the site from home or on your smartphone and you saw a cute guy hanging out by the bar in one of these clubs, you could either hurry down there and hope he was still there, or you could write him if the picture was tagged with his username. Based on the pictures featured on the home page, it was obvious that not everybody realized they were being photographed.

Louise clicked on *Thursday* to see who she could have met if she had been in downtown Copenhagen the previous night: some guys named Søsser, Herring, and Danny stood awkwardly with their arms around each other, smiling. The picture was blurry; Louise guessed it was taken from a cell-phone camera, and sighed when she realized there were eight pages of the same kind of tiny thumbnails. She would have to click and enlarge them to have any hope of making out the faces—and these thumbnails were just from one of the many downtown locations. She was starting to get a sense of how many pictures there must be for Friday and Saturday nights.

Tons of names and tons of drunken people. There were also pictures of people engaging in various types of transactions. She noted that she ought to tell Narcotics and Licensing about this while she was at it, surprised that people let themselves be photographed like this.

She kept going, zooming in on pictures, closing them again, and clicking the next one as fast as her laptop would permit. There were a few people her age! They were sitting at the bar drinking mixed drinks. The caption read, *Sip and Motor3*. Louise double-clicked *Sip* and pulled up her profile. There weren't any pictures on her profile, but you could email her. Louise closed that and tried *Motor3*. His profile included a good selection of photos.

Lars was back, although Louise hadn't noticed him come in. She was deep in concentration, staring at her screen. She had just realized there were pictures from the dating mixer out in Holmen, but since she was systematically moving back through time, she had only gotten to Saturday night so far. There hadn't been any sign of Bjergholdt in the places she had tried, though she knew there was only a minimal chance that she would suddenly recognize him if he was in one of the pictures. But he had been at the mixer, which meant that he was the kind of guy who went out on the town, so it was worth a try.

Heilmann stopped by periodically after that and looked over Louise's shoulder. The sergeant had been much quicker than Suhr to appreciate what Louise had found. The image quality of the mixer photos varied dramatically. In most of them, the lighting was so bad it was hard to see anything but blurry figures standing against a dark background.

"We probably won't be able to use them in a lineup with picture quality like that," Heilmann said before returning to her own office. "But if you find him, we'll get a tech to see if he can clean it up a little."

Louise saw a lot of old friends as she leafed through, clip by clip. Stine Mogensen and her friend Annette showed up in several of the pictures. Clearly it would take more than Duke and Friday night's experience to keep them away from the nightlife in the city.

He wasn't there, she determined, feeling empty inside without quite knowing why she had let herself get her hopes up so much during her search. She closed the album of photos from the mixer and moved on to last Thursday without much enthusiasm. She was just about fed up with the countless photos. She jumped when her phone rang, and glanced at the display but didn't recognize the number.

"Department A, Louise Rick speaking."

"Hi, it's Susanne. What did you think of my interview?" Confused and mentally depleted, it took Louise a second to remember who Susanne was and what interview she was talking about. She looked up from her computer screen and tried to snap out of it.

"I actually haven't had a chance to read it yet," Louise admitted, glancing over at today's paper, which was sitting on her desk. "But I have it right here. Were you happy with it?"

"Very. I just talked to Camilla, who told me that it got a lot of positive feedback. People want to support me, make sure I'm okay, and help me find a new place to live and another job," Susanne said, sounding happy.

"That's great!" It was amazing what an article like that could do. People came together when their fellow man was in need. "But remember to keep a low profile," Louise urged.

She noticed what a damper that put on Susanne's cheerful voice, and she regretted saying it immediately.

"I don't mean you shouldn't accept the help people are offering you," Louise hastened to add. "Just that you shouldn't rush into a

255

new apartment or job right now while the paper is set to follow your every move."

"I wasn't planning to," Susanne responded a little stiffly, continuing in a more businesslike tone, "but I agreed with Camilla that I would write a sort of diary about my life in hiding, about my thoughts, and what it's like having to move because you don't feel safe anymore."

Louise didn't know if she should laugh or chew Susanne out.

Susanne continued, "I actually called to say you don't need to worry about getting me a computer anymore. *Morgenavisen* is letting me borrow one."

Louise rested her forehead in the palm of her hand. She didn't know if it was bad or good for Susanne to have ended up in Camilla's orbit. Maybe it would help her make a clean break from her old life and create her new identity, or maybe it would turn her into a media sensation—some poor thing people felt bad about for a while and then forgot about again just as quickly.

"Okay, I'll shelve the request," Louise said, "but don't make any agreement with the newspaper that would allow readers to contact you directly, because then there's a risk *he* will."

Susanne mumbled something unintelligible. Louise predicted that *Morgenavisen* would provide an email address when they ran Susanne's diary. Doubtless there were plenty of readers who would make use of the opportunity to contact her. Louise would bring this up with Suhr and Heilmann.

"What phone are you calling from?" Louise asked.

Susanne's phone number should have shown up on her caller ID, if she was calling from her regular phone.

"It's a phone *Morgenavisen* gave me so I wouldn't have to use mine."

Now Louise saw what was going on. The newspaper was staking its claim. Camilla was on the story, and she was making sure no one else could get hold of Susanne. *Smart thinking, Camilla! Go in and ask for a raise*, she thought. At the same time, it told her that the paper obviously thought there could be more victims—that the story was big enough to headline all summer. Otherwise, they wouldn't have gone to such lengths to make sure they had the exclusive rights to Susanne's story. She pictured Camilla and her weekend in the countryside with her son and boyfriend. *Here's hoping her fairy tale won't be interrupted by a new rape*, Louise thought bitterly.

"Well, I'll talk to you soon," Louise said when she couldn't think of anything else. When you got right down to it, Susanne wasn't really doing anything wrong. She was just doing what most people would, and, as far as Louise could tell, at least her mother wasn't anywhere in the picture.

When Louise updated Suhr on this development, he decided he wanted to talk to Camilla himself and find out what her plans were for Susanne. He didn't want to see the case turn into a media circus, as he put it, but if the paper could guarantee that her address would remain secret and they filtered the emails she received, he didn't have any objections. Louise guessed that Camilla would humor him and agree to notify him right away if any interesting messages came in. Louise saw that Camilla had found a way to make sure she stayed one step ahead of the police. Now suddenly she was the one who would notify *them*, not the other way around.

Louise looked at her watch and realized she only had an hour to get home, shower, and change before she was supposed to meet Flemming. She quickly shut off her computer and raced out the door.

❧

Just a tad late and slightly winded, Louise stood peering at the densely populated bar counter, but there was no sign of Flemming Larsen. She walked over to an open table in the corner near the kitchen and had just sat down when he walked in the door.

"Have you been waiting long?" he asked apologetically.

She reassured him she had just gotten there herself. They moved into the restaurant section of the café, where he had made a reservation.

Louise felt awkward. She had more makeup on than she usually did for work. She was wearing a turquoise tunic from Pureheart—borrowed from Camilla—over her jeans, and for once she was letting her long, unruly curls fall freely. Flemming, on the other hand, looked like he had come straight from work.

"I got called out just as I was getting ready to come," he said, sensing she was feeling a little overdressed.

She had a sinking feeling in her stomach, involuntarily imagining that a new rape had been reported after she left the office.

He shook his head.

"A stabbing," he said. "I met Willumsen at the scene."

Louise shook her head in confusion, saying, "I thought Willumsen was away for a long weekend with his wife."

"He was, but he arrived right after me, so he must have ditched his wife at the hotel the instant Suhr called," Flemming said, smiling. "He feels sure this was a revenge killing. It was the same man who was released the other day for the murder of his ex-wife in Nykøbing Sjaelland we were speaking about at lunch. He was stabbed in the chest and the back. It looks like more than one attacker. Willumsen's guess is that the guy was bragging a little too loudly about the charges being dropped, which must have provoked the woman's family."

Louise listened without feeling anything. One murder case took over for another. The man had been going to go free, even though he had murdered his ex-wife. Now he was dead. Louise thought about the children, who had been sent abroad and no longer had a father or a mother to come home to.

She let Flemming order for them, watching him as he studied the wine list. She suddenly realized how much she longed for companionship, now that she was out and surrounded by people having a good time. She hadn't felt that in ages.

She finally gave in at four in the morning and let Flemming help her into a cab. She had had way too much to drink and smoked way too many cigarettes. Even in her fog, she was a little ashamed that she had gotten so carried away and out of control, but it had been a fun night.

25

When Louise woke up the next morning, her head was throbbing so violently that she could do nothing but lie there, pulling herself together until she could slowly push herself over the edge of the bed into a sitting position. They had mostly drunk gin after dinner, and the taste was still in her mouth. She got up and brushed her teeth and scurried back into bed, waiting for someone to pour her back into the bottle, as her father used to say when she was younger.

It had been a good evening, and even in the midst of her hangover she'd felt alive, as though something had been liberated inside her. She looked at the clock. She had an hour until she was supposed to meet Peter. Maybe she should cancel. Or maybe she ought to march right down to that café stinking of liquor and cigarette smoke and not give a damn.

❧

"Are you sure you're okay?" Peter asked uncertainly after they'd finished their second cup of coffee and had squared away all the practical matters about dividing up their possessions.

She nodded and asked, "How about you?" She had avoided asking before.

"Yeah, things are great," he said quickly.

That's a fucking lie. She could see that. Suddenly she noticed how he looked. He seemed sad, but was trying to hide it.

"I mean, obviously it's a bit of an adjustment," he added, watching her with an intent look that she didn't have the energy to interpret. "It's different."

She could imagine.

He looked at his watch and started getting ready to go. "We're going out to Lina's sister's place this afternoon. She's pregnant, and there's obviously a lot of baby stuff to talk about even though the little guy's not coming for another seven months."

Louise felt bad for Peter. He tended to use that sarcastic tone when he was starting to lose respect and to tune out.

The thought didn't hit her until she was back home, lying on the sofa. What would she do if he suddenly showed up at the door and wanted to move back in?

She closed her eyes, determined to push the thought out of her mind before she had a chance to start dwelling on it.

❧

When she woke up later in the afternoon, she made herself a big mug of tea, with plenty of sugar and milk, and then sat down in front of her computer. There were lots of new pictures from a wild Friday night on the town. She discovered to her amazement that there was a whole album from one of the places she and Flemming had been. She hadn't even noticed the photographer there, nor did she recognize any of the people in the pictures. She was forced to conclude she had been engrossed in the coroner's company.

She sat there idly, clicking through Copenhagen's night life. It took her tired brain several seconds to register what she'd seen.

He was with three girls, showing off for the photographer. He was standing on the far left, talking to someone who wasn't in the picture. His aristocratic profile stood in sharp contrast to pretty much everything else in the picture.

She clicked on the picture and zoomed in so it took up the whole screen, then scrolled down to the text box underneath it.

Prinzz.

So that's what he was calling himself now. She sat for a long time, staring, unable to remember the three girls' names. She saw only his name with those two Zs and wondered if it could belong to someone else. But there wasn't anyone else in the picture. Just the four of them.

She shivered a little as she went back to the start page and typed *Prinzz* in the site's search box. She couldn't tell if it was her hangover still wreaking havoc on her body, or if it was agitation, knowing he had been hanging out in the same part of town where she had been. She could have run into him. They actually could have been in the same place without her having realized it. She hit enter and found his profile. The album under his username was empty, but the profile did have a "Send Prinzz a Message" link. Louise sat there staring for a long time, and then her fingers started moving on the keyboard.

"I saw you downtown last night, but you weren't alone so I didn't want to bother you. Is there a place you usually go?" she wrote. Louise tried to imagine what Susanne would have written if it were her. Brief and not too self-confident at any rate. She signed it *TRIM* and pressed send, but regretted it right away. She should have thought it through when she was in a better mental state and not hungover. She wanted to arouse his curiosity, not set off his warning bells.

Shit, she thought, wishing she could take the message back.

She was still sitting there, trying to collect her thoughts, when an icon blinked to tell her she had a message in her Nightwatch inbox.

"Sometimes," he wrote succinctly.

Dumbfounded, she sat there staring. It had almost been too easy. Again, she worried that she had the wrong guy. Maybe this wasn't even Prinzz. She was so tired. Although her headache had abated, she was still thinking slowly, but she wasn't with it enough to come up with a plausible excuse to back out now and wait to reestablish contact once she was feeling better.

Another message from him: "Have I seen you?"

"No, I don't think so," she replied, starting to sweat. "You were surrounded by girls, so I totally don't blame you for not noticing me." It would be dumb to break off contact, she realized, since he was writing to her. If it turned out it really was him, she had to hold on, tooth and nail. She led the conversation to a neutral topic.

"Do you go out often?" she wrote.

"It depends. What about you?"

"No, not so much. I was just out with an old friend from school."

"Old? How old are you?"

She stopped to consider. Both Susanne and Christina Lerche were in their early thirties. It would be too much of a leap if she was much older.

"Thirty-three," she lied, adding that she hoped that wasn't off-putting.

"Not at all. Do you have kids?"

Yes or no, she wondered quickly. No, no kids to tuck into bed before dinner, she concluded.

"No, I haven't found the right guy yet," she wrote and then scolded herself silently. *Shut up, quick, this is too risky.*

"Or maybe he hasn't found you yet," was the speedy response.

"Good answer," she wrote.

Phew, she thought, noticing that her forehead was damp with sweat.

"What's your name?" he wrote, not acknowledging her compliment.

She wiped her brow with her sleeve and rubbed her temples. Then she quickly typed: "Call me Princess."

Louise jumped up all of a sudden and stepped back from the computer, unable to fathom the consequences of what she had gotten mixed up in. She went to the bathroom and splashed some cold water on her face. Her exhaustion was easing, along with the last traces of her hangover. She felt exhilarated; she was on to something. A wave of empowerment rolled up through her body. They had established contact. Now she just had to act sensibly.

She ought to contact Suhr or Heilmann so one of them could help decide how they should proceed. On the other hand, if she waited too long now, she risked his breaking off contact. He hadn't asked where she had seen him in town yet. Maybe he figured she'd seen him the night before. Or maybe everyone just took it for granted that people were checking the photos on Nightwatch because they knew it let you track down people you had seen in town.

She dried off her face and went back.

"Do you want to get coffee?" he had written while she was away.

She ran to the front hall to grab her cell phone from her purse. She quickly found Heilmann's cell number and called. It rang for a long time before it went to voicemail. Louise tried her home number, but there was no answer there, either. She heard a sound from her computer and knew she had received a new message. She left a voicemail for Heilmann, asking her to call back.

"Fuck," she said out loud as she hung up. It could be a long time before Heilmann called back, and she couldn't wait to respond to him. Irritated, she tried Suhr, who picked up after the second ring, but when she heard his voice, she could tell from his standoffish tone that she was interrupting something. She hung up, secretly rejoicing that her phone number wouldn't show up on his caller ID. What the hell would he have told her to do, anyway? They could run a trace on her computer on Monday if they thought that would give them anything new.

Again, she felt unsure if it really was Bjergholdt she had contacted. A man with so much on his conscience wouldn't be behaving so recklessly, right? Her thoughts were muddled; she couldn't tell Suhr that she was sitting at her computer writing to someone who might not even be their suspect. She needed to be a little more certain.

"That sounds nice," she replied. Then she hit return twice and continued, "I'm going out of town this weekend to visit my parents, but I'll be back Monday so maybe we can set something up when I get back?"

She sat there with a nervous knot in her stomach, waiting to see how he would react.

It took longer than before for him to respond. She wondered if she shouldn't have nailed down a specific time and was just about to write that they could decide on a time now when she received his response.

"Sounds good," he wrote. "What's your real email address? I'll send you a line Monday. Take care of yourself, Princess."

She sank, struggling to think clearly. The Hotmail account she had been using at work was just her initials, but that didn't go with TRIM at all. She felt like she'd been caught in a lie, and hid her face in her hands, struggling to try to think coherently. Finally, she gave up and wrote her Hotmail address, praying that he wouldn't get cold feet and ask her what TRIM, LR, and Princess had in common. But he just replied, "See you soon," a second after she pressed send.

❧

So, she had done it. They had a date to email each other on Monday. Suddenly she was starving. She went and opened her fridge, even though she knew there was nothing in it that would help her. Without even trying to fight her craving for a burger and a big container of fries, she shoved her feet into a pair of slip-ons and headed down to the street to get some takeout, replaying the exchange of messages in her head.

Had she written anything that could arouse his suspicion? Had she in any way said anything that didn't come across as natural? It occurred to her that in her eagerness to tone things down, she might have come across as uninteresting. Maybe he'd lose interest before Monday.

Her thoughts were racing, spinning into an enormous mish-mash by the time she got back to her apartment. She had ordered two cheeseburgers with extra bacon, even though there was almost no way she could eat more than one of them, but she felt like indulging. Feeling that her appearance screamed to all and sundry she'd been out most of the night— and wasn't particularly good at such things—she let herself back in through her building's main door holding a Jolly Cola and looked forward to collapsing.

26

Y ou've got to be fucking kidding me. You've been writing from your home computer after we set up a whole special work one just for that purpose?"

Michael Stig was leaning over Louise's desk sounding like a broken record. This was the fourth time he had repeated himself, and Louise was already fully aware that it might not have been the smartest decision. But she also knew that a civilian couldn't trace things back the way the police could, so she didn't quite grasp why it was apparently such a huge disaster.

"Well, first of all, we should have blocked your IP address," Stig had said at the investigative team's morning briefing.

The others had listened with interest as Louise told them about Nightwatch, and Heilmann had commended her for establishing contact when she'd had the chance. Even Suhr had seemed impressed, although Louise had pointed out several times that there was no way to even be sure she had contacted the right guy. She also explained the project she had Stine Mogensen working on, which was ultimately their best shot at contacting the suspect.

"Mogensen left the mixer with Bjergholdt that night," Louise reminded everyone present. "Last week I asked her to search for him whenever she was chatting online. They have chatted with each other before, so I thought maybe there was something distinctive about the way he expressed himself that she might recognize even if he were using a new username. But she hasn't found anything yet. So maybe this 'Prinzz' is just a wild-goose chase."

Louise said that mostly to tamp down their expectations.

Stig sat there shaking his head through the rest of the briefing. Louise wished he would just go back to focusing on his fucking Management Training Program. Finally, she couldn't take it anymore. "Would you give it a fucking rest!?" she snapped.

She avoided making eye contact with him even though he was all up in her face as he scolded her for using her home computer. He was making a big deal out of nothing, making it seem like her actions had been irresponsible and reckless. Which they had, she was fully aware of that. But he didn't need to keep harping on it.

❧

Suhr was standing in the doorway observing the drama without any change in his expression. It took a minute before Stig noticed him, gave everyone a quick nod, and left the room.

"Just keep going," Suhr said, ignoring the conversation he'd walked in on. "It won't be of real interest to us until we know for sure if it's him, of course. But don't be inviting him over to your place unless we're there."

Louise smiled at him and promised to be careful.

"The attacks we've seen from him so far aren't the kinds of things you get away with out in the open, so you just keep at it," Suhr encouraged.

She was glad that the lieutenant was being so low-key about the whole thing. There was still a long way to go, she thought, and she was sure Bjergholdt wouldn't even consider inviting her out to dinner until he was sure she was the type he was looking for. Which he couldn't know until they met in person. And she wouldn't be sure it was actually *him* until they met in person, either. Suhr's secretary interrupted them by coming in to let him know he had a visitor on his way up.

Louise looked at him askance. Suhr shrugged. "It's Susanne's mother," he said. "She's here to yell at me because I haven't found her daughter's rapist yet. Plus, now she's pissed that we moved her daughter, so she can't get in touch with her."

"When is someone going to talk to her, *really* talk to her," Louise asked, "…explain the situation and tell her that *she* is the reason Susanne doesn't want to have any contact for a while?"

Louise thought Jakobsen had already done that, but the woman obviously hadn't been clued in.

"Now," Suhr said, an anguished look on his face.

Unbelievable what all falls under the job description of a Homicide Division lieutenant, she thought, watching him leave. She secretly wished a curse on Stig that if ever he was promoted to lieutenant, he would immediately be inundated with stupid tasks like this.

❧

"I'll be in a little late tomorrow," Louise said when she ran into Heilmann in the hallway late that afternoon outside Suhr's office. She shared only that she had a doctor's appointment, and the sergeant was tactful enough not to ask.

Louise wasn't very hungry as she biked home, and decided she would just make do with a couple of open-faced sandwiches for dinner so she wouldn't have to stop and pick up any food. The whole way up to the fifth floor, she walked with her eyes trained on the steps in front of her, so absorbed in her own thoughts that she almost crashed right into the person sitting on the landing outside her door.

"What on earth are you doing here?" she asked, looking at Peter in surprise—but she already knew.

His overnight bag was sitting in front of the door. He nodded at it and shrugged.

Her insides went cold, and an image of Susanne and her mother flashed through her mind. If Peter wanted to move back in, Louise wanted to move to an unlisted address, too. She realized right away how childish that thought was. She stepped past him and unlocked the door.

"Come in," she said.

Her thoughts were in disarray. She had completely pushed the instinctive reaction she had on Saturday out of her mind, but now he was standing here, and she had no doubt as to why.

"It didn't work out?" she asked, heading into the kitchen to put the kettle on.

The atmosphere was awkward, and it was unreasonable of him to stay silent. But instead, Peter was leaving it up to her to break the ice and get the conversation going.

"I don't know," he finally said. "I think I need to really think things through."

That sounds sensible, she thought. Then the irritation hit her again. He hadn't even apologized about showing up unannounced, nor had he asked if this was a good time. It wasn't. She needed to go see if Prinzz had emailed. She'd been checking her Hotmail account from her laptop, but there hadn't been anything. She noticed she was feeling more and more nervous that Prinzz would back out at the last minute, and she had the irrational feeling she could force him to email her by sitting at her computer and staring at her screen. It had been on her mind all day, and her mind was going a mile a minute. She didn't have mental space left to devote to thinking about Peter's problems.

"So, what are you going to do?" she asked in a tone of voice that made it sound like his badminton game had been canceled.

"I miss you," he said.

Louise turned her back to him, wishing he would stop. "You can't just move back in," she said, surprised that he would think that was possible.

"I know that. I'm going to stay with Morten."

Louise couldn't think of anything to say, but was glad that at least he realized it would be better for him to sleep on a mattress at his buddy's place than to even consider sleeping on the couch at her place.

"I just wanted to let you know that," Peter said.

She shrugged. "Thanks, I guess," she replied, a little sarcastically.

She walked him to the door and stood there, watching him descend the stairs with his overnight bag over his shoulder. Her head was about to explode. She shut the door and stood there, lost in thought.

❧

When Louise logged in a little later to check if there was anything in her inbox, she found that Prinzz had written with a suggestion. "We could get coffee at Tivoli tomorrow, if you want."

Of course, she thought. He knows how easy it is to hide in the crowds at the popular old amusement park.

Camilla called and said she would drop by for a second and then hung up before Louise could tell her it wasn't a good time. Louise quickly emailed Prinzz back to ask where and when to meet.

"Café Viften, four o'clock," he replied succinctly, and then: "(You know what I look like.)"

"Cool," she wrote with no idea where Café Viften was. She sat there drumming her fingers for a bit. She sensed restraint in the tone of his brief message and wanted to keep the dialogue going to reassure herself that he wasn't thinking of backing out. Instead, she logged out of her mailbox and went to the kitchen to make herself a ham sandwich. She had just sat down to skim today's *Urban* when Camilla buzzed up from downstairs.

Louise guessed that she'd insisted on stopping by because Peter had called her.

"Hi, I'm a little busy so I can't stay long," Camilla said when Louise opened the door for her.

Louise smiled, shaking her head. *She* wasn't the one pressuring her friend to squeeze a visit into her busy schedule.

Camilla sat down at the kitchen table, hunching over a bit. "What the fuck is up with Peter?" she asked, eyeing Louise as though she expected an explanation. They briefly discussed how there was pretty much no chance in hell Louise was going to take him back, and Louise found it comforting that Camilla was tepid in her support of Peter, as well. Camilla listened to what Louise had to say, and disagreed only half-heartedly when Louise said the trust was broken and it was no use for them to try again.

When they ran out of things to say on that topic, Camilla pulled a handful of pictures out of her purse and spread them out on the kitchen table as she eagerly described Henning's idyllic farmhouse. There were also some pictures of Camilla and Henning holding hands.

Louise noticed again how attractive he was. Not flashy, but tall and dark-haired. Exactly Camilla's taste.

"That looks wonderful," she said, dutifully adding that she looked forward to visiting them out there.

"Couldn't you come out this week or next weekend sometime?" Louise dragged her feet. She felt guilty that she kept postponing on Camilla, so she tried changing the topic instead. "Do you talk to Susanne often?"

"Every day," Camilla replied. "I'm actually on my way over to see her now."

Louise raised her eyebrows, waiting for her to go on.

"We got such a response to her diary today," Camilla said. "We're drowning in email."

Louise hadn't been following all this.

"Susanne wrote a diary for us about her reaction to the rapist killing his next victim. She calls him a monster and says that in the pit of her stomach, she can picture what Christina Lerche's last minutes must have felt like. It was really very moving."

There was something sarcastic about Camilla's tone that bugged Louise.

"Well, she's right, you know," Louise exclaimed. "It could just as easily have been her. She was lying there hog-tied with tape

274

over her mouth for hours. If anyone would know what Christina Lerche must have felt, it's Susanne." It irked her that Camilla, who had been the one urging Susanne to share her story in the first place, was being so fucking condescending now that she had.

"Of course," Camilla said. "And she described it so well it really made people sit up and pay attention. I'm just so disgusted that that's what it takes these days to make the readers feel something."

Louise stopped feeling so defensive. "Maybe it's time for you to find a different job?" she suggested, as she had done countless times before.

Camilla shook her head, promptly dismissing the idea. "Why would I do that? Now that I finally know what it takes to make a compelling story!" she exclaimed, starting to gather and put away her pictures. "Well, I've got to head out to Roskilde. I've got a whole bagful of email we received for her today. I printed them out. Plus, a bouquet of flowers from the editor in chief. Høyer is pretty excited about this story, to put it mildly."

Louise could just imagine. She asked Camilla to say hi to Susanne for her and waved goodbye as she disappeared down the stairs.

Louise went back into her apartment and booted up her computer to see if Prinzz was feeling any more talkative. But there weren't any new messages, so she turned it off again and decided to keep tomorrow's coffee date to herself. She would involve the rest of the group once she was sure it was really him.

27

At nine o'clock the next morning, Louise was sitting in her doctor's waiting room, flipping through an issue of *Health* that she'd pulled out of the stack of old magazines. She had slept fitfully. Her fragmented dreams had been a bizarre cocktail of rapists, coffee, and pregnant bellies. She gave up a little after six and got out of bed to try to take charge of the thoughts spinning around in her head, but she couldn't shake her anxiety. Nervousness made her cross her arms over her chest to touch her breasts, confirming that they were indeed tender, and dread sat like a knot in her stomach at the thought of her coffee date later that day. Maybe she ought to tell Lars to come with her, she thought. But then, as Suhr had wisely pointed out, it wasn't as though Bjergholdt could do anything to her as long as they were out in public—and, besides, that wasn't actually what she was afraid of, she admitted to herself, tossing *Health* back onto the pile. Ultimately what really terrified her was that she would screw this up and scare Bjergholdt off—and that someone else could have done it better. But that wasn't true, she told herself with conviction. If anyone could establish contact with him, it was her.

"Louise Rick." Her doctor stood in the doorway, beckoning her. He had pulled her records up on his screen and was skimming through them quickly as he asked her to have a seat. "So, what can I do for you?" he asked, smiling at her.

"I'm afraid I'm pregnant." Louise stared at him, not really sure what else to say.

"Are you late?" he asked.

"No, not yet. I won't be until next week."

He raised his eyebrows. "Then it may be a little early to think you're pregnant," he said, pulling his chair over to her.

"I've been throwing up, walking around feeling sick to my stomach most of the time, and now my breasts are sore, too."

"When do you think you got pregnant?" he asked, clarifying by adding, "When did you last have sex?"

"A couple of weeks ago, but my boyfriend has moved out. We're not together anymore."

The doctor hesitated a bit before saying that nausea didn't normally set in until about five weeks, and that breast tenderness was not an accurate predictor.

If he had given her a paternalistic smile, she would have punched him, but his face remained neutral, and he continued very professionally, "I don't think you're pregnant. You're still taking your birth-control pills, aren't you?"

She nodded, but before he had a chance to go on, she objected, asserting that it could have happened anyway.

He said that he thought it was more likely that the breakup had upset her more than she wanted to admit.

"That type of distress can also cause nausea."

He stood up, walked over to a cupboard behind the desk, and took out a small sample packet, which he handed to her.

"These are seasickness pills. They should help with the nausea. Take one whenever you feel sick. But you should be prepared. It may take a little while before you're back to your old self."

She was going to protest, say she wasn't crushed over the breakup, that she was fine with Peter moving out, but before she had a chance, he reassured her, "The body usually has such a visceral response to something like this only right in the beginning."

She shoved the pills into her purse, sure that she wouldn't take them.

"So, you're saying that I can't be pregnant?" she asked, standing up.

He smiled at her and said that it wasn't impossible, but there was no reason to be concerned about it until she was sure her period was late.

She thanked him and hurried out.

When she was back down in the street below, she felt a little better. It was completely unreasonable of her to have gotten so worked up about potentially being pregnant, she thought, feeling something inside her relaxing. She realized how hysterically nervous she'd been. She hadn't been able to assess the potential consequences, but realized that having an abortion would not have been such an easy choice.

When she got to headquarters, she found a stack of reports on her desk with a note from Sergeant Heilmann asking her to read through them. She spread them out and thought, *What the fuck is this?* Again, she had the feeling they were going easy on her, but in a way, that suited her just fine. The thoughts whirling around in her head were slowly settling down. She realized she was feeling happier than the week before. With her crazy imaginings about her future put to rest, she was left with a little extra energy that was slowly starting to recharge her batteries.

After two o'clock, the minutes dragged. Their coffee date was just two hours away; Louise couldn't focus. She realized she hadn't given a thought to what her approach would be once she was sitting across from him. What would she say? How should she act? She looked at the time again and started packing up. It was no use preparing a strategy in advance. She'd figure it out at the café.

At twenty minutes to four she started walking toward Tivoli. Lars wasn't back yet, so she left him a message that she'd be back in an hour. As she left, she suddenly regretted not filling him in on her plans, but now she didn't know where he was, and she didn't have time to look for him.

She felt the butterflies in her stomach as she entered the park and walked past the small yellow Ferris wheel, following the gravel path around the end of the lake, looking for Café Viften. It was supposed to be over by the Golden Tower ride somewhere. She spotted the sign as she came around a turn in the path. The café was tucked back behind an ice cream stand.

Her heart beat faster as she approached and saw that the place

279

was packed with baby carriages. People were squeezed in around the tables, drinking coffee and eating cake. Louise stopped, partly hidden behind a thick tree trunk. She didn't see him. They were supposed to meet in five minutes. She surveyed the other diners to see if she could spot a guy on his own who might be Prinzz. Maybe she'd been emailing the wrong guy. But no one seemed to be there alone.

She studied a flyer hanging on a pillar next to the café. It listed live rock music on Friday night with a series of acts, but Louise wasn't reading them. Behind her sunglasses, she was watching people leaving their tables, making way for new diners to sit down. It was after four o'clock. She still didn't see a guy who looked like he was waiting for someone.

Restlessly she strolled quickly past the café and over to the other side of the entrance, so she could see the people approaching from the opposite direction.

There was a dark-haired man coming, but a second later she saw his wife and their young daughter. You don't show up ten minutes late to a date, she thought in irritation, and turned around to scan the area over by Faergekroen Brew Pub and the playground. Either you're there on time or you're not coming at all. A large group of Swedes had arrived and were now seated at a couple of different tables. They were trying to push their tables together so they could sit as one group.

Louise watched the scene unfold and smiled as an older woman in the group, in her eagerness to help, passed a chair to someone over the table, but lost hold of it so it landed right in the middle of a tray of desserts. Their loud voices drew all the diners' attention to the mishap.

When Louise tore her eyes away from the spectacle and moved

them back onto the people waiting to be seated, her eyes locked onto something. She recognized the dark hair.

❧

His silhouette was just as distinctive as she'd seen on the footage from the subway's CCTV cameras. The high forehead, the aristocratic expression with the Roman nose. He stood scanning the crowd, and when Louise started walking over to let him know she was there, she noted that he was taller and stockier than she had first estimated. Just then he turned toward her, and she stopped in shock.

Henning's eyes moved in her direction without noticing her. Evidently, he didn't know who he was looking for. Louise quickly pulled back. He walked over to the line by the cash register, still looking around, and she hoped he would get himself a cup of coffee and go sit down, which would win her a little time. She was breathing again, but she couldn't think straight.

She couldn't understand why she hadn't seen it before, but when you looked at his face straight on, you didn't notice the distinctive silhouette. She realized she'd never actually seen Henning from the side.

She was sweating as she fumbled for her cell phone in her bag to call Camilla and ask what the fuck Henning was doing in Tivoli. She knew that it was only a matter of time before he discovered that she was alone, too, and approached her. She stepped farther away so she was out of his field of vision but could still keep an eye on him.

She took a deep breath and tried to calm down, acknowledging that now she was really risking making a fool of herself if she made a wrong move. It was also crystal clear to her that it had been a mistake to come here alone.

She walked back and stood by the entrance to Café Viften so there was no doubt that she was waiting for someone. Sure enough, someone came right up behind her a few minutes later and said "Princess?" She turned around and found herself staring right up into the face of Camilla's boyfriend.

"Yeah," she said, nodding, wondering if Camilla had shown him pictures as well, in which case he would recognize her as Camilla's friend, the homicide detective. Or maybe he just believed she was who she'd said she was.

"It's, uh, I'm not the person you're supposed to meet…," he began.

His excuse was clumsy, and he was waving his hands around in the air a little. When Louise took a step back in surprise, he explained that unfortunately his brother was running late.

She stood there for a moment without responding, feeling neither relieved nor disappointed, instead trying to remember what she'd heard Camilla say about the brother. She couldn't remember anything other than that he'd been invited over for dinner one night when she had been there, too.

"Well, it's a little much to send someone else just because you're late," she said with a smile, her mind racing.

"He didn't have enough time to let you know he couldn't make it," Henning said with a shrug.

"It must have been an emergency," she concluded.

He nodded.

"We were having lunch here in Tivoli with my girlfriend, but then she had to go out to Roskilde for work, and then shortly after that one of my brother's clients was having trouble with a server that was down. So then he had to go over there. It wasn't any trouble at all for me to come over and let you know, since I was here already. Besides, I was waiting for my girlfriend to get back anyway."

Louise caught herself listening with her mouth agape as he continued.

"We're planning to see a show at the Glass Hall Theatre tonight, and it doesn't make any sense for me to go all the way home…" He kept talking, but Louise had long since stopped listening. She was thinking about Susanne. She didn't put much stock in coincidences or accidents, and she had a really awful feeling now.

She thanked him over and over again for having gone out of his way to wait for her, but as she started to walk away, he held out his hand. She stopped inelegantly and said a proper goodbye, thinking that it was going to be a little awkward when Camilla finally introduced them to each other.

When she was a little ways away from the café, she called the main ops desk at Police Headquarters. They picked up right away.

"This is Rick. We need to get hold of Susanne Hansson in Roskilde." She'd already pulled Susanne's phone number and address out of her purse. "I think the suspect we're looking for might be at her place right now."

They didn't waste any more time talking. The officer on duty was already dialing Susanne's number on another line and was ready to notify the Roskilde police if there was anything at all to back up Louise's suspicion.

"I'll call you back," he said tersely as he waited for Susanne to pick up.

Louise jogged toward the exit, trying to make herself calm

down. She picked up her pace, pushing her way past the people waiting in line to get into the park, darting across Tietgensgade in spite of the red light. Once she was safely across, she called Camilla in the hope that she was still in Roskilde with Susanne.

When Louise asked her what she was doing, Camilla replied, "I just walked into the office." Then she exhaled loudly. "I'm totally stressed out because I had to cut short a lunch date to go see Susanne."

"Why? What happened?" Louise interrupted before her friend had a chance to complain further.

"She was mad because her mother wrote in to the paper, defending herself against Susanne's piece saying she needed to get away. Now the mother is accusing the press of controlling her daughter. I think that's mostly what Susanne is upset about. I mean, she feels like she's finally just starting to have some control over her own life."

"Who were you having lunch with?" Louise tried to sound casually interested without seeming overly curious. She took long strides past the Glyptotek museum, hurrying toward Police Headquarters.

"Henning and his brother Jørgen. We're going to a show at the Glass Hall tonight. It was one I didn't think you'd be interested in, otherwise I would have invited you to join us."

"Do they know about any of the stuff with Susanne?" Louise asked urgently.

Before Camilla had a chance to respond, Louise heard the faint beeping noise that meant that she had another call.

"I have to go," she said just as Camilla started to answer. "I have another call." She hung up and then her phone immediately started ringing.

"Just relax. Everything was completely normal," the dispatcher responded from the operations desk, explaining that he'd just spoken to Susanne, who was having someone over.

"And it wasn't a man," the officer added before Louise had a chance to respond.

Louise stopped and exhaled.

"I gave her the number here at ops. If anything happens, I can get a patrol car out there right away. But as far as I can see on my screen, she lives at an unlisted address. Are you saying that the perp has tracked her down?"

Louise felt the anxious energy slowly draining out of her body, leaving it heavy and calm.

"I obviously overreacted," Louise said. "I guess I was seeing ghosts in broad daylight."

She entered Police Headquarters and took the stairs up to the second floor as her pulse settled back into a normal rhythm again.

Up in her office, she set down her purse and hung her jacket over the back of her chair. Lars was talking on the phone. He nodded to her briefly, concentrating on his conversation. Louise was annoyed at herself. Something had slipped away from her in the last couple of weeks. Usually her judgment was dead-on, but lately it seemed like she kept working herself up into a tizzy instead of tackling things rationally. She could have just asked Henning to call his brother, and she could have called Susanne herself instead of getting the operations desk involved. She'd better go give the dispatcher an explanation before he started spreading rumors that Department A had a new drama queen.

28

She clutched her neck, where blood was dripping from the cut he'd just made. It felt messy, the way it trickled down inside her blouse, between her breasts, and she didn't dare look.

The scent of freshly baked bread emanated from the kitchen. The coffee table was set with cups and lit candles.

He breathed out, a vein on the side of his neck throbbing. She glanced over at him without moving.

Her blouse was sticking. She bent her head down so her chin was resting on her chest, to stanch the bleeding. The pain seared her neck, and she thought maybe this was pushing more blood out instead; she raised her head so she was looking straight ahead again. She wasn't crying.

Moving slowly, he set the bread knife down on the coffee table.

She hadn't recognized the silhouette of his body through the frosted glass in the door when he rang the bell. She had not been prepared at all and didn't have a chance to react before he was inside.

With his arms in front of him in a defensive gesture, he had walked slowly toward her, assuring her that he didn't want to hurt her, just talk.

She had backed up, step by step, as he moved closer.

"You have to listen to me," he pleaded, when they were standing in the kitchen.

Oddly enough, she wasn't afraid. With her back to the refrigerator, she listened as he explained that he hadn't killed anyone. That the whole thing was a misunderstanding. There was something earnest and honest about his voice that made her believe what he said.

Her eyes moved down over his face as he spoke.

Suddenly she remembered those eyes. She wanted to move in closer. Woodland lakes, she thought. They were dark with a shimmer of green.

She stared desperately at the bread knife lying on the coffee table. The wound burned, and her body was paralyzed. The fear that had subsided when he started talking to her in his calm voice was back, wrapping itself around her like a mantle of ice. It had happened at that instant. She recognized the dangerous glint in his eye, and saw the distorted expression on his face. It had changed the second the phone rang. He ordered her to sit still and not pick it up. In a few quick leaps, he was out in the kitchen; when he came back, the serrations in the stainless-steel blade had sliced into the thin skin on her neck as he held her firmly in his tight grip and pressed.

"Answer it," he snarled.

She reacted mechanically, surprising herself with how calm her voice sounded.

She felt the blood spreading into a stain on her chest.

He gestured for her to stand up. He took the bread knife from the coffee table and was right behind her, leading her toward the closed door to the bedroom.

29

I don't think he knows the address," Louise explained, standing next to the dispatcher's desk in the middle of the large command center on the top floor of Police Headquarters, holding out her hands in an apologetic gesture. "But I suddenly had this suspicion that a reporter from *Morgenavisen*—who Susanne's been in touch with—might have let the address slip without thinking about it."

The officer smiled at her and said, "You really don't need to apologize. I would have been more than happy to dispatch Nymand and every other available uniform out to Roskilde."

He stood up and asked her if she wanted a cup of coffee. Telephones were ringing, and dispatchers were directing patrols and emergency responses to various addresses throughout the Copenhagen metropolitan area. She overheard a request for a

CSI team at a fire downtown, and it struck her how it was like stepping into another world, coming up here. The hectic life, the sound of the countless telephones and police scanners—they just didn't have that down in her division. There was a quieter, almost pious atmosphere down there, where people moved silently around in the dark, curving hallways, where footsteps echoed and everything seemed old-fashioned. Ops was the place at Police Headquarters that reminded Louise most of the other Copenhagen precincts she had worked at before she got promoted to Homicide.

He returned with two cups.

"I haven't heard from her, so there's no reason to be worried," he said, setting the cups on the desk. "I'm sure she's still sitting there chatting with her mother."

Louise stiffened and asked him to repeat, word for word, what Susanne had said.

"She said that everything was fine. And that she was just sitting there chatting with her mother."

Louise was already backing toward the door as he finished speaking.

❧

"We're going to Roskilde," Louise yelled to Lars, who was still at his desk with the phone to his ear. She quickly grabbed the keys to a patrol car from Heilmann's office and signed one out in the logbook. Heilmann must have gone home already. Her computer was off, at any rate.

Lars was right behind her as she bounded down the stairs.

"I was supposed to meet Bjergholdt in Tivoli, but he didn't

show. Camilla's boyfriend Henning came instead." She gave him a quick summary.

"Couldn't we just call Susanne and see if she's okay?" he asked sensibly as they sped down the highway.

Louise contemplated the option, "Obviously it's possible that I'm overreacting. We can certainly hope that's the case," she added. "But if Susanne was trying to tell us something on the phone, it must be because he was there. And if he is, calling could have disastrous consequences. He would immediately suspect she'd said some kind of code word."

Louise's head was spinning. Lars was in the passing lane, flashing his lights whenever someone didn't move out of his way quickly enough.

"Whatever she's doing, we can be 100 percent certain that she's not having a pleasant evening chat with her mother," Louise said emphatically. "Definitely not after her mother wrote an open letter to *Morgenavisen* that upset Susanne so much that Camilla was forced to cut her lunch short to drive out there and see her."

Suddenly, Louise was filled with doubt. Susanne had taken so many big steps in the past few weeks, done things she would never have done when Louise first met her. Maybe she asked her mother to come over after Camilla's visit so they could really talk things through. Louise was secretly relieved she hadn't had a whole emergency response team rush out to cordon off the area and storm the apartment.

She sighed deeply.

"I don't know what the fuck's going on," she said, running her hand through her hair. "I just have a terrible feeling. But I am fully aware I'm a little off my game these days, so I really don't know if my hunch is worth paying attention to or not."

Lars gave her a quick glance before focusing his concentration back on the road.

"I fucking thought I was pregnant," Louise blurted out, apropos of nothing.

She noticed that he slowed down a little and looked at her, so she hurried to add that it had turned out to be a false alarm.

"It was just my imagination," she said with a forced laugh. "That wouldn't have been a good idea. But, I don't think it would have ruined my intuition," she said, to bring the conversation back to Susanne.

"No, I'm sure it wouldn't," Lars said, pulling into the middle lane. "But obviously if you were preoccupied with all that, it might make you a little more sensitive than usual, you know."

It took them twenty minutes to drive to Roskilde. Traffic was actually moving along nicely the whole way out on Københavnsvej, but once they got to Røde Port it was backed up.

Louise sat in the passenger seat, drumming her fingers on the dashboard. She knew that would only irritate her more, but she couldn't stop. She was seething with annoyance, and the excess energy had to come out one way or another.

"Don't ride their bumper like that," she nagged Lars as they finally approached the parking lot in front of the cluster of two-story buildings where Susanne's ground-floor apartment was located. They parked out of view and approached the apartment through the other front yards so they couldn't be seen from Susanne's living-room or bedroom windows, only from the kitchen and bathroom.

"What are we going to do?" Lars asked as they stopped in front of the neighbor's apartment.

"I'll go over and knock, while you wait over here," Louise said.

"If she's sitting in there chatting with her mother, we'll go in and say hi. If he's there, you call it in to ops and get them out here while I see if I can grab Susanne."

Lars stopped, his phone out and in his hand. "Are you sure I shouldn't come in, too?"

Louise nodded quickly. "The whole thing will go smoothly. It's mostly just a matter of securing her. If he makes a run for it, we'll let him go and hope there's a patrol car nearby that can pick him up."

It looked as if Lars was going to protest, but Louise started walking before he could say anything.

She moved up the walkway through the front yard until she was right up against the building. With her back to the wall, she moved over to the kitchen window and peeked in.

The kitchen was empty. The door to the living room was ajar, but the crack was so narrow that it was impossible to see anything through it. She ducked under the frosted glass of the bathroom window and proceeded around the building to peer into the living room. Two tea lights were lit in small holders, and there were cups and a teapot on the coffee table. That calmed her down, but she couldn't see any people. The muscles in her body relaxed a little when she realized how unlikely it was that Susanne had been sitting there drinking tea with her rapist.

Louise walked back around to the front door and rang the bell, nodding to Lars to signal that there was someone home. No one came to open the door. Before ringing the bell again, she tried the knob and determined that the door was locked. This time, she held her finger on the ringer for several seconds and heard the sound cutting through the apartment's entryway.

She signaled to Lars that they were going in.

When he got close enough, she said, "Susanne wouldn't leave with the candles lit."

Louise rang the bell again and walked around to the other side of the building. With her hands against the glass, she peered in to see if the ringing doorbell had triggered any response. She watched her partner walk toward the shed and over the low, newly planted hedge that separated the front and back yards. She rushed over to help him find something they could use to shatter the glass in the front door. They found a couple of pavers in the shed.

"If they're in there, they know we're here," she said. "Let's get this over with."

Lars picked one of the pavers up in both hands and hammered it with all his might against the thick pane of glass in the front door. Louise expected it to shatter and was surprised that it yielded only enough to make a small hole. Lars kept hitting it until the hole in the heavy-duty glass was big enough that he could reach an arm through and unlock the door.

"Susanne!" Louise shouted into the apartment.

The air was silent. Instinctively she knew someone was there, and called out again. She opened the door and stepped in over the broken glass on the floor of the entryway.

"Susanne!"

She thought she heard a door open as she stepped farther in.

"Leave, or I'll kill her."

The voice was ominous, and the words were enunciated quietly and clearly. Louise guessed the voice was coming from the apartment's bedroom. She quickly turned to see if Lars had heard what had been said. She saw that he'd already pulled back and was calling ops for backup. They would contact the Roskilde Police right away, but she also knew it would take the negotiating team

293

at least an hour to arrive. She squeezed her eyes shut and tried to remember if she'd seen any of the crisis negotiators or tactical response folks around the division. Some of the officers were specially trained to handle hostage situations. But she was drawing a total blank.

Louise realized she would have to handle the situation herself. She had decided to go in, and now she couldn't just pull back and wait for the others to get here. *I have to talk to him myself if I want to keep him from taking it out on Susanne*, she thought. The local police would arrive soon to cordon off the area. The situation would be locked in, and she had to try to buy some time.

She took a step back and yelled that he should calm down, that she was here to help resolve the situation.

"I have a knife. Get out and close the door," he yelled.

Louise stepped back over the glass shards, thinking that it wasn't helping anything that they were standing around shouting back and forth at each other. She could win some time if she could get a real dialogue going with him.

"Couldn't we have this conversation over the phone?" she suggested through the front door.

He didn't respond.

She offered to toss her cell phone in and then call it. He still didn't respond.

"Jørgen." She pronounced his name loudly and clearly. "I really want to talk to you," she said, fully aware that she had taken a risk by using his name. It could either help or hurt her. And there was still the risk that she had the wrong guy. That it would turn out to be someone else in there with Susanne. Some other deranged lunatic who had now fixated on her as a result of the article and diary entries.

She took her cell phone out of her pocket and stepped back into the apartment again, over the glass on the floor of the entryway. She opened the door to the living room, squatted down, and slid the phone as far into the room as she could, then quickly got up and stepped back out the front door again to help him feel like she wasn't pressuring him.

❧

Lars was done talking to the command center.

"They're on their way," he said before handing her his phone so she could dial her own number. It rang for a long time before the voicemail recording said that Louise Rick was unable to take the call. She hung up and put the call through again. For the first time in days, the vague fog was gone from her brain. She felt present, her mind on high alert. She knew that she shouldn't underestimate the man she was dealing with. Sociopaths want attention, she reminded herself, and she was going to have to play his game if Susanne was going to make it out of there alive.

He answered her phone the third time she called, but didn't say anything. She could just hear breathing.

"Is Susanne alive?" she asked quietly.

"Yes," he confirmed after such a long pause that she almost gave up and decided he wasn't going to respond.

"Can I have some kind of sign?" she asked.

He didn't say anything, but Louise could tell he was moving. "Yes…" It sounded as if Susanne had forced the word out under duress.

"Susanne, this is Louise," she said, trying to sound as if everything were calm and relatively under control.

"Shut up," he said into the phone.

She ignored his rough tone and continued calmly, "If you don't do anything to her, I can help you out of this situation. You're calling the shots. Won't you tell me what this is about?"

But unfortunately, she had a very clear sense of what this was about. Jørgen knew that Susanne could testify against him if the police managed to find him. Karin Hvenegaard would also be able to ID him. Suddenly it occurred to her that she hadn't given a thought to Karin out in Rødovre since she had visited her. Maybe Jørgen had already paid her a visit. It wasn't hard to see that things were heating up for him.

Of course he's feeling threatened, she thought, his predicament becoming clear to her. The two aggravated sexual assaults were now the least of his troubles. The things he'd done to Karin and Susanne were serious enough, but Christina Lerche's death brought his crimes to another level.

Louise spoke firmly in a calm, quiet voice, and strangely enough she also felt calm on the inside. She wasn't thinking about the consequences of what might happen, just trying to win time. If she succeeded in talking him down enough, he might relent and accept the wisdom of coming out and letting Susanne go.

She continued in a controlled voice. "I know you didn't kill Christina Lerche," she said into her phone. "Her death was an accident."

She registered that several squad cars had already pulled into the parking lot. More would be coming to set up a perimeter. Now it was a question of keeping the dialogue going until the negotiating team got there and took over. There was a chance that they would succeed if she gently fed him everything he wanted to hear.

He still wasn't saying anything.

"It would go a long way if you came out on your own now," she continued. "Then you could keep the situation from spinning out of control."

It concerned her that he remained so quiet. When the silence and the faint static on the line continued, she got nervous that he'd put the phone under one of the couch cushions or somewhere else that would block the sound. He could have closed the door to the bedroom where Susanne was. Louise was suddenly struck by the chilling realization that he could be assaulting Susanne right now, even as she stood here, naïvely continuing to talk to him.

She went over to the door and knocked loudly. Leaned forward and listened.

"It's too late," the ominous voice finally said into the phone.

She couldn't be sure what he meant, if he meant it was too late for Susanne or for the situation as a whole. She hoped he meant the latter and seized on his words.

"It's never too late if you act rationally. It will benefit your case overall if you let her go now."

"I don't believe you. I can see the police."

"Those are just patrol officers. They're here to cordon off the area. That's the normal procedure before the negotiating team arrives to take over. I'm no expert, just an ordinary assistant detective."

"Negotiating team? You want to negotiate?"

"Yes," Louise said convincingly. "We want to make a deal with you so you make it out of this situation as levelheadedly as possible."

"So, you actually think I can get something out of this?" His tone was full of contempt.

She hoped he would bite so they could keep the conversation

going. She glanced at her watch. It would take another half hour at least before the team got out here from the city. That was a long time to wait, with things moving at this excruciating pace.

If he was desperate, he would start gushing like a waterfall, then demand they have a private plane waiting for him out at Roskilde Airport to take him out of the country and ask for anything at all that he could recall from similar situations in American movies. But he didn't do that. He didn't seem desperate in that way, didn't get carried away and ramble on, talking faster and faster. Instead it was like he was sitting there, weighing and contemplating each word he said.

She could hear Susanne crying in the background.

"If you let her go, I'll come in and take her place," Louise suggested.

"What am I supposed to do with you?" he asked, sounding surprised.

"You could talk to me."

Suddenly he seemed amused.

"But you don't even know me. Why would it help to talk to you?" he asked.

It struck Louise that he sounded like a businessman on a conference call, and she didn't really feel like she was bringing anything to the table that he would consider appealing.

She had a choice: tell him he was right, that maybe it wouldn't do him any good to talk to her, or brazenly lie.

"First of all, I can guarantee that I will do everything in my power to help you so that we can wrap this business up calmly and quietly and find a solution that you will be satisfied with," she said convincingly. "Let Susanne go, and I'll come in, and then we'll talk about it. I could also be your bargaining chip with the negotiating team if you'd rather wait for them and find out what they have to offer."

He mumbled something she couldn't make out. Then: "You don't know me, so you wouldn't understand me."

He sounded resigned.

Louise took a deep breath, inhaling the air deep down into her gut.

"Yes, I do," she said. "I know you, and you know me." Well, "know" was a bit of an exaggeration. But they *would* have known each other, anyway, if he'd shown up for their coffee date.

The silence on the other end of the phone became brooding. "Who are you?" he asked.

"Call me Princess," Louise said, leaning against the wall by the front door.

Silence. She started shivering, even though the sun was beating down on her. She had pushed them both all the way, to a place where a response was unavoidable.

She heard a sound from inside the house and turned to wave Lars over.

"I'm going in," she whispered. "Call headquarters and get them to send a patrol out to Karin Hvenegaard's place. He may have paid her a visit, too."

Lars looked away and was about to say something angry but stopped himself. She could tell from his clenched jaw muscles. Then he turned his face toward her again and put his hand on her shoulder.

"Watch out for him," Lars urged. "We don't know why he came here today, but he's already killed one person."

So far, she agreed with him.

"He's a hunted man," Lars continued. "If he lets her come out, it's because he thinks he can get more out of this situation if he uses you as a hostage."

Louise knew her partner was right, but honestly right now she was more afraid that Jørgen thought he would do better by holding on to Susanne.

She stepped back over to the front door and listened. She saw Suhr and Heilmann rushing across the parking lot, and she could tell that Suhr wanted to tell her something. But just then the door between the living room and the entryway opened and Susanne came into view, guided by an arm. She was bleeding from her neck and stood there frightened, staring at the floor. Her hands were tied together tightly in front of her, and Louise noticed that Jørgen hadn't used his usual cable ties. This looked like some kind of cord he'd found lying around in the apartment.

"She won't come out until you're in."

Louise quickly glanced at Suhr and, before he had a chance to object, stepped into the apartment and took up her position next to Susanne. She briefly considered trying to yank Susanne out the door with her so they could both be free, but she let go of the idea. If that didn't succeed, there was nothing else to fall back on. She put both her hands behind her head to signal that she was not armed and would not attack, and she noticed his grip on Susanne's arm loosen.

"Just go," she told Susanne.

Louise stood for a second, watching Susanne's back hurrying away from the building. An effervescent feeling of relief and victory managed to trickle through her before she felt a strong hand cinch in around her elbow and pull her into the living room, where she stumbled and struck the couch.

30

Jørgen stood there for a long time, watching Louise as she slowly got up and hesitantly sat down properly on the couch.

"You knew?" he asked, standing over her so she had to crane her neck to look up at him.

She shook her head. Immersed in another role, she was speaking as the girl who had seen him in town.

"I went to Tivoli to meet you, but you didn't come. I saw Henning instead."

She sensed his surprise when she mentioned his brother's name.

"Your brother is dating my best friend," she said.

"Camilla?"

He was still standing there, studying her. There wasn't anything aggressive or menacing about his appearance, and, somewhere deep inside her, that hurt. He seemed confused and uncertain, as if he had been forced into accepting a deal he didn't want.

"Yeah, Henning told me about your lunch together and about Camilla and how she had to go to Roskilde and how you left right after her," Louise said. "Did you follow her here?" she asked.

It took a little while before he nodded, as if he was considering whether he had anything to lose.

"You look like each other, you and your brother—at least from the side. When I saw Henning, I recognized his silhouette," Louise said and explained that she had seen Jørgen on the subway CCTV footage when he had walked Christina Lerche to her train at Kongens Nytorv.

He listened, but she couldn't tell what was going on in his head. "Suddenly I could see how it all might fit together," Louise said. "So, I came out here."

Louise did not dare mention that she had already known all that when she messaged him on Nightwatch. Even though he didn't seem particularly threatening right now, she was well aware that that could change in an instant. And there was something about his contemplative expression and the fact that he didn't seem stressed that made her extra-vigilant.

He was waiting for her to say more. Suddenly the silence felt interminable, and she sensed her own anxiety as she tried to think of something to say. She didn't dare glance down at her watch to see how much longer she had to stall.

"Camilla was the one who told me your name is Jørgen," Louise said.

She saw officers in SWAT gear walk past the window. They were getting into position, so she surmised the negotiating team had arrived.

"I didn't kill her," Jørgen finally said. He had taken a seat and was moving the fingers of both hands in and out of each other like gears engaging and disengaging. "I didn't do anything."

Louise refrained from commenting on that last remark, but she took it as an opening that might allow her to win his trust.

"I don't think that you killed her…intentionally," she added after a brief pause.

He pulled his hands back, as if he'd burned them, and then quickly leaned toward her.

"I didn't kill her," his voice was suddenly a hiss. "She wasn't dead when I left. She tricked me."

There was a clank as he moved his hands forcefully, knocking over an empty teacup. He stared intensely into Louise's eyes. "It was her own fault!"

She nodded to show she agreed with him. Suddenly there wasn't much time. She had been trying to drag things out to this point, but now the problem was whether she had enough time to talk him down before the SWAT team outside was ready to take over the conversation and she would have to make do with being a weapon in the negotiations.

She tried to reassure him. "She didn't die until you'd left the apartment," she said in a convincing voice. "The coroner called me and told me that it could easily have taken a fair amount of time before she died."

She could tell that he had heard the words but didn't understand what they meant. He was focused solely on having his innocence confirmed, she noted, which was classic behavior in these types of situations.

"You won't be charged with murder," she said, hoping he would find that comforting because he would undoubtedly be charged with manslaughter. Actually, she wouldn't be surprised if Suhr decided to charge him with second-degree murder anyway, since they were investigating the case as a death by aggravated battery.

"She wasn't supposed to die." His voice didn't have the same aggression in it, but it was still accusing. "She invited me over, and she was the one who wanted to take things into the bedroom."

Louise nodded silently as he spoke. Of course he would stubbornly maintain that what happened was consensual. He was guaranteed to do that when Susanne's case went to trial, too. So it would be up to Susanne and her lawyer to prove the opposite.

He glanced out the window, passively following what was going on outside. Traffic had been stopped; pedestrians were being held back. The only activity was of various police officers who had taken up positions in the parking lot and all around the perimeter of the building. Louise glanced over at the clock on the living-room wall. It felt as though she had been sitting across from him for hours.

"There wasn't anything wrong," Jørgen said, not really to Louise, more to himself, "but then suddenly it went wrong anyway. Completely wrong, obviously."

For a second she thought he was going to start crying. She wanted to ask him which part he thought had gone wrong, but didn't dare. She had the sense that that was precisely the problem—he didn't understand what the catalyst had been. He had had his own plans when he packed his rape case and headed off on his dates; if those plans couldn't be carried out to completion, perhaps he looked at that as something going wrong. That was a boil she had no intention of lancing right now. The forensic psychiatrist could deal with that one, because she was pretty sure there was a psychiatric evaluation in his future. She heard voices outside the front door, not voices so loud they were meant to be heard inside the apartment; they were just the sounds of people discussing something, which told her it was almost time. Her stomach tensed, and she could feel her pulse.

"I promise that you'll get the best defense attorney." Louise looked right at him. At first his eyes wandered, but then she managed to establish eye contact and she spoke slowly, with weight behind each word. "If we go out now, I'm sure Camilla will do everything in her power to help you."

She was just tossing things out there, but she got a response. She saw it in his eyes, and that made her proceed.

"The negotiating team is about ready to take over, so I can't do any more for you. And in a second the SWAT team will come in. If we walk out first, they will no longer consider this a hostage situation."

She was running out of things to say, and he seemed calmer now. She saw the officers in tactical gear and the sharpshooters taking up their positions.

"It would also be nice to get this wrapped up before too many media people show up," she added.

She had already noticed a number of photographers standing back behind the barrier that the police had set up.

"If anything goes wrong, I'm taking you with me when I run," he said after a long pause for consideration. His voice was once again a hoarse whisper.

She nodded, knowing he wouldn't have a chance to run off anywhere once they stepped out the door. He would be shocked by the size of the armed police response. She felt a pang in her heart for betraying him, given his mental illness and inability to control himself, and wished he would come with her now so he wouldn't have to go through the whole negotiation process. If he didn't come out voluntarily, they would send the elite anti-terror unit in after him. Of course, he wouldn't know it was them. He probably had no idea that in Denmark, taking someone hostage is classified as an act of terrorism, or that the very best-trained forces were always deployed to extract a hostage from a situation like this.

He got up and paced back and forth a little in the living room. "We'll go together," he said, giving her a look that she had a hard time interpreting.

His eyes were both ferocious and scared, but outwardly he still seemed calm, as though he was sure this whole scenario was taking place because there had been some misunderstanding. As if there had been a mistake. A wrong number. Something that didn't have anything to do with him. Louise was not entirely confident, but she stood up anyway and nodded, aware that this could end very badly.

"Is Camilla out there?" Jørgen asked, looking at her inquiringly.

"I don't know," Louise replied with a shrug. She hoped she wasn't.

He walked over slowly and stood in front of her. "I'll do it because you promised you would help me. And because I've decided that I would really like to get to know you."

She shuddered. *Whoa, does he really not get that that's not an option anymore?* she wondered. It struck her with even more clarity that he did not consider his assaults crimes. He was not picturing the charges the police would file against him later that night. *He is completely fucked up, and then some. He's a textbook sociopath!* ran through her mind.

"Why did you come see Susanne today?" Louise asked as Jør-gen began pushing her toward the door.

"She wrote in the paper that I'd killed someone. That's not true. She knows me and knows I'm not like that."

Louise's heart sank. There was no way she could look him in the eye. "You know, not all girls find it normal to be bound and gagged. It could easily seem frightening if that wasn't something you'd agreed on beforehand…"

She stopped talking because his face seemed to shut down. They were at the door.

"Wait a minute," she said as calmly as she could. "I'll call them and tell them we're coming out."

He watched her while she dialed and relayed a brief message to Suhr. Fear had taken hold of him, and there was nothing ferocious left in his eyes   just nervousness. His eyes wandered. He gripped her arm, ready to push her out in front of him when they opened the door.

"When you open the door, we'll walk slowly down the path through the front yard," she said urgently, worried that he might not understand what would happen if he moved too quickly.

He pushed the handle and opened the door. Suhr was standing at the end of the path, staring at them but not doing anything.

They took their first steps very slowly, like animals cautiously moving into unfamiliar territory. Jørgen pushed her ahead of him-self like a shield; once they'd made it a couple of steps beyond the front door, he suddenly stopped, taking in the whole scene. There were sharpshooters on several rooftops, aiming at him. Officers in tactical gear formed a ring all the way around the perimeter of the building. To Louise, the crowd of people loomed as an inscrutable mob, but it seemed as though he was memorizing the details.

With a violent shove, he pushed her forward. The motion was so brutal that Louise had the sense that he had planned to dart back into the house and stand his ground, but had decided that he probably wouldn't be able to pull her back with him. She saw Suhr subtly shake his head with his eyes locked on something behind her, either urging Jørgen not to do anything stupid so they could get this over with, or maybe sending a signal to a marksman who was probably up on the roof behind her.

Suhr started walking toward them. Behind him, the officers who would make the arrest were ready. Louise made eye contact with Lars and recognized a couple of the people who she knew were part of the negotiating team. They had withdrawn to the side and were standing in the neighbor's front yard, watching everything play out without their help.

Louise stopped and let Jørgen walk past her. He didn't turn to look at her as he slowly walked toward Suhr, but said, very softly, "I trust you."

She watched him as the tactical teams and officers in bulletproof vests swooped in to handcuff, search, and arrest him. She watched them walk over to the parked cars, where four men climbed in to sit with him in the back of a dark blue van. Louise vaguely registered Suhr walking over and standing next to her, and heard him ask if she was okay.

She shook her head and discovered that her legs were shaking underneath her. The strength was starting to seep out of her body. She wasn't okay at all, she thought.

The crime-scene investigators prepared to enter the apartment. It hit her that she didn't know what had happened to Susanne, but that would have to wait.

It took a little while before she noticed the photographers' flashbulbs aimed at her as well as Jørgen. Frightened, she turned around so her back was to them.

Lars came over, put his arm around her, and pulled her away. "Come on," he said, supporting her as they started walking over to the car. She saw Nymand, Roskilde's chief of police, approaching with his hand outstretched and a big smile. She looked the other way and picked up her pace.

Her partner opened the door and helped her in. Her muscles weren't obeying, her legs were trembling, and her hands were restless.

"Do you think he was planning to rape her again? He had tied her hands," Lars said as they drove back down Københavnsvej toward the highway. "Or did he come to kill her? Also, the uniforms they sent out confirmed that he had not gone to see Karin Hvenegaard."

Louise shook her head, trying to pull herself together. She just wanted not to think about it for a little while, but she could certainly understand that he was curious. He had been standing right outside, after all.

"He didn't come to kill her," she said. Talking about it made her feel like she'd overcome something. "He came to convince her that he hadn't killed Christina Lerche. To tell her that Christina had still been alive when he left her."

Lars nodded and proceeded to say what Louise herself had already thought. "Jørgen knew Susanne could identify him and that eyewitness testimony would be important at trial."

Louise explained Jørgen's reaction to Susanne's diary that the paper had published. "He felt like she was being unfair to him, blaming him for something he didn't do."

Lars glanced over at her quickly before picking up speed and moving into the passing lane on the highway. "What was he thinking?" he said. "Who goes on dates with a little kit full of paraphernalia for raping women?"

"I'm guessing that he would readily admit he has sadomasochistic tendencies and that he thinks that's just fine... which, I mean, I suppose it is, legally." Louise hurried to add, "If your partner is into that, too."

Lars moved back into the middle lane, lowered his speed a little, and listened.

"That just wasn't the case here," Louise continued. "I'm sure they probably agreed to have sex, but I don't think they talked about what kind of sex and when they would stop. At least Susanne didn't mention anything like that. Quite to the contrary, she had a very strong response when I asked her if she was into that kind of thing—if it turned her on to be tied up, beat up, and raped. I just can't believe that was something they'd discussed in advance, nor that the answer would have ever been yes."

Lars sat shaking his head as Louise spoke, and then said, "Hey, do you remember that case from a few years ago? The one where the upstairs neighbor arranged to have the woman who lived downstairs from him raped?"

Louise shook her head, not remembering the case Lars was referring to.

"The guy went online, claiming to *be* his downstairs neighbor, and he got in touch with a young guy he invited over to act out a rape fantasy. He pretended to be his downstairs neighbor, and he wrote that she would leave the door to the apartment unlocked for him when she went to bed. So, he could just let himself in. And that he should keep going, even if she screamed, so it would be as realistic as possible."

Louise was beginning to remember the case. For the first time she had felt in dead earnest that she wanted to see the balls cut off a guy. What that upstairs neighbor had done was so beyond the pale, but his punishment had seemed negligible.

"He had the keys because he'd once watered her plants while she was away on vacation. So he just stopped by a hardware store and had copies made," Louise added. "And the whole thing scared the shit out of that young guy."

"Yeah, he wasn't all that bright, was he," said Lars. "And the upstairs neighbor was convicted."

"Sick fuck," Louise said.

Reminiscing about old cases perked her up a little bit. Even though it had been a relatively brief case, she remembered it because the perp had thought the whole thing up with such malice.

Lars said, "This guy today, Jørgen, he's pretty fucked up, too. What was he like?"

"Basically, calm and quiet," Louise replied. "It seemed like he didn't actually get that he had committed a bunch of sexual assaults. He just feels misunderstood." Louise thought about it for a bit before continuing. "I'm having a little trouble figuring out how calculating he was. It really didn't seem like he was trying to hide. And that also fits with how it seemed more coincidental than planned that the subway security cameras didn't get a good shot of him. On the other hand, he was extremely meticulous about covering his tracks when he emailed the women, and he was careful not to leave fingerprints in their apartments."

"It seems illogical," Lars said, puzzled.

"Yeah." Louise nodded in agreement. Then a wave of guilt washed over her. "I just promised him one thing after another," she said. "Everything you can think of."

Lars didn't even glance over at her, just nodded and said, "Of course you did."

"We're all prostitutes before the Lord," she whispered to herself, tilting her seat back and leaning her body back into a position that helped her tensed muscles relax. "I would have promised him anything to get him to walk out of there."

"That's part of the job, and you did great," he said, giving her knee a squeeze. Then he admitted that Suhr had been tenser than usual while she'd been inside.

"But, of course, he was exceptionally pleased when Susanne came out," Lars hurried to add when he heard Louise sigh. "And I'm guessing there won't be a dry eye left when the papers print the pictures of him leading her away from the scene as her savior." Lars laughed a little before becoming serious again. "I've never seen him so quiet and desperate. He looked like he was holding his breath the whole time you were in there."

She didn't know what to think. It would certainly be understandable if he was angry that she'd acted without consulting him and deprived him of the opportunity to lead the charge.

"Should I take you straight home?" Lars asked.

She really wanted to take him up on the offer, but somewhere in the back of her head she could hear Jakobsen lecturing about how it was important for people to properly wrap up experiences like these so they didn't ossify.

"Camilla's dating his brother," Louise suddenly blurted out. She closed her eyes so she wouldn't have to see her partner's reaction, but she heard his outburst.

"What did you say?" he spluttered.

She was still squeezing her eyes shut. She described her meeting in Tivoli to Lars.

"At first I thought it was *him*. I recognized the silhouette. Turns out Henning is his older brother."

Lars had met Henning at the party out in Holmen, so he actually knew him better than she did, she thought, her body suddenly feeling heavy. Louise couldn't see how she'd ever be able to talk to Camilla about what had happened. Mostly she just wanted to dive down into the deep, inky darkness and not come back out until all the problems had been resolved and things were quiet up at the surface again. Right now, everything felt chaotic.

Lars was quiet for a while.

"Well, that sucks," he finally said. "For both of them."

31

Louise and Lars were the first ones back from Roskilde, but the rumors had already reached the division. Willumsen was standing in the doorway to their office, staring unabashedly at Louise. She noticed him there, but couldn't face listening to his blunt criticism about how she'd been rash and impetuous by entering the apartment. She made a point of continuing to stare straight ahead.

"We have an elite team of highly trained people who handle situations like the one in Roskilde," Willumsen began, once the silence in the room had grown awkward.

Louise wasn't listening. Or was pretending that she wasn't.

"And I wasn't planning on adding anyone else to that team," Willumsen continued.

He was speaking directly at her, even though Lars was sitting at his desk, too. The mood was gloomy, and she sensed that her partner was having trouble deciding whether he ought to leave the office so he wouldn't have to witness the imminent dressing-down, or whether he ought to stay and support her.

"I actually just said no to training any more folks from our division," Willumsen proceeded. "But it's dangerous to have people like you walking around, so maybe that was a mistake?"

Finally, Louise turned in her chair and looked at him. She had had just about enough. Just being here at the office instead of home in her bed required too much effort.

"I did what I could," she seethed. "There was no time to stand around outside and wait for backup. And it turned out fine."

Willumsen actually looked a little hurt by her assertive outburst.

"Lucky for you," he said, "I should have signed you up. You're cut out for it…"

What he was trying to say started to dawn on her. Of course he couldn't just say it straight out. That would have been too simple and unlike him, Louise thought, turning to face him and listening now, with interest.

"They're going to be training a new team," Willumsen said. "And as I said, we originally told them we weren't going to send anyone, but in light of today's events I think the situation has changed."

Louise felt a lump in her throat and realized how seriously unhinged she was. "Thanks," she said.

Just then, Toft and Stig came down the hallway and around the corner into her office. They ignored Willumsen and Lars and walked right up to her. Stig squatted down next to her chair while Toft sat down on her desk. They gave her looks that were so full of concern that she smiled.

"What is it?" she asked, looking from one to the other. "I'm fine. It's done. It went well."

On the way back to headquarters in the car, Lars had said that Stig had offered several times to go into the apartment and get her out, but Suhr had refused, snarling that he was more than satisfied to have Rick in there.

"What was he like?" Stig asked, succumbing to his curiosity. Louise shook her head. "He was actually really calm," she said, surprised that she didn't have anything more harrowing to tell him. Maybe she had a mental wall up, putting some distance from the fact that she had been face-to-face with a man who had committed a series of brutal rapes. She didn't feel any sympathy for him, and yet she had a hard time describing him as the calculating, cynical person they had been searching for.

It struck her again that Camilla might have been sitting around regaling Jørgen with tales of his own case when they were socializing together, without any sense of how catastrophic that could have been. He could have learned something from Camilla that triggered his response. But *desperate*? Based on her experience with him in the apartment, he really hadn't seemed desperate to her. "He didn't make any demands," Louise said, "but I promised him a ton of things I'll never be able to make good on." Suddenly she wished they would all just leave. She was tired, and her thoughts were whirling around in her head.

"Do you have someone who can come over and be with you when you leave here?" Willumsen asked genially.

Louise smiled. Willumsen rarely let the friendly side of his personality show, so she knew she ought to enjoy this rare glimpse.

Just then Heilmann walked in the door. "I can go with you," she offered.

Louise shook her head firmly. "I'm fine," she insisted. "I'd like to be alone."

"Be sensible, would—" Heilmann stopped as the sound of heels came clicking down the hallway. Everyone in the office turned to look at the doorway, where Camilla abruptly stopped and looked around with a questioning look, wondering if it was all right to interrupt them.

"Come on in," Heilmann said.

Toft and Stig had gotten up and moved over toward the door, as if they were afraid of being trapped in a room where things were about to get a little too intimate. Willumsen greeted Camilla briefly and then followed on Toft and Stig's heels. Willumsen had just gotten an extension on the pretrial detention of the immigrant woman's brother, so his group was between cases. Louise guessed he was still itching to charge the upstairs neighbor for perjuring herself during her deposition because she'd made up that story about hearing a noise in the apartment at one o'clock, but no one really believed the charges would stick. All the same, most people agreed it would be fitting revenge on a person who had interfered with the investigation so much that the police had been forced to let their suspect go. Of course, now he was dead—but still!

"What the fuck just happened down there in Roskilde?" Camilla asked, concerned, but unable to hide her curiosity.

She tossed her big shoulder bag into the corner and took her seat on the low bookshelf next to the door, quite at home in Lars and Louise's office. "I was hoping to find Lieutenant Suhr here," she said, looking at Heilmann.

Louise was guessing Suhr had already lined up the public defender so they could start questioning Jørgen that same night.

317

"Did something happen with Susanne?" Camilla asked with urgency.

Louise looked at her friend and tried to deduce how much she knew about the specific details of the story, because she had no doubt that Camilla was here in a professional capacity.

"No," Heilmann responded, "nothing too serious, but of course she is rather shaken up."

Camilla nodded, seeming very concerned. "I was just with her. He must have arrived right after I left."

Lars packed up his things and got ready to head home to his wife and twins. Louise hoped for his sake that they were already in bed. He must be more exhausted than he was letting on. She waved at him as he left, and thanked him for all his help.

Camilla said, "My editor ordered me out to Roskilde when we heard about it, but I figured the whole thing would be over before I got there and that it would make more sense for me to come here."

Smart, Louise thought, wondering how her friend had made it through security downstairs, since she apparently didn't have an appointment with anyone. It wasn't that easy to sneak into Police Headquarters, was it?

"What happened out there?" Camilla asked, training her eyes intently on Heilmann, but Heilmann shook her head and said, "Rick is the one who knows the most about it."

Camilla looked surprised and said, "It was you? I heard the negotiating team was down there, so I assumed one of them had gotten Susanne out."

Louise wasn't surprised that the story was already getting out. "He's a major sociopath, then, huh?" Camilla continued, scandalized. "What the fuck kind of person does something like this?" She shook her head, seemingly shocked. "He could have fucking killed Susanne...or you, for that matter!"

Yes, or you, Louise was about to add, but stopped herself. That wasn't the way to break the truth to Camilla.

"Do you think you could go home with Rick, so she doesn't have to be alone?" Heilmann asked, giving Camilla a somber look.

"Of course, Sergeant," Camilla answered without hesitation. Heilmann didn't know about Henning and the details that tied Camilla very closely to the drama in Roskilde. Heilmann would need to be filled in, Louise thought, but that would have to wait until after she'd had a chance to talk to Camilla.

"What about your editor?" Louise asked. "Are you sure you're free to take me home?"

"Of course. Terkel will just have to find someone else—"

They were interrupted by voices and footsteps in the hallway. It sounded like an invasion, there was so much commotion erupting through the silence.

When Suhr spotted Heilmann, he and his retinue stopped outside Louise's office.

"We're going to take Jørgen Zachariassen out to Vestre Prison once we're done here," he announced.

Louise didn't have a chance to react before she felt his eyes on her. "Prinzz" was surrounded by Toft, Stig, and his newly appointed defense attorney. Their eyes met the instant Louise glanced over in his direction. She tried to look away, but his eyes held hers.

"What the fuck is going on here?" Camilla burst out.

She was heading out into the hall when Heilmann grabbed her arm.

Jørgen reached out toward her, and in an instant Stig was all over him.

Suhr waved them on so no more words or looks could be exchanged.

"How much do you know about Jørgen Zachariassen?" Suhr asked, coming in and standing in front of Camilla.

Camilla walked over and took a seat in Lars's chair. "He's, uh, my boyfriend's brother. He didn't do this—it can't be him!"

Louise could tell that Camilla was starting to put two and two together.

"How much did he know about your setup with Susanne?" Louise asked.

Suhr moved closer to Camilla.

Camilla said, "Nothing! Nothing at all. You listen to me. He's a totally normal guy," she defended him. "He's a computer consultant, and he's totally normal. I simply cannot believe he raped anyone at all. Besides, he lived with a woman for years. They broke up two years ago, when she left him, but he has a totally normal life." Camilla was talking loudly and quickly. "You cannot seriously think it was him!"

"It's hard to think anything else since he was the one holding a knife to Susanne's throat a few hours ago. We just took a blood sample so we can run his DNA, and then we'll know for sure."

Camilla sat shaking her head as Suhr spoke. "What about Henning? Does he know Jørgen is here?" she asked, no longer listening to Suhr.

Suhr seized on the topic. "What was the relationship between the two of them like?" he asked, and was about to proceed when Heilmann signaled him to stop. With a brief arm gesture, Heilmann motioned toward his office.

Louise vaguely registered that Jørgen Zachariassen had been taken into Suhr's office, and the last thing she heard was Suhr's authoritative voice telling him, "You can take a seat there."

Then Suhr's door closed behind them.

Suddenly it was completely quiet. Louise looked over at Camilla, who was sitting there staring straight ahead as if in a trance. Slowly, Louise summoned the energy to move. She stood up, a little wobbly, walked over, stood right next to her friend, and started stroking her hair.

AUTHOR'S NOTE

The Silent Women is fiction. Everything could have happened, some of it did, but most of it came from my imagination, so the characters in this book do not bear any likeness to real people. The world in which the story is set has a fair amount in common with the real world, but I used authorial freedom to allow the Homicide Division to work throughout Copenhagen, even though they normally don't deal with cases in Frederiksberg. *Morgenavisen* and Nightwatch.dk are purely fictional.

As I wrote, it was crucial for me to familiarize myself with the real version of this world so I could create as realistic a portrayal as possible. Thus, I would like to express my heartfelt thanks to everyone who so graciously and helpfully welcomed me and took the time to answer my questions. My friend at the Forensic Pathology Institute and my friends at Department A with the Copenhagen Police deserve special thanks. Without their help, I could not have created this story about Louise Rick.

Any errors there may be are exclusively my own.

—Sara Blaedel

ACKNOWLEDGMENTS

From my very first publication and onward, I've been a stickler for thorough research, which is essential if the goal is storytelling that is believable, authentic, and realistic. I've had enormous help along the way. Special thanks go to Ove Dahl, former head of the Homicide Department, and to my now old friends at Copenhagen's Police Headquarters, without whose help the framework around Louise Rick wouldn't hold.

A big, fat, massive thank-you to Kurt Kragh and Tom Christensen, Flying Squad, who have been with me all along the way, and have generously contributed with talk and details as the book was in process. Deep gratitude for your time and compassion.

Heartfelt thanks go, as always, to my brilliant friend, forensic expert Steen Holger Hansen, who is there to help out when a plot needs to be spun together. Without you there would be no books.

Great thanks to my talented Danish editor, Lisbeth Møller Madsen, and to my publisher, People's Press. It's a pleasure to work with you.

ACKNOWLEDGMENTS

A billion thanks to my wonderful, super-smart American editor, Lindsey Rose, and to the spectacular, endlessly committed team at Grand Central. It is a thrill, an honor, and an enormous joy to work with you all. I appreciate every single effort you've made on my behalf. So happy to be here.

Thank you so very much to my fabulous and savvy American agent, the unparalleled Victoria Sanders, who works magic for me, and to your incredibly wonderful associates, the lovely and talented Bernadette Baker-Baughman and Jessica Spivey, whose great work, all around the world, leaves me filled with gratitude and aware of just how fortunate I am.

Thank you to the clever and tireless Benee Knauer, who knows what I am thinking and what I mean, and how to capture it perfectly. It means so much to know you are there, to have you behind and beside me.

I want to express my heartfelt appreciation to the American crime-writing community, and to my dear American readers. I cannot sufficiently convey how much your warm welcome has meant to me; you have made my dream come true. I love this country so much and I am delighted to call it my second home.

My warmest thanks must go to my son, Adam, whom I love with all my heart, and who has traveled every step with me along the way on this indescribable journey.

If you enjoy Sara Blaedel's Louise Rick suspense novels, you'll love her Family Secrets series.

An unexpected inheritance from a father she hasn't seen since childhood pulls a portrait photographer from her quiet life into a web of dark secrets and murder in a small Midwestern town...

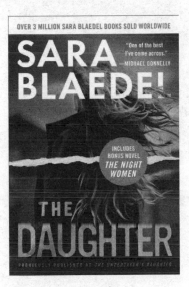

Please see the next page for an excerpt from *THE DAUGHTER*.

Available now.

1

What do you mean you shouldn't have told me? You should have told me thirty-three years ago."

"What difference would it have made anyway?" Ilka's mother demanded. "You were seven years old. You wouldn't have understood about a liar and a cheat running away with all his winnings; running out on his responsibilities, on his wife and little daughter. He hit the jackpot, Ilka, and then he hit the road. And left me—no, he left *us* with a funeral home too deep in the red to get rid of. And an enormous amount of debt. That he betrayed me is one thing, but abandoning his child?"

Ilka stood at the window, her back to the comfy living room, which was overflowing with books and baskets of yarn. She looked out over the trees in the park across the way. For a moment, the treetops seemed like dizzying black storm waves.

Her mother sat in the glossy Børge Mogensen easy chair in the corner, though now she was worked up from her rant, and her knitting needles clattered twice as fast. Ilka turned to her. "Okay," she said, trying not to sound shrill. "Maybe you're right. Maybe I wouldn't have understood about all that. But you didn't think I was too young to understand that my father was a coward, the way he suddenly left us, and that he didn't love us anymore. That he was an incredible asshole you'd never take back if he ever showed up on our doorstep, begging for forgiveness. As I recall, you had no trouble talking about that, over and over and over."

"Stop it." Her mother had been a grade school teacher for twenty-six years, and now she sounded like one. "But does it make any difference? Think of all the letters you've written him over the years. How often have you reached out to him, asked to see him? Or at least have some form of contact." She sat up and laid her knitting on the small table beside the chair. "He never answered you; he never tried to see you. How long did you save your confirmation money so you could fly over and visit him?"

Ilka knew better than her mother how many letters she had written over the years. What her mother wasn't aware of was that she had kept writing to him, even as an adult. Not as often, but at least a Christmas card and a note on his birthday. Every single year. Which had felt like sending letters into outer space. Yet she'd never stopped.

"You should have told me about the money," Ilka said, unwilling to let it go, even though her mother had a point. Would it really have made a difference? "Why are you telling me now? After all these years. And right when I'm about to leave."

Her mother had called just before eight. Ilka had still been in bed, reading the morning paper on her iPad. "Come over, right now," she'd said. There was something they had to talk about.

Now her mother leaned forward and folded her hands in her lap, her face showing the betrayal and desperation she'd endured. She'd kept her wounds under wraps for half her life, but it was obvious they had never fully healed. "It scares me, you going over there. Your father was a gambler. He bet more money than he had, and the racetrack was a part of our lives for the entire time he lived here. For better and worse. I knew about his habit when we fell in love, but then it got out of control. And almost ruined us several times. In the end, it did ruin us."

"And then he won almost a million kroner and just disappeared." Ilka lifted an eyebrow.

"Well, we do know he went to America." Her mother nodded. "Presumably, he continued gambling over there. And we never heard from him again. That is, until now, of course."

Ilka shook her head. "Right, now that he's dead."

"What I'm trying to say is that we don't know what he's left behind. He could be up to his neck in debt. You're a school photographer, not a millionaire. If you go over there, they might hold you responsible for his debts. And who knows? Maybe they wouldn't allow you to come home. Your father had a dark side he couldn't control. I'll rip his dead body limb from limb if he pulls you down with him, all these years after turning his back on us."

With that, her mother stood and walked down the long hall into the kitchen. Ilka heard muffled voices, and then Hanne appeared in the doorway. "Would you like us to drive you to the airport?" Hanne leaned against the doorframe as Ilka's mother reappeared with a tray of bakery rolls, which she set down on the coffee table.

"No, that's okay," Ilka said.

"How long do you plan on staying?" Hanne asked, moving to the sofa. Ilka's mother curled up in the corner of the sofa, covered herself with a blanket, and put her stockinged feet up on Hanne's lap.

When her mother began living with Hanne fourteen years ago, the last trace of her bitterness finally seemed to evaporate. Now, though, Ilka realized it had only gone into hibernation.

For the first four years after Ilka's father left, her mother had been stuck with Paul Jensen's Funeral Home and its two employees, who cheated her whenever they could get away with it. Throughout Ilka's childhood, her mother had complained constantly about the burden he had dumped on her. Ilka hadn't known until now that her father had also left a sizable gambling debt behind. Apparently, her mother had wanted to spare her, at least to some degree. And, of course, her mother was right. Her father *was* a coward and a selfish jerk. Yet Ilka had never completely accepted his abandonment of her. He had left behind a short letter saying he would come back for them as soon as everything was taken care of, and that an opportunity had come up. In Chicago.

Several years later, after complete silence on his part, he wanted a divorce. And that was the last they'd heard from him. When Ilka was a teenager, she found his address—or at least, an address where he once had lived. She'd kept it all these years in a small red treasure chest in her room.

"Surely it won't take more than a few days," Ilka said. "I'm planning to be back by the weekend. I'm booked up at work, but I found someone to fill in for me the first two days. It would be a great help if you two could keep trying to get hold of Niels from North Sealand Photography. He's in Stockholm, but he's supposed to be back tomorrow. I'm hoping he can cover for me the rest of the week. All the shoots are in and around Copenhagen."

"What exactly are you hoping to accomplish over there?" Hanne asked.

"Well, they say I'm in his will and that I have to be there in person to prove I'm Paul Jensen's daughter."

"I just don't understand why this can't be done by e-mail or fax," her mother said. "You can send them your birth certificate and your passport, or whatever it is they need."

"It seems that copies aren't good enough. If I don't go over there, I'd have to go to an American tax office in Europe, and I think the nearest one is in London. But this way, they'll let me go through his personal things and take what I want. Artie Sorvino from Jensen Funeral Home in Racine has offered to cover my travel expenses if I go now, so they can get started with closing his estate."

Ilka stood in the middle of the living room, too anxious and restless to sit down.

"Racine?" Hanne asked. "Where's that?" She picked up her steaming cup and blew on it.

"A bit north of Chicago. In Wisconsin. I'll be picked up at the airport, and it doesn't look like it'll take long to drive there. Racine is supposedly the city in the United States with the largest community of Danish descendants. A lot of Danes immigrated to the region, so it makes sense that's where he settled."

"He has a hell of a lot of nerve." Her mother's lips barely moved. "He doesn't write so much as a birthday card to you all these years, and now suddenly you have to fly over there and clean up another one of his messes."

"Karin," Hanne said, her voice gentle. "Of course Ilka should go over and sort through her father's things. If you get the opportunity for closure on such an important part of your life's story, you should grab it."

Her mother shook her head. Without looking at Ilka, she said, "I have a bad feeling about this. Isn't it odd that he stayed in the undertaker business even though he managed to ruin his first shot at it?"

Ilka walked out into the hall and let the two women bicker about the unfairness of it all. How Paul's daughter had tried to reach out to her father all her life, and it was only now that he was gone that he was finally reaching out to her.

2

The first thing Ilka noticed was his Hawaiian shirt and longish brown hair, which was combed back and held in place by sunglasses that would look at home on a surfer. He stood out among the other drivers at Arrivals in O'Hare International Airport who were holding name cards and facing the scattered clumps of exhausted people pulling suitcases out of Customs.

Written on his card was "Ilka Nichols Jensen." Somehow, she managed to walk all the way up to him and stop before he realized she'd found him.

They looked each other over for a moment. He was in his early forties, maybe, she thought. So, her father, who had turned seventy-two in early January, had a younger partner.

She couldn't read his face, but it might have surprised him that the undertaker's daughter was a beanpole: six feet tall without a hint of a feminine form. He scanned her up and down, gaze settling on her hair, which had never been an attention-getter. Straight, flat, and mousy.

He smiled warmly and held out his hand. "Nice to meet you. Welcome to Chicago."

It's going to be a hell of a long trip, Ilka thought, before shaking his hand and saying hello. "Thank you. Nice to meet you too."

He offered to carry her suitcase. It was small, a carry-on, but she gladly handed it over to him. Then he offered her a bottle of water. The car was close by, he said, only a short walk.

Although she was used to being taller than most people, she always felt a bit shy when male strangers had to look up to make eye contact. She was nearly a head taller than Artie Sorvino, but he seemed almost impressed as he grinned up at her while they walked.

Her body ached; she hadn't slept much during the long flight. Since she'd left her apartment in Copenhagen, her nerves had been tingling with excitement. And worry, too. Things had almost gone wrong right off the bat at the Copenhagen airport, because she hadn't taken into account the long line at Passport Control. There had still been two people in front of her when she'd been called to her waiting flight. Then the arrival in the US, a hell that the chatty man next to her on the plane had prepared her for. He had missed God knew how many connecting flights at O'Hare because the immigration line had taken several hours to go through. It turned out to be not quite as bad as all that. She had been guided to a machine that requested her fingerprints, passport, and picture. All this information was scanned and saved. Then Ilka had been sent on to the next line, where a surly passport official wanted to know what her business was in the country. She began to sweat but then pulled herself together and explained that she was simply visiting family, which in a way was true. He stamped her passport, and moments later she was standing beside the man wearing the colorful, festive shirt.

"Is this your first trip to the US?" Artie asked now, as they approached the enormous parking lot.

She smiled. "No, I've traveled here a few times. To Miami and New York."

Why had she said that? She'd never been in this part of the world before, but what the hell. It didn't matter. Unless he kept up the conversation. And Miami. Where had that come from?

"Really?" Artie told her he had lived in Key West for many years. Then his father got sick, and Artie, the only other surviving member of the family, moved back to Racine to take care of him. "I hope you made it down to the Keys while you were in Florida."

Ilka shook her head and explained that she unfortunately hadn't had time.

"I had a gallery down there," Artie said. He'd gone to the California School of the Arts in San Francisco and had made his living as an artist.

Ilka listened politely and nodded. In the parking lot, she caught sight of a gigantic black Cadillac with closed white curtains in back, which stood first in the row of parked cars. He'd driven there in the hearse.

"Hope you don't mind." He nodded at the hearse as he opened the rear door and placed her suitcase on the casket table used for rolling coffins in and out of the vehicle.

"No, it's fine." She walked around to the front passenger door. Fine, as long as she wasn't the one being rolled into the back. She felt slightly dizzy, as if she were still up in the air, but was buoyed by the nervous excitement of traveling and the anticipation of what awaited her.

The thought that her father was at the end of her journey bothered her, yet it was something she'd fantasized about nearly her entire life. But would she be able to piece together the life he'd lived without her? And was she even interested in knowing about it? What if she didn't like what she learned?

She shook her head for a moment. These thoughts had been swirling in her head since Artie's first phone call. Her mother thought she shouldn't get involved. At all. But Ilka disagreed. If her father had left anything behind, she wanted to see it. She wanted to uncover whatever she could find, to see if any of it made sense.

"How did he die?" she asked as Artie maneuvered the long hearse out of the parking lot and in between two orange signs warning about roadwork and a detour.

"Just a sec," he muttered, and he swore at the sign before deciding to skirt the roadwork and get back to the road heading north.

For a while they drove in silence; then he explained that one morning her father had simply not woken up. "He was supposed to drive a corpse to Iowa, one of our neighboring states, but he didn't show up. He just died in his sleep. Totally peacefully. He might not even have known it was over."

Ilka watched the Chicago suburbs drifting by along the long, straight bypass, the rows of anonymous stores and cheap restaurants. It seemed so overwhelming, so strange, so different. Most buildings were painted in shades of beige and brown, and enormous billboards stood everywhere, screaming messages about everything from missing children to ultracheap fast food and vanilla coffee for less than a dollar at Dunkin' Donuts.

She turned to Artie. "Was he sick?" The bump on Artie's nose—had it been broken?—made it appear too big for the rest of his face: high cheekbones, slightly squinty eyes, beard stubble definitely due to a relaxed attitude toward shaving, rather than wanting to be in style.

"Not that I know of, no. But there could have been things Paul didn't tell me about, for sure."

His tone told her it wouldn't have been the first secret Paul had kept from him.

"The doctor said his heart just stopped," he continued. "Nothing dramatic happened."

"Did he have a family?" She looked out the side window. The old hearse rode well. Heavy, huge, swaying lightly. A tall pickup drove up beside them; a man with a full beard looked down and nodded at her. She looked away quickly. She didn't care for any sympathetic looks, though he, of course, couldn't know the curtained-off back of the hearse was empty.

"He was married, you know," Artie said. Immediately Ilka sensed he didn't like being the one to fill her in on her father's private affairs. She nodded to herself, of course he didn't. What did she expect?

"And he had two daughters. That was it, apart from Mary Ann's family, but I don't know them. How much do you know about them?"

He knew very well that Ilka hadn't had any contact with her father since he'd left Denmark. Or at least she assumed he knew. "Why has the family not signed what should be signed, so you can finish with his…estate?" She set the empty water bottle on the floor.

"They did sign their part of it. But that's not enough, because

339

you're in the will, too. First the IRS—that's our tax agency—must determine if he owes the government, and you must give them permission to investigate. If you don't sign, they'll freeze all the assets in the estate until everything is cleared up."

Ilka's shoulders slumped at the word "assets." One thing that had kept her awake during the flight was her mother's concern about her being stuck with a debt she could never pay. Maybe she would be detained; maybe she would even be thrown in jail.

"What are his daughters like?" she asked after they had driven for a while in silence.

For a few moments, he kept his eyes on the road; then he glanced at her and shrugged. "They're nice enough, but I don't really know them. It's been a long time since I've seen them. Truth is, I don't think either of them was thrilled about your father's business."

After another silence, Ilka said, "You should have called me when he died. I wish I had been at his funeral."

Was that really true? Did she truly wish that? The last funeral she'd been to was her husband's. He had collapsed from heart failure three years ago, at the age of fifty-two. She didn't like death, didn't like loss. But she'd already lost her father many years ago, so what difference would it have made watching him being lowered into the ground?

"At that time, I didn't know about you," Artie said. "Your name first came up when your father's lawyer mentioned you."

"Where is he buried?"

He stared straight ahead. Again, it was obvious he didn't enjoy talking about her father's private life. Finally, he said, "Mary Ann decided to keep the urn with his ashes at home. A private ceremony was held in the living room when the crematorium delivered the urn, and now it's on the shelf above the fireplace."

After a pause, he said, "You speak English well. Funny accent."

Ilka explained distractedly that she had traveled in Australia for a year after high school.

The billboards along the freeway here advertised hotels, motels, and drive-ins for the most part. She wondered how there could be enough people to keep all these businesses going, given the countless offers from the clusters of signs on both sides of the road. "What about his new family? Surely they knew he had a daughter in Denmark?" She turned back to him.

"Nope!" He shook his head as he flipped the turn signal.

"He never told them he left his wife and seven-year-old daughter?" She wasn't all that surprised.

Artie didn't answer. *Okay*, Ilka thought. *That takes care of that.*

"I wonder what they think about me coming here."

He shrugged. "I don't really know, but they're not going to lose anything. His wife has an inheritance from her wealthy parents, so she's taken care of. The same goes for the daughters. And none of them have ever shown any interest in the funeral home."

And what about their father? Ilka thought. *Were they uninterested in him, too?* But that was none of her business. She didn't know them, knew nothing about their relationships with one another. And for that matter, she knew nothing about her father. Maybe his new family had asked about his life in Denmark, and maybe he'd given them a line of bullshit. But what the hell, he was thirty-nine when he left. Anyone could figure out he'd had a life before packing his weekend bag and emigrating.

Both sides of the freeway were green now. The landscape was starting to remind her of late summer in Denmark, with its green fields, patches of forest, flat land, large barns with the character-istic bowed roofs, and livestock. With a few exceptions, she felt like she could have been driving down the E45, the road between Copenhagen and Ålborg.

"Do you mind if I turn on the radio?" Artie asked.

She shook her head; it was a relief to have the awkward silence between them broken. And yet, before his hand reached the radio, she blurted out, "What was he like?"

He dropped his hand and smiled at her. "Your father was a decent guy, a really decent guy. In a lot of ways," he added, disarm-ingly, "he was someone you could count on, and in other ways he was very much his own man. I always enjoyed working with him, but he was also my friend. People liked him; he was interested in their lives. That's also why he was so good at talking to those who had just lost someone. He was empathetic. It feels empty, him not being around any longer."

Ilka had to concentrate to follow along. Despite her year in Aus-tralia, it was difficult when people spoke English rapidly. "Was he also a good father?"

Artie turned thoughtfully and looked out his side window. "I really can't say. I didn't know him when the girls were small." He kept glancing at the four lanes to their left. "But if you're asking me if your father was a family man, my answer is, yes and no. He was very much in touch with his family, but he probably put more of himself into Jensen Funeral Home."

"How long did you know him?"

She watched him calculate. "I moved back in 1998. We ran into each other at a local saloon, this place called Oh Dennis!, and we started talking. The victim of a traffic accident had just come in to the funeral home. The family wanted to put the young woman in an open coffin, but nobody would have wanted to see her face. So I offered to help. It's the kind of stuff I'm good at. Creating, shaping. Your father did the embalming, but I reconstructed her face. Her mother supplied us with a photo, and I did a sculpture. And I managed to make the woman look like herself, even though there wasn't much to work with. Later your father offered me a job, and I grabbed the chance. There's not much work for an artist in Racine, so reconstructions of the deceased was as good as anything."

He turned off the freeway. "Later I got a degree, because you have to have a license to work in the undertaker business."

They reached Racine Street and waited to make a left turn. They had driven the last several miles in silence. The streets were deserted, the shops closed. It was getting dark, and Ilka realized she was at the point where exhaustion and jet lag trumped the hunger gnawing inside her. They drove by an empty square and a nearly deserted saloon. Oh Dennis! The place where Artie had met her father. She spotted the lake at the end of the broad streets to the right, and that was it. The town was dead. Abandoned, closed. She was surprised there were no people or life.

"We've booked a room for you at the Harbourwalk Hotel. Tomorrow we can sit down and go through your father's papers. Then you can start looking through his things."

Ilka nodded. All she wanted right now was a warm bath and a bed.

"Sorry, we have no reservations for Miss Jensen. And none for the Jensen Funeral Home, either. We don't have a single room available."

The receptionist drawled apology after apology. It sounded to Ilka as if she had too much saliva in her mouth.

Ilka sat in a plush armchair in the lobby as Artie asked if the room was reserved in his name. "Or try Sister Eileen O'Connor," he suggested.

The receptionist apologized again as her long fingernails danced over the computer keyboard. The sound was unnaturally loud, a bit like Ilka's mother's knitting needles tapping against each other.

Ilka shut down. She could sit there and sleep; it made absolutely no difference to her. Back in Denmark, it was five in the morning, and she hadn't slept in twenty-two hours.

"I'm sorry," Artie said. "You're more than welcome to stay at my place. I can sleep on the sofa. Or we can fix up a place for you to sleep at the office, and we'll find another hotel in the morning."

Ilka sat up in the armchair. "What's that sound?"

Artie looked bewildered. "What do you mean?"

"It's like a phone ringing in the next room."

He listened for a moment before shrugging. "I can't hear anything."

The sound came every ten seconds. It was as if something were hidden behind the reception desk or farther down the hotel foyer. Ilka shook her head and looked at him. "You don't need to sleep on the sofa. I can sleep somewhere at the office."

She needed to be alone, and the thought of a strange man's bedroom didn't appeal to her.

"That's fine." He grabbed her small suitcase. "It's only five minutes away, and I know we can find some food for you, too."

The black hearse was parked just outside the main entrance of the hotel, but that clearly wasn't bothering anyone. Though the hotel was apparently fully booked, Ilka hadn't seen a single person since they'd arrived.

Night had fallen, and her eyelids closed as soon as she settled into the car. She jumped when Artie opened the door and poked her with his finger. She hadn't even realized they had arrived. They were parked in a large, empty lot. The white building was an enormous box with several attic windows reflecting the moonlight back into the thick darkness. Tall trees with enormous crowns hovered over Ilka when she got out of the car.

They reached the door, beside which was a sign: JENSEN FUNERAL HOME. WELCOME. Pillars stood all the way across the broad porch, with well-tended flower beds in front of it, but the darkness covered everything else.

Artie led her inside the high-ceilinged hallway and turned the light on. He pointed to a stairway at the other end. Ilka's feet sank deep in the carpet; it smelled dusty, with a hint of plastic and instant coffee.

"Would you like something to drink? Are you hungry? I can make a sandwich."

"No, thank you." She just wanted him to leave.

He led her up the stairs, and when they reached a small landing, he pointed at a door. "Your father had a room in there, and I think we can find some sheets. We have a cot we can fold out and make up for you."

Ilka held her hand up. "If there is a bed in my father's room, I can just sleep in it." She nodded when he asked if she was sure. "What time do you want to meet tomorrow?"

"How about eight thirty? We can have breakfast together."

She had no idea what time it was, but as long as she got some sleep, she guessed she'd be fine. She nodded.

Ilka stayed outside on the landing while Artie opened the door to her father's room and turned on the light. She watched him walk over to a dresser and pull out the bottom drawer. He grabbed some sheets and a towel and tossed them on the bed; then he waved her in.

The room's walls were slanted. An old white bureau stood at the end of the room, and under the window, which must have been one of those she'd noticed from the parking lot, was a desk with drawers on both sides. The bed was just inside the room and to the left. There was also a small coffee table and, at the end of the bed, a narrow built-in closet.

A dark jacket and a tie lay draped over the back of the desk chair. The desk was covered with piles of paper; a briefcase leaned against the closet. But there was nothing but sheets on the bed.

"I'll find a comforter and a pillow," Artie said, accidentally grazing her as he walked by.

Ilka stepped into the room. A room lived in, yet abandoned. A feeling suddenly stirred inside her, and she froze. He was here. The smell. A heavy yet pleasant odor she recognized from somewhere deep inside. She'd had no idea this memory existed. She closed her eyes and let her mind drift back to when she was very young, the feeling of being held. Tobacco. Sundays in the car, driving out to Bellevue. Feeling secure, knowing someone close was taking care of her. Lifting her up on a lap. Making her laugh. The sound of hooves pounding the ground, horses at a racetrack. Her father's concentration as he chain-smoked, captivated by the race. His laughter.

She sat down on the bed, not hearing what Artie said when he laid the comforter and pillow beside her, then walked out and closed the door.

Her father had been tall; at least that's how she remembered him. She could see to the end of the world when she sat on his shoulders. They did fun things together. He took her to an amusement park and bought her ice cream while he tried out the slot machines, to see if they were any good. Her mother didn't always know when they went there. He also took her out to a centuries-old amusement park in the forest north of Copenhagen. They stopped at Peter Liep's, and she drank soda while he drank beer. They sat outside and watched the riders pass by, smelling horseshit and sweat when the thirsty riders dismounted and draped the reins over the hitching post. He had loved horses. On the other hand, she couldn't remember the times—the many times, according to her mother—when he didn't come home early enough to stick his head in her room and say good night. Not having enough money for food because he had gambled his wages away at the track was something else she didn't recall—but her mother did.

Ilka opened her eyes. Her exhaustion was gone, but she still felt dizzy. She walked over to the desk and reached for a photo in a wide mahogany frame. A trotter, its mane flying out to both sides at the finishing line. In another photo, a trotter covered by a red victory blanket stood beside a sulky driver holding a trophy high above his head, smiling for the camera. There were several more horse photos, and a ticket to Lunden hung from a window hasp. She grabbed it. Paul Jensen. Charlottenlund Derby 1982. The year he left them.

Ilka didn't realize at the time that he had left. All she knew was that one morning he wasn't there, and her mother was crying but wouldn't tell her why. When she arrived home from school that afternoon, her mother was still crying. And as she remembered it, her mother didn't stop crying for a long time.

She had been with her father at that derby in 1982. She picked up a photo leaning against the windowsill, then sat down on the bed. "Ilka and Peter Kjærsgaard" was written on the back of the photo. Ilka had been five years old when her father took her to the derby for the first time. Back then, her mother had gone along. She vaguely remembered going to the track and meeting the famous jockey, but suddenly the odors and sounds were crystal clear. She closed her eyes.

"You can give them one if you want," the man had said as he handed her a bucket filled with carrots, many more than her mother had in bags back in their kitchen. The bucket was heavy, but Ilka wanted to show them how big she was, so she hooked the handle with her arm and walked over to one of the stalls.

She smiled proudly at a red-shirted sulky driver passing by as he was fastening his helmet. The track was crowded, but during the races, few people were allowed in the barn. They were, though. She and her father.

She pulled her hand back, frightened, when the horse in the stall whinnied and pulled against the chain. It snorted and pounded its hoof on the floor. The horse was so tall. Carefully she held the carrot out in the palm of her hand, as her father had taught her to do. The horse snatched the sweet treat, gently tickling her.

Her father stood with a group of men at the end of the row of stalls. They laughed loudly, slapping one another's shoulders. A few of them drank beer from a bottle. Ilka sat down on a bale of hay. Her father had promised her a horse when she was a bit older. One of the grooms came over and asked if she would like a ride behind the barn; he was going to walk one of the horses to warm it up. She wanted to, if her father would let her. He did.

"Look at me, Daddy!" Ilka cried. "Look at me." The horse had stopped, clearly preferring to eat grass rather than walk. She kicked gently to get it going, but her legs were too short to do any good.

Her father pulled himself away from the other men and stood at the barn entrance. He waved, and Ilka sat up proudly. The groom asked if he should let go of the reins so she could ride by herself, and though she didn't really love the idea, she nodded. But when he dropped the reins and she turned around to show her father how brave she was, he was back inside with the others.

Ilka stood up and put the photo back. She could almost smell the tar used by the racetrack farrier on horse hooves. She used to sit behind a pane of glass with her mother and follow the races, while her father stood over at the finish line. But then her mother stopped going along.

She picked up another photo from the windowsill. She was standing on a bale of hay, toasting with a sulky driver. Fragments of memories flooded back as she studied herself in the photo. Her father speaking excitedly with the driver, his expression as the horses were hitched to the sulkies. And the way he said, "We-e-e-ell, shall we...?" right before a race. Then he would hold his hand out, and they would walk down to the track.

She wondered why she could remember these things, when she had forgotten most of what had happened back then.

There was also a photo of two small girls on the desk. She knew these were her younger half sisters, who were smiling broadly at the photographer. Suddenly, deep inside her chest, she felt a sharp twinge—but why? After setting the photo back down, she realized it wasn't from never having met her half sisters. No. It was pure jealousy. They had grown up with her father, while she had been abandoned.

Ilka threw herself down on the bed and pulled the comforter over her, without even bothering to put the sheets on. She lay curled up, staring into space.

3

At some point, Ilka must have fallen asleep, because she gave a start when someone knocked on the door. She recognized Artie's voice.

"Morning in there. Are you awake?"

She sat up, confused. She had been up once in the night to look for a bathroom. The building seemed strangely hushed, as if it were packed in cotton. She'd opened a few doors and finally found a bathroom with shiny tiles and a low bathtub. The toilet had a soft cover on its seat, like the one in her grandmother's flat in Bagsværd. On her way back, she had grabbed her father's jacket, carried it to the bed, and buried her nose in it. Now it lay halfway on the floor.

"Give me half an hour," she said. She hugged the jacket, savoring the odor that had brought her childhood memories to the surface from the moment she'd walked into the room.

Now that it was light outside, the room seemed bigger. Last night she hadn't noticed the storage boxes lining the wall behind both sides of the desk. Clean shirts in clear plastic sacks hung from the hook behind the door.

"Okay, but have a look at these IRS forms," he said, sliding a folder under the door. "And sign on the last page when you've read them. We'll take off whenever you're ready."

Ilka didn't answer. She pulled her knees up to her chest and lay curled up. Without moving. Being shut up inside a room with her father's belongings was enough to make her feel she'd reunited with a part of herself. The big black hole inside her, the one that had appeared every time she sent a letter despite knowing she'd get no answer, was slowly filling up with something she'd failed to find herself.

She had lived about a sixth of her life with her father. *When do we become truly conscious of the people around us?* she wondered. She had just turned forty, and he had deserted them when she was seven. This room here was filled with everything he had left behind, all her memories of him. All the odors and sensations that had made her miss him.

Artie knocked on the door again. She had no idea how long she'd been lying on the bed.

"Ready?" he called out.

"No," she yelled back. She couldn't. She needed to just stay and take in everything here, so it wouldn't disappear again.

"Have you read it?"

"I signed it!"

"Would you rather stay here? Do you want me to go alone?"

"Yes, please."

Silence. She couldn't tell if he was still outside.

"Okay," he finally said. "I'll come back after breakfast." He sounded annoyed. "I'll leave the phone here with you."

Ilka listened to him walk down the stairs. After she'd walked over to the door and signed her name, she hadn't moved a muscle. She hadn't opened any drawers or closets.

She'd brought along a bag of chips, but they were all gone. And she didn't feel like going downstairs for something to drink. Instead, she gave way to exhaustion. The stream of thoughts, the fragments of memories in her head, had slowly settled into a tempo she could follow.

Her father had written her into his will. He had declared her to be his biological daughter. But evidently, he'd never mentioned her to his new family, or to the people closest to him in his new life. Of course, he hadn't been obligated to mention her, she thought. But if her name hadn't come up in his will, they could have liquidated his business without anyone knowing about an adult daughter in Denmark.

The telephone outside the door rang, but she ignored it. What had this Artie guy imagined she should do if the telephone rang? Did he think she would answer it? And say what?

At first, she'd wondered why her father had named her in his will. But after having spent the last twelve hours enveloped in memories of him, she had realized that no matter what had happened in his life, a part of him had still been her father.

She cried, then felt herself dozing off.

Someone knocked on the door. "Not today," she yelled, before Artie could even speak a word. She turned her back to the room, her face to the wall. She closed her eyes until the footsteps disappeared down the stairs.

The telephone rang again, but she didn't react.

Slowly it had all come back. After her father had disappeared, her mother had two jobs: the funeral home business and her teaching. It wasn't long after summer vacation, and school had just begun. Ilka thought he had left in September. A month before she turned eight. Her mother taught Danish and arts and crafts to students in several grades. When she wasn't at school, she was at the funeral home on Brønshøj Square. Also on weekends, picking up flowers and ordering coffins. Working in the office, keeping the books when she wasn't filling out forms.

Ilka had gone along with her to various embassies whenever a mortuary passport was needed to bring a corpse home from outside the country, or when a person died in Denmark and was to be buried elsewhere. It had been fascinating, though frightening. But she had never fully understood how hard her mother worked. Finally, when Ilka was twelve, her mother managed to sell the business and get back her life.

After her father left, they were unable to afford the single-story house Ilka had been born in. They moved into a small apartment on Frederikssundsvej in Copenhagen. Her mother had never been shy about blaming her father for their economic woes, but she'd always said they would be okay. After she sold the funeral home, their situation had improved; Ilka saw it mostly from the color in her mother's cheeks, a more relaxed expression on her face. Also, she was more likely to let Ilka invite friends home for dinner. When she started eighth grade, they moved to Østerbro, a better district in the city, but she stayed in her school in Brønshøj and took the bus.

"You *were* an asshole," she muttered, her face still to the wall. "What you did was just completely inexcusable."

The telephone outside the door finally gave up. She heard soft steps out on the stairs. She sighed. They had paid her airfare; there were limits to what she could get away with. But today was out of the question. And that telephone was their business.

Someone knocked again at the door. This time it sounded different. They knocked again. "Hello." A female voice. The woman called her name and knocked one more time, gently but insistently.

Ilka rose from the bed. She shook her hair and slipped it behind her ears and smoothed her T-shirt. She walked over and opened the door. She couldn't hide her startled expression at the sight of a woman dressed in gray, her hair covered by a veil of the same color. Her broad, demure skirt reached below the knees. Her eyes seemed far too big for her small face and delicate features.

"Who are you?"

"My name is Sister Eileen O'Connor, and you have a meeting in ten minutes."

The woman was already about to turn and walk back down the steps, when Ilka finally got hold of herself. "I have a meeting?"

"Yes, the business is yours now." Ilka heard patience as well as suppressed annoyance in the nun's voice. "Artie has left for the day and has informed me that you have taken over."

"*My* business?" Ilka ran her hand through her hair. A bad habit of hers, when she didn't know what to do with her hands.

"You did read the papers Artie left for you? It's my understanding that you signed them, so you're surely aware of what you have inherited."

"I signed to say I'm his daughter," Ilka said. More than anything, she just wanted to close the door and make everything go away.

355

"If you had read what was written," the sister said, a bit sharply, "you would know that your father has left the business to you. And by your signature, you have acknowledged your identity and therefore your inheritance."

Ilka was speechless. While she gawked, the sister added, "The Norton family lost their grandmother last night. It wasn't unexpected, but several of them are taking it hard. I've made coffee for four." She stared at Ilka's T-shirt and bare legs. "And it's our custom to receive relatives in attire that is a bit more respectful."

A tiny smile played on her narrow lips, so fleeting that Ilka was in doubt as to whether it had actually appeared. "I can't talk to a family that just lost someone," she protested. "I don't know what to say. I've never—I'm sorry, you have to talk to them."

Sister Eileen stood for a moment before speaking. "Unfortunately, I can't. I don't have the authority to perform such duties. I do the office work, open mail, and laminate the photos of the deceased onto death notices for relatives to use as bookmarks. But you will do fine. Your father was always good at such conversations. All you have to do is allow the family to talk. Listen and find out what's important to them; that's the most vital thing for people who come to us. And these people have a contract for a prepaid ceremony. The contract explains everything they have paid for. Mrs. Norton has been making funeral payments her whole life, so everything should be smooth sailing."

The nun walked soundlessly down the stairs. Ilka stood in the doorway, staring at where she had vanished. Had she seriously inherited a funeral home? In the US? How had her life taken such an unexpected turn? What the hell had her father been thinking?

She pulled herself together. She had seven minutes before the Nortons arrived. "Respectful" attire, the sister had said. Did she even have something like that in her suitcase? She hadn't opened it yet.

But she couldn't do this. They couldn't make her talk to total strangers who had just lost a relative. Then she remembered she hadn't known the undertaker who helped her when Erik died either. But he had been a salvation to her. A person who had taken care of everything in a professional manner and arranged things precisely as she believed her husband would have wanted. The funeral home, the flowers—yellow tulips. The hymns. It was also the undertaker who had said she would regret it if she didn't hire an organist to play during the funeral. Because even though it might seem odd, the mere sound of it helped relieve the somber atmosphere. She had chosen the cheapest coffin, as the undertaker had suggested, seeing that Erik had wanted to be cremated. Many minor decisions had been made for her; that had been an enormous relief. And the funeral had gone exactly the way she'd wanted. Plus, the undertaker had helped reserve a room at the restaurant where they gathered after the ceremony. But those types of details were apparently already taken care of here. It seemed all she had to do was meet with them. She walked over to her suitcase.

Ilka dumped everything out onto the bed and pulled a light blouse and dark pants out of the pile. Along with her toiletry bag and underwear. Halfway down the stairs, she remembered she needed shoes. She went back up again. All she had was sneakers.

The family was three adult children—a daughter and two sons— and a grandchild. The two men seemed essentially composed, while the woman and the boy were crying. The woman's face was stiff and pale, as if every ounce of blood had drained out of her.

Her young son stared down at his hands, looking withdrawn and gloomy.

"Our mother paid for everything in advance," one son said when Ilka walked in. They sat in the arrangement room's comfortable armchairs, around a heavy mahogany table. Dusty paintings in elegant gilded frames hung from the dark green walls. Ilka guessed the paintings were inspired by Lake Michigan. She had no idea what to do with the grieving family, nor what was expected of her.

The son farthest from the door asked, "How does the condolences and tributes page on your website work? Is it like anyone can go in and write on it, or can it only be seen if you have the password? We want everybody to be able to put up a picture of our mother and write about their good times with her."

Ilka nodded to him and walked over to shake his hand. "We will make the page so it's exactly how you want it." Then she repeated their names: Steve—the one farthest from the door—Joe, Helen, and the grandson, Pete. At least she thought that was right, though she wasn't sure because he had mumbled his name.

"And we talked it over and decided we want charms," Helen said. "We'd all like one. But I can't see in the papers whether they're paid for or not, because if not we need to know how much they cost."

Ilka had no idea what charms were, but she'd noticed the green form that had been laid on the table for her, and a folder entitled "Norton," written by hand. The thought struck her that the handwriting must be her father's.

"Service Details" was written on the front of the form. Ilka sat down and reached for the notebook on the table. It had a big red heart on the cover, along with "Helping Hands for Healing Hearts."

She surmised the notebook was probably meant for the relatives. Quickly, she slid it over the table to them; then she opened a drawer and found a sheet of paper. "I'm very sorry," she said. It was difficult for her not to look at the grandson, who appeared crushed. "About your loss. As I understand, everything is already decided. But I wasn't here when things were planned. Maybe we can go through everything together and figure out exactly how you want it done."

What in the world is going on? she thought as she sat there blabbering away at this grieving family, as if she'd been doing it all her life!

"Our mother liked Mr. Jensen a lot," Steve said. "He took charge of the funeral arrangements when our father died, and we'd like things done the same way."

Ilka nodded.

"But not the coffin," Joe said. "We want one that's more upscale, more feminine."

"Is it possible to see the charms?" Helen asked, still tearful. "And we also need to print a death notice, right?"

"Can you arrange it so her dogs can sit up by the coffin during the services?" Steve asked. He looked at Ilka as if this were the most important of all the issues. "That won't be a problem, will it?"

"No, not a problem," she answered quickly, as the questions rained down on her.

"How many people can fit in there? And can we all sit together?"

"The room can hold a lot of people," she said, feeling now as if she'd been fed to the lions. "We can squeeze the chairs together; we can get a lot of people in there. And of course you can sit together."

Ilka had absolutely no idea what room they were talking about. But there had been about twenty people attending her husband's services, and they hadn't even filled a corner of the chapel in Bispebjerg.

"How many do you think are coming?" she asked, just to be on the safe side.

"Probably somewhere between a hundred and a hundred and fifty," Joe guessed. "That's how many showed up at Dad's services. But it could be more this time, so it's good to be prepared. She was very active after her retirement. And the choir would like to sing."

Ilka nodded mechanically and forced a smile. She had heard that it's impossible to vomit while you're smiling, something about reflexes. Not that she was about to vomit; there was nothing inside her to come out. But her insides contracted as if something in there was getting out of control. "How did Mrs. Norton die?" She leaned back in her chair.

She felt their eyes on her, and for a moment everyone was quiet. The adults looked at her as if the question weren't her business. And maybe it was irrelevant for the planning, she thought. But after Erik died, in a way it had been a big relief to talk about him, how she had come home and found him on the kitchen floor. Putting it into words made it all seem more real, like it actually had happened. And it had helped her through the days after his death, which otherwise were foggy.

Helen sat up and looked over at her son, who was still staring at his hands. "Pete's the one who found her. We bought groceries for his grandma three times a week and drove them over to her after school. And there she was, out in the yard. Just lying there."

Now Ilka regretted having asked.

From underneath the hair hanging over his forehead, with his head bowed, the boy scowled at his mother. "Grandma was out cutting flowers to put in vases, and she fell," he muttered.

"There was a lot of blood," his mother said, nodding.

"But the guy who picked her up promised we wouldn't be able to see it when she's in her coffin," Steve said. He looked at Ilka, as if he wanted this confirmed.

Quickly she answered, "No, you won't. She'll look fine. Did she like flowers?"

Helen smiled and nodded. "She lived and breathed for her garden. She loved her flower beds."

"Then maybe it's a good idea to use flowers from her garden to decorate the coffin," Ilka suggested.

Steve sat up. "Decorate the coffin? It's going to be open."

"But it's a good idea," Helen said. "We'll decorate the chapel with flowers from the garden. We can go over and pick them together. It's a beautiful way to say good-bye to the garden she loved, too."

"But if we use hers, will we get the money back we already paid for flowers?" Joe asked.

Ilka nodded. "Yes, of course." Surely it wasn't a question of all that much money.

"Oh God!" Helen said. "I almost forgot to give you this." Out of her bag she pulled a large folder that said "Family Record Guide" and handed it over to Ilka. "It's already filled out."

In many ways, it reminded Ilka of the diaries she'd kept in school. First a page with personal information. The full name of the deceased, the parents' names. Whether she was married, divorced, single, or a widow. Education and job positions. Then a page with familial relations, and on the opposite page there was room to write about the deceased's life and memories. There were sections for writing about a first home, about becoming a parent, about becoming a grandparent. And then a section that caught Ilka's attention, because it had to be of some use. Favorites: colors, flowers, season, songs, poems, books. And on and on it went. Family traditions. Funny memories, role models, hobbies, special talents. Mrs. Norton had filled it all out very thoroughly.

Ilka closed the folder and asked how they would describe their mother and grandmother.

"She was very sociable," Joe said. "Also after Dad died. She was involved in all sorts of things; she was very active in the seniors' club in West Racine."

"And family meant a lot to her," Helen said. She'd stopped crying without Ilka noticing. "She was always the one who made sure we all got together, at least twice a year."

Ilka let them speak, as long as they stayed away from talking about charms and choosing coffins. She had no idea how to wind up the conversation, but she kept listening as they nearly all talked at once, to make sure that everything about the deceased came out. Even gloomy Pete added that his grandmother made the world's best pecan pie.

"And she had the best southern recipe for macaroni and cheese," he added. The others laughed.

Ilka thought again about Erik. After his funeral, their apartment had felt empty and abandoned. A silence hung that had nothing to do with being alone. It took a few weeks for her to realize the silence was in herself. There was no one to talk to, so everything was spoken inside her head. And at the same time, she felt as if she were in a bubble no sound could penetrate. That had been one of the most difficult things to get used to. Slowly things got better, and at last—she couldn't say precisely when—the silence connected with her loss disappeared.

Meanwhile, she'd had the business to run. What a circus. They'd started working together almost from the time they'd first met. He was the photographer, though occasionally she went out with him to help set up the equipment and direct the students. Otherwise, she was mostly responsible for the office work. But she had done a job or two by herself when they were especially busy; she'd seen how he worked. There was nothing mysterious about it. Classes were lined up with the tallest students in back, and the most attractive were placed in the middle so the focus would be on them. The individual portraits were mostly about adjusting the height of the seat and taking enough pictures to ensure that one of them was good enough. But when Erik suddenly wasn't there, with a full schedule of jobs still booked, she had taken over. Without giving it much thought. She did know the school secretaries, and they knew her, so that eased the transition.

"Do we really have to buy a coffin, when Mom is just going to be burned?" Steve said, interrupting her thoughts. "Can't we just borrow one? She won't be lying in there very long."

Shit. Ilka had blanked out for a moment. Where the hell was Artie? Did they have coffins they loaned out? She had to say something. "It would have to be one that's been used."

"We're not putting Mom in a coffin where other dead people have been!" Helen was indignant, while a hint of a smile appeared on her son's face.

Ilka jumped in. "Unfortunately, we can only loan out used coffins." She hoped that would put a lid on this idea.

"We can't do that. Can we?" Helen said to her two brothers.

"On the other hand, if we borrow a coffin, we might be able to afford charms instead."

Ilka didn't have the foggiest idea if her suggestion was even possible. But if this really was her business, she could decide, now, couldn't she?

"We *would* save forty-five hundred dollars," Joe said.

Forty-five hundred dollars for a coffin! This could turn out to be disastrous if it ended with them losing money from her ignorant promise.

"Oh, at least. Dad's coffin cost seven thousand dollars."

What is this? Ilka thought. *Are coffins here decorated in gold leaf?*

"But Grandma already paid for her funeral," the grandson said. "You can't save on something she's already paid for. You're not going to get her money back, right?" Finally, he looked up.

"We'll figure this out," Ilka said.

The boy looked over at his mother and began crying.

"Oh, honey!" Helen said.

"You're all talking about this like it isn't even Grandma; like it's someone else who's dead," he said, angry now.

He turned to Ilka. "Like it's all about money, and just getting it over with." He jumped up so fast he knocked his chair over; then he ran out the door.

His mother sent her brothers an apologetic look; they both shook their heads. She turned to Ilka and asked if it were possible for them to return tomorrow. "By then we'll have this business about the coffin sorted out. We also have to order a life board. I brought along some photos of Mom."

Standing now, Ilka told them it was of course fine to come back tomorrow. She knew one thing for certain: Artie was going to meet with them, whether he liked it or not. She grabbed the photos Helen was holding out.

"They're from when she was born, when she graduated from school, when she married Dad, and from their anniversary the year before he died."

"Super," Ilka said. She had no idea what these photos would be used for.

The three siblings stood up and headed for the door. "When would you like to meet?" Ilka asked. They agreed on noon.

Joe stopped and looked up at her. "But can the memorial service be held on Friday?"

"We can talk about that later," Ilka replied at once. She needed time to find out what to do with 150 people and a place for the dogs close to the coffin.

After they left, Ilka walked back to the desk and sank down in the chair. She hadn't even offered them coffee, she realized.

She buried her face in her hands and sat for a moment. She had inherited a funeral home in Racine. And if she were to believe the nun in the reception area laminating death notices, she had accepted the inheritance.

She heard a knock on the doorframe. Sister Eileen stuck her head in the room. Ilka nodded, and the nun walked over and laid a slip of paper on the table. On it was an address.

"We have a pickup."

Ilka stared at the paper. How was this possible? It wasn't just charms, life boards, and a forty-five-hundred-dollar coffin. Now they wanted her to pick up a body, too. She exhaled and stood up.

ABOUT THE AUTHOR

Sara Blaedel's suspense novels have enjoyed incredible success around the world: fantastic acclaim, multiple awards, and runaway number one best-selling success internationally. In her native Denmark, Sara was voted most popular novelist for the fourth time in 2014. She is also a recipient of the Golden Laurel, Denmark's most prestigious literary award. Her books are published in thirty-seven countries. Her series featuring police detective Louise Rick is adored the world over, and Sara is excited for the launch of her new Family Secrets suspense series in the United States.

Sara Blaedel's interest in story writing, and especially crime fiction, was nurtured from a young age. The daughter of a renowned Danish journalist and an actress whose career included roles in theater, radio, TV, and movies, Sara grew up surrounded by a constant flow of professional writers and performers visiting the Blaedel home. Despite her struggle with dyslexia, books gave Sara a world in which to escape when her introverted nature demanded an exit from the hustle and bustle of life. Sara tried a number of careers, from a restaurant apprenticeship to graphic design, before she started a publishing company called Sara B, where she published Danish translations of American crime fiction.

Publishing ultimately led Sara to journalism, and she covered a wide range of stories, from criminal trials to the premiere of *Star Wars: Episode I*. It was during this time—and while skiing in Norway—that Sara started brewing the ideas for her first novel. In 2004 Louise and Camilla were introduced in *Grønt Støv* (*Green Dust*), and Sara won the Danish Academy for Crime Fiction's debut prize.

Originally from Denmark, Sara has lived in New York, but now spends most of her time in Copenhagen. When she isn't busy committing brutal murders on the page, she is an ambassador with Save the Children and serves on the jury of a documentary film competition.